MW01678557

meet Dakota Lewis—retired air force lieutenant and man of wealth. This Native American warrior was about to undergo a secret mission involving none other than…Kathy Lewis, his gorgeous, estranged wife. Could this become a mission to reclaim their love?

Five wealthy Texas bachelors—all members of the state's most exclusive club—set out to restore the "Royal" jewels...and find true love.

* * *

Tycoon Warrior

SHERI WHITEFEATHER

Harlequin Mills & Boon

Desire

DID YOU PURCHASE THIS BOOK WITHOUT A COVER?
If you did, you should be aware it is **stolen property** as it was reported 'unsold and destroyed' by a retailer.
Neither the author nor the publisher has received any payment for this book.

First Published 2001
First Australian Paperback Edition 2001
ISBN 0 733 53209 8

TYCOON WARRIOR © 2001 by Harlequin Books S.A.
Philippine Copyright 2001
Australian Copyright 2001
New Zealand Copyright 2001
Except for use in any review, the reproduction or utilisation of this work in whole or in part in any form by any electronic, mechanical or other means, now known or hereafter invented, including xerography, photocopying and recording, or in any information storage or retrieval system, is forbidden without the permission of the publisher, Harlequin Mills & Boon, P.O. Box 810, Chatswood, N.S.W., Australia 2057.

All the characters in this book have no existence outside the imagination of the author, and have no relation whatsoever to anyone bearing the same name or names. They are not even distantly inspired by any individual known or unknown to the author, and all the incidents are pure invention.

This book is sold subject to the condition that it shall not, by way of trade or otherwise, be lent, resold, hired out or otherwise circulated without the prior consent of the publisher in any form of binding or cover other than that in which it is published and without a similar condition including this condition being imposed on the subsequent purchaser.

All rights reserved including the right of reproduction in whole or in part in any form. This edition is published by arrangement with Harlequin Enterprises II B.V.

Published by
Harlequin Mills & Boon
3 Gibbes Street
CHATSWOOD NSW 2057
AUSTRALIA

HARLEQUIN MILLS & BOON DESIRE and the Rose Device are trademarks used under license and registered in Australia, New Zealand, Philippines, United States Patent & Trademark Office and in other countries.

Printed and bound in Australia by
McPherson's Printing Group

SHERI WHITEFEATHER

lives in Southern California and enjoys ethnic dining, summer powwows and visiting art galleries and vintage clothing stores near the beach. Since her one true passion is writing, she is thrilled to be a part of the Harlequin Desire line. When she isn't writing, she often reads until the wee hours of the morning.

Sheri also works as a leather artisan with her Muscogee Creek husband. They have one son and a menagerie of pets, including a pampered English bulldog and four equally spoiled Bengal cats. She would love to hear from her readers. You may write to her at: P.O. Box 5130, Orange, California 92863-5130.

"What's Happening in Royal?"

NEWS FLASH, May—Everyone in the town of Royal is talking about a possible reconciliation of our favorite marrieds—Dakota and Kathy Lewis! 'Course, all those single gals are hoping it isn't true, as the swoon-inspiring former air force lieutenant Dakota Lewis proves a mighty catch. But this hunk's Comanche heart appears destined to belong to his beautiful wife, Kathy....

Seems the reunion began when woman-of-the-world Kathy returned to Royal unexpectedly to meet with our dashing Texas Cattlemen—her hubby, Dakota, included—behind closed doors. And where-oh-where did Kathy and Dakota disappear to soon after?

Perhaps our boys at the Cattleman's Club can finally give us some answers? We're waiting here with bated breath.... Stay tuned!

One

Retired air force lieutenant Dakota Lewis sat upright in a leather recliner, studying his home. Would the ranch look the same to Kathy?

Of course it would, he told himself a second later. He hadn't changed a thing. Not one cowboy novelty, not one Indian artifact. She would recognize every cow skull, every antler, every ceremonial pipe.

An ensemble of cedar, pine and mahogany made up Dakota's living room. He hadn't chosen pieces that belonged in sets. He preferred eclectic furnishings—hacienda-style trunks, tables topped with clay-colored tiles, mirrors framed in tooled leather.

He turned his attention back to his guests. They weren't discussing the mission at this point. Someone had made a reference to his wife. Was it Aaron Black? Sheikh Ben Rassad? Dr. Justin Webb? It wasn't Matthew Walker because Matt wasn't married.

No, but he was engaged. Happily engaged.

Hell, Dakota thought. What was wrong with him? The other men in the room were his friends, his peers. He had no right to envy them. They were all members of the Texas Cattleman's Club, the most exclusive gentlemen's club in the state. They were all wealthy—filthy rich, some might say. And they were all either happily married or happily engaged.

All except himself.

Dakota's estranged wife was due to arrive at his ranch any minute. Kathy had left three years before, a choice she hadn't even bothered to explain. Dakota had come home from an assignment to find her gone—her side of the closet empty, the scented lotions she favored no longer lined up on the bathroom counter. Two years of marriage shot to hell, and Dakota didn't know why. He had loved his wife, was certain she had loved him, too. Yet she'd walked out on him, saddling him with an emotional wound festering deep in his gut.

A wound that had become exceptionally active today. The top-secret mission the Cattleman's Club's members had come to discuss involved Kathy. She was the Foreign Service consular being teamed with Dakota. Together they would fly to Asterland, a small European country on the brink of a revolution.

The doorbell rang. Dakota excused himself from the other men and strode toward the entryway. Checking his watch, he tightened his jaw. Thirteen hundred hours. She was right on time.

Kathy stood on the other side of the door, slim and elegant, her thick, hard-to-hold hair coiled in a neat chignon. She wore a beige pantsuit and an emerald blouse that intensified the color of her eyes. Cat's eyes, he'd always called them. Exotic eyes and fire-tinted hair, features that belied Kathy's proper nature.

Neither spoke. Instead their gazes locked, and they stared at each other for what seemed like the longest moment of Dakota's life.

"It's good to see you," she said finally, extending her hand.

Polite pleasantries, he thought. What else could he do? This was business, and Dakota viewed his work as the number-one priority in his life. He wouldn't let anything stand in the way of an assignment, not even the pain shooting from his gut to his heart.

"It's good to see you, too," he responded, clasping her hand as though her touch wouldn't affect him. It did, of course. Her hand felt small and feminine, her skin soft and warm against his own.

He invited her in, cursing the memories threatening to surface. Her fragrance drifted to his nostrils like fresh strawberries smothered in cream. Kathy preferred scented lotions to heavy perfumes, aromas that never failed to make Dakota hungry.

Suddenly he fought the temptation to uncoil her hair, let it fall across her shoulders. He hadn't forgotten the woman he loved, hadn't forgotten how she looked soaking in the tub, her fiery tendrils slipping free from the pins that secured them, her long, sleek body creamy and smooth.

How many times had he watched her slide a washcloth down her arms and over her breasts? And how many times had he carried her, soaking wet, to their bed?

"Dakota? Are the others here?"

Kathy's question jarred him back to reality. Damn it. He stood in the tiled entryway, his hormones battling for control. How in the hell had he let that happen?

"Yes, they're here." He escorted his estranged wife to the living room, hating himself for the moment of weakness.

Like the Texas gentlemen they were, the other men rose as Kathy entered the room. Aaron Black came forward to hug her. How easily Kathy embraced Aaron, Dakota thought, wondering why a fist of rivalry gripped him hard and quick. Not only was Aaron blissfully married with a baby on the way, he was also a good friend, the American diplomat who had introduced Dakota to Kathy nearly six years before.

Kathy shook hands with the others, and soon they settled into their seats.

As Kathy crossed her legs, Dakota poured her a ginger ale from the wet bar. He didn't stop to ask her preference. He knew what Kathy's favorite soft drink was, and he still stocked the bar with it.

She thanked him quietly, the ice in her glass crackling. He poured himself a cola, opting to keep his hands busy. The urge to loosen her hair had returned.

How different they were, he thought, how opposite. Kathy was renowned for her grace and diplomacy, whereas Dakota was as rough-hewn as his taste in furniture, often solving matters with force.

Lifting his cola from the bar, Dakota took a swig, wondering if he should have spiked it with rum—something, anything to take the edge off. How could a woman skilled in conversation walk out on her husband without the slightest explanation? How could she ignore what they had meant to each other? The love? The passion?

Dakota didn't need to ask Kathy where she had been for the past three years. He already knew. She had gone to Washington, D.C., to serve in the Bureau of Consular Affairs, leasing a spacious apartment in an exclusive suburb and furnishing it with antiques. Prior to that, she had been on an extended leave of absence, debating whether to end her career. For Kathy, living abroad in the Foreign Service had become stressful. She wanted to remain in Texas. Or so she'd said.

Regardless, locating her in Washington had been easy. Keeping his distance had been the tough part. But Dakota figured Kathy didn't want to be confronted, didn't want him standing on her doorstep, demanding to know why she had left. So consequently, Dakota's pride—his hard-baked masculine ego—had managed to keep him at bay.

Sheikh Rassad drew Kathy into the meeting, pulling Dakota in as well.

"Are you familiar with the events leading up to this mission?" Ben asked her. "Are there any details that are not clear?"

"Aaron briefed me," she responded. "I know the Lone Star jewels were stolen. And I'm also aware that they've been recovered." She sat with her usual graceful posture, giving the sheikh her undivided attention. "Albert Payune, the Grand

Minister of Asterland, masterminded the robbery, intending to use the jewels to fund a revolution. Which is where Dakota and I come in. It's our job to make sure that revolution doesn't happen."

The sheikh leaned forward. "Aaron informed us that you are well acquainted with the king and queen."

"That's true. I'm very fond of the royal family, and I don't intend to see them lose their country." She placed her glass on a coaster, sending the sheikh a reassuring smile. "I've already made arrangements for Dakota to accompany me to Asterland for the queen's birthday ball. And since he will be visiting as my guest, his presence won't arouse suspicion."

Dakota listened, although he had already been briefed by Aaron. The plan had been carefully orchestrated. Dakota's initial arrival in Asterland must appear to be of a personal nature. And what could be more personal than traveling with his wife? They wouldn't need to fake their cover, at least not on paper. They would be playing themselves.

Almost.

They would have to pretend to be in the midst of a reconciliation, a couple mending their marriage.

Dakota glanced at Kathy, and she barely returned his gaze. She appeared poised and professional, but he could sense her uneasiness. The same uneasiness that swept through him.

How were they going to pull this off if they couldn't look at each other? Couldn't relax in each other's presence? Dakota glanced at Kathy again, his chest constricting with a familiar ache. Somehow, someway, they would have to. The future of a country was at stake. And this mission was far too risky for mistakes.

Kathy exhaled a quiet breath. When Aaron asked Dakota a question, he shifted his attention, giving her the opportunity to study him.

The years had been good to Dakota Lewis, aging him in a way that made him even more handsome, more rugged. He was half Comanche and half Texan—a tall, solid man with eyes that changed from brown to black, depending on his mood. His profile presented a determined jaw and high, slanted cheekbones. Everything about him boasted masculinity. His midnight hair, although short by most standards, was slightly longer than the military style he had worn while on active duty.

Active duty? Aside from allowing his hair to grow, retirement hadn't changed Dakota Lewis. He'd gone from Special Forces assignments to privately funded missions without a hitch in his long, powerful stride. Danger flowed through his veins like liquid; it was his life force, his blood. Kathy considered men like Dakota adrenaline junkies—men who would never give up the fight, the need to save the world.

Of course, adrenaline junkies didn't settle down with their wives. Instead they left them behind, left them alone to wait and wonder, praying frantically for their husbands' safe return.

How many assignments had he been on since she'd left? Did he miss her the way she had missed him? Or had his work filled the void? Dakota had loved her—that much she knew. Only he hadn't loved her the way she'd needed. Dakota's work had always come first. Kathy couldn't bear being second-best in her husband's heart.

And then when she'd lost the baby—

Her breath hitched. Oh, God. Don't think about the baby. Not here, not now. She placed a hand over her stomach. When would the pain go away, the ache of losing Dakota's child? How many years would have to pass? How many years before she stopped wishing every dark-haired toddler she saw was hers?

Dakota turned toward her, and she removed her hand from her stomach. Kathy had learned long ago how to keep her emotions in check, and she wouldn't give herself away now. Dakota didn't know about the baby. He had been in the Middle East tracking gunrunners when she'd miscarried—alone and afraid, missing her husband and crying for the baby they would never hold. A child she had wanted desperately.

"How well do you know Albert Payune?" Sheikh Rassad asked, catching Kathy off guard.

She lifted her chin and concentrated on the mission, the reason she had agreed to fly to Asterland with Dakota.

"I know Payune well enough to form an opinion of him," she responded. The sheikh's interest in Payune didn't surprise her, nor did his active participation in this meeting. She knew the sheikh's new bride had been formerly promised to Albert Payune in an arranged marriage. "Payune is a clever man, but he's arrogant, too. Much too vain to be considered charming. He isn't likable, but he knows how to command attention. He prides himself on power. Craves it, one could say."

"The perfect profile of a revolutionist," Aaron added. "It's quite possible Payune's sanity borders on his desire to succeed."

Matthew Walker joined in the conversation, mentioning his fiancée—Lady Helena of Asterland, a cousin to the royal family—a lady who shared Kathy's opinion of Payune.

Only Dakota and Dr. Webb remained silent. The doctor sat patiently, but Dakota rose from his chair and crossed the room, heading toward the cowhide-covered bar.

Kathy watched him. He moved like a long, fluid animal stalking his prey. It was the Comanche in him, she thought. The warrior preparing to count coup, his mental focus merging with his physical being. She recognized the look, the walk, the adrenaline charge that took him into the next battle, the next mission. This would be the man going after Albert Payune.

Had Dakota acquired another scar since she'd seen him last? Another mark of valor?

Kathy knew every inch of his body, every taut muscle, every hard ridge and flat plane. She also knew his hands were mildly callused, capable of inflicting pain or pleasure, depending on his objective. She had always been on the receiving end of pleasure, those large callused hands surprisingly gentle against her flesh. Dakota Lewis was as skilled a lover as he was a warrior.

Don't think about that now, she told herself. Focus on the mission. The reason she had agreed to help the Cattleman's Club.

When the meeting ended, the other men departed, leaving Dakota and Kathy alone. She clutched her handbag and stood. Suddenly the smell of wood and leather made her homesick. The ranch looked the same, the living room cluttered with rustic charm. Pillows, lamps, paintings, bronze statues—every piece told a Western story.

Was the bedroom the same? Had he kept the items she had chosen? The canopy bed, the hand-painted dresser, the horse weather vane sitting atop a Chippendale desk? The ranch belonged to Dakota, a custom-built home he had helped design ten years before. But when Kathy had married him, he'd asked her to redecorate the bedroom—fill it with her flair, her flavor. So she had combined formal antiques with Western relics, candles with cowboy boots, Waterford crystal with carved wood. The end result had pleased Dakota, especially the massive bed.

A bed Kathy had no right to remember. She didn't belong in this house. Loving Dakota didn't mean she could live with him, wait months on end for him to return from the missions that consumed him.

How ironic that they would come together for an assignment, for one of the secret operations engineered by the Texas Cattleman's Club. The members of that prestigious club weren't just established businessmen. They were Lone Star warriors, men who vowed to serve and protect.

Only Dakota hadn't protected her. He hadn't been there when she'd lost the baby.

"I think we should have dinner together tomorrow night."

Kathy blinked, then glanced up. How long had she been standing in the middle of Dakota's living room? And how long had he been watching her? "To synchronize our plan?"

"To get used to each other." He placed several empty glasses on top of the bar. "We can't go to Asterland like this. Acting like strangers. No one will buy our cover."

She let out an anxious breath. Right. The reconciled couple. The Foreign Service consular and her husband. "We still have some details to work out about the mission."

"We can do that over dinner. Which means avoiding a

restaurant. There are too many ears out there. I don't want to take the chance of being overheard.''

And she didn't want to have dinner with him at the ranch. She couldn't bear the familiarity. ''How about my hotel suite? We can order in.''

''That's fine.''

He walked her to the door, and as she turned to say goodbye, their eyes met.

Yes, she thought, struggling to hold his gaze, they needed to get used to each other. Three years, too many missions and a secret miscarriage had created a lot of distance between them. Pretending to be a reconciled couple wasn't going to be easy.

The following evening Kathy stood before a full-length mirror in her hotel room. She wore a white suit, gold jewelry and low heels. Reaching into her blouse, she lifted a long chain. Her wedding ring glittered on the end of it, a brilliant-cut diamond surrounded by emeralds. It was foolish, she knew, to wear it in such a manner, but she didn't have the strength to part with it completely.

It reminded her of wishes and dreams, a house full of children and growing old with the man she loved—a life where terrorists and gunrunners didn't take her husband away from home. As she slipped the chain inside her blouse, the ring thumped against her heart, out of sight but not out of mind.

Kathy tilted her head. Her hair was loose about her shoulders, the way Dakota liked it best. Quickly she twisted it into a neat chignon, her fingers working the heavy strands with deft precision. This wasn't about what Dakota liked. This was a business meeting, a professional dinner engagement.

When the room-service waiter delivered the meal, Kathy stood nearby, watching him set the table. Dakota would be arriving at any moment. She signed the bill and forced a smile, telling herself to relax. She had been in the company of dignitaries and heads of state. One tall, ex-military man, a dark-eyed Comanche, had no right to twist her stomach into a pretzel.

Five minutes after the waiter departed, a knock sounded at the door. She answered it, keeping her head high and her posture straight but not stiff. "Hello, Dakota."

"Hi." He smiled, a brief affection that gentled his raw-boned features.

She used to kiss the scar on his chin, she thought. And the one on his belly, too.

Kathy took a step back. What a thing to invade her mind—that masculine stomach, rippling with hard-earned muscle.

"Come in. I took the liberty of ordering our meal ahead of time."

"Great." He walked into the suite, his voice more casual than she had expected. But when he made a beeline for the phone and began dismantling it, she realized his tone was for show.

He talked about insignificant things as he swept the set of rooms for bugs, electronic devices that might have been planted by someone posing as part of the hotel staff. Kathy had already done a search, but she appreciated Dakota's professionalism. With her anxious behavior, she could have missed something. She wasn't accustomed to providing her own security.

"What are we having?" he asked, indicating his search had turned up clean.

"Prime rib," she responded, wishing she could relax the way a proper hostess should.

Tonight Dakota looked a little dangerous—black trousers, a black jacket and eyes as dark as his clothes. He used to complain that he didn't blend in well, that men in his field shouldn't stand out in a crowd. Of course, men in his field were masters of disguise, and he played the game to perfection. Kathy knew he had altered his appearance many times, his height the only feature he couldn't change.

"It smells good," he said.

"Yes, it does."

He scooted back her chair, and she took her seat, thinking they weren't off to a very good start. There was no level of comfort between them. None whatsoever.

She poured the wine, her hand steadier than her heart. He sat across from her, watching every move she made, his gaze filled with questions. Clearly he wanted to know why she had left.

Kathy wasn't ready to talk about personal matters, wasn't sure if it would even matter. Retired or not, Lieutenant Dakota Lewis was, and always would be, the ultimate soldier—a man drawn to the heat of battle. A wife longing for babies and domestic bliss had no place in his life.

Dakota reached for his wine, and Kathy toyed with her salad. But before the silence threatened to swallow them, he spoke. "Tell me about your relationship with the royal family."

"I consider Queen Nicole a friend," she answered, relaxing a little. "She is part American and enjoys having another American woman to talk to. Although she was born in Asterland, she was educated in the States and has a fondness for our culture."

"When were you assigned to the consulate in Asterland? You've been in Washington for the last three years."

So he knew where she had been. Well, of course he did. She couldn't very well hide from a man like Dakota, nor had she intended to. She had wanted him to come to her, wanted him to profess that she was more important than his work, that he would retire for good.

"I wasn't assigned to Asterland. I was brought in to handle a situation that involved Prince Eric." Queen Nicole's young son, a dark-haired little boy who had stolen Kathy's heart. "Prince Eric had gotten into trouble at a prestigious New England boarding school. He was on the verge of being suspended because his classroom behavior was too disruptive. And since the school officials weren't being particularly cooperative, Queen Nicole requested that an American consular assess the situation and report to her."

Dakota cut into his meat. "Your report must have impressed the queen."

"Prince Eric turned out to be a delightful child, which led me to believe his classroom behavior needed further investigation.'' Kathy adjusted the linen napkin on her lap. ''With the queen's approval, I brought in an educational psychologist. And the psychologist diagnosed Prince Eric with attention deficit disorder. Personally, I feel the boy had been treated unfairly. A learning disability isn't something that warrants a suspension.''

Dakota smiled. ''You've always been tuned in to kids. You could have been a teacher.''

Or a mother, she thought, swallowing the lump in her throat. Prince Eric had come into her life soon after the miscarriage, and bonding with the young boy had helped ease the pain of losing her own child. ''The queen transferred him to a boarding school that specializes in learning disabilities. He's doing well now. A determined fifth-grader.''

''It's hard to believe Prince Ivan came from the same family.''

''I know.'' Kathy pictured Prince Ivan. He was Eric's older brother, a grown man who abused his power and shamed his family. He had also been a menace to the town of Royal, a threat to the Cattleman's Club. But in the end, a cowardly act had consumed him. Rather than return to Asterland to face his family, the prince had committed suicide. ''Ivan is dead now.''

Dakota placed his fork on the table. ''But he's still creating trouble. Or his past deeds are. He's the one who convinced the king to appoint Payune to the position of Grand Minister. Payune and Ivan were thick as thieves.''

And at one time, the king, clearly blinded by parental love, had intended to abdicate the throne to Ivan. ''Prince Eric is nothing like his brother. He will make a fine king someday.''

''That's good to know. But if we don't stop Payune, young Eric will never get that chance.'' Dakota trapped her gaze, his dark eyes riveting. ''I hope to God Payune buys my cover. And yours, too. I'm going to have to convince him that you're a double agent.''

Kathy tried to look away, but couldn't. Dakota held her there, caught in his magnetic gaze. She wasn't able to respond; her mouth had gone dry. She reached for her wine, took a small sip.

His husky voice sounded gentle, low. "I'm sorry, sweetheart. I hate doing this to you, but I don't know how else to reach Payune."

Sweetheart. Kathy felt a pool of warmth settle deep in her belly. Dakota had used that endearment the first time they'd made love.

Show me what you like, sweetheart. Put my hands—

Oh yes, those hands. Those strong, callused hands—fingertips stroking her breasts, sliding lower, slipping between her thighs. He used to watch her climax, smile and watch, masculine pleasure alight in his dark eyes. Afterward they would kiss, and he would enter her, push himself deep inside, make it happen all over again. Every explosive, glorious sensation.

"Kathy?"

She started. "Yes?"

"Are you all right? Did that upset you?"

Yes, she wanted to say. It unnerves me that I can't stop thinking about us. That I can recall your touch, your smile, the feel of your mouth covering mine, the weight of your body, the rock of your hips. "No. I came into this mission knowing we would have to fool Payune. I'm prepared to play my part."

"You're absolutely sure? You don't have any second thoughts?"

"I'm ready for this assignment," she said, struggling to maintain her composure. "Aaron briefed me on all of the details." Dakota would present himself as a Texas billionaire willing to fund Payune's revolution for personal gain. And she would be painted as Dakota's shrewd wife—a woman who used a government job to her best advantage.

"Don't worry about me," she added. She wouldn't allow her thoughts to stray, wouldn't allow those disturbing images to cloud her mind. Because recalling Dakota's touch was possibly more dangerous than the mission.

Two

Kathy wore her hair up again, Dakota noticed, but the dry Texas wind had disturbed it, loosening several long, bright strands. She wore casual clothes—jeans and a short-sleeved cotton blouse, her shoulder nearly brushing his.

A bronze statue of Tex Langley, the founder of the Texas Cattleman's Club, stood like a monument behind them.

They sat on a park bench, but they weren't lounging on a leisure day. This was business, another meeting place where they wouldn't be overheard.

Sheikh Ben Rassad and his wife, Jamie, sat on the other side of the bench, a newly married couple looking far too much in love. Dakota resisted the urge to move closer to Kathy, to allow their bodies to touch. Although last night's dinner hadn't been a failure, it wasn't a complete success, either. They weren't exactly used to each other yet.

Dakota dug a booted heel into the grass. Maybe he should just kiss her and get it over with. Pull her onto his lap. Tug her hair loose. Slam his tongue into her mouth and devour the woman he had married.

After all, she was still technically his wife.

He glanced up at Ben Rassad. Yeah, right. Kiss Kathy now, here at the park, in front of his happily married friend. What the hell was he trying to prove? That he was an egotistical, envious idiot?

Dakota lifted a bottle of water and brought it to his lips, wetting his mouth and cooling his thoughts. Strange how things had worked out for Ben. The sheikh had been assigned to watch over Jamie when she needed protection, then ended up falling for her in the process. The feisty young woman had originally been a mail-order bride for Albert Payune, a union arranged by Jamie's father and Payune himself.

Luckily, Payune had backed out of the deal and never pursued Jamie any further. Which, in turn, had prompted this meeting—second-guessing Payune's actions—the man Dakota intended to take down.

"So, do either one of you have any idea why Payune had advertised for an American wife?" he asked, dividing his gaze between the other couple.

Jamie shook her head. "No, but we've talked about it. Tossed ideas back and forth."

"Like what, for instance?"

"Vanity, perhaps," Ben said. "Payune may have desired a young wife to boost his ego. Texas women are renowned for their beauty." He reached for Jamie's hand and held it lightly. "But there is also the possibility of revenge. Payune might blame the town of Royal for Ivan's suicide, and he planned to take one of our women as payment."

Dakota mulled over Ben's words, deciding anything was possible where Payune was concerned.

"I tend to think Sheikh Rassad was right the first time," Kathy said. "That Payune's ego was involved."

"Really?" When Dakota turned toward her, his hand brushed hers—an accidental touch that sent an electrical charge straight to his heart. He forced himself to concentrate on the discussion, but failed miserably. He noticed Kathy's hand was bare. She wore no rings. The wedding band he'd placed on her finger was gone.

Dakota looked over at Ben and Jamie. Both sat patiently as though waiting for Kathy to expound on her theory. Apparently he was the only one losing his train of thought. Damn it. He knew better than to allow his heart to get tangled up in this mission. Kathy had left him, and that was that.

Tightening his jaw, he turned toward her again. "So you think Payune wanted an American wife to make himself look good?"

She nodded. "It would enhance his public image in Asterland. Queen Nicole is well received in her country. And since she is part American, Payune may have been trying to find a wife he considered comparable to her." She shifted her gaze to Ben. "A beautiful Texan, just as Sheikh Rassad pointed out."

Dakota frowned. "If that's the case, then why did Payune let Jamie go? My contact in Asterland says he's no longer pursuing a wife, American or otherwise."

Kathy smoothed the wind-blown strands of her hair. "I don't know. But I've always had the feeling that Payune is enamored of Queen Nicole. Of course she's madly in love with her husband. She isn't the kind of woman to have an affair, and I'm sure Payune knows that."

"But he wants her." And in Dakota's opinion that made Albert Payune even more dangerous. Could there be an assassination plot brewing? If the king were killed during the revolution, Queen Nicole would be left a widow, free to accept Payune's affection. And if Payune controlled the queen and Prince Eric, then, in a sense, he would control Asterland, too.

Dakota figured Payune had three options: overthrow the Asterland government through a revolution, dispose of the entire royal family or kill the king and marry Queen Nicole.

But how could Payune possibly think the queen would turn to him? If she loved her husband, she wouldn't embrace the man who had assassinated him.

Or would she? Was Kathy wrong about Queen Nicole? Maybe the queen wasn't as madly in love as she claimed to be.

Wives, it seemed, changed their minds about such matters. Dakota knew firsthand that love wasn't all it was cracked up to be.

They were both experienced flyers—more than experienced. Kathy had lived abroad most of her life, and Dakota was a pilot, a man who belonged to the sky. But not today. Although they rode on a private, luxurious jet owned by a prominent member of the Cattleman's Club, they were anything but relaxed.

The pilot, thank God, was another retired air force officer, someone Dakota trusted implicitly. Flying to Asterland with Kathy was difficult enough, and the last thing Dakota needed to concern himself with was the competency of their pilot.

Kathy sat across from him in a cushioned chair. The jet offered an upscale, home-like setting, a penthouse apartment in the sky. Kathy fit right in. Dakota supposed he did, too—on the outside at least. He'd been born into money, even if he was the bastard son of a hard-nosed land baron, a man who'd left him a sizable inheritance. Dakota didn't fashion himself after his father, but he'd done his damnedest to earn the older man's respect.

Kathy paged through a magazine. It wasn't difficult to assess that she wasn't absorbed in its contents. Her mind was elsewhere. And rightly so, Dakota supposed. This mission had sucked both of them in, drawing them into an imminent vacuum.

Placing the magazine on a table, she looked up and asked, "Are you sure we're doing the right thing?"

Good God. She had second thoughts? Now? They were halfway to Asterland. "What do you mean?"

"Not involving the king and queen. I don't like deceiving them."

"We're not deceiving them. We're keeping this mission under wraps to protect them. The less people involved, the safer we'll all be."

Kathy frowned. "But it's their country."

And she was thinking with her heart instead of her head,

Dakota thought. Her friendship with the queen was blinding her judgment. ‘‘Kathy, we don’t know how many cabinet members are actually part of the revolution plot. If the king or queen put their trust in the wrong person, it would blow our operation sky-high. We can’t take that chance.’’

And Dakota had some concerns about Queen Nicole and Albert Payune. ‘‘Besides, how well do you really know the queen? She could have stumbled into an affair with Payune. That might be the reason he quit looking for a wife.’’

Kathy narrowed her eyes. ‘‘Queen Nicole hasn’t *stumbled* into affair, Dakota. I already told you she wouldn’t do something like that. She loves her husband.’’

And I thought you loved me, he wanted to say. ‘‘So women don’t cheat on their husbands? They don’t get themselves tangled up with other men?’’

‘‘Some do, I suppose. But not most. That’s a man’s game.’’

She picked up the magazine again, and Dakota kicked his legs out in front of him. A man’s game. Right. He hadn’t even looked at another women since she’d been gone. He studied Kathy’s professional attire, her slim, fashionable figure. When she flipped a page, he caught sight of a gold band glinting on her finger. She wore her wedding ring, the diamond and emerald design he’d had custom made for her.

Don’t take that as encouragement, he told himself. She’d put it back on for show, for the sake of their cover. ‘‘So have you been with anyone?’’ he asked, his voice gruff. ‘‘Did you leave me so you could sleep with another man?’’

Kathy’s complexion paled. ‘‘I can’t believe you’re asking me something like that.’’

He felt his muscles tense. Technically, they were still married. Neither had filed for a legal separation, much less a divorce. He had a right to know. ‘‘Well?’’

‘‘Of course not.’’ She lifted her chin and met his gaze, her eyes locking onto his. ‘‘What about you? Have you been with someone?’’

‘‘No.’’ He shook his head and made light of his loneliness, the years he’d waited for her to return. ‘‘The way I figure it, we've still got that piece of paper between us.'' As well as the vows they had taken.

For better or worse. Until death do us part. He had meant every word.

She let out an audible breath, her eloquent vocal skills suddenly failing her. ''I suppose it was best that we...discussed this issue. I...we...don't need any personal distractions on this mission.''

Yeah, and wondering if your spouse had a new lover would certainly fall under the category of a personal distraction. ''I agree. Now that it's out in the open, I won't mention it again.''

''Good.''

Her smile was tight, but the fear in her eyes had faded. Fear that he had been with another woman. The thought made him a little smug, as well as confused. If things like that still mattered, why hadn't she come home before now?

Dakota dragged a hand through his hair. She isn't home, Lieutenant Lewis. This is an assignment, a fake reconciliation. Get your facts straight.

They remained silent for the next twenty minutes, she, occupying herself with another magazine, he, staring out the window at the night sky. He would have rather been piloting the plane than sitting idle, thinking about how much he missed a closeness with his wife. Sure, they had spent some time away from each other, but due to the nature of his work, those separations couldn't be helped. And their reunions used to be nice. Damn nice. Nothing like this one.

''Dakota?''

He turned away from the window. ''Yes?''

''Why didn't you ever tell me the Lone Star jewels really existed?''

While he'd been thinking about her, she'd been thinking about the recovered jewels. Well, at least one of them had her mind on the mission. ''Only those associated with the Texas Cattleman's Club were supposed to know they existed.''

''Because of the legend?''

"Yes."

"So the story about that soldier is true?"

Dakota nodded. A Texas soldier had found the jewels during the War with Mexico and had brought them to Royal after the war, intending to sell them and make his fortune.

"When he came home, oil was found on his land. So he believed just owning the stones was lucky, and that they should remain in Royal."

"And now the Cattleman's Club protects them, and everyone else thinks their existence is just a legend. A story passed down from generation to generation."

"Yes, but Payune came across the truth somehow."

Kathy leaned forward, clearly engrossed in their conversation. But then she loved jewels, and the Lone Star gems were a rare, stunning collection. Too bad she would never see them, he thought. He would enjoy watching her eyes glow—those gorgeous green eyes.

"Any idea how Payune found out about them?" she asked.

"It's possible Prince Ivan had something to do with it. When he was in Royal, he asked a lot of questions. It would stand to reason that he heard about the legend. He probably told Payune about it."

"And Payune discovered the legend was true, from his comrade, Robert Klimt—the man who had stolen the jewels." Kathy reclined in her chair. "I'm so glad they were recovered. They haven't been safeguarded all these years to end up in the wrong hands."

"Funding a revolution no less." Dakota rose and headed toward a small wet bar. "Do you want a cold drink?" he asked.

She shook her head.

"Then how about a cup of hot tea?" He knew she added one teaspoon of sugar and a splash of cream to her tea. He wondered if she remembered little details about him or if she had chosen to forget. It wouldn't be hard to recall that he drank his coffee black or that he considered hot sauce a breakfast staple.

"No, thank you. I'm fine."

He poured himself a tall glass of soda water and returned to his seat.

Kathy placed the magazine on her lap. "Are you concerned about the queen's ball? I know how much you dislike social functions."

Dakota cocked an eyebrow at her. He didn't dislike all social functions, just the ones that required a tuxedo and served champagne instead of beer.

"No, I'm not concerned about it. I've been to plenty of fancy affairs." And they made him uncomfortable as hell, even the familiar Texas Cattleman's Club events. Dakota had spent more years in war paint and combat gear than he had in uniform. This ball, he figured, would be the worst part of the mission. Next to Kathy, he would probably look like a big, snorting Brahma. James Bond he wasn't. Not all undercover agents were that damned debonair.

"So you don't want me to brief you on royal protocol?" she asked.

Dakota scowled. "No, Miss friend-of-the-queen, I don't. I know how to behave around royalty. As you might recall, I spent twenty years of my life serving in the United States Air Force. I've picked up a few manners along the way."

She nibbled her bottom lip, then broke into an amused smile. "Miss friend-of-the-queen?"

He couldn't help but return her smile. Kathy knew him better than anyone. She knew darn well how he felt about attending the queen's birthday ball. "If the glass slipper fits, Lady Katherine."

She tossed her magazine at him. He ducked and shot her a playful grin, recalling how many times he used to tickle her on the living-room floor.

Dakota picked up the magazine, his grin fading. Somehow those tickling sessions would inevitably turn into foreplay. Hot, sexy kisses. Rubbing against each other through their clothes.

He looked over at Kathy and noticed her smile had disappeared, too. Just as well, he thought. The less tender memories they made, the better. Because when this assignment ended, they wouldn't be going home together.

The cottage the queen provided sat on a grassy cliff, the ocean below crashing upon a private stretch of beach. A cool, yet comfortable, sea breeze misted the May air, and clouds drifted lazily across an azure sky.

Kathy had stayed in the isolated cottage on several other occasions, and she adored the quaint, European charm. Window boxes displayed an arrangement of colorful flowers, and leafy vines clung to a white trellis. A scattered-stone walkway led to the front door. Inside was a collection of art and antiques, a cozy living area, two bedrooms, a fully stocked kitchen and two bathrooms decorated with hand-painted fixtures. French doors in each bedroom opened onto a lush, well-tended garden. A wrought-iron table sat amid perennial blooms in what Kathy considered an outdoor breakfast nook—a place to sip coffee and breathe the sea air.

The first thing Dakota did was search the cottage for concealed microphones, but Kathy expected as much. A frown furrowed his brow, she noticed. Was he preoccupied with the mission, or had he noticed the romantic ambiance—the vases of long-stemmed roses, the extravagant chocolates placed upon the master-bedroom bed? The big, quilted bed the queen's servants must have assumed Kathy and Dakota would be sharing?

He completed the search, and she stood beside their luggage. "We won't have daily maid service," she said. "There's a little bungalow behind the garden that was built as servant's quarters, but it's vacant. We've been provided with enough food, towels and linens to last through the week."

"Good. The less people around the better." He turned to look at her. "How did you manage that, anyway?"

"I informed the queen we wanted to be alone. She's fanatical about seeing to her guests' personal needs."

He frowned again. "Of course, our cover. Sorry, it was a stupid question."

With an answer that made them both wary, she realized. A married couple requesting privacy meant long, sensual baths, sipping wine by candlelight, feeding each other aphrodisiacs.

"I'll take the smaller bedroom," he said.

Kathy didn't respond, instead she followed him as he lifted her luggage and carried it to the master bedroom.

He placed her suitcase and garment bag on the bed, then turned toward the French doors and gazed out. "It's pretty here."

She moved to stand beside him. "There's a fountain in the center of the garden." And she thought of it as her own private wishing well, even if her wishes had yet to come true. "This cottage is in a world of its own."

"But it's not our world." With rigid shoulders, he turned away from the view, his mood switching from light to dark in one abrupt motion. "I have to meet with my contact soon. We can't get caught up in flowers and fountains. We're not on a holiday."

"I'm well aware of why we're here." Angry now, she continued to study the foliage. She wouldn't allow him to spoil the allure of her garden, a place where mystical creatures made magic. She wanted to believe that fairies fluttered around the flowers, and mermaids splashed in the ocean below.

"Kathy?"

She turned toward him with a hard stare. "What?"

He handed her one of the chocolates from the bed, an apology in his voice. "Truffles. They're your favorite."

She bit into the candy and savored the richness, the gentleness in his tone. "Is that why you offered me this room?" A silk-draped room with all the elements Kathy adored—scented candles, fresh-cut flowers, lace-trimmed sheers.

He smiled, but it fell short of reaching his eyes. He was worried, she realized. Worried about the mission, worried about being in an isolated cottage with his estranged wife. There was still so much distance between them, so much unnamed hurt. But how could she tell him that he hadn't loved her enough? That she needed more?

''You should unpack and get settled in,'' he said.

''I will.'' She searched his gaze. ''Who is your contact, Dakota? Have I met him before?''

He shook his head. ''No, but he's someone I've known a long time. A former intelligence officer, another skin.''

Kathy knew that meant Dakota's contact was Native American. ''Comanche?'' she asked.

''Apache. Goes by the name Thunder. If something goes wrong on this assignment, he'll get in touch with you, Kathy. He vowed to look after you.''

She didn't want to think about something going wrong, but she couldn't pretend the danger wasn't real. A man in Royal had been murdered by one of Payune's anarchists, and now they were on Payune's soil.

''Is Thunder a mercenary?'' She knew Dakota didn't consider himself a mercenary because serving merely for pay wasn't his objective.

Dakota nodded. ''Yes, but that doesn't make him someone you can't trust. He took a bullet for me. I owe him my life. We even look similar, like brothers.''

Feeling an emotional chill, she crossed her arms. How many bullets had Dakota dodged? How many times had his life been spared? ''Do you want me to unpack for you?'' she asked, hoping he would understand why she had offered. She needed to place his clothes in the closet, his shaving gear in the bathroom. She used to unpack for him whenever he came home from an assignment. To her it meant he would be staying, at least for a while.

He didn't answer. Instead he remained motionless, staring at her. Her husband stood so close, she could see every eyelash, every pore in his sun-baked skin. And now she remembered how it felt to stroke his face. That intense face—smooth in some areas, rough in others.

Kathy moistened her lips. She wanted to grip his shoulders, lean into him and press her body against all that male hardness, feel her bones dissolve while his tongue stroked hers.

''You better go,'' she heard herself say.

She had no right to want him, not now, not after all the

tears she had cried, the baby she had lost. Dakota would forever be walking away. There would always be another assignment, another mission—something more important than his marriage.

He left the cottage, and she decided not to unpack for him. Touching his clothes would only make her ache.

Hours later Dakota returned from his meeting to find Kathy in the garden. Rather than disturb the moment, he watched her. She stood beside the fountain, wearing a pale cotton dress that billowed softly in the breeze. Her hair fell loose from its confinement, long silky strands framing her profile. She belonged in the setting, he thought. The foliage reached out to her, colorful blooms and lush greenery graced by her presence.

He felt like an intruder. But he had some news, and it couldn't wait. Bad news, it seemed, never could.

"Kathy?" he said softly.

She turned. "Oh, hi. I didn't know you were back."

"I haven't been here long." He hated to spoil the serenity, the beauty of what he had come to think of as her garden. Her enchanted garden. He had no right to be there. Dakota wasn't a dreamer. To him life consisted of reality—hard, strong doses of it.

"Any new information?" she asked.

He nodded. "A valuable necklace was stolen last night, and Thunder is convinced Payune is responsible." Dakota shifted his stance. "It belonged to the Duchess of Olin. A rare ruby heirloom that will command a substantial price on the black market."

"Now Payune has another means to fund his revolution."

"That's right. He couldn't get his hands on the Lone Star jewels, so he went after the next best thing."

Kathy frowned. "How are we going to get around this? You can't very well infiltrate Payune's operation if he doesn't need the money you intend to offer."

"True. But Payune is still powerless until he fences the necklace." Dakota felt a surge of adrenaline rush through his veins, nervous energy he couldn't shake. This mission had become even riskier, and his wife was his partner. That thought didn't sit well. "I have to retrieve the necklace. Steal it back, so to speak."

Kathy's face paled. "How's that going to work? Payune will become suspicious of everyone who comes into contact with him. If the necklace is taken from him, he'll know that someone is trying to stop him from funding the revolution. And it won't take him long to look in your direction, not once you approach him with your cover."

"This won't affect my cover." Dakota resisted the urge to pace, to stalk the garden path. "The Duchess has a paste copy of the necklace. It's the one she wears in public, and it's extremely high quality—identical to the original. So all I have to do is switch them. Payune will never know he was robbed."

"Not until he tries to fence it and discovers it's fake."

"True, but that's the beauty of this plan." Because Kathy was still frowning, Dakota sent her a roguish grin. "Payune will think he nabbed the wrong necklace to begin with, rather than suspect foul play."

She chewed her bottom lip. "It could work."

"It has to. We don't have much time. Thunder thinks the necklace will be fenced right after the ball. Late that night. He has a pretty good handle on who's backing the sale."

"The ball is three days from now."

"Which is why I've secured a meeting with Payune tomorrow. I need to establish my cover before he tries to sell the necklace. If I wait to approach him, he just might put two and two together."

A light breeze blew the loose stands of Kathy's hair. "When are you going to switch the necklaces? You have to do it before the ball."

"Don't worry about it, sweetheart. I'll let you know when I've got the details worked out." Dakota was going to need her help. And Thunder's, too. It would take the three of them to pull this off.

He motioned toward the stone path leading back to the

cottage. "Why don't we go inside? I could use a cup of coffee." He had more news. Something that would take an emotional toll on Kathy, something he hated to tell her.

While Kathy brewed a pot of coffee, a wave of homesickness washed over Dakota. Not for Texas, but for her. He missed having her nearby, watching her do simple tasks. Her feet were bare, and more of her hair had come loose. He could almost imagine them snuggling in front of the TV, eating popcorn the way they used to.

Life had never been particularly simple for Dakota, but being married to Kathy made the world a better place. She brought out the good in him. Or at least he'd thought so. Kathy must have felt differently. A woman didn't leave a good man.

She handed him a cup of the dark brew. He carried it into the living room while she doctored hers with sugar and cream.

He lowered himself onto the sofa, and she entered the room and sat across from him in an overstuffed chair.

"I can tell there's something else going on," she said. "What is it?"

"You won't like it."

"Dakota. Quit stalling. That isn't like you."

"You're right." He wondered why he was trying to protect her from someone else's life. "There are rumors circulating about the king and queen."

She placed her coffee on a nearby table. "What kind of rumors?"

"That their marriage is in trouble."

She pushed a stray lock of hair away from her face, her posture suddenly tense. "I don't believe it. People like to make things up. Create scandals. That happens to every royal family."

"Don't hide your head in the sand, Kathy. Plenty of couples have problems. And royalty are like everyone else in that regard." Our marriage failed, he wanted to say. And we were supposed to be happy. Why not a king and queen?

She thrust her chin in a stubborn gesture. "This does not mean Queen Nicole is having an affair with Payune."

"I didn't say it did."

"But that's what you're thinking."

"No, it's not." He was thinking about his own life, about why Kathy had walked out on him. He wished to hell he knew what he had done wrong. But now wasn't the time to ask. Dakota had to concentrate on retrieving the stolen necklace, on trapping the revolutionists and sending them to jail.

This mission wasn't about the hole in his heart. It wasn't about the woman seated across from him, messy locks spilling out of her proper hairdo, her long slim body draped in a summer cotton dress. This romantic little cottage wasn't home, and he would do well to remind himself of that. Every chance he got.

Three

Kathy couldn't sleep. Tired of tossing and turning, she slipped out of bed, then stood before the French doors. She knew her garden was out there, and beyond it a grassy terrain dotted with wildflowers. Below the hills, a midnight ocean crashed upon the shore. She gazed out, but it was too dark to see anything but an eerie reflection of herself.

A woman in white silk, her hair a long, tousled curtain. She looked like a mysterious shadow. A faded image. The silhouette of a lady longing for her lover.

Suddenly she could see this woman, this shadow of herself, roaming the hills, the wind whipping through the night, a sheer nightgown clinging to her skin. She was naked beneath the gown, waiting for her lover to come to her. He was forbidden, she knew. But she wanted him. Wanted to tumble to the ground with him, tear at his clothes and feel his mouth ravage hers.

What am I doing?

Shaking off a sexual chill, Kathy reached for her robe. A thirty-two-year-old woman should know better.

What she needed was food. A sandwich might be a poor substitute for a good night's rest, but it would keep her mind off foolish fantasies.

Belting her robe, she made her way to the kitchen. She flipped on the light. The room was spotless. The appliances were white, the wallpaper a tiny floral pattern. The appeal was homey, but kitchens usually were.

Kathy opened the refrigerator and removed a package of ham. After spreading a small amount of mayonnaise on two slices of bread, she reached for the mustard. It was her favorite—a spicy French condiment. In her haste to combine the two flavors, she ended up with a glob on her finger. Lifting it to her mouth, she froze. The chill returned. This time it slid down her spine like a masculine hand brushing her skin.

She was being watched. She could feel his eyes on her. She hadn't heard him come into the room, but she felt him there.

Watching every move she made.

She squared her shoulders and turned. He stood in the open doorway, tall and silent, his stare dark and intense. He wore a pair of drawstring sweat pants, riding low enough to expose his navel. He looked big and powerful, almost frightening. His eyes were so black, his pupils no longer existed. He had spiked his hair with restless hands, the glossy strands a startling shade of midnight blue. A trick from the light, but it startled her just the same.

The muscles along his stomach rippled with each breath he took. Hard, barely controlled breaths.

He was angry. Or aroused. Neither thought gave her much comfort.

She wanted to leave the kitchen, retreat to the safety of her room. But she couldn't. Her sandwich was half made, and Dakota blocked the doorway. She had no choice but to continue her task, to convince herself his presence hadn't unnerved her.

"I can't sleep," he said.

Turning back to her sandwich, she barely glanced up.

"Neither can I. But then we both drank coffee later than we should have."

Although she avoided his gaze, she knew it remained fixed on her. He couldn't know about her fantasy, about what her imagination had conjured, yet she sensed he did. In her mind, she had been waiting for her lover. Her forbidden lover. And now he was here—the man she wasn't supposed to want.

The coffee hadn't kept him awake, Dakota thought. She had.

It had been three years. Three years since he'd made love, since he'd felt her warm, willing heat. And she stood in the kitchen wearing a silky robe, her hair spilling gloriously over her shoulders—that fire-tinted hair he ached to grasp, lift to his face.

She didn't look his way. Instead she continued to make her sandwich. No, he couldn't sleep. Because he had tossed and turned, remembering every kiss, every tantalizing taste. He had even considered going outside, walking the cliffs as if he would find her there. As if she would be waiting.

"Maybe I should eat, too," he said. He wasn't hungry, but he couldn't think of another excuse to get close to her, to stand beside her and torture the hell out of himself.

"Oh, okay." She moved to allow him room at the butcher-block isle.

He came forward, grazing her shoulder as he reached for the bread. She slipped by him to rinse a tomato. And when she turned back, her robe fell open.

He wasn't a painter, a man who made images come to life, but at this moment, this incredible, breathtaking moment, he sought to immortalize her. Kathy's nightgown was as filmy as a lace curtain, as sheer as a summer rain. Her nipples brushed the surface, and he imagined the fabric cool and sleek against her skin.

He lifted his head, and their gazes collided. The tomato fell from her hand and rolled onto the butcher block. And then nothing moved. Nothing made a sound.

"What's happening?" she whispered, her voice barely audible.

He heard her, yet he didn't. Her robe was still open, and heat rose between their bodies like steam. He knew they fought to breathe the same air.

Outside the wind grew angry with lust, forcing its way through the trees. He could hear it rattling the windows.

He fought the urge to push her to the floor, tumble and roll, tear at the wisp of silk and lace she wore. Wild, forbidden lovemaking. The wind was challenging him to take her. His loins hardened, his pulse quickened, his mouth went dry. He moistened his lips and imagined tasting hers.

What's happening?

The wind howled again, and Dakota gripped the counter. Damn the wind. Damn the ache in his groin. He stared at Kathy; she stared back at him. Her eyes shone like emeralds. Sensual. Catlike.

Damn her.

Damn them both.

"Nothing's happening," he said, masking the arousal in his voice, the huskiness that nearly made him hoarse. "Your robe came undone, and..."

She moved like lightning, a blur before his eyes. When he focused again, her robe was belted, snug and secure. She picked up the tomato as though trying to backtrack, make that other moment disappear.

She glanced at him quickly, then looked away. She couldn't meet his gaze, yet only moments ago those green eyes bore brazenly into his.

This was so damn awkward, he thought. It shouldn't be, but it was. He had seen every inch of her, caressed her most intimate places. They had showered together, licked beads of water off each other's skin. They weren't sexual strangers. Yet they were. Three years spanned between them—an eternity.

"Maybe we should talk about it."

"There's nothing to talk about." She studied the tomato she had cut into even little slices. "We're making sandwiches."

"I'm not hungry. I only said I wanted a sandwich so I

could get close to you. But I'm okay now. I got through it, and so did you.'' He tossed his bread in the trash. ''This is only our first night. We'll feel better in the morning. Normal.'' The wind would calm and the sexual pull would pass. Daylight would make everything all right.

She glanced up. ''Do you think so?''

He could hope. ''Sure. We just have to get used to each other.''

Much to his relief, Kathy smiled—a small, delicate tilt of her lips. ''Maybe I'll pass on the sandwich, too,'' she said. ''It's been a long day, and I could use some sleep.''

Dakota finally slept, not a deep, soundless sleep, but enough to help him function the following morning. He knew he would find Kathy in the kitchen. He could smell breakfast, the homey aroma of bacon sizzling and eggs frying.

He stood at the bathroom sink and splashed water on his face. A shower could wait. He couldn't recall the last time Kathy had cooked for him. It was a good sign, he thought. Apparently she had decided to put what had happened behind them.

As casually as possible, he entered the kitchen. ''Good morning. Is there anything I can do to help?''

She turned away from the stove, and for a moment, a suspended moment in time, their eyes met. And held.

He stood, riveted to the floor, the tiles cool against his feet. Don't let it happen again. Not now. Not today.

She blinked, and the air in his lungs whooshed out.

''You can set the table.''

''Sure. Okay.'' He opened the appropriate cabinet and removed the dishes. ''The bacon smells good. A great aroma to wake up to.''

''I figured we could both use a hearty breakfast.'' She motioned to the coffee pot. ''It's strong and dark, just the way you like it.''

''Thanks.'' Sidetracked now, he left the table half set. Pouring himself a mug of freshly perked coffee, he leaned against the counter and sipped. Was Kathy worried about his meeting with Payune? Was that the reason for this special treatment? Or was she trying to prove how normal staying in the same house could be?

Her hair was coiffed to perfection, he noticed, the fiery tresses twisted neatly, two pearl combs making an elegant statement. Her skin glowed flawlessly, her makeup applied with skill. She wasn't dressed to go out, but he sensed she would be before long.

Realizing breakfast was ready and he'd neglected his domestic duty, he gathered some silverware and napkins. The kitchen table matched the butcher-block isle, and a bay window presented a spectacular view.

She filled their plates and took a chair. He sat across from her and smiled. She had placed his favorite hot sauce on the table. Apparently she had supplied the queen's servants with a list of foods to provide, right down to brand name selections—items imported from a variety of continents.

He lifted the bottle, then poured the spicy sauce over his eggs. "You remembered."

"Of course," she responded in an easy voice. "How could I forget? You practically refuse to eat breakfast without it."

Was she as relaxed as she seemed? Or was she drawing from her social skills to fool him? Dakota thought Kathy would make a hell of a poker player. She could bluff with the best of them. He had no idea what was actually going on in her mind.

His one-track mind, on the other hand, had taken a dangerous turn. He imagined destroying her proper hairdo, bathing her lips with strawberry preserve, then licking it off with slow, erotic strokes. Apparently his social skills, as well as his table manners, weren't enviable qualities. It didn't take much to fuel his sexual appetite—a sunny kitchen and a tasty breakfast did him just fine. Now last night's haunting didn't seem quite so odd. The woman had been wearing see-through silk.

"Do you have an appointment later?" he asked.

"Tea with the queen. The palace is sending a car for me this afternoon."

A long, black limo, no doubt. He cocked his head. "That sounds downright snooty. Why didn't you tell me before now?"

She buttered her toast. "I always have tea with the queen when I'm invited to Asterland. This is nothing out of the ordinary. It won't arouse suspicion."

He shoveled a forkful of eggs into his mouth and swallowed, enjoying the trappings of a home-cooked meal. "Routine or not, you still have to keep me informed about everywhere you go, everything you do. Don't take anything for granted while we're here. Okay?"

She nodded solemnly. "Okay."

Dakota savored a slice of bacon, and Kathy added cream to her coffee, a drink he assumed she had diluted with extra water. He knew she preferred a milder brew.

She studied her cup, and he assumed her mind was on her audience with the queen.

Today they would both slip into their respective roles.

Hours later Dakota arrived at Albert Payune's home. A crenellated gateway, reminiscent of a medieval structure, led to the entrance of the Grand Minister's estate. The house itself wasn't quite so foreboding, but it reflected European craftsmanship with its stone-by-stone construction.

A butler escorted Dakota to a dimly lit office furnished with a large mahogany desk and leather wing-back chairs. But what caught Dakota's eye was an impressive collection of swords. Displayed on the paneled walls, they wielded military power, something Payune obviously admired.

"The Grand Minister will be with you shortly," the butler said, his English heavily accented.

"Thank you," Dakota responded, exaggerating his drawl. Today he was a big, tall, rich Texan—a businessman eager to make an unethical deal.

He didn't scan his surroundings for a safe. He knew Payune wouldn't keep the stolen necklace in his office. He would probably secure the heirloom jewels in his private quarters—the master suite where he slept. Thunder was working on a diagram of the estate, so it wouldn't be long before Dakota would have a floor plan to back up his instincts.

Minutes later Payune entered the room. A man in his early fifties, he stood with his shoulders squared and his head held high. He was neither tall nor broad. He was of medium height with a medium build, his physique toned and trim. He wore a dark suit with a silk ascot tie. And although his hair was thinning, he wasn't foolish enough to style it in one of those ridiculous comb-overs. Albert Payune carried his vanity with pride. He had an impeccable quality about him, but power-hungry rulers often did.

Payune extended his hand, and they exchanged a proper greeting.

Dakota had dressed carefully for the occasion. He couldn't present himself as a showy, loud-mouthed American, because that would belie his military background. But he still wanted to be easily identified with Payune's image of Texas, so he had worn a pair of custom-made cowboy boots and a 5X Royal Stetson he'd removed upon entering the house.

"Please, have a seat, Lieutenant Lewis."

"Thank you." Dakota settled into one of the wing-back chairs while Payune walked around to the desk. Referring to a retired officer by his rank was accepted as proper protocol, and a man in Payune's position would naturally adhere to decorum.

The butler appeared with a silver tray, offering both men snifters of brandy. When the servant departed, Payune lifted his eyes to Dakota.

"So you have come to discuss a business venture?"

"Yes, sir, I have." Dakota met the other man's detached gaze. "My partners and I intend to open a resort in Asterland with the biggest, grandest casino imaginable. But our only stumbling block is King Bertram." And for the sake of this mission, a proposal for the resort had been presented to the Cabinet under the guise of a Texas corporation. A proposal Dakota knew the king would not approve.

"I see." Payune swirled his brandy. "Am I to understand

that you want me to influence King Bertram to reconsider his stand on this matter?''

''In a manner of speaking.''

''You realize the king believes our country could not successfully support a venture such as yours. Our neighbors in Obersbourg have converted a portion of their palace into an exclusive gaming casino. How many resorts are tourists willing to visit? Asterland is still quite obscure.''

''So was Obersbourg before they opened their casino.'' And Dakota knew damn well Payune didn't intend to rule an obscure little country. He wanted to put himself and Asterland on the map. ''I'm talking about a full-scale resort—a five-star hotel, a spa, a country club and a PGA quality golf course. I have some of the wealthiest men in Texas in on this deal. And we don't intend to take no for an answer.''

Payune's demeanor was no longer detached. ''I've seen your proposal. And I must admit, it was quite impressive.''

''And so is the fact that you're going to govern Asterland someday.''

''You're mistaken. Prince Eric is heir to the throne.''

Dakota chose not to comment further. The Grand Minister was playing the loyal Cabinet member, feigning disinterest in the crown.

Payune placed his hands on the desk, then linked them together. ''As I said, the proposal for your resort was impressive, but I am puzzled by one thing.''

Dakota sipped his drink even though he had never acquired a taste for brandy. ''And what would that be?''

''Why, your wife, of course. Is she aware of your venture?''

Dakota's heart took a quick, forward leap. ''She's not only aware of it, she supports it without reserve.''

''But she is also a high-ranking Foreign Affairs consular.''

Dakota kept his gaze focused on his opponent. ''That's right, she is,'' he said, his tone implying Kathy used a government job to her best advantage. If Payune assumed Kathy's friendship with the royal family had been manipulated to influence the king to approve the resort, then all the better. But before the other man concentrated too deeply on Kathy, Dakota continued, ''I was hoping, sir, that you would help me get this project off the ground. If anyone can make this happen, you can.''

Payune sat with his head tilted at a regal angle. ''I appreciate your confidence, but I do not see how I can.''

''Maybe you could take some time to think it over.'' Dakota paused a beat, then leaned forward and dropped a hint about the impending revolution, making damn sure the other man wouldn't forget this meeting. ''My partners and I are willing to make it worth your while.'' A cash settlement he hoped Payune would be in dire need of within a matter of days. ''And with your involvement, I'm sure King Bertram would no longer stand in our way.''

Kathy walked with Queen Nicole along a stone path. Both women adored flowers, and strolling the castle gardens after a tea had become one of their favorite moments to share. Azaleas, poppies, tulips, irises—Kathy couldn't begin to name them all. There were also bridges to cross, statues to admire, bodies of water rippling with sunlight.

''This is like stepping into a painting,'' Kathy said.

The queen smiled as they passed a lily pond, then stopped to breathe the country air. ''And today we are in a Monet.''

Kathy turned to look at her friend. She thought Queen Nicole was one of the most beautiful women she had ever seen. With jet black hair and violet-blue eyes, she could have been a model. Even at fifty-three, she had a face and figure cameras loved. But for Kathy there was no envy, only admiration.

''You have been quiet on this visit,'' the queen said. ''Are you not well?''

''I'm fine. It's just been so long since I've shared a home with my husband.'' At least, she thought, that was a portion of the truth. She couldn't lead the queen to believe that her personal life was in perfect order, that her supposed reconciliation with Dakota had no flaws. The queen had come to know her too well for such a charade.

''You have not told him yet, have you?''

"About the miscarriage? No. And I'm not sure I can."

The other woman guided her toward a bench overlooking a sweep of irises. "If you want to have a life with him again, then you must."

But I'm only pretending I want a life with him, Kathy thought. So what good would it do to tell him about the baby? They couldn't alter the past. Dakota hadn't been there when she'd needed him. There was nothing either one of them could do that would change that.

"You could forgive him," the queen said as though reading her mind. "There is healing in forgiveness."

Kathy watched a butterfly light upon a flower. "I know." But how could she forgive him when she knew his work would always be more important than their marriage? "We're still attracted to each other." A dangerous attraction, she thought. "I can't think clearly when I'm around him."

No, she couldn't think, but she could feel. And fantasize.

She could still see herself waiting for him on the cliffs. Waiting for him to pull her to the ground, tear her nightgown and cover her body with his. And for one haunting moment last night, she knew he had wanted the same thing—desperate, forbidden lovemaking—a union they would have regretted later.

Queen Nicole sighed. "I have no right to give advice."

Jarred from her wayward thoughts, Kathy turned, then studied her friend's sad expression. "Forgive me for asking, but are the rumors true? Is your marriage troubled?"

"Yes, very troubled. Losing Ivan has put a strain on our relationship. The king refuses to mourn his son. He cannot cope with what Ivan did."

Kathy hadn't been prepared to discuss Prince Ivan, but she could see that the other woman needed to confide in someone—someone she trusted. "Most men don't grieve the way women do. They tend to keep their feelings inside."

Queen Nicole's voice quavered. "But the king is still too hurt and too angry to grieve. And until he forgives Ivan, our lives will never be the same." She lifted her face to the sun as though the warmth would help. "I, too, was destroyed by what Ivan had done. But he left us a note. He begged for our forgiveness.''

Kathy knew Prince Ivan had arranged a car accident that had taken the lives of a neighboring princess and her lover. Plus he'd tried to force the princess's sister, Anna, to marry him and merge their countries. So in remorse and shame, the Asterland prince had committed suicide rather than face his family. ''I'm sorry. I wish there was something I could say.''

''I grieved for my son when I buried him, and I found it in my heart to forgive him. I ask nothing more of the king.''

''I understand.''

Together they rose from the bench and walked side by side in companionable silence, the garden offering solace. Kathy had never doubted the queen's love for the king, nor had she suspected her of having an affair with Payune. And now Dakota could put aside his suspicion. What troubled the royal marriage was not another man.

Footsteps sounded on the walk, and a child with a radiant smile appeared. Ten-year-old Prince Eric had slipped through a path of trees, his fretful, red-faced nanny on his heels.

The queen laughed. ''He is so full of energy.''

And so beautiful, Kathy thought. The young prince had inherited his mother's jet-black hair and easy manner. His skin was tanned from the outdoor activities he enjoyed at his American boarding school, and his eyes were dark like the king's.

Like Dakota's.

Kathy realized Prince Eric looked the way she imagined a child of hers and Dakota's would look. Immediately she thought about the baby she had lost—the little boy or girl who should be toddling beside her.

''Mother, you told me I could visit with Kathy,'' the boy said.

''Yes, but I did not say you could give Nanny a wild goose chase.'' The queen cupped her son's cheeks, then whispered. ''Nanny is not so young anymore. You must show her the courtesy befitting her age.''

''Yes, ma'am,'' he responded.

Kathy knew the boy wanted to fidget. She couldn't help but smile. Prince Eric glanced over at her with a gleam in his dark eyes. When his mother released him, he came toward her with a proper greeting, and she responded in kind.

The hug that followed made her a little misty-eyed. "I've missed you, young sir."

"And I, you." He stood gazing up at her. "Mother says I may go to the ball. At least for a little while."

"I'm glad. I'll be there, too."

"Is your husband going to escort you?"

Kathy resisted the urge to skim his bangs from his eyes. "Yes, he is."

"So I will meet him?"

She thought of her lost child again. Dakota's child. "Yes," she said softly. "I would like very much for the two of you to meet."

Kathy sat beside Dakota in their rental vehicle, heading down a winding country road toward the beach. They had dressed for a casual outing, but Kathy assumed Dakota had business on his mind. They had a lot to discuss. The queen's birthday ball was tomorrow evening, and the necklace switch still hadn't been made.

Dakota parked the utility vehicle, and they remained silent for a moment. The private beach presented a narrow stretch of sand and a clear blue ocean bathing a scatter of large, jagged rocks.

Kathy smiled to herself. Mermaids lounged on the rocks when no one could see them, she thought—their long, luxurious hair blowing in the breeze, their iridescent tails swaying to the rhythm of the sea. Were there mermen? Or did the mermaids sing their siren's song for human males—men who didn't believe in fairy tales.

Men like Dakota.

"Let's go," he said.

He carried a blanket and a backpack, and she trudged beside him in a pair of lace-up boots. It wasn't a swimsuit day. The wind blew with a brisk chill, and the ocean roared with foaming waves. Both she and Dakota wore sweatshirts and jeans.

He picked a spot away from the tide and secured the blanket the best he could. They sat beside each other, and Kathy waited for him to speak. She could have kept silent for hours just watching the sea, imagining schools of glittery fish and sunken treasures sparkling with gold.

"Have you ever been through the maze at the palace?" he asked.

Kathy turned. "Just once. Prince Eric wanted me to play hide-and-seek with him, but I ended up getting lost. He had to rescue me, even though he was the one hiding. I felt a little foolish." And somewhat frightened. The garden maze was a labyrinth of tall, dark-green shrubs, a puzzle that had made her feel like Alice in Nightmareland.

"Did you ever make it to the center?"

She nodded. "Prince Eric guided me there." And she recalled a white gazebo, a porch-type swing and a lovely arrangement of seasonal blooms. "It was pretty, but not quite worth the trouble."

He frowned. "So you wouldn't remember how to get to the gazebo on your own?"

Kathy pushed a strand of hair away from her face. She had worn her hard-to-hold hair in a practical ponytail, but already wispy tendrils were coming loose. "Heavens, no." She studied the crease between his eyebrows. "Why? What's going on?"

"I'm going to switch the necklaces during the ball."

She had no idea what that had to do with the garden maze, but, regardless, his plan made no sense. "You can't. You're a guest at the ball. Nobody can be two places at once."

"It's the only time I can make the switch, the only time I can be absolutely certain of Payune's whereabouts." He sent her a wicked grin, his teeth gleaming. "And you're wrong, I can be in two places at once."

That slash of white in an otherwise dark face made him look like a rogue. She had to tell her girlish heart to behave. "I hope you're going to explain."

He moved closer. ''Of course, I am. This plan involves you.''

And that nightmarish maze, she thought with sudden doom. ''Go ahead.''

''Okay. We'll attend the ball—drink, dance and make our presence known to Payune. Then at 2030, we'll take a walk—stroll through the maze and neck a little on our way to the gazebo.''

Her heart bumped. ''Neck?''

The roguish grin returned. ''Kiss, nibble, paw each other like lusty teenagers.''

She couldn't catch her breath, so she forced herself to gulp the sea air. She didn't want to kiss him. Well, maybe she did. But because she did, she knew she shouldn't. ''That's hardly proper behavior at a royal ball.''

He raised an eyebrow at her. ''Don't get your sequins in a snit, Kathy. This is part of the mission. Payune might be watching us. He may even decide to follow. But if he sees us wrapped in each other's arms, he'll figure we're just out on a romantic, moonlit stroll.''

How did Dakota know her dress had sequins on it? she wondered testily, wishing she had brought an alternative ball gown. ''Payune is going to be that suspicious of us? Enough to follow us outside?''

''Hell, yes. He's not a stupid man. He understood the direction I was taking yesterday. I'm a former air force officer from Royal, Texas, with a Foreign Service consular for a wife. And to top it off, we're asking to be part of his revolution.'' Dakota blew a windy breath. ''I'd say that makes us the most interesting couple at the ball.''

He was right, of course. But necking for the sake of the mission irked her. Everything Dakota did was for some top-secret assignment, and now that included kissing her. ''So what happens next?''

''We go to the gazebo, retreat to a dark corner, and I slip away. From there I break into Payune's estate, switch the necklaces and return before anyone knows I'm gone.''

Panic rose in her throat as the sound of the ocean crashed in her ears. "You're going to leave me in the maze? Alone?"

His voice gentled. "No, sweetheart. Thunder will take my place. In the dark, we're virtually twins. Same height, same body structure."

Wonderful. She would be trapped in the maze with a stranger while Dakota took all the risks. "Why can't Thunder switch the necklaces?"

"Because breaking and entering are my areas of expertise, not his."

Kathy got a mental picture of a cat burglar—a tall, shadowy figure dressed in black. Dakota would do his part, and she would have to do hers. "It's a good plan," she said, reminding herself the future of a country was at stake.

"Thanks." He removed a sheet of paper from his backpack, and it snapped in the wind. "Now all we have to do is memorize the key to the maze."

"Is that a diagram of it?" she asked, leaning toward the paper.

He nodded. "Looks like one of those magazine puzzles, doesn't it?"

"Yes, it does." The pattern of the hedges had been outlined, along with a red line marking a zigzag path to the gazebo. She assumed the resourceful mercenary named Thunder had provided it.

"Come sit here so we can study it together."

Here, Kathy realized, undoubtedly meant between those long, denim-clad legs and against that big, broad chest. She frowned at the map. Didn't he have another copy? "Why do we have to share?"

"So we can snuggle. Payune won't buy our cover if we flinch every time we touch." He adjusted his position to make room for her. "Since we have to get physical at the ball, we may as well get used to the idea now."

Sure. Right. For the sake of the mission, she thought, hiding her frown. Settling herself between his legs, she leaned back, then held her breath. In spite of the chill, a sudden, unwelcome heat blazed through her body.

"Relax," he whispered, slipping his arms around her waist.

She let out the breath she was holding and tried to focus on the sway of the ocean, the color of the sand, the sprinkle of broken sea shells surrounding their blanket. But her concentration wavered. All she could think about was the pressure of her bottom nestled between his thighs.

He moved closer and nuzzled her neck. He smelled like a familiar brand of aftershave, the one he had always worn. She swallowed and searched for a place to rest her hands.

"You still feel stiff," he said.

Well, so did he, she thought, lowering her hands to her own lap. But then his stiffness was beneath his zipper, and that probably didn't count.

"I'm fine," she responded. But when he tugged at her earlobe with his teeth, she wasn't fine. She wanted to turn her head and capture his mouth, remember the first time they had kissed. The last time. Every time in between.

He held the maze key out in front of her. The paper rippled in the wind. "Don't let it blow it away," he told her.

She grabbed it and held on for dear life. She felt him removing the decorative band from her hair, dislodging her ponytail. She knew he liked her hair loose, liked to run his hands through it, liked to mar her proper image.

"Do you still think about me, Kathy?"

In bed. He wanted to know if she climbed under the covers at night and thought about him, imagined the stroke of his tongue, the rock of his hips. That hard, powerful body thrusting into hers. "Yes."

He placed his hand over hers, then began tracing the pattern of the map. When his jaw brushed the side of her cheek, his beard stubble grazed her skin. "I think about you, too. About all the things I used to do to you." His voice turned low—hushed and aroused. "The naughty things you used to do to me."

Kathy moistened her lips.

The naughty things you used to do to me.

Suddenly the secluded beach called out to her—the allure of the wind, the scent of the sea, the passion of the sky. Now she remembered the last time they had made love. The way they had rolled over the bed, tugging at each other's clothes. His labored breathing, her hand closing over his arousal. The forceful kisses, the soft moans, the silky sensations. She had lowered her head to taste him, take him into her mouth while he'd fisted her unbound hair and raised his hips, his gaze following every urgent stroke.

"You used to watch," Kathy heard herself say. You watched that night, she thought, that wild, bittersweet night.

"And you used to make me crazy," he responded, scraping his jaw against her cheek once again. "So good. So crazy."

Her heartbeat thudded in time with his, but she knew he wouldn't kiss her, wouldn't ease the forbidden hunger flowing through their veins. Instead he would make them both wait until tomorrow night. The mission, Kathy thought. As much as they lusted after each other, they still needed an excuse—even for a kiss.

Four

Dakota walked down the hall, then stopped when he saw Kathy through her open doorway. She stood in front of a full-length mirror, checking her appearance. When she smoothed her dress, he allowed himself a long, languorous look.

The emerald-colored gown clung to her curves in a lithe, elegant shimmer. The fabric, a watery satin, caught the light each time she moved. The neckline, decorated with a row of sequins, revealed a hint of cleavage. Her skin looked warm and smooth next to all that icy green.

Her hair, he decided, had been styled with him in mind. It fell loose about her shoulders in thick, scarlet waves, both sides adorned with a diamond-and-emerald-studded comb. It appeared deliberately messy, yet fashionable. He could touch it, twine it around his fingers, lift it to his face, and no one would know. It was, Dakota thought with a smile, a hairstyle created for lovers.

When she turned his way, her hand flew to her heart. "Oh my God! You scared the daylights out of me. How long have you been standing there?"

Long enough to get turned on, he almost said, his smile tilting a little crookedly. "Just a few minutes."

Her eyes, he noticed, had been enhanced with a smoky liner. The dark, sultry illusion made them appear even more catlike. "You look incredible, Kathy."

She tilted her head, and diamonds winked at her ears. "Thank you."

She slipped into satin pumps, and he wondered what she had going on under her dress. A corset-type bra? Silk panties? A garter belt and thigh-high hose? He moved into the room so he could enjoy her mouthwatering scent. He knew she had layered her favorite body products: powder, lotion, a strawberry mist. She smelled good enough to eat, so he imagined lathering her with whipped cream—a taste from her nipples—a line down her belly—a sweet, sexy flavor between those long, gorgeous legs.

She would purr, he decided. Press herself against his mouth and make throaty little sounds.

When she glanced up, he shoved his hands in his pockets and feigned a casual air. He wasn't behaving like an officer or a gentleman. But damn it, he wanted her. Wanted to bathe her with the afterglow of a warm, wet orgasm.

"You look handsome, Dakota."

He blinked, his blood still pumping lust through his veins. Struggling to focus, he glanced at his starched white shirt. He wore a traditional black tux with a pair of onyx cufflinks. Kathy had always liked the way he looked in formal attire. "Oh, yes. Thanks."

She opened a sequin evening bag and placed a lace handkerchief, a gold compact and a tube of lipstick inside. Then reaching into the closet, she removed a shimmering green jacket that matched her sleeveless dress. "I'm ready."

They walked toward the front door, then he turned and headed into the kitchen. "I forgot something." Opening the fridge, he removed a windowed box. "It's a wrist corsage." A delicate floral design he couldn't resist—a white orchid with gold ribbon and a spray of baby's breath shimmering with emerald glitter.

"How did you know?" she asked, reaching for the flower, her voice soft with feminine wonder.

"That it would match your gown?" he watched her slip the corsage around her wrist. "I didn't. I ordered it because it reminded me of you." And because he knew it would complement the diamonds and emeralds sparkling on her finger—the engagement ring and wedding band he had given her.

An hour later they arrived at the palace, then stood with the other guests in a receiving line, waiting to pay their respects to the royal family. The king stood tall in a uniform that displayed his commander-in-chief status. Dakota assumed Payune drooled inwardly over that uniform, since the impressive armed forces rank came with the crown.

The queen glittered in a diamond tiara and a sparkling gown, and young Prince Eric wore a serious expression, even though boyish excitement brightened his dark eyes.

The ballroom dominated nearly an entire floor. Crystal chandeliers glimmered from the ceiling and leaded-glass doors led to the gardens. Tables in the dining area were set with candles, polished silver and fine linens. A velvet curtain with gold tie-backs signaled the entrance to the dance hall.

Dakota wasn't the least bit nervous, but he was no longer out of his element. Tonight's agenda put him in control. The ball was now a crucial part of the mission.

As the festivities got underway, Kathy spoke to a great number of people—most of them as noble as their prestigious European titles. Dakota kept one eye trained on Albert Payune and noticed the Grand Minister kept an equally close eye on him.

Kathy excused herself from an elderly duke, and Dakota escorted her to the expansive buffet. It was, he thought, the most impressive spread he had ever seen. Each delicacy was a work of art, but Kathy had told him that renowned chefs from around the world had been flown in to prepare the menu. Serving platters brimmed with deviled quail eggs, gingered capon, crab soufflé, tender meats, fresh vegetables and exotic fruits. The dessert tables displayed decadent cakes, parfaits, tortes, tarts and meringues.

They filled their plates and sat beside each other in their designated seats. Kathy sampled a lobster crepe, then looked up and smiled. Their gazes locked in an intense stare, and Dakota knew their minds had connected. Yesterday's erotic admission billowed between them like a warm, sensual cloud. Both still fantasized about being in each other's arms—aroused and naked.

Her tongue darted out to taste the crepe, and he nearly groaned. He wanted to kiss her. Here. Right now. In front of the king and all of his fancily attired court.

But as other guests occupied their table, Dakota reined in his hormones. And while they ate their meal, they engaged in varied conversations.

On occasion Dakota glanced at Payune from across the room and noticed Payune kept stealing glances at the queen.

After dessert and coffee, the king and queen danced the first waltz. Dakota and Kathy stood with other guests, watching the royal couple glide across the floor.

"They look so right together," Kathy said, her voice tinged with sadness.

Dakota frowned. His wife was still upset by the queen's troubled marriage. Or was it the reminder of their own broken vows that she thought of tonight? He sensed this was not the moment to ask her to dance. Instead he suggested they explore the alcoves in the ballroom, and she readily agreed.

The first windowed section held a pair of seventeenth-century Venetian chairs, and the second displayed borders of rose-covered silk and a marble table.

Kathy examined a gilded vase on the table, and Dakota moved closer. "Did you wear your hair like that for me?" he asked, studying the tumbling red tresses she normally struggled to contain. He would not allow her sadness to linger. Not tonight.

She hesitated, then met his gaze, her eyes as illuminating as her gown. "Yes," she said softly.

"Because you knew I would want to run my hands through it?"

"Yes," she whispered again.

He skimmed her cheek. She hadn't reapplied her lipstick. Her lips were moist and slightly parted, just waiting for his. Dare he kiss her now? Inside the palace?

He dropped his hand. He couldn't. There were too many guests milling about, too many foreign dignitaries, dukes and counts, lords and ladies.

"Excuse me. Ma'am? Sir?" a voice said.

Dakota cursed his lack of focus. Someone had managed to approach without his knowledge. And at the very moment he had been debating a kiss, no less. He raised an eyebrow at Kathy. She, too, seemed surprised. Unsure of what to expect, they turned simultaneously.

Prince Eric stood before them. In spite of his regal posture and proper tuxedo, the boy's appearance made Dakota smile. The child's thick black hair rebelled from a slick side part, a cowlick fighting desperately for control. Apparently the young prince had hair as hard to tame as Kathy's.

They responded to the boy as protocol dictated, and Dakota decided Prince Eric owned not an ounce of pretension. He was being groomed to rule an old-world country, but his manner put both Dakota and Kathy at ease.

"Are you a United States Air Force lieutenant?" the boy asked Dakota, clearly wondering why he wasn't in uniform.

"I retired from duty four years ago," Dakota told him.

"Are you a pilot?"

"Yes. Do planes interest you?"

"Yes, and cowboys, too," came the youthful response. "I attend a boarding school in America."

Dakota resisted the urge to slip Kathy a sideways glance. He supposed he looked like a forty-one-year-old cowboy with his rugged skin and hard-earned crow's-feet. His Texas drawl certainly fit the cowboy mold. Dakota didn't have a lot of experience with children, so the last thing he had expected was admiration from an adolescent prince. It boosted his pride with a masculine sort of awe.

"So you like horses, then?"

Prince Eric nodded, his voice a little quieter. "But I prefer a Western saddle to the hunt seat," he said as if the admission might earn him a European scolding. A security officer in the royal service stood a non-intrusive distance away, keeping a careful eye on the boy.

Dakota smiled. He doubted the stoic-faced guard had heard, and even if he had, who would tattle on a future king?

For a moment Dakota thought to invite the child to his ranch. He could teach the young prince about Comanche horsemanship. In Dakota's culture, a boy didn't merely learn to ride. He had to be a trick rider, practice picking up objects while his mount traveled at full speed. And the ten-year-old prince, with his rebellious hair and dark, curious eyes, would make a quick study. European royalty, he thought, with a Comanche soul.

Dakota shook off the notion, realizing he had allowed an unexpected paternal urge to get the best of him. He couldn't extend an invitation to Price Eric, he thought, a twinge of regret constricting his chest. Who would explain his true marital status? Who would tell the child that Kathy no longer lived at the ranch? It was bad enough the young Prince would be burdened by his parents' personal problems. He didn't need to be dragged into Dakota's as well.

After Prince Eric departed, Dakota and Kathy returned to the main ballroom. As they left the charming alcove, Kathy's heartbeat quickened. Heading toward them was Albert Payune, his steely blue eyes focused directly on her.

There was no way to avoid him. Soon they would come face-to-face with the man who had been watching them for most of the night. Did Payune know that Prince Eric had looked upon Dakota with youthful admiration? Or that Dakota had smiled affectionately at the child? The rightful heir to the Asterland throne?

Payne shifted his gaze to Dakota. "Lieutenant Lewis," he said in a formal greeting. "Are you enjoying the ball?"

"Yes, thank you. And you, sir?"

Such stifled pleasantries, Kathy thought, her pulse refusing to relax. How could Dakota stand there looking so calm?

Because it was his job, she reminded herself. Her husband thrived on danger.

"It is a lovely affair," Payune responded in an unemotional tone. He turned to Kathy, trapping her with a cool smile. "Mrs. Lewis, you look simply stunning."

She forced herself to meet those frosty blue eyes. "Thank you."

He held her gaze, and she knew he was testing her, waiting to see if she squirmed. She lifted her chin a notch, even though she feared the pounding of her heart would give her panic away.

"Your husband came to see me the other day," Payune said. "We had quite an interesting chat."

She glanced briefly at Dakota. He didn't come closer, didn't coax or comfort her in any way. But the Grand Minister studied them with keen interest. Assessing their body language, she assumed.

"Yes, he told me," she said. "And I do hope you will consider his offer."

"We shall see. For now, it is much too grand a night to concern ourselves with business." He reached for her hand and brushed his mouth over her knuckles in the same manner he had brushed off her statement. "But I would be honored, Mrs. Lewis, if you would save me a dance."

"Of course." She wanted to snag her hand back and wipe it on her dress. Even his lips were cold.

Dakota moved in with a smile, touching her with sudden familiarity. She did her best not to collapse in his arms.

"My lovely wife promised me a tour of the gardens. Didn't you, darling?"

"Yes, I did. The grounds are breathtaking."

"Do not detain her for too long, Lieutenant." Payune split his cool gaze between them. "I am looking forward to that dance."

The instant Kathy and Dakota stepped outside, she allowed herself a nervous shiver.

"Are you cold?" he asked. "Do you need your jacket?"

"No, I'm fine. The air feels good." She took a deep,

cleansing breath. Already she could smell sweet, earthy scents rising from the flowers. She would draw from their beauty, she thought. Their magic. Surely the palace gardens had resident fairies, little winged creatures who would keep them safe.

They walked arm in arm for a short while, taking the stone path that would eventually lead to the maze. As they came upon the queen's traditional rose garden, he spoke in a hushed tone. Other guests explored the grounds, their voices a distant buzz.

''You did fine, sweetheart.''

''He's suspicious of us.''

''Of course, he is. I expected as much. He isn't the sort of man who puts his trust in others. Not even those he considers allies.''

And that worried her. Payune might accept Dakota's offer, might bring him into the revolution, but her husband would be watched. Maybe too closely.

Before she could ask if he thought they were being followed, Dakota stopped to draw her into his arms. Needing him, she came willingly. He dipped his head and his breath fluttered across her cheek, then brushed her lips.

The kiss was tender and protective, and she welcomed it from deep within her soul. Roses flourished all around them—a gathering of soft, velvety petals—long, sturdy stems and prickly thorns. Beauty and danger, her mind warned.

This man.

This moment.

Their tongues touched lightly, ever so lightly. It was a tease, an awakening. He tasted of Russian vodka. Just a little, she realized, just enough to induce a slow, warm intoxication.

She let the sensation steep her, heat and melt and pull her into a dreamy state. He licked her bare shoulder, grazed it with his teeth. She clung to him, felt a shift in his stance. She inhaled his cologne, wanting to breathe him into her lungs, into her body.

He nuzzled her neck, then lifted his head and brought his face next to hers. ''We have to go. We can't stay here.''

"I know." Somewhere in the back of her foggy mind, she heard voices. Someone was speaking French. A language as fluid as their kiss.

Although flood lights lit the gardens, shadows danced across their path—dark, leafy shapes—tall, billowy figures. Their feet scraped the stone walk, scattering pebbles. The natural perfume from the roses had disappeared. Beyond them lay an endless carpet of grass, and in the distance a dark, ominous structure.

The maze stood like an ancient castle, ghostly and foreboding. The music from the palace seemed ghostly, too—a lonely waltz drifting into the shadows.

"It looks haunted," Kathy said. And if someone followed, they couldn't be sure. Payune could have sent a tail—a dark figure who blended into the night. There were too many shrubs, too many trees in which to take cover.

They cut across the grass; it was damp and freshly mowed. She felt her shoes sink into the moisture.

The opening of the maze beckoned, and she feared that first step. It would swallow them, and then Dakota would disappear.

They followed the path they had memorized. It went on forever, twists and turns, fake passageways, clever openings. There was enough light to keep from stumbling, but not enough to make her feel safe.

The gazebo surfaced like a mirage, but it, too, seemed haunted. The swing rocked on its own, just a little, just enough to frighten her. A spray of flowers grew from the soil—blooms too unusual and too exotic to name. Nothing felt familiar. Nothing felt right.

The night had eyes, she thought.

Dakota took her hand and guided her into a corner—a tall, rectangular shape that led to another geometric cove.

And then his mouth came down on hers.

Hard.

So hard she locked her knees to keep herself from falling.

There was no time to think, no time to dwell on ghosts and

swings and heady-scented flowers. His hands, those big, powerful hands circled her waist and pulled her flush against him.

This was no phantom lover, no figment of her imagination. He was real, solid, built of bronzed flesh and unyielding bones. She explored the breadth of his shoulders, the tapering of his waist, the muscles that jumped in his stomach.

And while arousal flooded her system, he played with the zipper on her dress, sliding it down, then back up again—cupping her bottom, pressing heat against heat.

She heard sounds. Her sigh. His low growl. The slice of her zipper.

He delved into her hair, and she felt it fall into his hands, tumble over his wrists and down his arms.

He kissed her, over and over, sipping and tasting. Her nipples tingled against the silk of her bra, the satin of her dress.

They made love through their clothes, she thought. There was no other way to describe the sleek, sliding motion. The pressure building upon need. The hot, fumbling strokes.

But they didn't have long. It would end too soon—this glorious, wicked sensation. And it wasn't enough, not nearly enough.

He gentled the kiss, then drew back to look at her, his breathing a series of husky pants. Moonlight slashed across his face—the razor edge of his cheekbones, the sensual shape of his lips, the hard, smooth line of his jaw.

"I wish I could take you. Here. Right now."

She understood, and the thought made her dizzy. He wanted to lift her dress, remove her panties, untuck his shirt, open his trousers.

Suddenly she didn't care if the night had eyes. She could almost feel him moving deep inside her, each powerful thrust urging them to completion. "Then stay with me," she whispered.

He rubbed his forehead across hers, his voice quiet—broken words only they could hear. "I can't. You know I can't."

Yes, she knew. But the fear had returned, and she didn't want to lose him. It was always the same fear, the one that had surfaced soon after she'd married him. He would go away and never come back.

Don't do this to me, she wanted to say. Don't make me remember why I can't be your wife. Not now. Not while I'm here in your arms.

"Close your eyes," he told her.

She did as he asked, and he carried her to the connecting cove. As her feet touched the ground, he kissed her. A touch that fluttered across her lips like the elusive wings of a butterfly.

She could still smell the woodsy scent of his cologne, but when she opened her eyes, she looked into the shadowy face of a stranger. Dakota was gone, and in his place stood the man called Thunder.

Payune's estate wasn't far from the palace, and Thunder had left everything Dakota needed, including a vehicle that took him to a grassy field laden with foliage. Dakota parked between two gnarled old trees, then brought the night optics to his eyes. He could see the stone wall that surrounded the Grand Minister's estate. He had studied the floor plan of the sprawling estate, and he knew the home contained three safes. The necklace could be in any one of them, but he was banking on the one located in the master suite.

Dakota adjusted his gloves. He had already slipped on a pair of dark coveralls and changed his shoes. There was nothing left to do but switch the necklaces and return to Kathy's waiting arms.

What would happen to Kathy if he foiled this mission? Dakota started across the field, his mind suddenly troubled. Thunder would take care of her. The other man had given his word.

A burst of masculine rivalry surged through his veins like a charge of angry adrenaline. Yeah, that was all he needed. A guy who looked like himself taking care of his wife.

His face shielded by a ski mask, Dakota scaled the wall, grateful Payune wasn't a fan of guard dogs. Or dogs in general. All Dakota had to think about was the household staff, and a skeletal crew at that. Apparently Payune didn't trust employees of the royal service any more than he trusted a Doberman or a rottweiler not to turn on him. But then Payune was a man who had plenty to hide, and people as well as dogs could usually smell a rat. Especially if they lived under the same roof with one.

Taking to the shadows, Dakota disengaged the alarm, a tedious task of stripping and rearranging wires. He did the same with the phone lines, knowing he would have to reverse the process after he switched the necklaces.

Dodging flood lights and a security camera, he ascended the terrace like a mountain climber claiming Mount Everest, then stood beside the door that led to the master suite, his back to a stone wall.

Get in and get out, he told himself. Kathy was waiting.

Frowning, he picked the lock. That's right. Kathy waited in the maze, in a dark, cozy corner with Thunder—an Apache with the heart of a rogue and a smile to match. Women loved the hell out of that guy. And Dakota trusted him. Until now.

Payune's private suite came into view, but Dakota didn't waste time assessing the man's ostentatious taste in art and antiques. There were three sets of connecting rooms. He turned to the wall that contained the built-in safe and grinned. This was too easy—a scene from an outdated television show. An aristocratic portrait with a stolen necklace behind it.

He went to work on the safe and what he didn't find had him cursing under his breath. That out-dated television script had just thrown him a Hollywood curve ball. There wasn't a ruby in sight.

The library or the office? he asked himself. Which safe was it in? He checked his watch and thought about Kathy. With Thunder.

He slipped out of Payune's suite and took up residence in an unlit corner of the hallway. The servants' quarters were in the back of the house, and he could only hope the household staff had tucked themselves in for the night. And if not, he had already mapped out every escape route imaginable.

The stairs descended in a circular motion, a slick polished

banister guiding the way. He took each step soundlessly. But as he made his way toward the library, he spotted a flood of light streaking beneath the kitchen door. Not a security light like some of the others burning throughout the estate. This bright flash said that someone was working in there.

His senses went into full alert. Freshly baked bread. A pot of simmering soup. The contented hum of a plump, elderly cook.

Footsteps sounded. Foreign voices spoke. Maids, two of them. He stood like a masked statue, his body molded to the side of an antique hutch taller and wider than himself. The women entered the kitchen, and he heard feminine chatter and bowls clanking. Apparently the cook had prepared a late-night meal.

When the rat is away, Dakota thought, his mouth splitting into a grin—the household staff will gossip and play.

A push of pure adrenaline led him into the library. He went right to his mark, pulled out the false front on a bookshelf and uncovered the safe.

The rubies glittered like blood, and a surge of excitement shot straight to his groin. With his mind on his wife, he slipped the necklace into a pouch, leaving the fake for Payune.

Years of experience kept Dakota on track, even though Kathy occupied his thoughts. He completed the job and returned to the palace grounds. With a pounding heart, he followed the twists and turns in the maze, then stopped when he saw them.

Kathy and Thunder.

They stood near the gazebo, leaning toward each other, their shadowed faces much too close. Thunder could have been him, Dakota thought. No one would suspect that the man gazing into Kathy's eyes was an imposter. He looked like her husband.

Her lover.

A knot of jealousy twisted Dakota's gut. He mimicked the caw of a raven, signaling his return—a call Thunder would recognize.

The other man leaned a little closer to Kathy, then took her hand and guided her toward the section of the maze where Dakota waited. Kathy didn't seem aware of what was happening, but Dakota knew she couldn't see him, not when a tall, dark shrub stood between them.

"I'll be right back," Thunder whispered as he moved away from her.

Like hell you will, Dakota thought, even though he knew Thunder didn't intend to keep his word.

A moment later, the two men came face-to-face, but neither dared speak. Dakota handed over the pouch containing the necklace, and Thunder grinned before he stole into the night, letting Dakota know he had enjoyed every minute of his assignment.

Wonderful. His wife and the guy who had taken a bullet for him. How was that for an equation?

Dakota slipped around the hedge and, in spite of the darkness, Kathy recognized him instantly. She threw her arms around his neck and practically melted in his arms.

He stroked her hair and smiled. Apparently he had been missed.

Their mouths came together then, more in relief than passion, but an overwhelming pleasure squeezed his heart. At that mind-spinning moment, he felt loved.

Beautifully, thoroughly loved. An illusion, maybe. But a damn good one.

"We can't stay," he whispered as they came up for air. "We have to go back." The job had taken longer than he'd expected, and they couldn't afford to arouse Payune's suspicion anymore than they already had.

"I know," she responded, stroking his face as though his features might disappear if she didn't touch him.

They walked back to the palace, but before they re-entered the ballroom, Kathy stopped and let out a breath. "Do I look a mess?"

He smiled. Her hair fell about her shoulders in gorgeous disarray and her cheeks as well as her lips were flushed. "You look thoroughly kissed, sweetheart."

She didn't return his smile. "I have to freshen up before anyone sees me." She glanced down at her shoes. "Oh, goodness. They have grass stains."

He suppressed an amused grin. Her shoes were green to begin with, an emerald satin that matched her dress. "I don't think anyone will notice. But I'll escort you to the nearest powder room, so you can get yourself together. Okay?"

"Thank you."

"Kathy?" He took her hand. "Afterward, will you dance with me?"

She went stiff, her hand suddenly cold. "I promised *him* a dance."

And Payune would be waiting, Dakota thought. "Don't worry, you'll get through it. And if he tries to monopolize your time, I'll cut in." Dakota wanted to hold her, just once more. In spite of the sexy things they had said to each other earlier, he knew they wouldn't be sharing the same bed tonight. Stars still lit up the sky and flowers still scented the air, but the moment had passed.

"What am I supposed to say if he asks where we've been? We've been gone a long time, Dakota."

He guided her to the door. "Just tell him we got lost in the maze." It was, he thought, as close to the truth as they could admit. Even to themselves.

Five

Two days after the ball, Dakota entered Albert Payune's home, an invitation extended by a phone call early that morning. The butler escorted him to the parlor, and Payune told the servant not to disturb him. Besides Payune, there were three other men already in the room. Dakota recognized all of them. Two were low-level Asterland cabinet members—willing participants in the impending revolution, he assumed.

And the third?

Dakota locked gazes with the average-looking man. He could have been anyone's neighbor, European or American. With his wavy brown hair and relaxed stance, he didn't appear to have a sinister bone in his body. Dakota knew otherwise. Mark Delray, as he had just been formally introduced, was a hired assassin. They had never met before, but Dakota had seen Mark's photograph in a top-secret military file. Different name, but that average, nice-guy face was one he wasn't likely to forget.

Someone was going to be murdered. Today, tomorrow or

possibly the day after. Soon, he thought, the assassin would strike soon. Dakota glanced around the room and hoped to hell he wasn't the intended recipient of Mark Delray's hit.

Kathy had practically worn a hole in the carpet. What was taking so long? Where was Dakota? She peered out the window. Dusk had begun to settle in the sky. A bright orange sun was setting, a silvery moon hiding somewhere, waiting to take its place.

Feeling claustrophobic, she headed out the front door and down the scattered-stone walkway until she reached the grassy cliffs. She needed to breathe, needed to feel the wind on her face.

There was no one to call, no one to spill her worries to. How long could a meeting with Payune take? Dakota had left six hours ago.

Six hours. Six days. At the moment she couldn't distinguish the difference. All she knew was that he hadn't returned, and she feared for his safety.

Thunder would contact her if there was trouble. She tugged on an errant strand of hair as it fell free from its pinned coiffure. What if Thunder didn't know Dakota was in trouble. What then?

She stared out at the hilly terrain. The beauty mocked her mood. The sky was ablaze with a fiery glow and wildflowers dotted the hills with a lavender hue.

She spotted a familiar SUV in the distance, a white Mercedes ML moving up the winding road. "Thank you, God," she whispered.

Dakota parked the vehicle, and she stood watching him, the wind playing havoc with her hair. She couldn't run to him, no matter how much she wanted to. If she took that first step, she would probably burst into tears and cry in his arms, shake uncontrollably and kiss him senseless.

So she waited instead, her feet bare, the hem of a pale blue dress billowing in the breeze, her heart as fiery as the setting sun. Suddenly she wanted to kiss him, taste and tug and pull him to the ground. She wanted to feel those muscles bunch beneath her hands, hold him and never let go. He was safe. He was safe.

He exited the car, then caught sight of her. For a moment he stood motionless, watching the way she watched him. And then he smiled, a flash of white in that dark handsome face.

He came toward her, then stopped just shy of touching. "It's over," he said. "Or it will be in the morning."

"Over?"

"Payune and the others will be arrested tomorrow. I found what I needed to know and passed the information to Thunder."

"And Thunder contacted the Royal Police?"

Dakota nodded. "Payune is expecting the money tomorrow, but that's not what he's going to get."

Kathy released a sigh of relief. If her feet weren't planted so firmly in the grass, she might have lost her footing and toppled over. "You did it."

"We did it," he corrected gently. "I couldn't have pulled this off without you."

She blinked back a collection of tears. The sun had disappeared, but the sky was still a haven of color. Magenta streaks blazed through slashes of orange and beams of midnight blue. It was beautiful, and so was he—this tall, powerful man.

"Kathy?"

"Hmmm?"

"They were going to kill the king."

Her heart went still, much too still. But rather than respond in a frightened voice, she waited for Dakota to continue. "It wasn't Payune's original plan. But when he heard that the royal marriage was in trouble, he got this insane brainstorm."

Dakota pulled a hand through his hair, spiking the thick, ebony strands. "Payune tried to convince me that the king was emotionally disturbed, just like Prince Ivan."

Kathy's heart was no longer still, it pounded with a hard thump. "They were going to murder King Bertram and make it look like a suicide."

"That's right. And in Payune's warped mind, Queen Nicole would have eventually turned to him for solace. Of course Payune didn't admit to any of this outright, but one of the other cabinet members got my attention on the sly.''

''How?'' she asked, picturing Dakota in that risky situation.

''He was pouring drinks for everyone. And when he handed mine over, he whispered, 'follow me.' I knew he meant after the meeting. At first I was concerned that I was being set up for a hit. But then, something—instinct, I guess—told me he was going to make some sort of confession.'' Kathy fought a shiver, and Dakota continued. ''So after the meeting I followed him to a deserted road.''

''And he told you about Payune's plan?''

''Yes, he did. And he's willing to cooperate with the Royal Police. He never expected this to come down to murder, but he didn't know how to approach the police without arousing Payune's suspicion.''

Kathy battled another chill, realizing how often Dakota had been exposed to dangerous situations. ''How did this cabinet member know you were out to get Payune?''

''He didn't. He just figured an American businessman wouldn't want to be implicated in the assassination of a king.''

She tipped her head and looked up at the sky, then back at Dakota. ''I'm so glad it's over.''

''Me, too.''

They stood staring at each other, and she nearly lost her breath. ''I'm going to miss this cottage.'' And she would miss him—those piercing black eyes and that Comanche smile.

''It is kind of magical.'' He moved closer, brushing his body against hers, his lips just a heartbeat away.

A pounding, drumming heartbeat.

He lowered his head, and she closed her eyes. There was no time to think, to rationalize. There was only Dakota's mouth covering hers.

He tasted as clean as the elements, as spicy as the scent of his cologne. She stood on her toes and clung to him. Heat burned throughout her body, making her breath catch in her throat. She arched to feel as much of him as she could, but it wasn't enough.

While he kissed her, she tugged his shirt from his trousers, then unbuttoned it, searching for muscle and male flesh. The wind snapped the tails of the fabric, pulling it away from his chest. She grazed him with her nails, and he shifted his hips and deepened the kiss.

His hands were suddenly everywhere, all over her, sliding and roaming. He went after the front of her dress, popping buttons as he did. Dragging his lips down the column of her neck, he unhooked her bra. Kathy moaned and bit his shoulder. Dakota tongued her nipple.

She held him against her breast and watched him suckle. A blade of moonlight glinted off his hair, and she realized dusk had slipped into darkness. Her bra remained slack, falling against her body.

No, there was no time to think. No time to care about anything but how he made her feel. She had become part of this enchanted world—the cliffs and the trees and the ocean crashing below. She pictured the waves rising and swelling, bathing the rocks in crystalline sheets. Just as Dakota bathed her—with his mouth, his tongue.

She buried her hands in his hair while he licked, then pulled on those short spiky strands as he closed his teeth around her. It was gentle. It was rough. An ache that brought both pleasure and pain.

When he stepped back to look at her, a light breeze blew across her nipples, chilling them.

"Tell me you want more," he said.

Her breath rushed out of her lungs. "I do." She wanted everything. Every touch, every kiss, every slick, hot sensation he could give her. "I want more."

As he pushed her dress from her shoulders, Kathy felt it pool at her feet in a flutter of pale-blue lace.

Their gazes locked in a magnetic pull. His eyes were black against the night, dark and compelling. And his face, so close to hers, was hard and smooth and mildly abrasive. She stroked his skin, memorizing him beneath the stars.

He didn't remove her panties. Instead he skimmed her

tummy, then slid his hand under the elastic. She rocked against his hand, and he stroked—a gentle, rhythmic pressure.

He pushed a finger deep inside, and she gasped. More. Yes, she wanted more. He kissed her, took her mouth while he made her unbearably wet.

She tasted desire in his kiss, felt it blaze like a neon moon. She gripped his shoulders and lost herself in his touch—his hand moving between her thighs, those long, callused fingers teasing and arousing.

Deeper.

Wetter.

"Let it happen," he whispered.

She had no choice. The wind rushed through her hair, spilling pieces over her shoulders and down her arms. One strand adhered itself to her nipple, to the moisture he had made. His fingers surged into her with exquisite force. Desperate, she kissed him so hard, they both gasped for air.

Need clawed like talons, and she rubbed against his hand—against the pressure, the friction, the fire she couldn't control.

And then suddenly the world stilled, and there was nothing but the sound of her release. She heard it rip from her throat and echo into the night before she closed her eyes and let herself tumble.

Kathy collapsed in his arms, so Dakota held her in a soft, quiet moment. The moon sent fiery streaks through her hair, and her skin glowed with a passionate sheen. She was beautiful. So beautiful. Bathed in the afterglow of the climax he had given her.

He brushed her cheek, and she made a kittenish sound. She was still dazed, still caught between silk and sensation. He ran his hands down the sides of her body, down the long, lithe curves. Her tummy was flat, her hips lean yet womanly, her breasts full, nipples taut and aroused.

He was aroused, too. So damn aroused.

His shirt flapped in the wind, and he wondered if she was cold. She wore nothing but a pair of lace panties. Blue lace and smooth, creamy skin.

"I'm taking you inside." He swept her into his arms, and she clung to him, her hair falling free from its confinement. It spilled over her shoulders like a scarlet ribbon, reminding him of Christmas and birthdays and all the holidays he had missed holding her.

Tonight they would make up for lost time. Tonight, he thought, carrying her to the master bedroom, they would make love.

He placed her on the bed and turned on a lamp. An amber bulb lit the room, illuminating with a soft glow. There were fresh flowers on the nightstand, and he knew she had picked them. They were wild, the same lavender blooms that dotted the cliffs. Everything in the room was decidedly feminine—pillows the color of champagne, window sheers trimmed in lace, a quilt as silky as her skin.

It made him feel erotic, a little forbidden—a man stealing into a lady's chamber at night.

Oh, yes, he thought, as he unbuckled his belt, this cottage was haunted. A sexual haunting he had no will to stop.

"Let me touch you," she said.

"Go ahead," he challenged, his shirt gone, belt undone, trousers unzipped. "Touch as much as you want. Wherever you want."

Painfully aroused, he stood before her while she sat on the edge of the bed and looked up at him. She skimmed his belly, gently abrading him with her nails. And then she leaned forward and pressed her mouth to the scar just below his navel.

His stomach was corrugated with muscles, and each and every one of them jumped, sending a cool, clean shiver straight to his groin.

Damn it. He closed his eyes, then opened them, realizing they had forgotten something. One simple, important little thing.

"I didn't bring any protection." Three years of celibacy had left him without a reason to think about it. Until now. "Tell me we can risk it." They had taken risks before. But Kathy knew her own body, knew when it was safe.

"I..." Something flashed in her eyes. Pain? Sadness? He couldn't be sure, wasn't certain if he wanted to know. Suddenly their emotions were too close to the edge. They were half naked, looking into each other's eyes, stripping each other's souls.

He skimmed her cheek. "Kathy?"

Her breath hitched. "I want you to love me."

"Then I will."

He discarded his boots and shed his belt, then lowered himself to the bed. She reached for his trousers, and together they battled to remove them.

Soon his pants landed at the foot of the bed along with his briefs. She still wore those pale blue panties, so he slipped them off, tugging the lace from her hips.

The sheets smelled sweet, like Kathy, like fresh-picked berries on a summer morning. He imagined living there, in this bed, with her by his side.

They could feed on each other, sustain themselves with sex. Luscious, wild strawberry-scented sex. It was an insane notion, but it made him smile.

And then she reached between their bodies, and every coherent thought slipped from his mind. He surged hot and greedy into her palm, and she closed her fingers around him.

His pulse pounded. He wanted to slam into her, take her as hard and fast as he could. Yet he wanted to savor and touch and kiss and make the urgency last.

Pinning her to the bed, he cuffed her wrists with his hands. Her hair was everywhere, a mass of scarlet ribbon tangling over her shoulders, down her arms, across the pillow. One silky wave curled around one taut, rosy nipple. She was his fantasy. She had always been his ideal, and he had wanted her from the first moment he had seen her.

She looked up at him, seducing him with those exotic green eyes. She must have been a cat in another life, he thought. A lean, leggy creature with claws.

She struggled against his restraint, rising to nuzzle his chest, purring like the feline he imagined her to be.

He smiled and held her down again. Hot and restless, she moved beneath him, challenging him to take her, to make her wet and slick and quivering with lust.

Dakota nearly lost his mind. Releasing her wrists, he slid down her body, over those smooth, feline curves. Placing his mouth against her, he kissed between her thighs. Kissed and licked while she bucked and made throaty little sounds.

He could hear the wind outside, knew it had picked up speed. The same speed as the rhythm of his heart. The beating, the pounding, the rush of excitement.

He tasted her release, felt her orgasm rise and swell, but it still wasn't enough. Not nearly enough.

He needed more. So much more.

Dakota rose above her, then entered her with a deep, sensual stroke. She raised her hips, and together they moved in unison—lovers who relished the pleasure, the warmth, the familiarity of each other.

They couldn't stop kissing, touching, feeling—giving sensation, taking it back.

They rolled over the bed until she straddled him, rode him while he watched. Her hair fell forward, a portion of it still pinned, the rest tangling over her body like fiery vines. She was a goddess, he thought, an enchantress, a mermaid from the sea, a siren from the sky. She was everything he had ever wanted in a lover.

He couldn't think about missing her because she was here, riding him, milking his body with hers. Heat shot through his belly and blazed through his loins, begging for a release. Begging for the strength to hold on. Just one more minute, one more warm, wet spiraling second.

She grasped his hands, locked on and held. He watched her, his vision blurred, his need edgy. And when that last second spun out of control, he threw back his head and let himself fall.

Hours later Dakota opened his eyes, trapped between waking and sleeping. The room was dark, not pitch black, but still too dark to focus. Someone touched him. A hand in his hair, fingertips skimming his shoulder.

He didn't stir. Instead he wondered if he dreamed, if he wasn't awake at all. He slept alone each night, yet there was a woman beside him. The lotion scent of her skin drifted to his nostrils, melding with the lusty lingering of sex.

Kathy. His mind came awake, and his body responded. He grew hard and achy between his thighs—the kind of pressure a woman could relieve. But not just any woman. He wanted his wife.

He turned, shifting in her direction, and her breath caught. He could see her shadow—the outline of a heavenly body with tumbling hair.

"I thought you were asleep," she said.

"I was." He squinted to bring her into focus, but she was still ghostlike. It was the cottage, he thought. The haunting. "You don't have to stop touching me."

"I stayed awake because I wanted you again." She slid down beside him, her leg brushing his. "Before morning."

He struggled to make sense of her words. If she wanted him she could have him now and in the daylight. "We won't turn into pumpkins. Or whatever happens in fairy tales."

"Maybe we will." She ran her hands down the front of his body, over the planes and ridges, muscles that formed his stomach. "Maybe tonight is just a fairy tale."

A tightness, a pain constricted his heart. He understood why she had remained awake. Tomorrow their loving would end. She wasn't offering to come back to him, to become a part of his life again.

What they had was now. His haunting. The darkness that shielded their past and kept them from a future.

He should have turned away, but he couldn't. If this moment was all they had, then he'd take it.

He reached for her, and she moved into his arms. They kissed and then caressed, their hands slipping into a languid rhythm. It was like dancing on a wave, floating on the edge of a dream. Yes, he thought. She was a mermaid, a goddess of the sea. And he couldn't keep her. Nor would he try.

After tonight, he would let her go.

"Kathy," he whispered her name, and she lifted her hips to accept his penetration. His deep, warm strokes.

There were no urgent thrusts. No groping or fumbling. No torn clothes or breathy pants. This was quiet, gentle loving—a joining that came from the heart.

And one Dakota would never forget.

Two days later Kathy held a gold vase, a gift from Queen Nicole and King Bertram. It was truly over. Albert Payune, the other revolutionists and the hired assassin were in jail. The cabinet member who had cooperated with the police would receive a lesser sentence for exposing the murder plot.

She studied the sparkling sapphire imbedded in the vase. King Bertram was a gracious man. Both he and the queen had thanked Dakota and Kathy personally, offering a valuable gift in honor and gratitude. The Asterland government had also promised that Payune would not be able to spread the word that the Lone Star jewels actually existed. The legend would be protected.

"Kathy?"

She turned to the sound of Dakota's voice. He hadn't stepped foot in the master bedroom since the night they'd made love. She had awakened that morning to find him gone. Later she'd discovered he'd left the cottage to roam the hills, then tie up the loose ends of their mission.

"Have you finished packing?' he asked.

"No, but I'm nearly done." She tried to avoid his gaze, but couldn't quite manage. Those Comanche eyes held her captive, trapping her in deep, dark emotion.

"It's beautiful, isn't it?" He motioned to the vase. "Kind of an unusual shape, though."

Should she tell him? Kathy wondered. Tell him why her vase had a curved indentation and his rounded on one side? Apparently he hadn't examined them closely enough to make the connection. "They're a set."

He blinked. "What?"

"The vases."

He reached for the jeweled object, a small frown creasing his brow. She watched as he ran his hand over the gold, following the shape. "It means something, doesn't it? Something significant?"

Kathy released a quiet breath. "They represent love. They're very old and valuable. There aren't that many in existence, and in Asterland when they're given as a gift, they're always given to a couple, sometimes on their wedding day."

Kathy glanced down at her hand and realized she still wore her wedding ring, the diamonds and emeralds Dakota had given her. She noticed Dakota still wore his, too. But he had chosen white gold and onyx. A design that didn't resemble a wedding band—a ring that rarely interfered with his undercover work. It was a piece of jewelry that looked natural on an Indian man, whether he wore it on his left hand or switched it to his right.

"Love." Dakota cleared his throat as if to clear away a sudden huskiness. The discomfort in his eyes wasn't hard to miss. "You didn't tell the queen about our cover, did you? She thinks we've reconciled. That we're making a fresh start in our marriage."

"I didn't have the opportunity to tell her." Kathy folded a blouse and placed it in her suitcase, giving herself something to do. "And after she and the king gave us the vases, it seemed too late. The gesture had already been made."

Shifting the object in question, Dakota's frown deepened. "Mine fits against yours." He lifted his gaze. "Like our bodies."

"I think that's the idea." She knew her voice sounded rigid, but she couldn't relax her throat. He had practically abandoned her after they'd made love. But then what had she expected? For him to say that he would retire for good? That their marriage was more important than the next mission? Sex wouldn't change that, no matter how incredible it had been.

To ease some of the tension building in the room, she took the vase and placed it on the bed. "I don't think the symbolism was meant just for us. I think the gift was also the queen's way of saying that she and the king are trying to work through their differences.'' And for that, Kathy was deeply relieved. Not only did the monarchs truly love each other, they had a child to consider—a ten-year-old boy.

''That's good.'' Dakota stood with impeccable posture, a military stance that fit his tall, broad stature. ''They're a nice family,'' he said, revealing an affection for Prince Eric that mirrored her own.

''Yes, they are.''

Telling herself not to dwell on dark-eyed children, she glanced at the wilting wildflowers on the nightstand and realized the extent of her loneliness. She hadn't been in the mood to walk the cliffs, enjoy the scent of the ocean or pick lavender flowers. All of those pleasures reminded her too much of Dakota. Even the garden was a sad reminder. Making wishes and imagining fairies seemed foolish now.

''Are you going back to D.C.?''

She looked up. ''No, I'm not. I'm leaving the Bureau.''

''For good?''

''Yes. I gave my notice before we came here.'' A decision that had been a long time coming.

Dakota hooked his thumbs in his jeans, suddenly looking more like a cowboy than a retired air force officer. Why hadn't she noticed his Wranglers and embroidered Western shirt before? His lizard-skin boots and tooled leather belt? He had well-dressed Texan written all over him.

Kathy closed her suitcase. Maybe she hadn't wanted to notice. Maybe she found the image just a bit too sexy.

''So what are you going to do?'' he asked.

''Head up a satellite office for my parents' business.'' Her grandfather had founded a successful import/export company. Kathy's family had been living abroad for as long as she could remember. So joining the Foreign Service had seemed like a natural step. But now she wanted to live in the States, someplace other than the Capitol.

''So where are you going to set up shop, so to speak?''

She lifted her chin. ''In Royal.''

His jaw nearly dropped. ''You mean Texas? Where I live?''

She narrowed her eyes. ''As you may recall, I lived there once, too.'' After Dakota had retired from the air force, Kathy had taken an extended leave of absence from the Foreign Service, hoping for a quiet, domestic life at the ranch, one Dakota had never given her. In spite of his retirement, the dangerous missions continued. ''I like Royal. I have friends there.''

''Of course you do.'' He softened his voice. ''So you've rented an apartment already?''

''No, but I intend to. I've already arranged for a moving company to ship my belongings to Royal.''

''Oh.''

They stood in awkward silence after that, Dakota staring at his boots and Kathy reorganizing cosmetics in her makeup bag, hoping to look busy enough for him to just leave her be.

Finally he lifted his gaze and broke through the quiet. ''You're welcome to stay with me. You know, just until you find a place.''

Her heart leaped forward with a hard thump. ''Do you think that's wise?''

''Why wouldn't it be?'' he responded a bit too easily. ''Since we've already gotten each other out of our systems, it just might be possible for us to be friends. There's certainly no harm in trying.''

Gotten each other out of our systems. Maybe Dakota was right. Maybe it was time to accept him as a friend. She had lived in limbo long enough. And so had he. They both needed to come to terms with their broken marriage and move on with their lives.

''Thank you.'' She forced a casual smile. ''I promise I won't wear out my welcome.''

''Don't worry about it.'' He returned her smile, then offered to carry her suitcase out to the car. This tall, gorgeous man who still made her heart beat much too fast.

Six

Dakota was back in Texas and wondering if he'd gone crazy. He'd left Asterland behind, but he'd brought Kathy with him—to the ranch, the house they'd once shared. She was in the guest room he'd offered, and she'd been holed up in there all day.

He squared his shoulders and headed in the direction of her room. They couldn't hide from each other. Both had agreed to embrace friendship.

He knocked, then stepped back a little. Embracing friendship wasn't the same as embracing each other.

She opened the door, and he cursed a sudden, unwelcome jolt of lust. Her hair, damp from a late-day shower, fell loose about her shoulders. And she wasn't wearing a bra. He could see the faint outline of her breasts through a printed cotton dress.

"Hi," she said.

"Hi." Dumbstruck, he couldn't think of another thing to say. Why had he gone to her room? What had he hoped to accomplish?

"Are you settled in all right?"

"Yes. Thank you."

So polite, he thought, so proper. Even with damp hair and no bra. "Are you hungry? It's lunchtime," he added hastily. Her nipples were erect, poking against the flowers on her dress.

She tucked a lock of wet hair behind her ear. He could smell her shampoo. "Are you fixing lunch? Or are you going out?" she asked.

"I thought I'd fix something here. Mrs. Miller did some shopping for me this morning." And he didn't have the slightest idea what to make. Lunch had been an afterthought, just something to talk about.

Kathy let the door fall open. Behind her Dakota could see the unmade bed. The sheets probably smelled like strawberries by now, like her hair and her skin.

"So Mrs. Miller still works for you?"

He pulled his eyes away from the bed. "Yes, and she hasn't changed a bit."

Kathy smiled. "Same starched gray hair, same white uniform, same squeaky white shoes?"

"That's her." And the housekeeper's non-meddling, get-the-job done personality suited him just fine.

"Can you give me a few minutes before lunch? I still have to dry my hair."

"Sure. No problem."

He made his way to the kitchen, opened the refrigerator and rummaged through the groceries. What in the hell had possessed him to invite Kathy to stay with him? Self torture? He hadn't gotten her out of his system. Not by a long shot.

Forcing himself to concentrate on food, Dakota decided on grilled cheese sandwiches and a black bean salad. The salad took a lot of dicing and slicing, but it contained some of his favorite ingredients: bell and jalapeño peppers, onions, cilantro, parsley and Roma tomatoes.

Kathy entered the kitchen just as he poured the Southwestern mixture over a bed of lettuce and garnished it with lime wedges.

"I should have known you would make something spicy."

He glanced up to acknowledge her, and when she turned toward the dining room, he noticed her dress was one of those great little backless numbers. Talk about spicy. "You know me. A creature of habit." Hot food and sleek redheads. His tastes would never change.

While she took it upon herself to set the table, he grilled the sandwiches. Maybe spending time together at the cottage had made things easier on them. They fell into a domestic pattern as if it were routine. But then, it used to be. They had always shared kitchen duties.

They sat across from each other at an early Texas table scarred with over a century of wear. It suited Dakota's lifestyle as well as the rugged surroundings. His home wasn't a showcase for wealthy living, nor was it actually a working ranch. He owned horses because they gave him pleasure and steers because he enjoyed hosting an occasional Friday-night jackpot for amateur cowboys. And since his ranch hands tended to the animals as nonintrusively as Mrs. Miller tended to the house, he was able to protect his personal life. No one gossiped about Dakota Lewis. Not anymore. He had worked damn hard to be regarded as something other than a billionaire's half-breed, bastard son. High society, he knew, wasn't always kind.

He looked across the table at Kathy. She ate the food he'd prepared, even scooped a diced jalepeño into her mouth. In spite of the disciplined, air force officer image he'd carved out for himself, she used to tell him that he liked everything hot and fast, that he lived on pure heat and adrenaline.

Dakota watched her sip a frothy glass of milk. As if Miss proper-and-pretty had room to talk. The woman was downright wicked in bed, and the stuffy society types she'd dated before him hadn't satisfied her need for hot, fast sex.

"When is Mrs. Miller coming back?" Kathy asked.

Dakota blinked. Answering a question about his no-nonsense housekeeper while he had been thinking about hot-and-fast sex with his gorgeous wife wasn't an easy transition for his male brain to make.

"Wednesday afternoon." He reached for his coffee, hoping the caffeine would snap his senses back in order. "Her schedule hasn't changed." The older lady didn't live at the ranch. Instead she worked four days a week, whether Dakota was home or away on an assignment.

Kathy lifted her napkin. "Does she know I'm here?"

"Yes, I told her."

"So she understands it's just a temporary stay?"

He tried not to frown. "Yes." It hadn't been easy telling the housekeeper that his wife was sleeping in one of the guest rooms. His pride, he supposed, along with his heart, had taken a bruising just saying the words out loud. "There won't be any misunderstandings." Nor would he pressure Kathy about why she had left in the first place. Eventually he would ask, but for now he would do his best to concentrate on friendship.

Dakota tilted his head, pushing the brim of his Stetson back a notch. West Texas was a sight to behold, even before the break of dawn. The moon peeked through a menagerie of clouds as they moved across a vast, deep-blue sky.

Dakota turned toward Ben Rassad. "Do you paint?" he asked, wondering how someone would go about capturing a crescent moon or a shifting cloud.

"No," the sheikh answered. "But I appreciate those who do."

Ben, too, seemed mesmerized by the sky. But Dakota supposed once a man lived in Texas, there was no turning back. The Lone Star state flowed through his veins, whether he was an Amythrarian sheikh or a Comanche pilot.

"The others should be here soon," Dakota said, focusing on their purpose. The Texas Cattleman's Club didn't normally hold pre-dawn meetings in the middle of a park, but this meeting was probably the most significant gathering this group would ever have. The recovered Lone Star jewels would be hidden on this brisk May morning. The private park, which housed the Cattleman's Club and an old adobe mission, also offered acres of greenery. Neither the exclusive gentlemen's club nor the historic mission was visible from the spot they had chosen, but the park, with its tree-lined paths and seasonal blooms, was as familiar to Dakota as his own home.

"Tex is waiting," Ben noted.

Dakota smiled. In 1901, Tex Langley had founded the Texas Cattleman's Club, and these days the rugged oil baron stood in the form of a prestigious bronze statue erected just a few feet away.

Dr. Justin Webb and Matt Walker arrived together. And like Dakota, both the surgeon and the horse breeder sported Western hats and boots. Minutes later diplomat Aaron Black joined the group, and the men greeted each other quietly.

Other than nesting birds and curious squirrels, there wasn't a sign of life seen or heard within miles. The gated park was deserted, and the road that led to it as dark as the night sky.

"So this is it," Matt said, studying the designated location.

Dakota nodded. A small reflecting pool was under construction. The forms had already been set and the rebar was in place, leaving rows of soil between round metal rods. All they had to do was bury the tiny, sealed case containing the priceless gems and wait for the unsuspecting contractors to arrive to pour the concrete.

While the other men stood in the shadows, Dakota dug a deep, narrow hole with a small camper shovel, and Matt placed the airtight case inside. Their only light was a solitary beam from a flashlight. Even the moon respected their silent task, its crescent shape slipping behind a cluster of trees.

The jewels had been originally hidden in a secret passageway in the old mission, and securing them this time seemed simple by comparison. But Dakota knew what each man had risked in an effort to recover the gems. Their lives, as well as those of the women they loved, had been laden with danger. The triumphant moment belonged to all of them.

Dakota stepped away from the burial site. The moon had resurfaced, bathing the ground with a soft silver glow. It seemed fitting somehow—ceremonial to a Comanche who believed Mother Earth provided all things sacred.

Leadership. Justice. Peace. Those three words shone in the eyes of every man present. The Lone Star jewels. A red diamond, a black opal and a two-carat emerald, represented an unspoken mantra—lifelong values they vowed to uphold.

With satisfied nods, Ben, Matt and Justin departed. They had agreed beforehand that Aaron and Dakota would wait for the construction crew.

The diplomat headed out to his truck and returned with a thermos and two plastic cups. He placed them on a nearby bench. "Shall we?"

"Sure," Dakota answered. "And I'm glad it was you and not Justin who supplied the coffee."

Aaron poured the steaming brew, and they grinned at each other in the dark. It was a running joke that the doctor had acquired a taste for week-old sludge that accumulated in the bottom of a pot.

"So how does it feel to be back on American soil?" Aaron asked.

"Good. It's where I belong, I suppose." Even if an edge of restlessness had begun to set in. For Dakota the end of an assignment often left him anxious.

The other man lifted his coffee. "If you get hungry, my wife sent along some pastries. They're in the truck."

"Thanks. Maybe later." Although Dakota considered Aaron a close friend, they went on to discuss insignificant things. Aaron wasn't one to pry, and Dakota wasn't one to offer details about his personal life. Aaron already knew that Kathy had left the Foreign Service and was staying with Dakota until she found a suitable place of her own. What else could be said of his broken marriage? Dakota had offered Kathy a guest room at the ranch so they could pursue friendship. He wasn't supposed to want her so badly, wasn't supposed to hurt every time he thought about the past. Admitting how he felt would solve nothing.

An hour after the sun came up, Aaron opened the gate for the construction crew, a trio of men who routinely repaired the hardscape at the park.

Dakota leaned against a tree as they poured the concrete. After the barricades were placed, he and Aaron would discuss another construction matter with the crew, but only for the sake of their cover. The American diplomat and the retired air force lieutenant would remain at the scene to protect the Lone Star jewels one last time.

A small breeze billowed Dakota's jacket. Within days the pool would be filled, and only those who had made a vow to the Texas Cattleman's Club would know that three priceless gems lay beneath the reflection of Tex Langley's statue.

Kathy knew she was alone. Dakota had left the ranch in the wee hours of the morning. The master bedroom was next to hers, and she'd heard his shower running at an ungodly hour.

Squinting at the sunlight streaming through the windows, she slipped on her robe, then stepped into the hall. Glancing over her shoulder, she noticed Dakota's door was slightly ajar.

She had no right to enter the master bedroom, but she couldn't seem to stop herself. Immediately the bed drew her toward it. She ran her hand along the wood and imagined Dakota sleeping there, his long muscular body tangled in the sheets. He was a light sleeper, a man who always seemed to have something on his mind.

The room looked the same. He'd kept it just the way she had decorated it. The horse weather vane still stood atop a Chippendale desk, the window valances still matched the fabric on the canopy bed and a hand-painted dresser displayed a collection of Indian baskets and crystal candelabras.

Kathy released a shaky breath. Still scanning the dresser, she noticed a familiar item was missing. A framed photograph. A picture of herself and Dakota on their wedding day. She moved closer and reached for the top drawer. Had he buried it beneath his clothes? Or had he destroyed it?

"What are you looking for?"

Caught in the act, Kathy froze, her fingers wrapped around the brass handle. "I apologize," she said as she turned toward him. "I shouldn't have come in here."

He stood, tall and rigid in black jeans, leather boots and a lightweight jacket. The brim of a cowboy hat shielded his eyes, but she knew they were fixed on her.

"I asked what you were looking for."

He made her feel like a criminal, the woman who had once shared this room with him, slept in the canopy bed, kept her undergarments folded in the drawer she had been opening. "I wondered where our picture was," she answered honestly.

He jutted his chin toward the dresser. "It's in there. I couldn't look at it. Not every day."

"I'm sorry," Kathy whispered, not knowing what else to say. His tone was guarded, but pain edged his words. She knew she owed him an explanation, yet she didn't know where to begin.

Neither spoke after that, and Kathy felt the room closing in. She glanced back at the dresser and imagined their picture hidden beneath his clothes. It made her sad and guilty. He deserved better than a woman who had just walked away, a woman who couldn't bring herself to admit why she had left. But the loss of their child and the loneliness she had suffered wasn't something she could put into words. It wasn't fair, but it made her realize that she and Dakota had never really been friends. Their courtship had been a whirlwind romance based on passion, not communication. And their marriage had been much the same.

Dakota followed her gaze to the dresser. "I don't burn candles anymore. I don't know why I still keep them around."

She understood his meaning. Their wedding picture used to sit between the crystal candelabras, and they used to make love by candlelight, touch and kiss while blue and gold flames sent shadows flickering across their skin.

"I'm sorry," she said again. Sorry that she had hurt him. Sorry they hadn't been able to share more than just their bodies. But she knew he hid his deepest emotions. She had seen him laugh, but she had never seen him cry. Not even at his father's funeral.

He tossed his hat onto the bed. "I'm sorry, too. I didn't

mean to sound so harsh earlier. I just didn't expect to come home and find you in my room.''

She wasn't sure whether to leave him alone or stay and talk. He still seemed guarded, yet his tone had softened, his apology sincere. ''You left while it was still dark.''

''Texas Cattleman's Club meeting.'' He unzipped his jacket, then dragged a hand through his hair. ''We secured the jewels.''

And he seemed unsettled, she thought, a little edgy. But hiding the jewels meant the mission was truly over and he had become an out-of-work soldier again, a man without a purpose. Staying home never suited Dakota, and that was one of the reasons Kathy had left. She had wanted some normalcy in their marriage, but he had been satisfied with their whirlwind relationship, with stealing moments between his never-ending missions.

''Are you sure it's okay for me to stay here?'' she asked, wondering if it had been a mistake.

''Of course, it's okay.''

He came toward her, so close she could smell the wind on his clothes, the fading scent of his aftershave. She lifted her face to his and wondered if he was going to kiss her. If he did, she would kiss him back. She could feel the sexual magnet, the energy that drew them together. They couldn't talk, but they could touch. Yearn for each other.

He toyed with the collar of her chenille robe. ''What happened to the silky one?''

''I didn't think I should wear it around you.''

He moistened his lips. ''Afraid I wouldn't be able to control myself?''

She swallowed. ''It's been known to happen.'' He was too tall, too dark, too dangerously handsome. His mouth was inches from hers, his breath warm. He would taste like the elements, she decided, like a warrior who belonged to the night.

He skimmed her cheek with his, then stepped back and grinned. ''So you decided to wear this grandma getup instead?''

For a moment Kathy only stared. He'd gone from brooding to sexy to silly within the blink of an eye. And she remained in a daze, waiting for him to kiss her. She lifted her hand to her face, to the spot he'd just touched. "Grandma getup?"

"Yep. You look cute, though. Kinda sweet and fuzzy."

She couldn't find it within herself to return his smile. He teased her, but the humor hadn't quite reached his eyes. They were black, with a sort of feverish glow. He was aroused and pretending he wasn't. If she bumped against his fly, she'd feel the evidence of his desire. This was her punishment for invading his room, she thought. She should have stayed away.

He stepped back even farther. "Kathy?"

"Yes?"

"I danced with other women at the Texas Cattleman's Club ball. It was months ago, but I just thought I should mention it. You know I'm not one for fancy social events, but I felt more or less obligated to be there."

"And you felt obligated to dance." She tried to keep her voice steady. She had no right to be jealous. She had, after all, walked out on him. "It doesn't matter, Dakota. You didn't do anything wrong."

"Have you danced with other men?"

She sent him a twisted smile. "I danced with Payune. Remember?"

He didn't seem amused. "That's not what I mean."

"There were political functions in Washington. I suppose I danced a few times." But she couldn't remember who her partners were. "I don't understand why you brought this up."

"Because you've lived alone for three years. And I keep thinking that there must have been men interested in you. Someone must have asked you on a date."

The look in his eyes startled her. The macho, possessive glare. She had already told him that she hadn't slept with anyone, but apparently he couldn't stand the image of her even having dinner with another man. "I didn't go on any dates."

His gaze softened. "So what did you do?"

"Worked." Came home to an empty apartment and

thought about her husband, wondered what he was doing, wondered if his next assignment would be a greater risk than the last, if he would be captured or killed. "I adopted a dog."

"Really? That's great."

"I'm glad you think so because I'm picking Sugar up at the airport tomorrow. A friend from Washington is putting her on a plane for me."

"Sugar? That's your dog's name?"

Kathy nodded. "She belonged to an elderly lady who lived in my building. And when Mrs. Leone died, I just sort of inherited her dog. But Sugar is a little angel. I adore her." The Maltese had gotten her through some sad and lonely times, making her separation from Dakota bearable. "She loves everyone. And she's quiet. You won't even know she's around."

"Your dog is welcome here, Kathy. You have to stop acting like you're putting me out. I invited you, remember? We agreed to be friends."

"Yes, friends," she said, wondering if that was truly possible.

The following day Kathy returned from the airport with the Maltese in tow. She walked into the living room, and Dakota looked up from his newspaper and smiled.

The dog was pretty much what he had expected. Little old ladies had lapdogs that wore bows on top of their heads, and Kathy had inherited Sugar from a little old lady. He had to admit the pooch was cute—silky white fur and a face with round eyes and a delicate muzzle. He figured the Maltese didn't weigh any more than four or five pounds.

Placing the paper on the coffee table, he came to his feet. "So this is Sugar?" He reached out to pet the dog and received a high-pitched doggie yip in return.

Kathy's head whipped up. "What happened?"

"I don't know." Dakota nearly stammered. "I guess she's scared or something."

"But she likes people." Kathy adjusted Sugar in her arms. "She never acts that way."

"She just got off a plane, and this is a new environment. Hell, she's bound to be nervous."

"I suppose you're right." Kathy stroked the dog's head. "Maybe I should put her down and let her get used to the place."

Sugar decided she liked the couch. She curled up on a cowhide pillow, and Dakota thought she looked like a toy—a little, white fluffball on his rugged sofa. Yep, she was cute, even if he thought hair bows on canines were kind of sissy. But this one was a female, so he supposed that was okay.

He inched closer, then knelt to let the dog sniff his hand.

Sugar bared her teeth and snarled.

Caught completely off guard, Dakota jerked back, lost his balance and landed flat on his startled butt.

Behind him, Kathy gasped. "Oh, my God! Are you all right?"

"Of course, I am."

"Did she bite you?"

"No." With as much masculine pride as he could muster, he stood and squared his shoulders. He outweighed Sugar by a good hundred and eighty pounds. And he was an ex-military man trained in survival tactics. A former para rescuer who flew planes into enemy territory, rescued hostages, defused mines, tracked gunrunners across the desert. He had done it all, in and out of the service.

"I wasn't expecting her to snarl at me," he said, explaining away the humiliation.

"I'm so sorry. She's never done that to anyone before." Kathy reprimanded Sugar, and the dog dropped her ears and whined, making Dakota feel like a heel.

"I'm sure it won't happen again," she told him.

"Don't worry about it." He met Kathy's gaze, and she caught her bottom lip between her teeth. "Don't you dare laugh," he warned.

"Why would I?" she asked, a bit too innocently.

"Oh, I don't know. Maybe because your little dog knocked me on my ass."

"You should have seen yourself, Dakota."

Her lip quivered, and they both burst into laughter. But when footsteps sounded in the entryway, Kathy sobered immediately.

"That must be Mrs. Miller," she said.

Dakota nodded. He knew Kathy and the housekeeper hadn't seen each other yet, but he figured they were about to. Mrs. Miller would say a predictable yet impersonal hello before she began her chores.

Dakota studied his wife. As though suddenly conscious of her appearance, she fussed with the loose strands of her hair—that luscious, heavy hair she had twisted into its usual chignon. This afternoon she sported tan trousers and a lemon-colored blouse. Yellow suited her. Even the sunny robe she'd worn yesterday had turned him on. She'd looked as frothy as the meringue on top of a pie.

Mrs. Miller entered the room like a broom-wielding militant, shoulders back, head held high, short gray hair resembling a helmet. She could have been a nurse with her crisp white uniform and thick-soled shoes. It amazed Dakota that even after a thorough housecleaning, she departed as starched and white as she had arrived.

"Good afternoon, Lieutenant," she said, greeting him as she had for the past ten years.

"Good afternoon," he responded as the older lady turned toward Kathy.

He watched as they acknowledged each other. Kathy stepped forward and smiled. "It's nice to see you again."

"Thank you. It's a pleasure to see you as well."

The conversation was neither strained nor friendly. Dakota had no idea if Mrs. Miller liked Kathy, but he wasn't sure if the older woman liked him, either. The housekeeper rarely smiled, even during the holidays when she filled the cookie jar with red-nosed reindeers and jolly Santas.

Mrs. Miller smoothed her immaculate dress, then turned and spotted the dog curled up on the couch. "Oh, my."

"That's Sugar," Kathy said. "But she's a little nervous today."

As the older lady headed toward the sofa, Dakota searched

for a more appropriate warning. Be careful. Watch yourself. That adorable little fluffball is actually a junkyard Doberman in disguise. But before he could utter a single word, Sugar wiggled her behind and gazed up at Mrs. Miller with adoring eyes.

"Aren't you precious?" the housekeeper crooned in a sing-song voice Dakota had never heard the no-nonsense woman use before.

Kathy beamed like a moon in June, and within minutes she and Mrs. Miller were discussing Sugar's upkeep and habits. The dog ate a select brand of canned food, played indoor fetch games, required periodic trips to a groomer and enjoyed being walked on a silver leash that matched her glittery collar.

Dakota had never felt so left out, so big and undeniably male. And then it hit him. *Male.* That was it. Sugar probably didn't know what to make of him. She wasn't used to men. The Maltese had been coddled and protected by women.

He watched the pooch leap into Kathy's arms, watched as Kathy's expression turned soft and gentle.

Dakota swallowed around a lump in his throat. Somehow he was going to have to earn that little dog's trust. At the moment Sugar seemed to hold the key to Kathy's heart—a heart he longed to feel beating in time with his own. Because in spite of all of his friendship talk, Dakota couldn't deny the truth.

He was still in love with his wife.

Seven

Later that afternoon Dakota offered to accompany Kathy on her home search. Royal had plenty of upscale apartment buildings since it was a bustling, exclusively rich town surrounded by oil fields and sprawling ranches.

The temperature rose to ninety degrees, but the West Texas wind blew, making the heat bearable. Kathy still wore the lemon-colored blouse, and her hair still rebelled from the pins struggling to secure it. Wispy tendrils fluttered around her face, reflecting sunlight like sparks of fire.

They took the stairs and followed the apartment manager to 6B, then waited while the woman unlocked the door. Kathy had specific tastes, but she hadn't been nearly as selective as Dakota. He had found fault with the previous apartments they'd looked at, but he had good reason. Plain and simple—he didn't want his wife leaving the ranch. He liked having her around. He wanted to keep her.

He loved her.

"This is nice," Kathy said as they entered.

Dakota frowned. ''It's all right.''

A gas fireplace dominated the living room and two large windows offered a spectacular view of Royal. The appliances in the spacious kitchen were new, and the dining area boasted a brass chandelier.

''That won't look right with your furniture,'' Dakota said. ''It's too modern for antiques.''

''It's fine,'' Kathy responded and moved on to explore the bedrooms.

The master suite presented another view, this one from a rather large balcony. Dakota couldn't find much fault, but he was damned determined to try. ''I'll bet lugging groceries up and down stairs is a nuisance. And then of course there's that balcony.''

Kathy stepped onto the feature in question. ''What's wrong with it?''

He moved to stand next to her, out of earshot from the building manager. ''Could be dangerous.''

She sent him a strange look. ''It seems sturdy enough to me.''

''Of course, it's sturdy. I was referring to the rail. Sugar might be able to fit through the bars.'' He approached the rail, playing out his drama. ''It's a long way down, sweetheart. And there's nothing to pad the fall. I don't think you should risk it.''

Kathy studied the opening between the bars with a critical eye. ''Sugar's body is bigger than that. She couldn't fit through there.''

Dakota scraped a booted foot on the cement. He was certain Kathy would have given that scenario more thought. ''Maybe you're right. But she could get her head stuck. Animals do that sort of thing all the time.''

That appeared to do the trick. Kathy frowned and stepped closer to the rail. ''You know, that's actually possible.''

''Of course it is.'' He resisted the urge to flash an overly smug, overly macho smile. ''Did you think I was making these things up? I've been trained to spot potential hazards.

And this apartment isn't right for you. I sensed it the moment we walked in."

She gave him another one of those strange looks, and he lost the urge to grin, his machismo not quite so smug. Had he really said something that ridiculous, laid it on that thick? Trained to spot potential hazards? In an upscale Royal apartment?

"How about some lunch?" he suggested, hoping to distract her. Did he really want her to know that he was deliberately thwarting her effort to find a suitable place to live?

Kathy accepted his invitation, so Dakota decided on the Royal Diner, a typical greasy-spoon-type place that served typical greasy-spoon-type food. He had a hankering for casual atmosphere and a messy hamburger. He'd been to enough fancy balls and eaten enough deviled quail eggs to last a lifetime.

They scooted into a vinyl booth and grinned at each other like kids sharing a private joke. The paper placemat the waitress slapped in front of them boasted, The Royal Diner—Food Fit for a King! Yet King Bertram stopping in for a bowl of chili and finding it to his liking presented a ludicrous image.

Dakota ordered a bacon cheeseburger, and Kathy chose a club sandwich. He drank coffee while she sipped iced tea.

"I really thought I would find an apartment today," she said.

"You know what the problem is?" he asked without giving her a chance to answer. "You should be living in a house and not an apartment. Someplace with a yard for Sugar and privacy for yourself." Someplace like the ranch, he thought. He had a fenced yard the pooch could play in and a big canopy bed just waiting for Kathy.

"You know, I think you're right," she responded, her eyes sparkling with sudden enthusiasm. "I should start looking at rental houses instead."

Dakota wondered if he was an idiot. Here he was hoping to keep her, yet he hadn't asked why she'd left in the first place. Lifting his coffee to hide a frown, he took a sip. And why hadn't he asked?

Because deep down he feared the answer. Kathy might have left for a very simple, very devastating reason. She might have fallen out of love with him. And if that was the case, there wasn't much he could do about it.

Or was there? If she had loved him once, couldn't she love him again? If they spent enough time together, would those feelings come back?

The waitress delivered their lunch, and as they sampled their food, the jukebox played a country ballad. The sound of silverware clanking and voices chattering could be heard above the music, but the song managed to soothe Dakota's soul just the same. Kathy had chosen to live in Royal. That in itself seemed like a good sign.

He searched her gaze. "Do you ever think about the first time we met?"

A small smile touched her lips. "Charity dinner at the Texas Cattleman's Club. You were in uniform."

"And you were in white silk." A dress as cool and sleek as the woman wearing it. He'd taken one long, luxurious look and decided he'd wanted her. As to how he intended to win her over, he hadn't been sure. "I didn't think you would be interested. You were so refined, so elegant. Your type rarely gave me the time of day."

"My type?"

"You know what I mean." He took another bite of his burger and swallowed. "Do you think it was fate, us meeting like we did?" He had been stationed at Aviano Air Base in northeastern Italy at the time, but was home on leave. And she had come to Royal to visit Aaron before she left for Italy to replace a consular who had taken ill.

"That we met in Royal, but both ended up at the same Italian village?" She glanced down at her sandwich, then back up. "The Italy part might have been fate, but Aaron suspected I wanted to meet you. I think that's why he invited me to the charity dinner."

Stunned, Dakota leaned against the table. "I don't understand. Did Aaron mention me? Tell you I was a decent guy or something?"

Kathy stirred her tea a little nervously. ''Yes, but I saw your picture first. Aaron had some photographs from a friend's wedding, and you were the best man. So when I came across your picture, I think I said something like 'Wow. He's gorgeous. Who is he?' '' She clanked her spoon against the glass. ''Pretty shallow, I guess.''

Shallow? It was the best damn thing he'd heard in years. ''Why didn't you ever tell me this before?''

''In the beginning it would have been too embarrassing. And later on, it didn't seem important. We never talked about how we had met.''

Something in her voice bothered him. Something that said they weren't as close as he liked to remember. Dakota reached for his coffee, pushing his worry aside. Why dwell on the past? Instead he would do his best to focus on the future.

The following afternoon Kathy paced her bedroom, wondering what to do with herself. She couldn't seem to concentrate on anything other than overwhelming guilt. She could barely face herself in the mirror, let alone face Dakota every day.

Was he waiting for her to approach him? Waiting to hear why she had walked away from their marriage? A week had passed since they'd returned from Asterland, but she had yet to say a word.

It wasn't fair. He had a right to know. The baby had belonged to him, too.

Kathy slipped on a denim blouse, then zipped her jeans. She knew Dakota was at the barn, spending some time with the horses.

Exiting the house through the back door, she ventured into the Texas air. She could have taken one of Dakota's trucks, but decided the walk would do her good. Once inside the courtyard, she stopped to take comfort in her surroundings. Greenery had a way of soothing her, and the yard was lush with potted blooms. Beyond the Spanish tiles and rustic patio furniture lay a thick carpet of grass. This was her favorite spot at the ranch, a place to sip coffee in the morning and watch the stars light up the sky at night.

She opened the gate leading to the rest of the property. The land was flat, wide open and picturesque in a vast, Texas kind of way. As she walked, her boots kicked up dust. The soil wasn't fertile, but it reflected the sun in warm, golden shades.

The breezeway barn stood strong and solid, a building alive with the scents and sounds of the horses Dakota loved. He had an incredible facility, designed with the recreational cowboy in mind—an indoor and outdoor arena, fenced pastures, wash racks, a hot walker, an enormous tack room, hay storage and RV buildings. He didn't want for anything, she thought, except maybe the truth from his wife.

Kathy didn't need to enter the barn. Dakota stood beside a hitching post, saddling a big, black gelding. She couldn't help but admire her husband, the breadth of his shoulders, taper of his waist, those long legs covered in time-worn denim. And his rear, she thought, that taut masculine rear.

She walked toward him, and he turned and smiled, making her guilty heart flutter. He still affected her, still had a way of making her limbs watery and her breath catch.

"Hi," she said. "Are you going for a ride?" It was a dumb question with an obvious answer, but she couldn't think of anything else to say.

"Sure am. Do you want to join me? It's a great day to hit the trail. Not nearly as hot as yesterday."

Kathy brushed a stray hair from her eye. He sounded so relaxed, so friendly. And she was a nervous wreck, at least on the inside. Maybe on the outside, too. She couldn't seem to keep her hands still. She batted away another hair, a useless effort in the wind.

"Okay," she answered, thinking she would probably return to the ranch wobbly-legged and sore. "But I haven't been on a horse in a while. I'm a little out of practice." And anxiety-ridden. Could she really talk about the miscarriage today? Talk about their lost baby on this warm, breezy Texas day?

"Then you should ride Serenity," he said, suggesting Kathy's favorite mount. "She'll be good to you."

Serenity had been named well. The mare, a leopard Appaloosa, nuzzled Kathy in a gentle welcome. "She hasn't forgotten me."

Dakota placed Kathy's saddle on a nearby stand. "You're not easy to forget, sweetheart."

And neither was he, she thought, sending him a shaky smile. Not a day had passed without him entering her mind.

They mounted their horses in silence. The main trail led to a dozen smaller paths, the next as boundless as the last. The vegetation was sparse and the ground level for as far as the eye could see, but the land was rich with history. Wars, cattle drives, the building of railroads, the discovery of oil. Every rock, every cactus, every speck of dirt told a story.

They rode for nearly two hours, with Kathy taking in familiar sights, scenery she enjoyed. In the distance, windmills turned, pumping water from the earth.

"Do you want to stop?" Dakota asked as they came upon one of the few shade trees on the trail.

Kathy nodded, anxiety setting in once again. If she intended to tell him, then it should be now, while they were away from the ranch—away from the memories that lingered in the halls of the house they once shared.

She slid from her saddle, and Dakota took Serenity's reins. He hobbled the horses, returning with a blanket under his arm. Dakota never traveled on horseback without a blanket. It was, Kathy decided, the Indian in him, the nomad running through his veins. The Comanche were a wandering tribe, a people who had once roamed West Texas, then later fought to keep the Lone Star plains as their home. Another piece of history, she thought, another lost battle.

They sat beneath the oak and sipped bottled water.

"I'm going out of town tonight," he said.

Kathy's heart made a fast, nervous leap. "Another assignment already?"

He shook his head. "No. Business in Lubbock."

"Oh." She released an audible breath. Business in Lubbock meant the shopping centers Dakota owned. Commercial property was the major source of his income. The Texas Cattleman's Club missions had nothing to do with money. "How long will you be gone?"

"A few days."

Apparently that was all the information he intended to share. But Kathy knew Dakota didn't enjoy the corporate world. It wasn't dangerous enough, she supposed.

He removed his Stetson and handed it to her. "You'd better wear my hat on the way back or you'll end up with a sunburn."

"Thanks." Kathy placed the hat beside her. She had the fair, sensitive skin common to most natural redheads, even though she lacked the freckles and fiery temper often associated with scarlet hair. But Dakota used to say that her passion was red, that her appetite in bed was the color of fire.

She felt her cheeks warm. "I'm probably pink already."

"A little." He tapped her nose in an affectionate gesture, and her nipples pebbled.

"This is nice," he said.

She blinked. "Nice?"

"The weather. The horses. You and me. It reminds me of our days in Italy."

It had been wondrous—falling in love with a pilot, holding his hand and stealing kisses in tiny cafés. Aviano Air Base was thirty minutes from the beach and thirty minutes from the mountains. A more romantic location didn't exist.

He reclined on the blanket. "Lie down with me."

Kathy caught her breath. She couldn't resist—not his crooked smile, his Texas drawl, the long fluid line of his body.

She lowered herself to the blanket. Being next to him was more than nice.

"I think we're turning out to be pretty good friends," he said. "Don't you?"

She nodded, knowing she couldn't bear to spoil this moment, this warm, tender feeling. She couldn't tell him why she had left. At least not today.

* * *

Kathy answered the phone at 10:00 p.m., surprised by the masculine voice on the other end of the line. Dakota rarely called when he was away on business.

"What are you doing?" he asked.

"Nothing, really." She glanced at her bed. Sugar was curled up on a pillow. "I was thinking I might make some hot chocolate. Maybe read for a while."

"Are you in the kitchen?"

"No. My room."

"And you're alone?"

Kathy gripped the phone. "Sugar's here."

Dakota sounded strange, not quite himself. She looked around nervously. Was he worried the house was bugged? He could be involved in another mission, something he hadn't told her about. Or someone from his past might have surfaced. Dakota had probably made plenty of enemies over the years.

"Are you on the cordless phone?" he asked.

Was he really in Lubbock? "Yes."

"Good. I want you to go to my room."

"Okay." Heart pounding, she walked down the hall, then entered the master bedroom. He hadn't made the bed before he'd left, but other than that, the room was tidy. Nothing looked disturbed, nothing out of place. "I'm here."

Dakota's voice softened. "Go to the closet and pick out one of my shirts."

Kathy frowned. His instructions were getting stranger by the minute, but he appeared to have a distinct purpose in mind, something he needed her to do. Meet him somewhere? Bring him a shirt? It made no sense.

She stepped into the walk-in closet. Neat, organized, very Dakota. Casual wear at one end, dress clothes at the other. She tried to ignore the empty rack that used to be hers. He hadn't filled the space. It remained vacant.

"What kind of shirt?" she asked.

"It doesn't matter. You choose."

She reached for denim, soft and well-worn—a long-sleeved

shirt with pearl-front snaps. She liked how he looked in blue, it made his eyes appear darker, his skin more golden.

"Do you have one?"

"Yes."

"Put it on the bed."

If they were being bugged, she thought, someone was listening to an odd conversation. But maybe that was the idea. She removed the shirt from the hanger and did as he asked. "Done."

"Good girl. Now tell me what you're wearing."

Kathy froze. She looked around, caught sight of the canopy bed—the tousled covers, his denim shirt. There were no electronic bugs, no old enemies lurking. She wasn't in any danger. And there was only one reason why she couldn't hang up on him.

His voice. The husky, sensual sound of his voice.

She adjusted the phone. "I can't believe you're doing this to me."

"I'm lonely, Kathy. I miss you."

She closed her eyes. She missed him, too.

"Are you wearing a dress?" he asked.

She shook her head, then realized he couldn't see her. "No." He wanted to see her, she thought. He wanted to picture her in his mind. She opened her eyes. "A blouse and a skirt."

"Nylons?"

"No. My legs are bare."

She heard him swallow. "Take your blouse off."

Kathy sat on the edge of the bed. Could she do this? Could she play this forbidden game? She touched his shirt. Dakota's scent lingered in the room, the woodsy note of his cologne drifting through the air.

"Kathy?"

"I'm taking it off," she said, reaching for the top button on her blouse.

"Is it green? Emerald, like your eyes?"

"Yes." But even if it wasn't, she would have told him what he wanted to hear. She wanted to fuel his imagination, make him warm and aroused. She glanced at her hand and realized she still wore her wedding ring. "Where are you, Dakota?"

"In a hotel room."

She pictured him lying on a bed, his chest bare, his back braced against a wooden headboard. His room-service dinner would be untouched, except for a bottle of imported beer. She could almost taste the alcohol on his lips, taste the intoxicating flavor.

"Are you wearing jeans?"

"Yes."

She let the blouse fall from her shoulders. "Are they unzipped?"

His voice turned rough. "As far down as they'll go."

Suddenly the image in her mind intensified. The contrast of his skin against crisp, white sheets. The broad expanse of his chest, the narrow line of his hips. His sex, full and erect, pressing against his jeans.

Kathy couldn't stop the heat between her legs, the silky moisture. "I'm in my bra and panties." She had dropped her skirt to the floor, where it pooled at her feet.

Dakota groaned, and she knew he had lifted his hips. "Tell me what you look like," he said. "Every detail."

She walked to the mirror, the phone cradled against her ear. She looked aroused, her cheeks flushed, her lips slightly parted. "My hair is pinned up, but it's starting to fall." Just the way he liked it, she thought, tangled and messy. And the color of her bra, she told him, was called autumn gold. She had ordered it from a catalog, along with matching panties. The bra was seamless and sheer, the panties decorated with a hint of lace.

"I can hear the wind," she said, turning toward the window. She could almost feel it blowing through her hair, cooling her face. With her head tipped back and her eyes closed, she unhooked her bra, then slipped off her panties.

"Are you naked?" he asked, his voice a husky whisper above the wind.

"Yes." For him, she thought. Naked for him.

"Put my shirt on, Kathy. Put it on and climb under the covers. I want you in my bed."

The shirt could have been his hands. It caressed her, brushed her nipples, slid between her thighs—rough yet gentle.

And the bed. She pressed her face to the pillow and imagined him there. His scent. The weight of his erection. His mouth covering hers.

Kathy brought the phone to her lips and smiled. Tonight they would make love in their minds. Warm, wet, languorous love. A beautiful, erotic fantasy.

Kathy answered the door, and found herself face-to-face with Violet Tenewa, Dakota's Comanche mother.

"Kathy!" the other woman exclaimed. "Honey, I had no idea you were back."

"I'm not. I mean, I am, but..." How could she explain her presence at the ranch to her mother-in-law? "I'm just a temporary houseguest. Dakota invited me to stay until I find another place to live."

Violet's smile fell. "Oh."

Kathy stepped away from the door, praying this wasn't going to be an awkward reunion. She adored Dakota's mother. Violet was a striking, independent woman. Even at sixty-two, she looked as exotic as her name. Her silver-streaked hair fell in a straight, black curtain, complementing a golden complexion and deep-set eyes.

"Would you like to come in?" Kathy asked. "Dakota isn't here, but I'd love to visit with you."

"Thank you. I'd love to visit with you, too."

Kathy made a pot of coffee and warmed the pastries she had baked the day before. Coffee in hand, they sat in the living room, the aroma of cinnamon wafting between them.

"Where is Dakota?" Violet asked.

"He had some business in Lubbock. He's been gone a few days."

Violet reached for a cinnamon roll. "Have you heard from him?"

"Yes, he called." And seduced me over the phone, she thought, her skin suddenly warm. "He should be home later this afternoon."

Neither spoke after that. Small talk didn't seem appropriate. Kathy had walked out on Violet's son—a subject that certainly outweighed the weather.

"I'm sorry," Kathy said finally, struggling to find a simple way to explain the burden in her heart. "I never meant to hurt Dakota. When I left, I kept hoping that he would come to me. That he—" She paused, her eyes beginning to mist. "That he would tell me that I was more important than his work." She swallowed past the emotion and met the other woman's gaze. "I suppose that sounds foolish, especially to someone as independent as you. Your life with Jack was so unconventional."

"Oh, honey. It doesn't sound foolish at all."

Kathy scooted to the edge of the sofa. "Then you understand why I left?"

Violet pursed her lips. "I suppose I do. Except it's a little difficult for me to accept because he's my son. I want to believe that Dakota was a perfect husband, even if he wasn't."

Kathy's eyes turned misty again. "I never stopped loving him."

Violet squeezed her hand. "Now that part I truly understand. I know it's possible to love a man who always has other priorities. Who makes you feel like you're second-best in his heart."

Unable to conceal her curiosity, Kathy blinked away her tears. "Dakota's father?"

Violet nodded. "If Jack Lewis wasn't caught up in an important business deal, then he was attending a social function with his wife." She released a heavy sigh and went on, "I realize that I shouldn't have been involved with a married man, but I honestly believed he was going to divorce his wife and marry me. Jack and Sharon had one of those society marriages. There wasn't any real love between them."

"We've never talked about this before." Kathy knew Violet had been Jack's mistress, but she had no idea Dakota's mother had wanted something more. "I assumed you were comfortable with the arrangement."

"No, I never was."

"But you were with him all those years."

"Yes, all those years, and he was still married to Sharon. They even died together."

A boating accident, Kathy recalled. "I'm sorry. I had no idea." Which seemed disrespectful to Dakota's mother. Most women would prefer to be a wife than a mistress.

"I was nineteen when I met Jack. Nineteen and naive. I left him once, though. I was devastated that I was about to give birth, and my baby's father still hadn't made arrangements to marry me. So I went to South Dakota to stay with a friend." She sent Kathy a woman-to-woman smile. "Two months later I came back to Texas."

Kathy returned Violet's smile. "And presented Jack with a son."

"An illegitimate son. Something Dakota never let himself forget."

Both of their smiles faded. "But he hasn't made an issue of it, at least not to me. I was under the impression it didn't matter to him all that much."

"It mattered." Violet reached for her coffee, then took a sip. "Being the illegitimate son of a prominent man wasn't easy, even if Jack treated him well. Dakota tried very hard to legitimize himself, to be accepted by his father's peers. And I suppose serving his country was a way of proving his worth. Dakota enlisted at seventeen, a boy on the verge of manhood."

And now Kathy understood why her husband didn't enjoy high-society events. They reminded him of a time when he wasn't welcome. "It must have made things easier on Dakota that Jack and Sharon didn't have any children. At least he was Jack's only son."

"That's true, but his father being intimate with two women

was still a problem. I don't think Dakota understands the true concept of marriage—how much work is involved or how much a couple has to give of themselves. In that respect, Jack was a poor role model.''

Kathy nodded. It made sense. All of it. Unlike his father, Dakota had remained faithful to his vows, but he still didn't consider marriage the number-one priority in his life. His career had always come first.

''Dakota still doesn't know why I left. I can't seem to bring myself to say the words out loud. At least not to him.'' And that sounded like an excuse, Kathy thought. Feeble and unfair. But there was the baby she had wanted so badly—the part of her heart she had lost.

Violet frowned. ''Has he asked? Has he questioned you about it at all?''

''No.''

''Then maybe he isn't ready to face the past. Maybe he needs a little more time to sort out his feelings.''

Kathy cocked her head, considering the possibility. ''I hadn't thought of that.'' She hadn't thought of anything but her guilt, her secret, her own loss. But what Violet suggested provided a small measure of relief. Kathy wasn't ready to talk about the past, and Dakota wasn't ready to hear about it. ''After I left, did he confide in you? Did he say anything?''

''Not a word,'' the other woman responded in a soft, almost sad voice. ''At first he closed himself off completely, and later he threw himself into his work, doing all of those dangerous things that he does.''

Kathy lifted her coffee. Dangerous things. She understood that phrase well. ''So he—'' As a pair of boots sounded on the Spanish tile, she nearly spilled the hot drink.

Dakota.

''He's home.'' She looked up at Violet, and they both waited for him to enter the room.

Eight

While Kathy battled a bout of nervousness, Violet stood and approached her son. Had he overheard their conversation? Kathy wondered.

She stole a quick glance and decided he hadn't. It wasn't in Dakota's nature to eavesdrop.

"Mom." He hugged her, then stepped back. "It's good to see you."

"Kathy said you were in Lubbock."

He nodded. "I had some business to take care of with Dad's properties."

Kathy shifted on the couch. Strange, she thought, how Dakota still hadn't taken mental possession of the shopping centers Jack had left him. He still referred to them as his father's—a man who had influenced him more than she had realized.

Violet resumed her seat, and Dakota turned toward Kathy. "Hi."

"Hi." She met his gaze, her heart leaping into its teeter-totter mode. Why couldn't she look at him without experiencing a physical reaction? "I wasn't expecting you back so soon."

"I had a meeting this morning, but it ended early."

He held her gaze, and her heart continued to flutter. He wore a tan T-shirt, faded blue jeans and distressed leather boots—clothes too casual for a business meeting. Apparently he had changed before coming home.

Kathy chewed her lip. Were those the Wranglers he had worn during their telephone conversation? Unable to help herself, she glanced at his fly, then back up to his face. He flashed a bedroom smile and made her hot all over.

Are you wearing jeans?

Yes.

Are they unzipped?

As far down as they'll go.

Violet cleared her throat, and Kathy felt like a teenager who'd been caught lusting after an older boy. Her nipples tingled against her bra, not a good thing to happen when the older boy's observant mother occupied the same room.

Dakota looked away and pulled a hand through his hair. "So, Mom, what's going on? What made you stop by?"

"Do I need a special reason to come to your house?"

"No, of course not."

Violet's eyes, Kathy noticed, sparkled with amusement. But her big, strong, Comanche son revealed something rare—an embarrassed flush coloring his bronzed cheeks. Of course, he had been caught behaving like a teenager, too—sending Kathy a provocative, I'm-thinking-about-sex smile.

Dakota moved toward a leather recliner and sat. Careful, it seemed, not to cast his gaze in Kathy's direction. He focused on his mother instead.

Unwelcome silence ensued, and Kathy wished her heart would quit bumping against her breast. Violet couldn't possibly know that she had climbed into Dakota's bed while he was gone, or that his shirt had brushed decadently between her naked thighs.

Two or three minutes passed, but still no one spoke. They

just sat there, Kathy and Dakota avoiding eye contact, and Violet splitting her amused gaze between them.

"Actually I did stop by for a reason," she admitted finally.

Grateful for the reprieve, Kathy's breath rushed out of her lungs. Dakota, too, seemed grateful his mother had decided to let them off the hook. He leaned forward in his chair.

"As you know," Violet said, "I'm on the board of directors at the West Texas Indian Center, and we need some volunteers to help out with an event next Saturday."

"What kind of an event?" Dakota asked.

"A carnival to raise money for the Foster Care Mentor Program."

Apparently more relaxed, Dakota strode to the bar and poured himself a soda water. "Oh, yeah. You mentioned that program before."

Violet explained to Kathy. "Since we're not able to place all of the children in Indian homes, we're trying to secure weekend foster parents. It's actually called respite care, but we prefer to think of it as our Mentor Program."

"That sounds wonderful," Kathy responded. "Role models are important." Especially to kids from troubled homes, she thought sadly.

"So you'll help out at the carnival?" the other woman asked.

"I'd love to."

Violet looked at Dakota, and he placed his drink on the bar. "Sure, Mom. Me, too."

"Good." She smiled at both of them. "I should get going. I still have more volunteers to recruit." She hugged Kathy, then took her son's arm as he walked her to the door.

Kathy busied herself carrying coffee cups and the leftover pastries into the kitchen. A minute later, Dakota came in and grabbed one of the sweets.

"I enjoyed visiting with your mom," she said before the lone moment trapped them into another awkward spell.

"I imagine she was surprised to see you. I should have called her and told her you were staying here."

"That's okay." Kathy didn't want to think about telephone

conversations, not when she couldn't get the other night out of her mind.

She rinsed the cups and placed them in the dishwasher, then turned to see Dakota licking icing from a cinnamon roll.

He smiled that sexy smile, and she swallowed.

"Do you want a bite?" he asked.

She wanted to bite him. Kiss and nibble. Taste that warm, dark, tantalizing skin.

Struggling to respond in a dignified voice, she cleared her throat and then remembered why Dakota's mother had done that earlier. "No, thank you," she managed.

Sugar trotted into the kitchen and saved Kathy's sanity. The dog made a wide circle around Dakota to get to her.

"She still doesn't like me," he said.

Kathy opened a can of dog food, glad the Maltese had given her another busy task. "I know, I'm sorry. I just don't understand it."

"I do." He leaned against the counter, his shoulder nearly brushing hers. "Sugar isn't used to men."

And he was definitely a man, she thought, cursing her quavering heart. Dakota Lewis was as rugged as his gender came.

She filled the dog's bowl, hardly blaming Sugar for being nervous around him. "Then I suppose it will take time."

Time she wouldn't allow herself to have. Soon she would have to find another place to live.

Dakota knew he didn't have much time. Several days had passed since he'd returned from Lubbock, and he'd barely seen Kathy. She spent every free moment looking at rentals. How was he supposed to win his wife back once she moved out?

Call her? Make love on the phone?

The idea had merit, but it wasn't the same as a flesh-to-flesh encounter. He missed holding her, missed being her husband.

And his progress with Sugar was slow, too. He opened the box of dog treats he kept in his room and stuffed a few in his pocket. He bribed the Maltese whenever Kathy wasn't around, although it didn't appear to do him much good. The dog still wouldn't get close enough to take the treat from his hand. He would set it on the floor, and she would wait until he backed away before nabbing it.

He strode down the hall, then entered the kitchen where he found Sugar with Mrs. Miller. The dog danced happily around the older woman's feet as she cleaned.

He assessed the situation. Little white dog. Big, dark Comanche man. Unless he got some outside help, his chances were slim to none with that pooch.

"Good morning, Mrs. Miller."

She looked up from her sponge. "Hello, Lieutenant."

He stood at attention, but why, he couldn't be sure. Mrs. Miller was hardly his superior. "I need a favor from you."

She took a break from her chore. "Yes, sir. What is it?"

"I want you to help me make friends with the dog." He eyed Sugar and noticed her ears had perked. "I'm not having much luck on my own."

Mrs. Miller cocked her head, giving him the same curious look as the dog. "What seems to be the trouble, Lieutenant?"

Dakota didn't ease his stance. At the moment he felt far from casual. What he felt, he realized, was tense. Out of his element. "Sugar doesn't appear to like men."

"Oh, my. That could present a problem."

She glanced at the dog, then back at Dakota, her bottom lip quivering. Was she suppressing a smile? he wondered. No-nonsense, never-cracks-a smile Miller?

"I don't suppose we can put you in a dress," she said, her lip quivering just a bit more.

Dakota raised an eyebrow at her. He supposed the image was funny, but he hadn't pegged the housekeeper as the smart-aleck type. Deciding he liked this side of her, he grinned. "Why not? I've got great legs."

She finally smiled. And when she did, her entire face came alive. "I hope it won't come to that." She reached down and scooped up the dog. "Say hello to her. How you talk to an animal is important."

Okay, now he felt stupid. Sugar, her gold hair bow angled

like a crown, looked like the queen bee in Mrs. Miller's arms, just waiting for him to make an ass out of himself.

"Hi, Sugar," he said.

The dog turned her white fluffy head away, and Mrs. Miller snorted. "Your voice is too deep."

Dakota frowned, wondering what in the hell he had gotten himself into. "It's called testosterone. I can't help it." Hadn't they already discussed the fact that he was a man?

"Of course you can help it," she scolded. "Haven't you ever talked to a baby?"

A baby? "Actually, no." His lifestyle didn't lend itself to pink and blue bundles. Dakota didn't know diddly about kids, especially the diaper-clad variety.

Mrs. Miller tsked, and he wondered if she had given up on him. She placed the Maltese on the floor, then asked, "So what have you been doing to get Sugar's attention?"

He reached into his pocket and produced the doggie treats. The older woman made another disapproving noise. "I think we can do better than that."

"Better than that" turned out to be pan-fried bits of filet mignon. "Grandma's making you something special," Mrs. Miller told Sugar, who sat sniffing the air.

Grandma? Dakota shook his head. He sure as hell hoped that didn't make him the dog's—

"Daddy's going to help," the gray-haired lady added, shooting him a you-better-get-involved glance. "Aren't you, Lieutenant?"

Daddy seasoned the steak, thinking he'd just lost his mind. All this fuss for a five-pound mutt.

They waited for the meat to cool. Sugar let out a few anxious yips, wiggling impatiently on the floor. Dakota didn't make a move without Mrs. Miller's instruction. The housekeeper had taken charge, giving orders the way his mother sometimes did, outranking him with feminine skill.

"Now you can feed her," she told him. "One piece at a time."

He knelt and offered the treat. As badly as Sugar wanted

the steak, she didn't forget herself. She looked up at Mrs. Miller and whined, clearly pleading for help.

"Go on," the older lady urged. "He won't hurt you."

The dog inched closer and took the meat. Dakota grinned, feeling like he'd just scaled a mountain. He continued hand feeding Sugar, and by the time she'd devoured the last piece, the pooch was sitting on his lap.

Mrs. Miller smiled. "You realize we've just spoiled her for life?"

"It's for an important cause."

"I know," the woman said gently. "It would be nice if Kathy and Sugar moved in permanently. I like your wife, Lieutenant. You're good for each other."

"Thank you." His heart went soft. "I think so, too."

On Saturday morning, Kathy woke with the sun. It was too early to get ready for the carnival, so she brushed her teeth and slipped on her chenille robe, preparing to start a pot of coffee.

Sugar roused from her spot on the bed and followed Kathy into the hall. But as they passed Dakota's room, the dog nudged open the crack in the door.

"Sugar, no!" Kathy's warning came too late. The Maltese had already darted inside.

Without a second thought, Kathy went after her, then stopped when she neared the bed. Dakota was still asleep, the sheets tangled around his waist, the quilt kicked away from him. His face, she noticed, was dark and angular, the tiny lines around his eyes prominent in the morning light. Black hair spiked against his pillow, and beard stubble shadowed his jaw.

He looked warm and touchable, she thought. Like the man she had married, yet slightly changed. She wanted to tame his hair, skim his cheek. But she knew better. He wasn't hers anymore. Too much time had passed, too much heartache. And he was still a soldier. Soon there would be another mission. Dakota wouldn't remain idle for long.

So why was she here, standing in his room, longing for

what could never be? What had possessed her to get this close to him?

Good grief. Sugar. One long, stolen glance at Dakota and she had forgotten about the dog.

"Sugar," she whispered, looking around the room. "Come on, sweetie, we have to go."

A movement from the bed caught her eye, and a familiar being emerged from beneath the rumpled quilt—two black eyes, a mass of silky white fur and a half-cocked metallic bow.

Kathy sent the dog a scolding glance, keeping her voice hushed. "What are you doing in his bed? You don't even like him."

As if determined to defy Kathy's words, Sugar picked her way around the tangled sheets and settled herself right next to Dakota, snug against his bare chest.

Kathy had to smile. The big man and the little dog were an odd, but tender sight. Sugar's white paw rested on Dakota's arm, and he nuzzled closer, stirring in his sleep.

She turned to leave them alone, but only got as far as the door.

"Kathy?"

She turned back to see Dakota squinting at her. She should have known he would awaken. Dakota was a light sleeper. She assumed it came from his military background, night after night of sleepless combat. "I'm sorry I disturbed you. I was looking for Sugar."

"She's right here. Did I oversleep?"

"No. It's still early."

He sent her a boyish smile. "Wanna join us?"

She did. God help her, she did. "No. I'm already up. I think I'll just go start a pot of coffee. Maybe fix an omelet."

He glanced down at the dog, then straightened her bow in what seemed like a paternal gesture. Kathy steadied herself. The image in her head made her knees weak—Dakota with the child they should have had—a dark-eyed, dark-haired little girl dressed in ruffles and ribbons.

"Sweetheart?"

"Yes?" She responded to the endearment, hating that it made her weaker, more vulnerable, achy inside.

"If you give me a few minutes, I'll help you with breakfast."

"Just meet me in the kitchen when you're ready." She forced her legs to carry her down the hall, wondering how she was going to survive the carnival—an event overflowing with dark-eyed, dark-haired children.

Kathy started the coffee and by the time the hash browns were cooking, Dakota arrived with Sugar in tow. He had showered, shaved and zipped himself into a pair of jeans.

He made his way around her, the Maltese at his heels. Kathy couldn't help but wonder what had turned Sugar around. Had the dog looked at him this morning and decided he was just too gorgeous to ignore?

They fixed breakfast and sat across from each other at the dining-room table, their plates filled with potatoes and eggs.

"So, have you found a house yet?" he asked.

Kathy shook her head. "No." None of the rentals seemed quite right. They were all too big for one person, too spacious and lonely. She wanted charming and cozy, like the cottage in Asterland. Or a place that would make her feel warm and woodsy, like Dakota's ranch. She needed the perfect, permanent home, something her living-abroad parents had never provided.

"What about office space?" he asked, pursuing their conversation.

"I haven't looked." She had been too busy scouting Royal for a house that probably didn't exist. "But I guess I'd better start. My parents are anxious for me to get this location up and running."

He lifted his coffee. "Do they know you're staying with me?"

"Yes." And they approved. They didn't understand why Kathy had left Dakota in the first place. One lost baby, her mother had told her, didn't mean that she couldn't have another. And Dakota had been a soldier when she'd married him, so walking out on him two years later made no sense.

Kathy's pragmatic parents didn't understand the dreamer in her, the old-fashioned girl who wanted an enchanted garden, a house full of children and a husband who cared more about saving his marriage than saving the world.

Hiding a frown, she sipped her juice. Her mother had been the first to suggest Royal as a satellite location. That didn't mean her parents were playing matchmaker, did it? Her proper, professional, business-minded parents? No. That couldn't be.

A small, whining noise jarred Kathy from her thoughts. "Is that Sugar?" She looked around to see the dog sitting at Dakota's feet. "Is she begging?"

"No," he answered hastily. "She's just watching me eat."

Watching him eat? "You've been feeding her table scraps, haven't you?" No wonder Sugar followed him around like a lovesick fool. It was food she was after, not masculine attention.

Dakota winced. "Maybe I've given her a few bites here and there. But it wasn't my idea. Mrs. Miller put me up to it."

His boyish excuse sounded impossibly endearing. "And why would your housekeeper do that?"

"Because I asked her to help me make friends with your dog."

A burst of moisture rushed behind Kathy's eyes. She blinked, refusing to cry over breakfast. It had to be, she thought, the sweetest, silliest thing he had ever done. She smiled and reached across the table for his hand. "Sometimes you surprise me."

His fingers curled around hers. "You surprise me, too."

Sugar leapt onto Dakota's lap, and Kathy laughed. Suddenly she was looking forward to spending the day with her husband, even in the company of dark-eyed, dark-haired children.

Beneath the Texas sun, a small park in Midland had been transformed into a carnival, its grassy spaces filled with merriment. It wasn't a large affair, not the kind with those whiplash-type rides, but it was entertaining nonetheless. It reminded Dakota of being a kid himself, of the Halloween festival his elementary school used to host every October. His mother had been involved in that, too. Dakota figured being on the board of directors at the Indian Center was a lot like being a PTA mom for Violet Tenewa. Only these days, she had more than one child to look after. She had taken on a caseload of foster kids.

Dakota sniffed the air, the aroma of hot dogs and buttered popcorn teasing his senses. Kathy had been placed in one of the concession stands, and he could see her from his post at the shooting gallery. She wore slim-fitting jeans and a buckskin-colored T-shirt, a thick ponytail bouncing high on her head. She seemed right at home, filling cartons of popcorn and handing out candy apples.

Looking up from a customer, she noticed him watching her, then graced him with a quick, ladylike smile.

He returned the smile, feeling like a tall, love-struck adolescent, a Comanche youth just coming into his own.

They lost eye contact over the crowd, and Dakota glanced back at the prizes lined on the shelves—the stuffed animals and plastic toys. Suddenly he wished Kathy had been a part of his early years. Maybe if they had been childhood sweethearts, their lives would have been too connected for her to sever the tie as she had.

A middle-aged man placed a stack of tickets on the counter. "For the boys," he said, a friendly smile working its way across his face.

Dakota took the tickets and scanned "the boys." Three of them, each a different shade of brown. Foster kids, he thought, and a fair-skinned foster dad who believed in rainbows. It made him like the man, respect him for doing something Dakota would have never considered. Kids, no matter what their shape or hue, were foreign to Dakota.

"You're Violet's son, right?" the foster dad asked, as each boy claimed a rifle and studied the ducks moving across the target.

Nodding, he extended his hand. "Dakota Lewis."

The other man gave a hearty shake. "Bob Calhoun." He motioned to the child at the end of the row, his voice suddenly quiet. "That one's Jake. He's Comanche. Violet said I ought to mention that. You know, since Jake's in the program."

In other words, Dakota thought, Jake was in need of an Indian mentor. A Comanche, he supposed, wondering if his mom was lurking somewhere, watching his befuddled expression.

What did he know about being a mentor? Jake appeared to be about five, with thick brown hair and skin about the same color as Dakota's. A mixed-blood, he surmised, like himself.

The boy wiggled as he fired at the ducks, even though his tongue darted out in a gesture defining serious concentration. Dakota figured all kids that age were squirmy and active. No, he wouldn't know what to say or do with someone that small.

The tallest of Bob's boys earned himself a prize. Dakota let him pick through the toys, his foster brothers crowding him in excitement as he chose a plastic snake. He looked up at Dakota with a ready smile. "I'm Scott. Me and him are Cherokee," he said, nudging the boy on his left. "Just like Bob's stepdad."

So Bob had been raised in an Indian home. Somehow that made sense. The rainbow was a part of his upbringing. Dakota assumed Bob's stepfather was a mentor to the two Cherokee boys.

"Nice to meet you guys, I'm Dakota. I'm from the Comanche Nation."

"Cool." Scott put his arm around the third child. "So is Jake."

At the mention of his name, Jake flashed a gap-filled grin. He was the littlest of the bunch and the most wiggly. Dakota resisted the urge to smooth his hair. For an instant, Jake reminded him of Prince Eric.

The kids went back to their rifles, and Dakota returned to Bob.

"You know, Jake has a twin sister," Bob said. "Pretty girl named Jenny. She lives with us, too." He motioned toward another booth and chuckled. "She's with my wife. Those two are determined to bring home a goldfish."

Twins. He could only assume Jake and Jenny were a package deal. A boy and a girl who needed a Comanche mentor, someone who could help them stay connected to their roots. It made him wonder how they had ended up in foster care in the first place. Were they orphaned? Abused? Neglected?

When their tickets ran out, Bob and his lively brood said goodbye and headed in the direction of the goldfish toss, Dakota staring after them.

Fifteen minutes later, Violet arrived with Dakota's replacement. Rather than accuse his mother of setting him up, he strolled the carnival grounds with her, waiting for Kathy's shift to end.

"Tell me about them, Mom."

"Jake and Jenny?" She took his arm as they passed a vendor selling Texas trinkets. "Their father is Comanche, but he's been out of the picture for quite a while. And their mother is in rehab for drug abuse." When Dakota frowned, Violet squeezed his arm. "She's not a bad person, she just got caught up in something bad. She loves her kids, and she's working hard to stay clean."

"That's good."

"Jake and Jenny are perfect for the mentor program. They're doing well at Bob's, but he isn't familiar with Comanche practices." She stopped to gaze up at him. "They're sweet kids, and they're mixed-bloods, Dakota. Like you."

He let out a breath, confused by his emotions. "You don't have to push so hard. I've already decided to come into the center and find out more about the program. But, Mom—"

"Yes?"

"I can't make any promises."

She kept her eyes on his. "It's enough that you're thinking about it."

Was it? he wondered. Thinking and doing weren't the same thing. He didn't know if he had what it took to make a difference in Jake and Jenny's lives. What if they sensed his uneasiness? His inexperience with kids? And how many Saturdays would he be free to mentor? Thunder had already contacted him about the possibility of another assignment.

Nine

At dusk Kathy and Dakota sat on the lawn, the carnival twinkling around them. Enjoying each other's company, they sipped ice-cold lemonade and ate a variety of junk food.

Kathy savored the sweet, sugary taste of cotton candy melting on her tongue. Her fingers were sticky, but she didn't care. It made her feel young and free, a girl without a care in the world. She hadn't felt that way in a long time. Life had a way of crushing those moments.

Dakota munched on chili dogs dripping with melted cheese. He spilled a glob on his jeans, wiped it with a napkin and grinned.

"Do you ever wish we had known each other when we were kids?" he asked.

Kathy reached for her drink, the question surprising her. Dakota wasn't a dreamer. He didn't try to turn people or places into something they weren't. They had grown up worlds apart, and she assumed he accepted their differences.

"I've thought about it." But the fantasy never played out

quite right. "Since you're nine years my senior, I don't think we would have been friends."

"I forgot about our age difference." He chuckled. "And here I was picturing myself as your first lover. Sixteen-year-olds parked in an empty field, kissing and groping."

She laughed, too. "When you were sixteen I was seven. And when I was sixteen, you were twenty-five."

After polishing off two chili cheese dogs, he attacked a carton of fries. "So much for that romantic illusion."

Kathy leaned back, wondering what had made him imagine such a thing in the first place. Was it the carnival? The teenagers holding hands and stealing kisses? When dusk arrived, so had the Texas youth—long, lanky boys in cowboy hats and girls with fresh, pretty faces.

"I didn't know kissing and groping in the back of a pickup was romantic," she said, angling her head to study him. He had been long and lean as a youth, too. Or so he appeared in the photographs his mother kept in leather-bound albums. And his first vehicle had been a shiny red Ford, much like the truck he drove today.

"It is to sixteen-year-old boys." Lifting a fry, he dunked it into a plastic cup brimming with ketchup. "And I did my fair share."

"Should I be jealous?" Once the words were out, she could have kicked herself. They might be legally married, but they were no longer a couple. Jealousy didn't fit into the equation.

He didn't appear to notice her blunder. Either that or he was having too much fun reminiscing to care. "You know who drove the boys in Royal wild?" he said wistfully. "Lori Lynn Thorton and her thirty-six-double-Ds."

Kathy found herself amused. He sounded ridiculously male. "Was she your first?"

"In my dreams, maybe." He shoved a fry into his mouth. "Lori's older brother was a body builder. Mr. Universe or something. I swear, the ground rumbled when he walked." Dakota went after another fry. "Hell, Lori's probably still a virgin."

"Yes," Kathy quipped, nudging his foot with her own. "Poor Lori Lynn and her double-Ds. She probably joined a convent. Took a vow of chastity."

He pushed back, his boot against hers. "Yeah, and Mr. Universe probably has love handles and a beer belly by now."

They looked at each other and laughed, their feet still touching. It felt strangely intimate, she thought. Casual and loving.

When their laughter faded, Kathy let the wind caress her face. The air was light and stirring, the noise from the carnival almost dreamy and far away. And the sky, she noticed, was painted with streaks of lavender and soft shades of blue.

She finished her drink and thought about what Dakota had called his romantic illusion. No, he hadn't been her first lover, not in the literal sense, but he had been the first man to awaken her desires. To bring her to a mind-spinning climax, to melt her bones and heat her skin, to leave her dizzy and trembling.

He knew, of course. During a fainthearted moment in Italy, she had told him. And he had reacted with sheer masculine pleasure, pushing his tongue into her mouth and carrying her swiftly to his bed.

She remembered how incredible that moment had been, how smooth and seductive, the mountain air blowing in through an open window, billowing the curtains.

Wondrous love. Deep, possessive strokes. She could still feel him moving between her legs, promising a lifetime of forever. He had asked her to marry him that night, his eyes dark and intense, waiting for an answer.

"Kathy?"

She placed her cup against her forehead, realizing how warm she had become. How suddenly warm. "Yes?"

"Are you okay?"

She blinked and lowered the cup. "What?"

"You seem a little out of it."

"I'm thirsty," she said, as if that should account for her dazed behavior. "My drink is gone."

He handed her his, and she placed her mouth on the straw,

thinking she could taste him there. It was, of course, her imagination, her weakness. The part of her that still fantasized about him, that let herself remember the past.

"I was just thinking about Asterland," he said.

She allowed the lemonade to cool her, then took another slow, steady sip for safe measure. They had made love in Asterland, and that was something she hoped he didn't want to discuss. Not now, not while her body was already wandering in that direction. She couldn't pour the drink over her skin, even if it craved something cold and wet.

"You were?"

He nodded. "I was wondering what you thought of Thunder."

Relief flooded her system. Thunder she could deal with. "I liked him. He was nice."

"Nice?" Dakota made a disbelieving face. "Women don't refer to him as *nice.*"

Her senses, thank goodness, were returning. And to prove it to herself, she handed Dakota the lemonade. "Then how do they refer to him?"

"Oh, I don't know. A hunk. A flirt. A womanizer. Something along those lines."

"Well, I thought he was nice. The perfect gentleman."

The look he gave her could have split hairs. "Now I know you're lying."

And now she knew her conversation with Thunder hadn't reached Dakota's ears.

Dakota misses you, Kathy.

He told you that?

No, but I recognize the signs.

"Did you know Thunder was married?" she asked.

Dakota's jaw nearly dropped. "Well if that's the case then he's been cheating big-time. Boy, did he play a number on you. Pretending to be blissfully wed."

She shook her head. Trust a man to jump to that conclusion, especially a man whose father had kept a wife and a mistress. "He's not married now. It was a long time ago."

"So he's divorced?" Dakota asked, his tone quieter.

She nodded. "He didn't say why. Just that things didn't work out." And it was Thunder's wife who had filed the papers, that much Kathy sensed.

Dakota drew his knees up. "I guess I shouldn't have said what I did. But he's never mentioned an ex-wife to me. Then again, we rarely talk about our personal lives."

No, she thought, but they go on missions together, dodging bullets and trying to save the world. How ironic that neither one of them could save something as sacred as a marriage. They were more like brothers than they knew.

"I just spoke to Thunder a few days ago." Dakota collected their empty food containers and shoved them in a bag. "He might need my help."

Kathy's heart slammed against her chest. "With what?" she asked, although she knew. An assignment. An undercover mission. More bullets. More danger.

"Thunder has been tracking the leader of a prominent terrorist band for years. And just recently, he got another lead. Whether or not it will pan out remains to be seen."

She forced out a breath. "So if it pans out, he'll need you."

"Yes, but it will probably be a while. Thunder could be tagging this lead for months. He won't bring me into it until he's certain that he's on the right track."

How could Dakota sound so casual, so relaxed? Didn't he know what news like that did to her?

Of course, he didn't. And he never would. Because even if she told him, it wouldn't matter. She was back in Royal, and Dakota was caught up in another mission.

A knot formed in Kathy's stomach. Soon she would have to contact an attorney about filing for divorce. What other choice did she have?

Dakota Lewis was a soldier, not a husband. Nothing would stop him from pursuing his life's work. Ending their marriage was the only answer. Even is she still loved him.

The weekend wasn't over. The sun rose on Sunday, even if Kathy's heart refused to shine. The decision she had made yesterday left her cold and shaken.

Divorce. The word sounded so final, so permanent—a legality she had been avoiding for three long, hopeful years. Three years of waiting for Dakota to come to her, to choose their marriage over his work. But hiding her head in the sand wasn't going to change the facts. She was back in Royal, and Dakota hadn't thought twice about getting involved in another mission. When Thunder needed him, he would go. And she would be left alone.

Again.

Remembering where she was, Kathy took a deep breath and told herself to relax. The weather was perfect for a poolside barbecue, and Sheikh Rassad had gone to great lengths to entertain his guests. A buffet table displayed a variety of side dishes, many from Ben's homeland, including several large platters of *hummus* and baskets of pita bread. Of course, the thick prime cuts of beef being seasoned for the grill were pure Texas.

Kathy studied her host and decided he and his wife were an unusual, stunning pair. Ben stood tall and lean, a proper man with copper skin and exotic gray eyes. Jamie, on the other hand, was petite, blond and as spirited as her smile.

"They make an interesting couple, don't they?"

The comment came from Aaron's wife, Pamela. She sat next to Kathy, nibbling on a small variety of salads. Pamela had a quiet charm about her, a former elementary school teacher with twin dimples and a scatter of freckles.

Kathy smiled at the other woman, thinking her young students must have adored her. "Yes, they do."

Pamela reached for her drink. "The food is wonderful. I've never had some of these dishes before." She pointed to a bulgur wheat salad on her plate. "This is my favorite."

"It's called tabbouleh." Kathy was familiar with Middle Eastern food. One of the advantages, she supposed, of being a world traveler. "It's fairly simple to make. I'm sure Ben's housekeeper will give you the recipe."

"I'll have to ask her. I'm eating as healthily as I can."

Of course she was, Kathy thought, with a tug of admiration

and a twinge of envy. Pamela was five months' pregnant, her tummy a small mound beneath a light cotton blouse. Aaron would be a father in the fall.

Kathy resisted the urge to place her hand on Pamela's stomach, to feel the flutter of life. She remembered being pregnant all too well—the thrill, the maternal warmth. She knew the stages of prenatal development, the miracle growing and changing in Pamela's womb. The miracle that had once lived in her womb.

Refusing to dwell on her own loss, Kathy pictured Pamela's child instead. Tiny fingernails forming, a strong, steady heartbeat, an active little creature kicking its legs and sucking its thumb.

"Are you hoping for a boy or a girl?" she asked, knowing it must be the universal question posed to a mother-to-be.

"It doesn't matter. A boy who looks like Aaron would be wonderful. But having a daughter would be special, too. All those adorable, frilly little clothes." Pamela placed her hand on her tummy in a natural gesture. "If my doctor requests an ultrasound, we're going to ask the technician not to tell us what the baby is. We like the old-fashioned idea of being surprised."

Kathy nodded in agreement. Waiting and wondering had to be one of the pleasures of expectant parenthood—choosing two sets of names, decorating a nursery with either sex in mind.

Pamela kept her hand on her tummy, even when she turned to glance over her shoulder, drawing Kathy's attention to Aaron and Dakota.

The men stood Stetson to Stetson, each with a bottle of beer in hand. Kathy assumed the party was for the Texas Cattleman's Club members who had recovered the Lone Star jewels. It was a close-knit group, and Ben seemed happy to provide a casual, festive afternoon.

Kathy amended her thought as Matt Walker and his fiancée, Lady Helena, headed toward her and Pamela. The party was for the *couples* who had recovered the jewels, those who shared a common bond. She supposed in that sense, she and Dakota were a couple, too.

Matt placed Lady Helena's plate on the table and lingered for a moment, his hand on her shoulder. She looked back at him with quiet intimacy, and Kathy and Pamela exchanged a glance, their hearts tugging. Lady Helena was still recovering from substantial burns, making the use of her left hand nearly impossible. She also walked with a slight limp, but that didn't make her any less beautiful in Matt's eyes.

"Ladies." He stepped back and tipped his hat, brushing his fiancée's cheek before he detoured to the ice chest and joined Dakota and Aaron.

Lady Helena took her seat and followed his progress. "The women are sampling the buffet, and the men are drinking beer." She smiled and placed a napkin on her lap, her movements careful and slow. "I don't suppose they will be interested in food until those steaks are grilled."

"Deep down, they're just cowboys," Pamela said, indicating the masculine show of boots and trophy belts. "Even the sheikh."

Lady Helena nodded. "That may be true, but he is the only man keeping his wife exceptionally close by."

"I noticed that, too," Kathy added. But she also noticed the tender smiles passing between the newly married couple. The sheikh's young bride all but glowed.

She glanced at her plate, a lump forming in her throat. It made her long for the days when she and Dakota had first fallen in love. The romance and passion, the stolen glances and heartbeats of excitement.

Could she really divorce him? Take that final, devastating step?

Pamela rose. "I can't resist another helping. Just one more salad before the main course." She rubbed her protruding tummy. "And I do have the excuse that I'm eating for two."

As the pregnant woman flashed her dimples and headed for the buffet, Kathy and Lady Helena laughed. Aaron's wife was a true delight.

A quiet, reflective moment ensued, and Kathy gazed out at

the scene before her. A Texas-style terrace led to the pool, but an arrangement of pillars and statues resembled the ruins of a classic temple. The sheikh's ranch was a Royal oasis—a unique blend of culture and eclectic architecture. Beyond the pool, an array of colorful blooms charmed the Western landscape with tropical beauty.

"Kathy?"

She met Lady Helena's gaze and realized the other woman had been watching her. "Yes?"

"Thank you so much for what you did. I owe you and Dakota my deepest gratitude, but I don't know how to repay you."

Kathy's eyes misted. Lady Helena was the daughter of an Asterland count, and she had been waiting to return to her homeland to plan her wedding. But the threat of Payune's revolution had kept her from fulfilling that dream. And now that Payune was in jail and her country was safe, Lady Helena and Matt Walker would fly to Asterland to arrange a traditional European ceremony.

"We've already been rewarded by the king," Kathy responded. "And your happiness is gratitude enough. The way Matt feels about you makes it all worthwhile."

"Thank you." The blonde tilted her head. "He is such a wonderful man."

And they deserved a long and happy marriage, Kathy thought. Their union was just beginning—as hers and Dakota's was ending. But she had no right to envy Lady Helena, no right to fixate on the emptiness in her own soul. Today was a celebration, a party of goodwill and cheer.

Pamela returned to the table and the three chatted until a friendly commotion caught their attention. Kathy turned and found herself staring. The last of the guests had arrived. Dr. Justin Webb and his wife Winona apologized for being late, but no one minded their tardiness. Angel, their six-month-old daughter, had just awakened from an overdue nap.

The baby, graced with golden curls and bright blue eyes, clung to her mother with a chubby-cheeked smile. And at that tender moment, Kathy's arms began to ache. She wanted the chance to hold Angel, for as long as the child would allow.

Dakota was having a wonderful time. The steak was thick and juicy, the grilled corn dripping with butter, the beer cold and thirst-quenching. Ten adults gathered at one long table, eating great food and exchanging lively conversation.

He sat next to Kathy, thinking she'd never looked prettier. She wore a breezy spring dress and strappy beige sandals. Her hair fell loose about her shoulders in a shining burst of scarlet waves. He also noticed that she couldn't keep her eyes off the baby.

Little Angel was propped on Winona's lap, waving her hands and making kiddy sounds. And although she had already eaten her own mushy food, that didn't stop her from attacking the contents on her mother's plate.

How did parents do it? he wondered. How did they entertain someone so small? Did they baby-talk and make goofy faces from sunrise to sundown?

"Would you like me to hold her?" Kathy asked Winona. "I've finished my meal."

The other woman removed a squished strawberry from the little girl's hand. "Are you sure you don't mind?"

"No, not at all. I couldn't eat another bite. I've been to the buffet table twice, and you're just getting started."

"In that case, I accept." Winona sent Kathy a grateful smile and came around to their side of the table. Placing her daughter on Kathy's lap, she told the child to be good.

Dakota wondered if that was possible. In spite of Angel's ethereal name, a devilish glint shone in those big blue eyes. Then again, cherubs smiled the way she was smiling, their cheeks pink and chubby.

Her smile widened, and he grinned. She had one tooth, one tiny white chip poking out of her gums.

While Angel bounced on Kathy's lap and laughed, Dakota made one of those ridiculous faces just to amuse her. But when Kathy looked over to see the child's source of entertainment, he stopped acting like an idiot and picked up his corn. Making faces was one thing, getting caught quite another.

Angel laughed again, and he bit into his corn. The cherub seemed pleased that they'd fooled Kathy, even if he hadn't intended to make a game of it.

"What are you giggling about?" Kathy asked the baby.

Me, Dakota wanted to say. He had made Angel laugh. And it felt good, he realized. Babies had never paid much attention to him in the past, but he supposed that was partly his own fault. He wasn't overly animated nor did he have a smooth, soothing voice. He was big and broad and uncertain of how to connect with a being so much smaller than himself.

But he had done all right today. Angel seemed to like him.

Kathy fussed adoringly with the little girl, brushing a curl from her eye, fixing her T-shirt when it rolled up her belly. Angel sported a casual yet lacy outfit, complete with matching socks and a ruffled collar. Sugar and spice, Dakota thought. The description fit the child and his wife. They made a beautiful, feminine picture.

From across the table, Winona and Justin watched, pride glittering in their eyes. Angel was their miracle, a baby who had literally been left on Winona's door step. Dakota couldn't help but wonder how it would feel to save something as precious and tender as a child. At the moment, it seemed far more important than anything he had ever done.

A jolt of unexpected longing constricted his chest. Would a child have made a difference in his marriage?

He glanced at Kathy, and Angel laughed again, catching him off guard. He grinned back at her, but this time his wife turned and trapped his gaze.

"So you're the reason she's been giggling all this time?"

He shrugged, his grin still in place. "I guess she thinks I'm funny looking."

The smile that spread across Kathy's face was as sappy as his, and he thought this had to be the strangest, most heartwarming moment they had ever shared. He felt warm and wooly and kind of stupid inside, but he liked the feeling so he kept smiling, even if a flutter of self-consciousness had crept in.

There probably wasn't a person at the barbecue who hadn't noticed his uncharacteristic behavior.

Angel leaned forward and held out her arms, and Kathy's expression softened. "She wants you to hold her."

His pulse jumped, and something akin to panic shot through his veins. Hold her? Him? The big, brutal soldier? What if he dropped her? Damaged the little imp for life? Or what if she decided he wasn't so entertaining up close? What if she squirmed and cried?

Angel made a loud, impatient noise and waved her dimpled arms, demanding the attention he was afraid to give.

"Okay, now. Don't fuss." He placed his hands around the child's waist, handling her as carefully as a ticking bomb. A feminine temper tantrum would only make matters worse.

Angel came to him readily, no tears, no tiny-female fits. Instead she hugged his neck and snuggled against his shoulder. He looked across the table at Justin, who studied him from beneath a straw Stetson, a father watching his baby girl cuddle in another man's arms.

"She smells good," Dakota said, nuzzling the child.

Justin cocked an eyebrow, a slight quirk to his lips. "Did you think my daughter would smell bad?"

Dakota flashed a chagrinned grin. "No." But he hadn't expected to feel like the sun had chosen to shine exclusively on him. Angel's body was soft and warm, her skin a blend of sweet, comforting scents—powder and lotion and flowers blooming along heaven's pearly gates. He stroked her back, then patted her bottom, the rustle of diaper a curious sound.

Angel wasn't exactly still, but she wasn't a concealed bundle of explosives, either. She toyed with his shirt and moved her head back and forth, her hair tickling his chin.

I want one, he thought, turning to meet Kathy's gaze. A shimmering, misty gaze, he noticed. A woman thinking she wanted one, too.

Was it possible that their sudden fantasy could already be taking shape in Kathy's womb? They had made love in Asterland without protection, and mistakes often produced miracles.

Before Dakota could monopolize Angel's time, the baby decided she wanted to try her luck with Ben. She latched onto the sheikh, and the transfer was made. Ben got a syrupy look on his face, and Dakota laughed. One bright-eyed little girl was turning the Texas Cattleman's Club macho militia to mush.

Within twenty minutes Angel had charmed her way around the table, until Justin claimed her for good. Once she was in her daddy's arms, no other man stood a chance.

After the dishes were cleared, the sheikh's loyal housekeeper appeared with a frothy cake, pastel icing dotted with sugared roses.

Ben nodded to the elderly woman and guided his wife to the head of the table. ''We would like to thank all of you for coming to our home,'' he said. ''This is a special time for Jamie and me, and we are proud to announce that—''

''I'm pregnant!'' his spontaneous young bride blurted, raising the hem of a pale blue blouse just enough to expose a glimpse of her navel.

The customarily proper Ben laughed and kissed her smartly on the lips, and a blast of excitement followed. The women rushed Jamie with exuberant hugs, and the men clapped Ben on the back and pumped his hand. Even Angel squealed in baby wonder.

Dakota congratulated the beaming couple, then stepped back to absorb the joy, the sheer enchantment of life.

God permitting, he and Kathy would be next.

Ten

Kathy exhaled a ragged breath, her emotions a mass of conflicting energy. Being happy for your friends and sad for yourself presented an uneasy combination. She craved a cup of herbal tea, her Irish grandmother's remedy for relaxation.

''Can I get you anything? Tea? Coffee?'' she asked Dakota, slipping off her sandals. Bare feet helped, too. And curling up in an oversize chair.

''No, thanks. I had coffee at Ben's.'' He removed his hat and hung it on a nearby rack.

She nodded and headed into the kitchen. Searching through the tea bags, she chose a lemon flavor promising to lift her spirits. Tea from the microwave wasn't as soothing as tea from the stove, so she set the water to boil and waited.

She could hear Dakota playing with Sugar, tossing the dog's favorite ball so the Maltese could romp down the hall. The chipper little bark should have snapped her out of this confusing depression, but somehow it only managed to intensify her loss.

Kathy carried the steaming brew into the living room, then frowned when Dakota and Sugar followed. She wasn't up for company or conversation, but she couldn't explain why she needed a few quiet moments of solitude. It would mean alerting Dakota to her mood, something she preferred not to do.

Dakota settled onto the sofa, and Sugar leaped up beside him, a striped ball in her mouth. She dropped it and nudged him, pursuing lapdog attention. He obliged with several gentle strokes. Satisfied, Sugar closed her eyes, one paw guarding the ball.

They made a touching pair, a domestic sight that hurt Kathy's grieving heart. She sipped the lemon tea, praying for the promised lift. Wallowing in self-pity at the expense of someone else's good fortune placed her in a selfish, unhealthy light, even in her own bleak eyes.

She knew better. God help her, she did.

Tucking her feet beneath her, she studied the fireplace. Although the weather wasn't permitting, she imagined burning logs just to calm herself. Winter was her favorite season—mistletoe, evergreens and the woodsy scent of a crackling fire.

"I had a great time. Didn't you?" Dakota asked.

"Yes." But it had been too much for one day. Too many happy couples, too many pregnant women. One moment at the barbecue she had been fine, the next floating through the reverie and wishing Angel was the baby she had lost.

"Are you tired, sweetheart?"

She glanced up from her drink. "Do I look tired?"

"A little. But you look pretty, too."

She wanted to squeeze her eyes shut and make the world go away. How could she look appealing, the woman who wanted to cry because her friends were either getting married or having babies? She didn't deserve pretty.

The tea wasn't working. Kathy's emotions were fighting a losing battle. And contemplating divorce while others found happiness was the self-inflicted culprit. She had spent the past three years pretending divorce wasn't a viable option. At least not to her. If Dakota had made the choice, then she would have told herself that he'd never really loved her, that it had all been a mistake. But that hadn't happened. No papers were served, no irreconcilable differences charted. Instead they stayed in limbo, legally married with no future to speak of.

And wasn't that worse? she asked herself. Worse than no decision at all?

''You seem happy,'' she told Dakota. Which, of course, made her even more sad. There would be someone else in his life someday. Someone who understood the soldier in him, who supported his causes. He was too magnetic, too easy to fall in love with, too attractive to ignore.

''I do feel good,'' he announced. ''But I enjoy casual get-togethers.''

Kathy tilted her head. Maybe he would choose a string of lovers instead of just one. Sex without serious commitment worked for plenty of men. And wasn't that the lifestyle he had leaned toward before their relationship developed? People did that after divorce, didn't they? Reverted back to their old ways?

Not everyone, she thought. She couldn't see herself dating at all, let alone the type who had come before Dakota—Ivy League heirs who appreciated proper, mundane dinners and suggested she cut her unruly hair into a more suitable style.

She would rather remain alone and remember the tall, dark-eyed man waiting for her on the cliffs. Her forbidden lover. The husband she couldn't keep.

She released a weary sigh. How typical. And tragic. Casting herself as the heroine in an ill-fated legend—a woman wandering through life like an aimless shadow, her heart longing for what could never be.

As Dakota removed his boots and placed them under the coffee table, Sugar stirred, then settled beside him again. ''Angel sure is a cute little girl.'' He shook his head in amazement. ''Imagine discovering a baby on your doorstep. Thinking you hear an abandoned kitten, but going outside and finding a child instead.''

Because Kathy couldn't bring herself to picture such a confusing yet magical scenario, she responded simply. ''Winona and Justin are wonderful parents.''

He sought her gaze. "Yes, they are. In that regard, it was the right doorstep."

And ours was the wrong one, she thought, wishing those dark eyes weren't exploring hers. Why was he watching her so closely? Did he sense her uneasiness?

She set her tea on a nearby table and tried to relax. She didn't want to be found out. Not now, not with the dark cloud of divorce weighing on her mind, with images of Dakota finding other lovers.

"Kathy," he said, still studying her.

It was too late, she realized. He was going to ask why a festive barbecue had made her so sad. She held her breath and waited, wondering what she would say, how she would convince him that she was fine.

"Is there a chance you might be pregnant?"

Oh, God. She gripped the cushioned chair, her heart tackling too many beats. "Why would you—?"

"We didn't use protection in Asterland."

"I'm not." She let out the breath she had been holding, forcing her voice to remain steady. Every cell in her body ached, right along with her pounding heart. "You don't need to worry."

"I wasn't worried. I was actually hoping." He paused to shift his posture, move closer to the edge of the sofa. "I've never really thought about having kids. At least not consciously. And then today it hit me."

Dizziness swept through Kathy, making her legs weak. She untucked them, then placed both feet on the floor, searching for solid ground, for stability she couldn't quite find.

"I'm not pregnant." And his wish, his hope had come much too late. Their baby was gone.

"Are you sure? Did you take one of those drugstore tests?"

"There was no need." She felt as though she were floating outside herself, pushing away pain from the past. Pushing as it drifted toward her, waiting to connect. "I didn't miss my period."

"Oh." He dropped his gaze, then lifted it a second later. "We should have had kids when we had the chance, when things were right between us.'' Reaching for Sugar, he stroked the dog's sleeping form. ''I can't help but think it would have made a difference in our marriage.'' His smile was a little sad, a little wistful. ''You would have made a terrific mother. And I could have learned to be a dad.''

Kathy didn't burst into tears. Instead they trailed slowly down her cheeks, one right after the other, burning as they went.

When Dakota leaned forward, she held up her hand to ward him off, to keep him from coming closer. It was time to tell him about the baby, but she couldn't if he touched her.

''Don't,'' she whispered. ''Just give me a minute.'' A minute for three years of loneliness. It sounded absurd.

Wiping her eyes, she stared at her husband, the man who waited with a concerned expression. The man who suddenly wanted to be a father.

Dakota knew he had said something hurtful. Somehow he had hurt Kathy without meaning to. ''Tell me, sweetheart. What's wrong?''

She continued to stare, more through him than at him, her red-rimmed eyes vacant, the sound of her voice distant. ''There was a baby. But I miscarried. Three years ago.''

''I don't understand.'' He blinked, struggling to grasp her words. It wasn't something he expected to hear, to comprehend. ''Why didn't you tell me when you found out you were pregnant? When…?'' He let his next question drift, unable to say it out loud.

''Because you weren't here. Not during any of it.'' Her voice broke a little, and he knew she forced back another flood of tears, another knot of emotion. ''I had no way to reach you. You were on a mission. Gone for months.''

And she had lost their child. The baby he had thought about today. The baby they should have had. He tried not to picture her, but his mind's eye refused to listen. He saw her in his head—her tummy swollen, the life inside her flourishing one week, its tiny heartbeat gone the next.

''Did you tell anyone?''

''I was waiting for you.'' She brushed at her dress, her

fingers curling until they clutched the fabric. "I didn't suspect I was pregnant until weeks after you'd gone. So I waited, hoping you would come home soon."

"But I didn't." And to him, one day of the mission had seemed like the next. It had been a long, grueling ordeal—a dangerous operation that kept him from contacting his wife. "I thought about you, always." But that hardly mattered, he realized. His thoughts hadn't protected Kathy or their child.

She glanced away. "I thought about you, too. Wondered exactly what you were doing, who you were with, if you were safe. I was happy about the baby and worried about you at the same time."

He didn't know how to respond, not through the overwhelming pain and guilt. Was it stress that had caused her to lose their child? "How far along were you?"

"When I miscarried?" Avoiding eye contact, she released an erratic breath. "Almost three months. Eleven weeks. I was just getting over the morning sickness."

Suddenly her answer made it all too real. Too vivid in his mind. He should have returned from his mission to find a healthy, happy, pregnant wife. He should have kissed her tummy, brought her breakfast in bed, shopped for teddy bears, chosen a color for the nursery.

"It happened at home," Kathy said. "In this house. I suppose I should hate staying here, but for some reason I don't. Maybe because I was happy here once."

Dakota prayed she could be happy there again, that they could get through this. He didn't want to lose his wife. Not a second time.

"Were you alone?" he asked.

"Yes. I came home from the market and while I was putting away the groceries, I got this terrible cramp." She clutched her stomach as though still feeling it. Feeling the loss of their child. "I called the doctor right away, but I knew it was too late." Rocking a little, she stared into space, into the memories filling her head. "I didn't buy much at the store. I had this craving for a peanut butter and banana sandwich."

Someone should have been there with her, he thought.

No, not just someone. He should have been there. Her husband.

She kept her hands wrapped around her middle. "I don't even like peanut butter. Not really."

Dakota wished she would look at him, scream and yell, tell him that she hated him. It would be easier to bear than watching her droop like a wilting flower, delicate petals ragged and torn.

"I'm sorry," he whispered. "So sorry."

Finally she turned, "I left this house two weeks later. I couldn't stay here. I couldn't wait for you anymore. I didn't just lose our baby. I lost us."

"I know." He remembered coming home to find her gone, to find himself living with emptiness. "Let me help you get ready for bed. You're exhausted. You should lie down." Dakota rose to his feet. He needed to hold her, and she needed warmth and comfort. Her eyes were still edged with tears. She wasn't through crying. Tonight they would spill from her heart.

She didn't take the hand he offered, so he stepped back, a lump forming in his throat.

"I don't need your help," she said, her voice quiet. "I fell apart a long time ago. I'm not falling apart now."

But she was, he thought. She was barely holding on. She had waited so long to tell him about the baby. Much too long.

She stood and faced him. "We can't change what happened. It's over. It's done. And I don't want to talk about it anymore."

Dakota nodded and let her pass, not knowing what else to do. On silent feet, she walked down the hall toward her room. The day had shifted into night, early evening with an early moon shining through the living-room windows.

After closing the blinds, he left the sleeping dog on the sofa and carried Kathy's cup into the kitchen. Leaning against the sink, he pictured her there, three years before, pregnant with his child.

His child.

Today he had held a baby for the first time—a tiny girl

who smelled sweet and powdery, a girl with fair hair and bright blue eyes.

Pouring the leftover tea down the drain, Dakota watched it disappear. Like Angel, their baby would have been beautiful. It would have inherited his Comanche skin and Kathy's Irish smile—a child whose dark hair would have shimmered in the sun with streaks of auburn.

Dakota sank to the floor, mourning the life he had never got to know—a son or daughter who should have grown into a wondrous little being.

Two hours passed before he glanced up at the clock. While he'd sat on the floor, trapped in emotion, what had Kathy been doing? Battling exhaustion? Hugging her knees to her chest?

Rising, he pulled a hand through his hair. He couldn't leave her alone. Not tonight. They both needed comfort, whether they lay awake or succumbed to sleep.

A pale glow spilled from beneath her bedroom door. He stood, gazing down at the light. It wasn't her bedroom, he corrected, a frown taking root in his brow. It was the room they had decorated for guests. Kathy didn't belong there. She belonged with him.

He didn't think to knock. Opening the door, he slipped inside.

She was awake, wearing the same sleeveless dress, her hair a golden shade of red—a fiery halo enhanced by the illumination of a single amber bulb. Fragility sprinkled over her like a spring rain, each teardrop as delicate as spun glass. Some clung to her lashes, others slid down her cheeks.

How could she look so lost, yet so beautiful?

Their eyes met, but neither spoke. She held a pillow against her stomach while another supported her back, cushioning the headboard. The quilt was rumpled, the sheets only mildly disturbed.

He wanted to carry her to his room, to the bed they once shared, but he doubted she would welcome such a powerful intrusion. If he touched her, it would be with her permission.

He stopped in the center of the room, praying she wouldn't

turn him away. He should have knocked, respected her privacy.

"Can I stay?" he asked. "Can I sit with you?"

She nodded, and he came toward the bed.

"You should try to sleep." He reached for a tissue on the night stand, then settled beside her. Tilting her chin, he dried her tears.

She leaned into him, her head on his shoulder, the scarlet halo vivid against the white background of his shirt. He intended to get her a nightgown, to dress her for bed, but he didn't want to lose the connection. So he held her instead.

Even in the amber light, he saw shadows beneath her eyes, pale lavender circles, swollen from tears. She felt as fragile as she looked, her slim, elegant body draped in a wrinkled dress.

"I should have told you sooner," she said. "I meant to."

"It's okay. None of this is your fault." He lifted the sheet and tucked it around her. Pressing a kiss to her forehead, he felt her breath stir against his neck just as her eyes drifted closed.

And while she slept, he thought about how much he loved her.

Kathy awakened at daybreak and found herself next to Dakota, a printed sheet balled at their feet. They were both dressed in the clothes they had worn yesterday, but his shirt fell open and the top button of his jeans lay undone. His belt was gone, she noticed. Sometime in the middle of the night he had removed it.

He looked rumpled and gorgeous, his jaw shadowed with just a hint of beard stubble. And his hair, as black and coarse as a winter night, spiked against a pillow. The bedding suited him, the wash of Sante Fe colors complementing Indian skin.

Allowing her gaze to roam, she locked onto his hips, onto those unfastened jeans. The waistband of white briefs were barely visible, and a stomach rippling with muscle moved with the inhale and exhale of sleeping breaths.

She glanced away deliberately, but came back a moment

later. Was he aroused? Drifting in and out of naughty dreams? His fly bulged, a masculine rise beneath deep-blue denim.

Palms itchy to touch, she lifted her gaze, and it collided with his.

Blushing wasn't welcome, but her cheeks heated just the same. She had been caught studying his hips, his navel, his sex.

They stared at each other, neither sure what to do or say. She hadn't expected to feel this way, not on the morning after an emotional cry. But last night's tears had vanished with the dark, and now Kathy couldn't think beyond the awkwardness of lust.

He arched a long, sturdy body, stretching a mass of muscle and sinew, and she swallowed, her throat dry as dust.

"Morning," he said, his voice still rough from sleep.

"Hi." Her nipples pebbled against her bra, chafing uncomfortably. "We slept in our clothes." Obvious as her statement was, it was the only coherent sentence that came to mind. Her bra was, after all, part of her clothing.

He grabbed hold of his shirt tail. "Yeah, we did."

Kathy nearly smiled through her nervousness. Apparently he lacked vocal skills on this odd morning, too.

A second later, a heavy breath expanded his impressive chest. She chewed her bottom lip and decided he didn't need to say anything brilliant or compelling.

Even as she told herself having him would be wrong, her rational side refused to obey. She struggled for control and lost.

She needed him. One last time.

"I don't want to talk," she said. Not about important things. That would spoil the moment. The slow, shy heat slipping between them.

"Then we won't. Not now." He moved closer, just enough to send a silk-wrapped shiver down her spine.

"Touch me," she whispered, inviting his caress.

He unbuttoned the front of her dress with infinite care, and the gentleness made her dizzy. The simple white bra and cotton panties weren't designed for seduction, but she saw pleasure shining in his eyes as he discovered them.

Their mouths came together, and they sipped from each other, sunlight spilling like wine. She removed his shirt, then brought her hands to his chest and smoothed her palms over warm, solid flesh. He had the body of a warrior, strong and toned, with a line of dark, silky hair that grew from his navel to his sex.

Kathy reached for his fly, lowered the zipper and smiled when his stomach flexed with a taut quiver.

He kissed her again, this time hard and deep, tongue to luscious tongue. She swayed with sensuality. Dakota was half-naked and fully aroused. As he unhooked her bra, a groan rose from his throat.

"Tell me what you want," he said, trailing a finger down her belly.

Her bra went slack, her breasts aching. "You. I want you."

"Where?"

Battling her next breath, she pressed her thighs together. Suddenly she wanted him there, his mouth and his tongue, but she couldn't bring herself to voice the words.

He nipped her ear. "You said it on the phone that night. I asked what makes you crazy, and you told me."

But he had been miles away in a hotel room, not poised above her, waiting for an answer. "Then you already know."

Removing her bra, he lowered his head and nuzzled her nipples. She slid her hands into his hair and struggled to hold onto the short, spiky strands. He was teasing her, moving slowly down her body, turning heat to hunger, satin to sensation.

"Is this what you want?" He lifted her hips and brushed his mouth over her panties, over the swatch of virginal cotton.

"Yes," she whispered. "Please. Yes."

He complied, pulling her panties down and discarding them. She clutched the sheet and let the fever take control. The blinding heat and cool shivers. The moisture. The edgy need of knowing what came next.

"You taste sweet," he said, opening her fully, licking and sucking, pressing her erotically against his mouth.

Kathy clung to the fever, holding fast and tight, until the stab of his tongue, the deep, wet strokes drove her to a quick and ruthless climax.

In the next spiraling moment, he was naked, nuzzling tenderly. "Do you want me to use protection?"

Barely recovered, she nodded, and he reached for his wallet on the night stand.

"I kept hoping this would happen between us, but I didn't know where or when, so..." His words drifted as he fingered the foil packet. "Are you sure we should use it?"

Her answer came out shaky. "Yes."

"Okay." He lowered his mouth to hers, stealing her breath and the sudden sadness with it.

Now, they both knew, was not the time to talk about babies.

Sheathed in a condom, he entered her, sliding hard and heavy between her legs. She touched his cheek and arched to accept him, thinking how much she loved him. How much she would miss him.

Their eyes met, and they slipped into a smooth, sleek rhythm, watching each other with longing and intensity.

She wrapped her legs around him, and he made a primal sound. She welcomed every sensation, every shiver, every ragged pulse. He kissed the side of her neck, breathed in the fragrance of her hair. She could feel his heart beating against hers, pounding as he withdrew and entered her again, heightening the magic. The pleasure of making love.

Desire swam in her head, like the flow of a long, luxurious current, the water warm and inviting. Touching him, she lingered over the play of muscles, over powerful arms and a stomach tightening with each sexual thrust.

Pressure battered upon need, and the water rose like a tide. Desperate, she took his mouth, kissed him until greed devoured. Him. Her. Both of them together.

They shuddered and strained, arched and bucked, then fell in each other's arms, lovers forbidden once again.

Eleven

Kathy slipped on her robe. She wanted to stay in bed with Dakota all day, but she knew that would only prolong the inevitable. ''I have to leave soon.''

He wore his briefs and nothing else—nothing but skin as smooth and solid as a bronze statue. ''Why? Where are you going?''

''To look at a house.''

Dakota frowned and reached for his jeans. ''Why can't you stay here with me? This is your home. This is where you belong.''

She sat on the edge of the bed while he stood and zipped his Wranglers. Watching him, she tightened the belt on her robe. ''No, it isn't. Nothing has changed. You know about the baby, and we made love again. That doesn't solve the turmoil in our lives.''

''So we'll make things right.'' He skimmed her cheek with callused fingers. ''We just need some time, that's all.''

She blinked, willing herself not to cry. He made it sound

so simple. "I didn't leave because I lost the baby, Dakota. I left because you weren't there when I needed you."

"I know." His voice turned rough with tenderness. "But I'm here now, and we can start over. We can have other children. I love you, Kathy. So damn much."

An arrow lanced her heart, magnifying the ache already there. His claim wasn't enough. The dreamer in her wanted to believe that love healed all wounds, but deep down, she knew better. "You're going on another mission with Thunder."

He sat beside her. "But that could be months from now. Or it might not happen at all."

"What if we decided to stay together and I was pregnant months from now?" Couldn't Dakota see that the cycle would repeat itself?

"Then I wouldn't take the mission. Thunder could get someone else to help him. It doesn't have to be me."

Such easy words to say, she thought. But they wouldn't be easy for him to fulfill. She studied him, this dark-eyed, dark-haired man she had married. He looked every bit the warrior, his face leaner, bones more pronounced. His work suited him, the missions that kept him focused. It was all he had ever known. An honor-roll student at seventeen, he'd graduated from high school early, gone to his parents and told them that he wanted to join the air force. And, recognizing his determination, they'd granted their consent.

Kathy couldn't compete with that, and she would be foolish to try. She had learned her lesson well. "You would go crazy staying home," she told him. "I've seen how restless you get."

"But we're not talking about for the rest of my life—" He paused, then held her gaze, his eyes as dark and cloudy as a foggy night. "Are we?"

She took a breath, let it out slowly. Dakota's panic had already set in. It surfaced in his expression, the muscle working in his jaw, the lines beginning to crease an otherwise smooth forehead.

If only dreams could take the form of reality. She wanted

to keep him forever, live in the fantasy of her choosing. But Dakota was what he was—a soldier who could never be a conventional husband.

"Kathy?" he persisted.

"I can't expect you to change, and it wouldn't be right to ask you to try." She lifted her chin and tried to keep her thoughts calm and logical, her hands folded quietly on her lap. She had fallen apart last night and couldn't bear to let it happen again. "We don't want the same things. We're too different from each other."

He stood, his shoulders broad, his chest bare. He looked big, powerful and combating a myriad of emotion. "Opposites attract. It's what brought us together."

"And what pulled us apart." Her hands fumbled now, looking for something to do. "You wouldn't be content to stay home. You agreed to help Thunder with his mission because that's who you are. A soldier out to save the world."

He rolled his shoulders, the muscles bunching. The movement reminded her of a caged animal fighting its confinement. The battlefield was Dakota's wilderness, she thought, his natural element. And civilization, no matter how much he conformed to it, would always be his cage.

"I was a soldier when you married me."

"I know, but you only had a year left of active duty." She smoothed her tangled hair, hating that she couldn't keep her hands still. "I was eager for you retire. Eager for us to settle down."

"You never told me that. You never said a word."

"I didn't think I had to. I assumed that's what retirement meant to you, too."

He sat beside her again, the bed shifting from his weight. "It scared me a little. Being retired, I mean. I was thirty-seven years old and idle for the first time in my life. I couldn't imagine lounging around in my socks. Or fishing half the day away. Reeling in some poor unsuspecting trout when I could be making a difference somewhere." He turned to look at her. "But I liked the idea of you being home, safe and secure, waiting for me. That part felt right."

And it was the part she couldn't handle. Kathy wanted to pretend this wasn't happening, that their marriage wasn't ending. Yet she wanted to lure him back to bed, back into her arms, into that current of sleek, silky possession. "Sex is the only thing we have in common. It's the only form of communication that works for us."

He glanced at the tumbled sheets. "Is that why you slept with me?"

"No." She brushed his hand, then drew back, the contact too familiar. "I needed to hold you again. To make love with you just one more time."

Breathing shouldn't hurt, but as Dakota inhaled the strawberry-scented air, an overwhelming pain rose in his chest. The room smelled like her, like lotion and shampoo. Why hadn't he noticed that before? He loved her fragrance, her sweet, feminine aroma.

He pulled a hand through his hair. The room smelled a little like sex, too. A hint of the lovemaking they had just shared.

Just one more time.

It couldn't mean anything else. Kathy was leaving him. And this time it would be for good, the final act he had feared all along.

"You're divorcing me, aren't you?"

She clutched the front of her robe, her hand as shaky as her voice. "It's the only thing left to do. The only thing that makes sense. We'll never be able to get on with our lives if we don't end it."

He laughed, a bitter, humorless sound. "And here I thought if we spent enough time together, you would fall in love with me again." His eyes burned, but he knew he wouldn't cry, at least not outwardly. Tears would only humiliate him, and he already felt a sense of emasculation.

"Spending time together makes me hurt," she said. "And I don't need to fall in love with you again because I never stopped loving you."

Her admission should have pleased him, given him a measure of satisfaction, a glimmer of hope, but he couldn't see beyond the despair of divorce. "That makes a hell of a lot of sense."

"Have you ever looked up *love* in the dictionary? Read its various meanings?" Still clutching the robe, she tilted her head. "I have. I know them by heart."

Dakota wasn't in the mood for a collegiate rendition of love. "You know almost every word by heart. In a variety of languages. Why would this one be any different?"

"Because I used to think there were some definitions missing." Kathy steadied her gaze to his. "It doesn't say that love heals. And it doesn't say anything about happily-ever-after, either. But now I understand why those things aren't mentioned."

Because love hadn't healed her broken heart, he realized. And because she had lost faith in happily-ever-after.

Studying her, he frowned. What had happened to his wife? To the woman who relished fairy tales, who dreamed of knights in shining armor and ladies in long, flowing dresses?

I happened to her, he thought. The man who spoiled her fairy tale, who left her alone when she needed him most.

"I still believe in love. Or I want to." He reached for her hand, held it lightly in his. "Can't we start over? Give it one more try? If you don't want me to go on any more missions, I won't. I'll stay here with you instead."

"That won't work." She curled her fingers, her nails grazing his palm. "Eventually you would resent me for clipping your wings. For holding you down when you're desperate to fly."

"You're wrong. I could never resent you." True, he had no idea what staying home would be like. He had never been completely comfortable in a quiet, domestic setting. Making a difference in the world was the only thing he knew, the only true calling he'd ever had. And he used to think that Kathy understood that, loved him for it. But she was right. They didn't communicate well.

Dakota glanced at his rumpled shirt. He had to admit that the idea of giving up his work made him nervous. What would he do with himself? How would he fill his time? And would he lose a part of himself? The man who needed to make a difference?

The questions, the insecurities were boundless. This wasn't something he could have predicted, and it made him disoriented. But if Kathy asked him to stay home, he would. At the moment that didn't appear to be an option. She seemed convinced it was too late.

He linked his fingers through hers, but she tugged her hand away. Not in anger, he thought, but in pain. She was wounded, as fragile as a fledgling with a damaged wing.

She stared straight ahead, her voice quiet. "After I left, I prayed for you to come to me."

And say the words he was saying now, the words that were suddenly too late. How could he blame her for being wary? For not believing in him?

She rose from the bed and headed toward the dresser. "I should get ready to go." She fumbled through the top drawer, gathering fresh undergarments.

She still looked fragile. But the unexpected shyness struck him most of all. They had made love less than an hour before and now she balled a pair of lace panties in her fist as if it embarrassed her to let him see them.

It made him feel like a stranger, a lonely soul aching for familiarity. If she divorced him, this is how it would end. They wouldn't remain friends. There would be nothing left but faded memories.

And then she would meet someone else.

Dakota tensed against the pain, the fear he couldn't dismiss—Kathy finding solace in the arms of another man.

Who would be her next lover? A handsome young politician searching for the perfect partner? Or maybe a widower who already had children, someone who understood her need for family?

She motioned to the connecting bathroom. "I'm going to take a shower now. I don't want to be late for my appointment."

He nodded. Her appointment to look at a rental house. God. How could he lose her? How could he let this happen?

Dakota watched her disappear into the other room, wishing he knew how to save his marriage.

Two days later, Kathy stepped into the kitchen, following the aroma of Colombian coffee.

Mrs. Miller stood at the counter rinsing dishes. She turned and smiled, and Kathy greeted her, surprised by the housekeeper's chipper expression. She could only assume that the older lady's newfound friendship with Dakota was the cause.

Kathy poured herself a cup of coffee and diluted it with hot water, noting the strength had been brewed for Dakota.

"Can I fix you some breakfast?" Mrs. Miller asked.

She added sugar and cream to her cup. "No, thank you. This will do."

"Lieutenant Lewis is in the backyard. He wants to talk to you when you have some time."

"Oh." She looked up, a twinge of nervousness setting in. "All right."

Crossing to the back door, Kathy walked through the courtyard, then stopped when she saw Dakota. He stood, leaning against a shovel, staring at a section of freshly tilled ground. Long and lean in a pair of threadbare jeans and a simple T-shirt, he was a striking sight to behold.

Sugar sniffed around his feet, pawing the earth, her white muzzle dusty with compost.

Kathy moved froward, telling herself to relax. It wasn't easy being around Dakota. Divorce still hovered over them like a murky cloud. "I think my dog is going to need a bath," she said, conjuring an airy voice and a manufactured smile.

He adjusted the shovel. "True, but she's been having a blast out here."

"So I see." Sugar dropped a stone into a hole she had dug and proceeded to bury it. She reminded Kathy of a mischievous little girl playing in her Sunday best. A fancy gold bow and a heap of rich soil presented an amusing combination.

They didn't speak for a few minutes. Instead they watched

the dog, the sun shining brighter than usual. It was, Kathy thought, a beautiful day to be outdoors. It almost chased that cloud away, making her forget the turmoil in her life.

"When did you take up gardening?" she asked, breaking the silence.

He grinned a bit boyishly, a white flash against tanned skin. "This morning."

As her heart forgot its natural beat, she glanced away from that devastating smile and studied the trays of potted herbs. Gardens were her weakness, even though she had never attempted to start one herself.

"I've always been fascinated by herbs," he said. "Their healing and cooking properties. But I never asked my gardeners to plant them because it's something I wanted to do myself."

She didn't need to ask why he had chosen to pursue this task. He was home and feeling idle, needing to fill his time, the restlessness that normally left him eager for another mission.

Maybe he had the right idea. Kathy itched to dig in the dirt, to lose herself in manual labor, as well. Dakota wasn't the only restless soul. "Mrs. Miller said you wanted to talk to me."

He nodded. "Thunder called earlier."

"He did?" She looked up at the sky, focused on the vast, dream-like serenity before allowing the harshness of reality to overwhelm her. "About the mission?"

"Yes. He still doesn't know if it's going to happen or not, but he should have more information in a few weeks." Dakota implored her to meet his gaze. Beneath the brim of a tan cowboy hat, his eyes sought hers. "I told him I wasn't sure if I was available. That he may want to consider contacting someone else."

Her mouth suddenly dry, Kathy swallowed. "Do you want to be available?"

"Not if you would prefer I stay here."

"This should be about what you want, Dakota. The decision has to be yours." Reaching up, she secured a bobby pin.

Her topknot was loosening, spilling errant strands of hair. It made her feel messy and disorganized, not in control.

"I'm confused," he admitted. "I love you desperately, and I want to stay married and raise a family. But I'm having trouble making a conscious choice to give up my work. If you ask me to, I will. Right now, that's the best I can do."

"I appreciate your honesty. But I don't want to be responsible for forcing you to stay home." In time it would destroy him, and she couldn't live with the emotional destruction it would cause. Neither could she live with the nature of his work, no matter how desperately they loved each other. "It looks like we're at a crossroad."

"I suppose," he said, his expression grim. "How about if we take a couple weeks to think about it? Don't make any decisions until then. You won't move out or file any papers, and I'll take some time to deal with everything that's happened." He paused to study her. "You haven't found a house yet, have you?"

"No." And what he proposed seemed logical. A few weeks of reflection would give them the opportunity to prepare for what lay ahead. The calm, she thought, before the storm. "I did lease an office, though. Not far from the Royal Diner."

He managed a smile. "I guess you won't go hungry at lunchtime." The smile faded, and he adjusted his hat. "Will you give it a couple of weeks, Kathy?"

"Yes." She fixed her hair again, nearly jabbing a bobby pin into her scalp.

"Good." He leaned the shovel against a shiny red wheelbarrow, but it slid to the ground with a thump. Sugar barked at it, then went about scattering dirt.

The dog's busy paws were the only movement. Dakota and Kathy both stood silently, nearly frozen like statues. It reminded Kathy of the recess bell at one of the elementary schools she had attended. She couldn't recall which school exactly, but she remembered that her playmates used to freeze in silly positions when the bell rang. Kathy, of course, never acted foolishly. She always stood with impeccable posture, her hands at her sides.

"So you're ready to set up shop?"

She blinked, only hearing a portion of his question. "I'm sorry. What?"

"Your office. Are you anxious to get things going?"

She shook away the recess-bell memory, wondering if she had been a dull child, too mature for her own good. "Yes, I'm looking forward to it."

"So what is it you'll be doing? We haven't talked about it. Other than it will be a satellite office your folks asked you to head up."

"I'll be managing the export operations for domestic companies my parents are affiliated with. Besides hiring distributors and reps, I'll be in charge of advertising, marketing and promotions. There's plenty to do."

"Sounds like you'll need help."

She nodded. "As soon as I get the office set up, I'll be interviewing for a secretary and an assistant."

"Well, I'm glad you found a convenient location."

"Me, too."

A hush fell over them again, the kind of silence that had them staring at each other in discomfort. She fussed with her hair for something to do, and he dug his work boots into the soil.

How could she divorce him? she wondered. Sever their tie completely? Then how could she not? He was willing to give up his work for her, but it wasn't what he truly wanted to do. And she hadn't anticipated a complication like that. In her dreams, Dakota never regretted the decision. He was eager to leave the danger behind.

But those were glorified fantasies, she reminded herself. This was reality. Kathy looked away from Dakota. In two weeks they would discuss their decisions. *Two weeks.* What could possibly change in such a short amount of time, other than Thunder's details about Dakota's next mission?

"I guess I better get these planted," he said, indicating the trays of potted herbs.

Kathy should have nodded her head and used this moment to escape, but suddenly she didn't want to. She wanted to lift the plants to her nose and inhale each sweet, earthly fragrance.

"Do you need some help?" she heard herself ask.

"I—" He paused to look at her, move his gaze from the top of her head to the tips of her Italian shoes. "In those clothes?"

She lifted her chin under the tight scrutiny. "I'm wearing jeans." And a white cotton blouse with a lace collar. And butter-soft leather flats sporting a designer label. She should have said that she intended to change, but that seemed dull and proper, like a child who didn't have enough spunk to make the freeze bell enjoyable. "Yes, in these clothes. My blouse can be laundered." She slipped off her shoes and stood in her bare feet. "And I like the feel of dirt between my toes."

He arched a black brow. "More like mud since we're going to be watering these plants."

She shrugged. "That's okay."

"All right." He didn't smile, but he sounded amused. "Then let's get to it."

Sugar, her nose and paws still covered in compost, sent Kathy a doggie grin when Dakota turned his back to retrieve the plants. Surging with excitement, she patted the dusty Maltese. Her first gardening experience. She felt like an eager virgin.

Dakota set the trays near their work area. "I hope you know more about this than I do."

She placed her shoes out of the line of fire. "That depends on how much you know."

"Gee, I'm so glad you offered to help," he said, his voice tinged with pleasant sarcasm. "Now I know we're going to kill every last one of these. By tomorrow morning they'll be needing a decent burial."

"We'll do no such thing." She lifted a plant she thought was dill, then checked the label with a smug expression.

"They're going to be healthy and happy. We'll even talk to them if we have to."

Dakota shook his head. "If you say so."

"I do." She sniffed the dill. "This one makes a fabulous dip."

"It's good for an upset stomach, too," he added. "My mom used to make a tea out of it with white wine."

"See." Kathy smiled and placed the pot back on the tray. "We know more than we think we do."

"A barefoot woman, a dirty dog and three bags of compost." He handed her a pair of work gloves and grinned. "What more could a man want?"

"Nothing, Lieutenant Lewis." She grabbed the gloves and stole his hat, her heart tagging longingly after his. "At the moment you've got it all."

Twelve

Dakota was nervous. He hated to admit it, but it was true. Kathy had promised to be home by 1500 hours. And he sure as hell hoped she was on time. This afternoon, patience wasn't his strongest virtue.

Jake and Jenny were due to arrive at 1530. This would be their first unchaperoned visit with Dakota. Seven-year-old twins. What in God's name had he gotten himself into? What did he know about mentoring second graders?

He checked his watch and cursed. He couldn't do this without Kathy, at least not today.

Striding into the kitchen, he removed a half gallon of milk and considered taking a swig from the carton. It used to burn his mom when he did that during his teenage years. But what good would it do to defy her in his own house? She wasn't even there.

He retrieved a glass and shook his head. Great. Now he was punishing his mom for nudging him into the mentor program. He poured the milk and swallowed it in one long, thirsty gulp.

A feminine sound rapped his attention. He cocked his head. The sexy snap of high heels on the entryway. Dakota left his glass on the counter and followed the clicking noise.

Catching sight of Kathy, he stopped. A cream-colored jacket nipped her waist and a matching skirt exposed long, slender legs. Suddenly aroused, he glanced at her feet, not surprised that she made a pair of professional-looking pumps sound wicked.

He moistened his lips, and she adjusted the briefcase in her right hand. How many of these silent, hungry moments would he be forced to endure? Dakota couldn't think of a damn thing to say. In fact, he couldn't think at all, not beyond the visceral emotion of wanting her.

Almost a week had passed since their agreement, six days of torture. Neither seemed any closer to a solution. He wanted her to remain his wife; she wanted him to be content giving up his work.

"I did my best to get here on time," she said.

Dakota's mind stumbled for a moment, then kicked into gear. The kids. She had come home to help him mentor. "I appreciate it. How was your day?"

"Fine. I'm still interviewing." She placed her briefcase on a small antique table in the foyer. "How are you doing?"

"Okay."

"Are you sure? You seem tense."

He pulled a hand through his hair. "I'm a little nervous about this, I guess. You know, having the twins here." It was, he supposed, the center of his anxiety this afternoon. That and wanting his wife. Missing her. Praying she wouldn't divorce him.

She stepped closer. "You shouldn't be. You've already spent time with Jake and Jenny."

"At their house, with Bob, his wife and the social worker present. Somehow, this doesn't feel the same."

"But you've been approved for the Mentor Program. That has to mean something."

He wished his misgiving wasn't so obvious. It made him feel inadequate. But he supposed his limited experience with children spoke for itself. He couldn't pretend that being certified as a weekend foster parent made him an expert.

"I'm anxious to meet them," she said.

"I'm glad." He needed her today, more than ever. "They're twins, but they don't seem that much alike. But there is the boy-girl thing, I suppose." He led Kathy into the living room. "I'm worried that they're a little small for their age. When I first saw Jake I thought he was around five. But he and Jenny are seven."

"Children develop in stages." She gave him a reassuring smile. "I'm sure they'll catch up."

Dakota worried more for Jake then Jenny. He remembered some of the smaller boys in school being picked on. But that wasn't a cross he'd had to bear. The unkindness he'd endured had come in the form of whispers and unclean looks. Not so much from kids but from adults. His mom may have been an active PTA parent, but she had also been sleeping with a prominent member of the community—a married man.

Kathy glanced at her watch. "I should change."

Dakota nodded. "Slip on a pair of jeans and boots. The kids are interested in seeing the horses." Which he hoped would be his saving grace. At Bob's house there had been all sorts of toys to entertain the twins.

She moved past him, the picture of professional beauty, her wild hair coiled in a tidy topknot, her designer suit simple yet elegant.

Sugar roused from her favorite napping spot and followed Kathy. She stooped to greet the dog, and Dakota tilted his head. Too bad, he thought, that Kathy hadn't leaned forward. He would have enjoyed a little more leg, a glimpse of thigh. Cradling himself between those creamy thighs occupied a good portion of his thoughts these lonely, troublesome days.

The doorbell pealed. Dakota let out a breath and answered the summons.

"Hi." He invited Bob and the children into the house. Bob wore a mail carrier's uniform, signaling the end of a workday. The kids were dressed for the ranch. Jenny had a dark-haired doll with her, and Jake had his hands in his pockets. Both stared up at him with curious faces—wondering, he supposed, how much fun he was going to be.

Dakota smiled, wishing he were more like Bob. The other man had a relaxed, easy manner, an unmistakable dad-like quality.

They chatted in the entryway and, before Dakota knew it, Bob hugged the kids and said goodbye, leaving Dakota on his own.

He guided the twins into the kitchen and offered them a soda. He had asked Mrs. Miller to stock up on kid-type food, so now the cupboards were filled with crackers, chips and snack cakes oozing with gooey filling.

"My wife is getting her boots on," he said. "Soon as she's ready, we'll head out to the barn."

Jake wiggled and hummed while he drank an orange pop, and Dakota was glad the boy hadn't chosen one of the caffeine colas.

Jenny, her dark-brown hair fashioned in two long ponytails, placed her doll on the counter.

Dakota studied the toy. "Hey, she's wearing boots. And fringe, too." The doll appeared to be attired for a Texas hoedown. "What's her name?"

The girl gave him a look that said he had just asked the dumbest of dumb questions. "Barbie," she replied.

And everybody, including Dakota, knew who Barbie was.

Insecurity looming over him, Dakota wondered if he should ply the kids with snacks. Or would that spoil their dinner? Mrs. Miller had suggested hamburgers with a side of macaroni and cheese, then ice cream for dessert.

Kathy entered the kitchen and saved the moment. "Well, hello." She flashed a radiant smile. "I've heard a lot about the two of you."

Five minutes later they walked to the barn. And as Jake bubbled with excitement and Jenny reached for Kathy's hand, Dakota's heart gave a warm, yearning lurch. With a light breeze blowing and spring blooming, he felt a sudden, amazing sense of family.

* * *

Kathy held Jenny's hand, wondering how many times she had dreamed of moments like this. Herself and Dakota enjoying the ranch, dark-eyed, dark-haired children beside them.

Jake, who carried a bag of carrots for the horses, had a charming grin, just crooked enough to make him look mischievous. And Jenny, precocious, ladylike Jenny, was a child beyond her years. They were both delightful, enchanting in their own special way.

Upon entering the barn, Dakota directed them to the first occupied stall. "This is Kathy's mare," he said. "Her name is Serenity."

The horse came forward and poked her head out, pleased by the introduction.

"Can I give her a carrot now?" Jake asked, eager to make friends with Serenity.

Dakota smiled. "Sure. But let me get you something to stand on, then show you how to feed a horse correctly." He found two empty crates and placed them on the barn floor, helping each twin onto one. Next he cautioned both children to keep their hands flat and offer the carrot in their palms. "Otherwise the horse might nip your fingers."

Jake laughed as Serenity took the treat from him, and Jenny held perfectly still watching the animal with curious intensity. "She has spots like a leopard," the girl said.

Dakota glanced at Kathy, and she could see that Jenny's observation impressed him. "That's because Serenity is a leopard Appaloosa. All Appaloosas have spots, but the leopard appy is white with dark spots, kind of like the jungle cat."

Jenny turned toward the next stall. "What kind is this one? It doesn't have any spots."

"Nomad is a quarter horse. He's my personal favorite, the one I ride most of the time." The horse snorted and Dakota stroked its nose.

"Nomad wants a carrot, too," Jenny told Jake, moving her crate so the boy could accommodate the animal. She assumed the role of the older, wiser sibling, even though she had entered the world only minutes before her brother.

Taking a step back, she looked up at Dakota. "You called Serenity a mare. Does that mean she's a girl?"

"Sure does."

"What's a boy horse?"

"Nomad is a gelding."

"Oh." She stood quietly for a moment, pondering his answer. "Then what's a stallion?"

Dakota's head whipped up to catch Kathy's gaze. She smiled and shrugged, amused by his shocked expression. Apparently he had no idea how bright and curious a young child could be. He would have to handle this one on his own, she thought. Jenny and Jake were his charges.

He frowned, then let out a heavy breath. Jenny waited patiently for his response, her head cocked.

"A stallion is boy, too."

"So Nomad is a gelding and a stallion?" Jenny prodded, confused by his simple answer.

Dakota swallowed, and Kathy placed her hand on the girl's shoulder, wondering if she should come to Dakota's rescue. The big, tough soldier looked as though he had lost his voice.

"No," he said finally. "Nomad isn't a stallion. He's called a gelding because he—" Dakota paused, possibly rethinking his statement. "He won't ever be a father."

Jenny studied the horse with an expression bordering on pity. "So Serenity and Nomad can't have babies together?"

"That's right. But Serenity could have a foal with a stallion if she wanted to." He appeared to notice Jenny's sympathy for the quarter horse. "And most people ride geldings instead of stallions. So you don't have to feel bad for Nomad. He's not particularly interested in being a dad."

Her worried expression softened. "A foal is a baby horse?"

Dakota nodded, relief bringing a smile to his lips. "You don't miss anything, Jenny. Do you?"

"Neither do I," Jake interjected in typical kid fashion, making sure he didn't lose out on any attention. "Can I ride Nomad, Dakota?"

"Not today, sport. I'd have to give you some lessons, and

I can't do that without making sure it's okay with your social worker first."

"You can ask our mom, too." Jake pushed his bangs out of his eyes. "Mrs. Newberry takes us to see her every other weekend. You can come with us."

Kathy assumed Mrs. Newberry was the social worker. She glanced at Dakota and waited for him to answer.

"I'll talk to Mrs. Newberry," he said. "And we'll let her decide when I can meet your mom. All right?"

"Kathy, too," Jake added. "I want Kathy to meet our mom, too."

Her heart tugged. Being included in something so important to Jake felt wonderful, but it tied her to Dakota in a way that made her sad. Next week they were supposed to discuss their marital status—the choices they needed to make. Choices Kathy was afraid to face. If she asked Dakota to give up his work, he would. But she couldn't see basing their reconciliation on a forced issue, on his desperation and guilt.

She met Dakota's gaze, and he smiled, making her heart hurt even more.

He hoisted Jake up, and the boy laughed. Kathy still had her hand on Jenny's shoulder, the connection easing her a bit. Today was for the children.

"In the old days, one of the first things a Comanche kid learned to do was ride," Dakota said. "Both girls and boys were taught to ride with and without a saddle. But the boys had to try harder because they were expected to do tricks."

"How come?" Jake asked, interest alive in his dark eyes.

"Because it was part of their training to become warriors. When a boy was young he had to learn to pick up objects from the ground while his horse was running full speed. At first, these were small, light objects." Dakota placed Jake back on his feet and continued. "But as the boy grew older, heavier things were used. So by the time he became a man, he was able to rescue an injured warrior. Pick him up from the ground and swing him across his horse."

"But that must have hurt the guy who was bleeding," Jake said, clearly searching for the logic in Dakota's story.

"Maybe, but it was better than leaving him there to be killed by the enemy. And usually two men performed this task together, both lifting the fallen warrior at the same time. There wasn't much else they could do. They didn't have ambulances in those days."

Jenny gazed up at Dakota. "Can you ride like a warrior?"

He smiled at the little girl, then knelt to bring himself to her level. "I've never rescued anyone on horseback, but I can do a few tricks."

Kathy struggled with her next breath. Maybe he had never lifted a fallen comrade onto his horse, but he had spent a good portion of his life flying into enemy territory and rescuing downed airmen who would have otherwise died. And hostages, Kathy thought. How many innocent civilians had he rescued? Dakota Lewis was more than a warrior. To those he had saved, he was a hero.

"Will you ride for us?" Jenny asked. "Show us some tricks."

"Sure."

He winked at the girl, then glanced at Kathy. She managed a shaky smile and told her lovelorn heart to be still. Now wasn't the time to miss him.

Jake and Jenny went home and evening brought moments of reflective silence. Although sadness had edged portions of the day, Kathy couldn't deny how much she had enjoyed watching Dakota with the children.

He would have made a loving, attentive father.

She excused the thought and concentrated on loading the dishwasher instead. She had no business drifting over that emotional line.

Dakota came up behind her. She heard his booted footsteps, smelled the faint note of his cologne blending with the earthy scents of hay and horses.

She turned to look at him, unable to control the attraction rising inside her. The excited flutter. The yearning. The need to hold and touch.

"Would you like to sit outside for a while?" he asked. "Maybe have a glass of wine?"

"That sounds nice." She dried her hands and released the top button on her blouse, certain fresh air would do her good.

He poured two glasses of zinfandel and offered her one. She accepted the drink, and he opened the backdoor. Wine in hand, she slipped past him, leading the way to the courtyard.

Just as she'd imagined, the air was cool and fresh. She took a seat at the wrought-iron table and tipped her head to the sky. "It's a beautiful night." A vast strip of velvet showcased a glitter of stars, and a three-quarter moon shone with a silvery haze.

Dakota settled across from her, angling his chair so he could stretch his legs. The heel of a boot scraped the courtyard's Spanish tile. "It was a beautiful day, too."

Kathy nodded and studied her husband. The illumination from the patio lamps highlighted his eyes and shadowed those arresting cheekbones. She thought his face resembled that of a nineteenth-century warrior, a man marked by a hardened lifestyle, the risks that had become part of his nature. When he lifted his wine, it struck her how delicate the glass seemed in his large, callused hand.

"Children are amazing, aren't they?" He smiled and rolled his shoulders. "Active, too."

She couldn't help but return his smile. Now he looked like a forty-one-year-old warrior uncovering one of the seven wonders of the world. "You were terrific. Jake and Jenny adore you."

"Thanks. I couldn't have made it through the day without you, though. I think I would have been overwhelmed."

"I'm glad I could help."

How polite they were, she thought. Two people on the verge of ending their marriage, of abandoning the love they still felt. It made no sense, yet it made perfect sense. They cared too much to destroy each other with anger. So they held on by their thumbnails, afraid to let go.

"This must be how parents feel," Dakota said. "You know, after their kids are in bed."

Because her thoughts had strayed in a different direction, it took Kathy a moment to comprehend his words. "You mean the quiet? The close of a busy day?"

"Yeah. I'm tired, but it's a good kind of tired. Rewarding."

In spite of the wine, she vowed to keep a clear head. His admission pleased her, but slipping into a fantasy would only end up shredding her emotions. Jake and Jenny were someone else's children.

They sat quietly after that, both lost in thought. She gazed into the backyard where their herb garden flourished, spilling sweet, harmonious scents into the air. Breathing in that air, she shook her head. The garden wasn't theirs, it was his, along with the rest of the ranch. She had only been borrowing his possessions, stealing into his life. The temporary wife, longing for more.

"Kathy?"

She placed her glass back on the table, wondering if he had read her mind. His tranquil expression had tightened. "Yes?"

"Do you remember me mentioning that Thunder called last week?"

She nodded. It wasn't something she was likely to forget, nor was the fact that Thunder would be calling again, expecting Dakota's final answer. "You discussed his latest mission."

"Among other things." He kept his legs stretched out before him, his boots dark against the clay-colored tile. "I asked Thunder about his marriage. It wasn't any of my business, I suppose, but I asked him anyway."

"And did he tell you?"

"Yes. His wife lost their baby, too."

Kathy couldn't breathe. For one lonely moment all the pain came rushing back. Forcing oxygen into her lungs, she willed herself to sit and listen, to keep her eyes dry and her hands steady.

''It wasn't like our situation, though,'' Dakota said. ''They got married because she was pregnant, so when she miscarried, their relationship ended. He said there was no reason to stay together.''

''And do you believe that was all there was to it?'' she asked.

''No, but I didn't see the need the press Thunder about it. To me, it was obvious that he had loved her. I could hear it in his voice.''

Kathy's hand wasn't as steady as she had hoped, so she avoided lifting her glass. ''Did it help? Talking to someone else who has been through it?''

''In a way, yes. And now that I know about Thunder's child, I understand why this mission is so important to him. The terrorist he's been tracking is responsible for opening fire on a group of tourists. One woman was eight months pregnant. And although she pulled through, the baby didn't.''

A lump formed in Kathy's throat, but she didn't respond. She dropped her hands to her lap and waited for Dakota to continue, knowing he had more to say.

''I want to be here for you, be the best husband possible.'' He glanced up at the sky as though drawing emotional strength from the elements. ''Yet I want to help Thunder catch this guy. For the baby who didn't survive the shooting. For the baby Thunder's wife lost. And for our baby, the child we should have had.''

She kept her hands on her lap, her fingers numb from gripping her jeans. ''I'm confused. Are you asking for my permission to go? Or are you asking me to tell you to stay home?''

''Neither. You said the choice has to be mine, and you're right. But I do want you to understand why I'm considering this mission, and why the decision is weighing on me. It isn't giving up my work that scares me. It's giving up the good I can do.''

"What about us?" she asked, blinking back tears. "What about our marriage?"

"That's the hardest part." He trapped her gaze, his voice breaking a little. "Because losing you scares me most of all."

Thirteen

Dakota walked into the backyard, then stopped when he saw Kathy. She knelt at their garden, mothering the plants. She didn't appear to be aware of his presence, so he remained silent, taking the opportunity to admire her.

Her hair, shimmering in the late-morning sun, cascaded over her shoulders. She sported a blue work shirt tied at her waist and a pair of faded jeans, cuffed at the ankles. Because her feet were bare, he smiled. She really did like the feel of dirt between her toes.

He moved closer, his smile fading as anxiety coiled in the pit of his stomach. His decision-making two weeks were up. And Thunder would be calling for an answer. Soon. Most likely today.

As he approached, his boots made slight indentations in the grass. The garden, small enough to look cozy yet large enough to require stepping stones, thrived just beyond the lawn.

Kathy turned, gazed up at him and shielded her eyes with

her left hand, where the wedding ring he'd given her still sparkled. She hadn't removed it since they'd returned from Asterland.

Why? he wondered. Was she hoping she wouldn't have to? Hoping he would live up to her fantasy and give up his work? The decision that scared him senseless.

"Hi," she said.

He knelt beside her. "How long have you been out here?"

"A while. It's so peaceful."

It was, he thought, as a warm breeze blew the loose strands of her hair. The Texas sun offered warmth and an illusion of safety, something he knew Kathy needed. But it wasn't her own safety she feared for, it was his.

He wanted to brush a strand of hair from her cheek, but he kept his hands still instead, not trusting himself to touch her. Even the lightest caress might lead to a kiss. And that was his illusion of safety. His need.

"Were you talking to our plants?" he asked, knowing she had already watered them hours before. The soil remained slightly damp, just enough to make the ground cool.

"Maybe a little," she admitted. "They looked sort of lonely."

He scanned the herbs. But to him, they didn't look lonesome at all. They grew in pretty clusters, keeping each other company with a variety of shapes and colors. It was Kathy who appeared lonely, she who seemed to long for companionship.

She fingered a sprig of parsley, then drew back. "They're not our plants, Dakota. They're yours."

He frowned, pressure creasing his brow. "That's not true. Everything here belongs to both of us."

She shrugged. "Legally, maybe."

He didn't like the direction their conversation was headed. It sounded like divorce talk, common-law jargon. Rather than continue on the same vein, he said what was in his heart. "I love you, Kathy."

She lifted her gaze to his, her eyes as green as their surroundings. "I love you, too."

Dakota took a deep breath. Such beautiful words. Shouldn't they be enough?

Maybe they were, he thought, at least for the moment. Suddenly the tension eased between them, making the sun feel warmer, the plants smell more fragrant. He picked a grouping of leaves and tucked them behind Kathy's ear, giving in to the need to touch her.

"Peppermint." Before the leaves could slip from her hair, she secured them, brushing Dakota's hand as she did. "It's my favorite."

"I know. Mine, too." The scent was cool yet comforting, as clean and refreshing as a playful kiss on a spring day. It was, he realized, the way being married to Kathy made him feel.

Enraptured. Being with her brought joy and contentment. And so did everything else he wanted to share with her—the ranch, the horses, the newly planted herbs. And the children. Jake and Jenny, who basked in the attention Kathy favored upon them.

"I made sun tea." She pointed to a jar sitting in the center of the yard.

Dakota smiled. It looked like an offering, a gift to the elements, to the beauty of the morning. Strange how something so simple could seem so important. So homey. "Do you think it's ready?"

She nodded. "Are you thirsty?"

For a kiss, he thought, telling her he would love a glass of tea.

"Just give me a few minutes. I'll add some ice and sugar."

"And mint." He plucked more leaves and handed them to her, thinking she looked like an island goddess, with her emerald-colored eyes and bare feet.

"And mint," she repeated.

He watched her walk across the grass and lift the jar. As she proceeded to the house, her hair blew around her like a vibrant curtain, each strand shining beneath the sun.

Dakota studied the garden. They were common herbs, but they fascinated him, made him feel connected to the earth.

Maybe he would take another trip to the nursery and let the kids get involved. He remembered seeing a mint that smelled like chocolate. Jake and Jenny would probably get a kick out of planting that.

Glancing up, he noticed Kathy coming toward him, minus the iced tea he'd been expecting. "Isn't it strong enough?"

She stood for a second, her expression strange, her eyes cloudy. "You have a phone call."

"Oh." He came to his feet, then stopped, reality taking hold. He didn't need to ask who was on the other line. He already knew. It was Thunder, awaiting his answer. The decision Dakota had momentarily forgotten about.

Kathy walked beside Dakota. They entered the house together, neither speaking. She'd known this day would come, and she'd known how it would make her feel. Alone, sad, lost.

Dakota paused in the kitchen and stared at the telephone. "I'll take it in the study," he said. The study was the room Dakota used for personal business.

Kathy nodded, and he lifted his hand and grazed her cheek, his touch gentle. She wanted to lean into him, kiss him, hold him. But she didn't. The phone call wouldn't disappear, and she couldn't pretend it wasn't important, that it didn't symbolize the end of their relationship.

They stared at each other, both silent. Finally he turned away and exited the kitchen, leaving her alone.

Kathy studied the blinking telephone. She stood dead still until the light quit flashing, an indication that Dakota had picked up the line in the other room.

The jar of tea sat on the counter, the freshly picked mint beside it. Returning to her task, she filled a glass pitcher with ice and poured the tea into it. She had to keep herself busy, keep herself from tears.

Kathy added sugar to the drink, then watched it sink to the bottom of the container and crystallize.

How could two people in love be losing each other?

Her heart constricted. Deep down, she knew the answer.

And it shamed her. She hadn't given their marriage a chance, hadn't believed in the power of love.

It was her fault, all of it. She was the one who had left, who had walked out on her husband without an explanation. He had been a soldier when she'd married him, that fact remained. And she had loved him for being strong and caring, for trying to make the world a better place.

But she had left him for the same reason.

Because she had blamed him for the loss of their child. Blamed him for something that was out of his control.

As Kathy stirred the tea with a wooden spoon, ice cubes clinked against the pitcher. Dakota wanted to dedicate his next mission to the baby they had lost. And he wanted to make the world a safer place for future children.

Children he hoped to have with her.

How could she fault him for that? How could she divorce a man with that kind of honor and integrity?

She couldn't. God help her, she couldn't. Dakota's passion for justice was part of his spirit, part of the warrior she had fallen in love with. And she had no right to ask him to be less than what he was. If she had to share him with the world, then she would.

The tea forgotten, Kathy began to pace. How long would Dakota's phone call take? How long before she could look into his eyes and tell him that she wanted to remain his wife, no matter what the cost?

Thirty minutes passed, and Kathy's decisiveness turned to anxiety. What if Dakota no longer trusted her? What if she had ruined their chance at happiness? How could she convince him that she wouldn't run away again, that she would wait for him, mission after mission?

She wasn't sure what to say, what to do to prove herself.

"Kathy?"

She spun around at the sound of her name.

Her heart in her throat, she stared at Dakota. His T-shirt was untucked, his jeans soiled from the garden. He had raked his hands through his hair, leaving the short, ebony strands in disarray. But to her, a more handsome, more noble man didn't exist.

"Yes?" she asked.

"We need to talk."

Kathy came toward him, her limbs shaky. They headed for the living room where Sugar snuggled on a leather recliner. The dog's ears perked when she saw them. Kathy sat on the sofa, and Dakota stood in the center of the room as though gathering his thoughts.

"I told Thunder I'm not taking this mission," he said.

His admission startled her, causing a quick, unexpected gasp. "You can't do that. You can't give up something that's so important to you."

He sat beside her. "Other things are important, too." He turned to face her, his voice quiet. "And I don't want to lose you."

"But you can't do this just for me."

Dakota took her hand. "It isn't just for you. It's for me, too. Something happened over these past few weeks, Kathy. Moments of contentment I hadn't understood until now. I want to wake up everyday with you beside me. And I want to grow beautiful things together. Flowers, babies."

She wanted that, too. She longed to see her tummy swollen with his child, longed to feel the flutter of life. She slipped her fingers through his, grateful for the physical connection. "But what about the terrorist? What about your need to catch him?"

A frown creased his forehead. "It still exists. But saving my marriage is more important. Even Thunder understood."

"I shouldn't have asked you to make that choice." She looked into his eyes and prayed he would accept her words, believe the truth in them. "I want you to take that mission."

He shook his head. "But I can't leave you alone."

She lifted their joined hands. "Yes, you can. And I promise to wait for you. Forever if I have to."

"You're forcing me to go? I decided to stay home, and you're forcing me to go?" A smile tugged at the corner of his lips. "We're quite a confused pair."

Kathy felt like smiling, too. Crying, smiling, holding him inside her heart. "We're in love. I think it goes with the territory. And I'm not forcing you to do anything. But I think we both need closure, and this mission is it."

"Like starting over where we left off?"

She nodded.

"Does that mean we should renew our wedding vows?"

Her breath rushed out her lungs. He trusted her. She could see the depth, the beauty, the emotion in his eyes. "Do you want to?"

He took her in his arms. "What do you think?"

Before she had the chance the answer, he kissed her, his mouth, his tongue brushing hers. Kathy meant to deepen the kiss, but he drew back.

"If I take this mission," he said. "Then it's going to be my last one. Okay?"

He didn't honestly expect her to argue, did he? "If that's what you want."

"It is. There are other ways to make a difference. The world is full of orphaned and abandoned kids. Children who need parents." He gazed into Kathy's eyes. "I hope you're interested in a big family." A grin teased one corner of his lips. "I'm really into this dad thing."

She closed her eyes, then opened them, testing the dream, the perfection of the man she had married. Not only did he want to raise their own babies, he wanted to adopt. He wanted to give his home and his heart to those who needed him. He would still be saving a piece of the world, but this time with love. He couldn't have said anything that would have pleased her more. "A big family is all I've ever wanted."

"Then that's what we'll have."

She pictured the ranch, alive with tiny faces and happy voices. "I think Jake and Jenny will approve."

"I'm glad they've become a part of our lives. But it's even more important that they have a caring mother, someone who's trying hard to win them back."

"You're incredible, Lieutenant Lewis." She stood and held

out her hand, offering him the security of her touch. The warmth of her body. The start of their future.

Dakota accepted her hand, and she led him to her room. There she collected the gold vase the king and queen had given her. She handed it to Dakota, and they proceeded to the master bedroom. Sealing their emotional declaration, he placed her vase beside his, joining the two pieces as one. Next he removed their wedding photograph from his drawer and centered it between two candles.

Lighting the candles, he smiled, anxious to see the fiery glow dance over Kathy's skin. It was daytime and the sun streamed through the windows, but the candles added a touch of magic, an element of quiet romance.

They turned toward each other and began to undress. While he removed his own clothing, he watched her untie the blouse at her waist, slip the faded jeans from her hips. Her bra and panties fluttered to the floor in a wisp of yellow lace. And then she stood naked before him—a seductive angel, her hair falling in tantalizing waves.

They came together in a kiss, her aroused nipples brushing his chest, his hands sliding down her back, over lean, luscious curves. She smelled as fresh as the Texas breeze, like the mint leaves still tucked behind her ear.

"I love you," he said.

"I love you, too." Her voice was breathy, soft and alluring. "Always."

She nuzzled his neck, then slid her mouth down the center of his chest until she dropped to her knees and kissed his navel. His stomach muscles jumped as her hair tickled his skin. He knew what she intended to do, and he had no will to stop her.

She closed her fingers around him, setting the rhythm for her tongue, her mouth. Dakota lowered his head and watched, his blood running through his veins like a warm river. A current of pure need.

Candlelight shimmered in her hair, sending streaks of gold tumbling through the scarlet mass. He tugged a handful, reveled in the texture while she seduced him with slow, intoxicating strokes, her mouth gentle yet greedy.

She kissed her way back up his body, and they tumbled onto the bed, pulling at the covers as they did. He couldn't get enough of her. This woman who was his wife, his lover, the lady of his heart. She had given him the most important gift of all. She loved him for who he was, for the man life had made of him. He couldn't ask for anything more.

He licked the tips of her breasts, smiled when her eyes glittered like emeralds. Beautiful Kathy. She arched as she reached for him, playful as a kitten, erotic as a cat.

He settled between her thighs, took comfort in being there.

"No protection this time." She slid her hands through his hair. "I want you inside me, only you."

Dakota touched her cheek. Not using protection might make her pregnant. He understood her wish, her hope. She had found healing in their reunion, just as he had. The past was over, the hurt and the pain gone. Tonight was perfect for creating a new life.

He entered her, found her warm and willing, wet and inviting.

Together they moved, peppermint leaves and candles scenting the air. He was home, Dakota thought. Wrapped in the luxury of forever.

Epilogue

Dakota, attired in a buckskin shirt, led a pinto, an exceptional horse he had purchased for this occasion. Pinto horses had been prized by his Indian ancestors for their color and stamina.

Stopping at the fence that separated the courtyard from the path that led to the barn, he waited, the horse patient beside him.

A gathering of guests waited as well, quiet and respectful of the ceremony about to take place.

Kathy's father, Harold, opened the gate and escorted his daughter onto the dirt path. Stunning in a three-piece buckskin dress, she took Dakota's breath away. The beadwork was bright and intricate, the leather heavily fringed. Her hair fell loose about her shoulders, shimmering like fire beneath the Texas sun.

Dakota offered Harold the pinto, a ceremonial gift representing a bride price in the Comanche culture. As the older man guided the horse back to the corral, Kathy came forward and reached for Dakota's hand.

Their eyes met, and they smiled. This was the renewal of their wedding vows. No words were exchanged, but the message was clear. In a modern version of an ancient tradition, Kathy had just accepted Dakota as her husband. It was simple, yet beautiful—a moment neither would ever forget.

A whoop of appreciation sounded from their guests, and Dakota and Kathy turned to the festive commotion.

Dakota scanned the sea of faces and spotted his mom, Kathy's mother and Mrs. Miller, the three looking happy and proud. A beaming Jake and Jenny stood with their full-time foster family, and beside them were the men and women who had participated in the Lone Star jewel mission.

Sheikh Rassad, wearing a kaffiyeh with his traditional robes, held his wife's hand. Dr. Webb and Winona took turns entertaining baby Angel, and Aaron and Pamela caught Dakota's eye and smiled. But the couple who seemed to relish the ceremony most deeply were Matt Walker and Lady Helena. Soon they would be married, too.

Within a heartbeat, hugs and good wishes were granted, along with laughter and handshakes. Angel squealed and flashed Dakota a one-toothed grin. He nuzzled the little girl's cheek and winked at Kathy. Making babies was constantly on their minds.

Dakota escorted his bride to the courtyard where buffet tables of catered food and a tall, white cake awaited. A band had been hired to play soft country ballads—music to sway by.

As the guests filtered into the festively decorated area, Dakota kissed Kathy's hand. The Lone Star jewels mission was over, but he knew the hidden stones still sparkled.

Leadership. Justice. Peace. The secret mantra the Texas Cattleman's Club members had chosen to honor still guided their lives. But so did another word.

Love.

Each man, including Dakota Lewis, had found his one true

love. The woman who would share his home, his soul, his world. The woman who had become the shining gem of his heart.

* * * * *

A Cherokee Knight.
A Dragon Slayer.

Sarah couldn't keep her eyes off Adam. He stood before her, his thumbs hooked in his pockets—a stance that made the female in her take notice.

He took a step toward her. "We still haven't talked about what happened earlier."

"We're just friends." The statement sounded foolish, even to her own ears.

"I keep telling myself that. We're just friends. There's nothing happening between us." He laughed, a rough-textured sound that faded as quickly as it came on. "That's a lie, at least for me. I can't help myself. I want you. And I can't pretend that I don't." He moved closer, until they were only inches apart. "You're my midnight seduction, sweet Sarah."

Her heart thumped wildly. She wanted to kiss him, seduce him, feel him branding her skin. Mist and moonlight, she thought. Fairy tales and fantasies. She craved all of that and more.

But wanting Adam didn't mean she had the courage to take him.

Cherokee

SHERI WHITEFEATHER

Harlequin Mills & Boon

Desire

DID YOU PURCHASE THIS BOOK WITHOUT A COVER?
If you did, you should be aware it is **stolen property** as it was reported 'unsold and destroyed' by a retailer.
Neither the author nor the publisher has received any payment for this book.

First Published 2001
First Australian Paperback Edition 2001
ISBN 0 733 53209 8

CHEROKEE © 2001 by Sheree Henry-Whitefeather
Philippine Copyright 2001
Australian Copyright 2001
New Zealand Copyright 2001
Except for use in any review, the reproduction or utilisation of this work in whole or in part in any form by any electronic, mechanical or other means, now known or hereafter invented, including xerography, photocopying and recording, or in any information storage or retrieval system, is forbidden without the permission of the publisher, Harlequin Mills & Boon, P.O. Box 810, Chatswood, N.S.W., Australia 2057.

All the characters in this book have no existence outside the imagination of the author, and have no relation whatsoever to anyone bearing the same name or names. They are not even distantly inspired by any individual known or unknown to the author, and all the incidents are pure invention.

This book is sold subject to the condition that it shall not, by way of trade or otherwise, be lent, resold, hired out or otherwise circulated without the prior consent of the publisher in any form of binding or cover other than that in which it is published and without a similar condition including this condition being imposed on the subsequent purchaser.

All rights reserved including the right of reproduction in whole or in part in any form. This edition is published by arrangement with Harlequin Enterprises II B.V.

Published by
Harlequin Mills & Boon
3 Gibbes Street
CHATSWOOD NSW 2057
AUSTRALIA

HARLEQUIN MILLS & BOON DESIRE and the Rose Device are trademarks used under license and registered in Australia, New Zealand, Philippines, United States Patent & Trademark Office and in other countries.

Printed and bound in Australia by
McPherson's Printing Group

SHERI WHITEFEATHER

lives in Southern California and enjoys ethnic dining, summer powwows and visiting art galleries and vintage clothing stores near the beach. Since her one true passion is writing, she is thrilled to be a part of the Harlequin Desire line. When she isn't writing, she often reads until the wee hours of the morning.

Sheri also works as a leather artisan with her Muscogee Creek husband. They have one son and a menagerie of pets, including a pampered English bulldog and four equally spoiled Bengal cats. She would love to hear from her readers. You may write to her at: P.O. Box 5130, Orange, California 92863-5130.

To the Cherokees who inspired this story—
Annie Dear-Johnson for her strength and sensitivity; Lisa Kelly and her daughter Mandi for their beauty and heart; Kona Bruckner and her children, Amy, Bryon and Jeremiah for their triumph; Christine Tevis and her sons, Bobby, Bruce and Bryon (my favorite little artist) for following Windrunner's path.

I would also like to acknowledge Barbara Carlton for teaching her son about his Cherokee heritage and Barbara Ann Tucker, my Texas friend, for the lovely letters and powwow pictures. And to another Barbara, my proud and supportive mother-in-law, many thanks for encouraging us to consider alternative medicine whenever one of us is ailing. Unfortunately we don't always listen, but the characters in this book took your advice to heart.

And finally to the countless readers out there expressing an interest in the American Indian culture, this recipe is for you:

INDIAN FRY BREAD
(from various sources)

Cornmeal or flour for dusting board
2 cups flour
1/2 tsp salt
1/2 tsp baking powder
1/2 cup instant dry milk
3/4 cup water
Oil or shortening for deep frying

Dust pastry board. In a mixing bowl, stir flour, baking powder, salt and powdered milk. Add water in small amounts, stirring until the mixture reaches the consistency of bread dough. Knead until smooth and elastic. Cover and let rest for ten minutes. Heat oil or shortening in a deep frying pan. Pull off a palm-size mound of dough, roll into a ball, then flatten into a 6-inch disc. Fry one at a time on both sides until golden. Serve hot, sprinkled with powdered sugar, drizzled with honey or covered with taco fixings. Makes about 4 servings.

One

Sarah Cloud entered the break room, her productive day nearing its end. She didn't own Ventura West, a successful skin care salon in the San Fernando Valley, but she took pride in working there. She enjoyed soothing her clients with a refreshing mask and a quiet shoulder massage. They relied on her to make them feel whole, to sweep them away from the hustle and bustle of their harried L.A. lives, if only for an hour each week.

Removing a small container of orange juice from the refrigerator, she looked up. Tina Carpenter, the sweet but airbrained receptionist, stood in the doorway.

"You're never going to believe who's here," the young woman said, her eyes wide and bright. "It's that doctor-type guy from the clinic next door."

Sarah smiled, amused by Tina's definition of the holistic practitioner. Of course it wasn't his profession that mattered to the women in the salon. All were in agreement that their new neighbor was by far one of the most attractive men they had ever seen. Sarah had no idea what to think, since she had yet to catch even a quick glimpse of him. Not that she cared. Southern California overflowed with tall, tan, muscular men.

Tina flashed an excited grin. ''Guess what? He wants to talk to you. And he even said it's personal. I wonder if he's going to ask you on a date or something.''

Baffled, Sarah capped her orange juice. A date? With a woman he'd never even met? Not likely. ''Are you sure it's me he wants to talk to?'' This wouldn't be the first time Tina had misconstrued a message. The receptionist was the owner's niece—an inept but permanent employee.

''Of course I'm sure, silly.'' Tina grabbed her arm. ''Come on. He's waiting.''

Sarah approached the reception area, then slowed her pace when she saw him. He stood near the front window, almost out of place amid the elegant ambiance of the salon. He wasn't what she had expected. He wore dark indigo jeans and a blue button-down shirt, the sleeves rolled to his elbows. But it wasn't his ranch-style attire that made her stop and stare. She knew immediately that the color of his skin hadn't been enhanced by the sun, his golden complexion and strong, chiseled profile suddenly reminding her of home. An uncomfortable reminder.

When he turned, their eyes met. And then held. She wanted to look away, but couldn't. He was too unusual to be considered classically handsome. Each riveting feature battled for dominance—eyes too deep, a mouth too full, cheekbones so prominent they could have been sculpted from clay.

He was a mixed blood, she realized. But how mixed she couldn't quite tell. He wore his hair long, but it was brown instead of black, secured at his nape in a thick ponytail.

Sarah took a deep breath, more uncomfortable than ever. She hated being reminded of home.

He came toward her, his height overwhelming. She had been wrong. California wasn't overflowing with men like him. His masculine presence commanded attention, but his smile generated warmth. No wonder no woman within breathing distance could keep her eyes off him. Tina leaned over the reception desk, and Claire, the flamboyant makeup artist, craned her neck to get a good look at his backside.

"Hi," he said. "I'm Adam Paige. I work next door."

Sarah extended her hand, sensing he waited for her to do so. Apparently he had been taught the same protocol. A man didn't touch a woman without invitation, not even in a greeting.

The handshake sent an electrical charge straight up her arm. She drew back quickly, keeping her voice polite and professional. "I'm Sarah Cloud. How can I help you?"

He pushed at his shirtsleeve, shoving it further up his arm. "Vicki Lester suggested I stop by. She's a patient of mine."

Sarah nodded. Vicki was a client of hers, too. And a friend. Vicki lived in the same sprawling apartment complex. "She didn't tell me to expect you," Sarah said, hoping she didn't sound too distrustful. How could her friend neglect to mention this man and all his rugged beauty?

"I saw Vicki this morning," he explained. "After her appointment, we got into a serious conversation. When I told her about what's going on in my life, she thought I should talk to you."

His life? I'm an esthetician, Sarah thought, not a psychologist. If he had problems, the best she could do was ease him with a facial—lift the tension from his forehead, massage the stress from his shoulders.

She glanced up at those broad shoulders and swallowed. Then again, talking might be better. She actually found herself attracted to Adam Paige—a man whose golden complexion and Indian cheekbones reminded her of why she'd left home. "Would you like to sit down?"

He glanced around, caught Tina's eye and returned her smile, indicating to Sarah that the bouncy blond receptionist appeared to be eavesdropping.

"Maybe we could go across the street to the juice bar instead," he said.

"Sure, that's fine." Sarah had some time to spare, and a cold drink sounded good. She'd left her orange juice on the table, and now her mouth felt unusually dry.

He opened the door for her, and they stepped onto the sidewalk in front of the salon. Ventura Boulevard buzzed around them. Late-day traffic gathered at a red light while summer tourists explored what locals simply called the Valley.

Sarah looked over at Adam as they crossed the street, and he sent her a devastating smile. If she hadn't been wearing sensible shoes, she would have tripped over her own feet.

Curious, she glanced down at Adam's feet, wondering what sort of shoes he wore. Lace-up ropers, she saw, California style. No dust, no scuffed toes. In spite of his Western appeal, Adam Paige with the chiseled profile and heart-stopping smile had most likely been born and raised in the Valley.

Sarah lifted her gaze, realizing a case of nerves had set in. Suddenly she felt like the troubled Oklahoma girl she had been. The one who had come to L.A. with nothing more than a battered suitcase and a need to break free of her past.

After Sarah's mother died, her father had found solace in the bottle, drinking his way into oblivion. And as much as she loved her dad, walking away from him had become her only option. She had learned firsthand how deceptive alcoholics could be, how irresponsible and hurtful.

She glanced toward the sky and recalled his last broken promise, the last devastating lie. She'd graduated from high school two weeks before, and had come home from a new full-time job to find her dad in the backyard. He was dressed in grubby clothes, the old jeans and T-shirt he wore when tending the rose bushes that bloomed every summer. The flowers Sarah loved, the only beauty left in their run-down yard.

Standing in the setting sun, she watched her father reach into a planter and dig below the dirt. And then her breath caught, the threat of tears stinging her eyes.

The bottle that glinted in his hand could have been a knife. When he dusted it off, twisted the cap and took a drink, a sharp pain sliced through her—the sickening stab of betrayal.

He turned and their eyes met. And at that painful moment, she knew. He wasn't her father anymore, the man she had once admired, the Cherokee warrior who used to tuck her in at night. Too many scenes like this one had destroyed those warm, tender feelings. For Sarah, there was nothing left but emptiness.

Neither said a word. She didn't accuse, and he didn't apologize. They only stood, staring at each other. His graduation gift to her had been an impassioned promise, an ardent vow of sobriety, and that gift had just been shattered, along with Sarah's eighteen-year-old heart.

"We're here."

Blinking, she turned to see Adam, not her father, watching her. "I'm sorry. What?"

"The juice bar."

"Oh, of course."

Once inside, they ordered their drinks and sat across from each other in a small booth. Sarah fidgeted with her cup. Adam studied her, his gaze scanning the length of her hair.

"Vicki told me that you're originally from Tahlequah," he said. "And that you're registered with the Cherokee Nation."

She stiffened at the mention of her hometown and her heritage, her memories still too close to the edge. "Yes, I am. Is this what you wanted to talk to me about?"

He nodded, his voice tinged with emotion. "I just found out that I was born in Tahlequah and that I'm part Cherokee, too. I know that sounds strange, but up until a little over a month ago, I had no idea that I was adopted."

Sarah released a heavy breath. He was born in Tahlequah? This gorgeous Californian? No wonder he reminded her of home.

She didn't want to discuss his newly discovered Cherokee roots, but after his personal admission, how could she just get up and walk away? The least she could do was give him a moment of her time, no matter how uncomfortable the subject made her.

"You were adopted by a white family?" she asked.

"Sort of," he answered. "My father was English, but my mom was Spanish and Italian. I always figured my coloring had come from her. You know, all that Latin blood." He glanced down at his drink, then back up. "My parents died when I was in college. They were killed in a plane crash."

"I'm sorry," she whispered. Grief was something that still haunted her. She knew how it could destroy, claw its way into a person's soul. And at this oddly quiet moment, Adam's soul could have been her own. Their gazes were locked much too intimately.

Adam didn't respond. He couldn't. Everything around him had gone still. There was nothing. No one but the woman seated across from him. He wanted to touch her. Make the invisible connection between them more real.

Was it Sarah's eyes that captivated him? Those dark, exotic-shaped eyes? Or was it her hair—the lush black curtain? Her skin was beautiful, too. Clear and smooth and the color of temptation.

Before Adam's imagination took him further, he blinked away his last thought, breaking their stare. Sarah picked up her juice, and he sensed her uneasiness. Was the connection between them loneliness? Was she as alone as he felt? Within the span of a month, everything familiar in Adam's world had changed. He'd moved, switched jobs and stumbled upon his adoption.

"I've been storing some things that belonged to my parents," he said finally. "Mostly personal items, but there were two tall file cabinets from my dad's office. They were filled with old business records, but I kept them anyway." He glanced at Sarah's slender hands, recalling the shock tied to his discovery, the way his own hands had shaken. "I moved recently. Not a major move, just to a place that's closer to work. But since I was reorganizing and packing, it seemed like a good time to clean out those files."

"You found something, didn't you?"

"Yes." He swallowed back the pain, the lump that had formed in his throat. "There was a document from an adoption agency. It was in a manila envelope with some old tax records. I guess that's why I didn't see it before." He swallowed again, then released a heavy breath. "I discovered that

I was born in Tahlequah, Oklahoma, to a Cherokee woman named Cynthia Youngwolf.'' Leaning against the table, he searched Sarah's eyes, hoping for a miracle. ''Do you know anyone by that name?''

She shook her head. ''Tahlequah is the Cherokee capital. There's a large Indian population there. It would be impossible to know everyone.''

Adam's heart sank. ''I've been trying to find her, but nothing has panned out. First I checked with the Oklahoma phone directory, and then I placed some personal ads in newspapers. After that, I listed my name with one of those adoption search agencies.'' He hoped his biological mother was looking for him, too. Looking for the son who had lost his adoptive parents.

Surely Cynthia Youngwolf wondered about him. What woman wouldn't think about the child she had given up?

''This whole thing has been pretty overwhelming.''

''I'm sorry I wasn't able to help,'' Sarah said.

Adam studied her face, features that were strong yet delicate. Vulnerable yet proud. Were other Cherokee women as compelling?

What did his mother look like? And who was his father? Were they secret lovers? Too young to raise a child? He had questions, and no one but Cynthia Youngwolf could answer them.

And what about his parents? The ones who had raised him? Why hadn't they told him that he was adopted?

He couldn't control the turmoil, the jumbled emotions that left him feeling hurt and confused. Why had they lied to him, pretending he was their biological son? They'd had so many opportunities to tell him, especially during all that family counseling.

And what about the critical events leading up to the therapy? Were there subtle hints? Quiet innuendoes? Something, anything that marked the truth?

Yes, he thought, his heart striking his chest. There was.

Adam had been seventeen at the time, a tall, rangy boy with fire in his blood. And two weeks earlier, he'd gotten caught stealing a pint of whiskey from the local market, the place where his mother bought groceries.

Adam had lied, of course, insisting he'd swiped the liquor on a dare. Yet that hadn't stopped his parents from cornering him, from trapping him with one of their mandatory talks. But why? He knew they hadn't found the other bottle, the one he kept hidden in the trunk of his car.

"We picked up some literature," his father said.

Slumped on the couch, Adam glanced up at his dad. His mother sat in nearby chair, twisting the tassel on one of the pillows she'd embroidered. His dad was tense, and his mom was jittery and fretful. Things didn't look good.

"Literature?"

Ronald Paige nodded, a quick, hard jerk of his head. "About alcoholism."

Irritated, he righted his posture. "And what's that got to do with me?"

"You drink, Adam. You drink a lot."

"That's bull." He dragged a hand through his hair and ground a booted heel into the carpet. "I party on the weekends once in a while. That doesn't make me an alcoholic."

"It's more than that, and you know it. You're addicted. All the signs are there."

All the signs are where? he wondered. In some stupid brochure his parents had latched onto? "I'm not going to sit here and listen to this." When he stood, he topped his father by several inches. "You guys are freaking out. Making something out of nothing."

"And you're out of control. You don't even seem like our son anymore."

"Really? Well maybe I wished I wasn't. All you ever do is hassle me." Turning to leave, he caught sight of the look that passed between his parents. A look that said something secretive, something he couldn't quite name.

Shrugging it off, he slammed the front door and headed for his car, grateful the whiskey was still there.

A horn honked and Adam jolted, realizing where he was. He sat in the juice bar, staring blindly out a window. Taking a deep breath, he let it out slowly. He had come a long way since his bout with the bottle, and, up until their untimely death, his parents had remained by his side. The loving, supportive family that had kept his adoption a secret. None of it made sense.

He turned to face Sarah, hoping she could help him unscramble this puzzle. "Do you still have family in Tahlequah? Will you ask them if they've ever heard of Cynthia Youngwolf?"

Her eyes shifted focus. Instead of meeting his gaze, she studied her drink, her tone distant. "My family…my father doesn't live in Tahlequah anymore. He's in another part of Oklahoma now."

"I see," Adam responded, although he didn't. All she would have to do was ask her father about a name, yet she appeared reluctant to do so. Why? he wondered. Why wouldn't she make one simple phone call? And why had her shoulders tensed throughout portions of their conversation?

One minute he saw attraction in her eyes, the next detachment. Warm. Aloof. Gentle. Afraid. She appeared to be all of those things. And that made him want to touch her even more, reach for her hand and hold it. This woman, he thought, this dark-eyed mystery, was connected to his birthplace, a heritage he knew nothing about.

The Cherokee books he'd purchased helped, but they weren't enough. Reading didn't combat the loneliness. He needed more than just words on a page.

He needed human contact.

He needed Sarah.

Adam started. He needed a woman he'd just met? Was he losing his mind? The last of his sanity?

No, he thought. He wasn't crazy. A woman born in Tahlequah, a stunning Cherokee with dark eyes and long, flowing hair. He couldn't have dreamed her if he'd tried. Sarah was the answer he had been waiting for.

She glanced at her watch. "It was nice meeting you, Adam. But I should get back to work."

"I'll walk you," he offered.

They stood on the street corner, and as she brushed his arm, a ray of hope shot through him—an awakening from one of his ancestor's arrows. No, he wasn't about to give up on Sarah Cloud. Somehow, some way, he would break through her defenses, unlock the mystery surrounding her. And in the process, he intended to find his biological mother. The woman who had given him life.

The next week Sarah paced one of the facial rooms, checking and rechecking her supplies. Adam Paige was her next appointment. A facial. The man had booked a facial. Not that she didn't have other male clients. She encouraged men to take better care of their skin, yet the thought of touching Adam made her palms tingle and her pulse race.

She sanitized her hands for the tenth time, a nervous habit, she supposed. And one she'd just acquired. Checking her watch, she exhaled a shaky breath. Maybe he would fall asleep during the facial the way some of her other clients did. It would be easier touching him if he slept.

Sarah let out an anxious laugh. Mrs. Whipple snored during her procedure, but then Vivian Whipple was nearly eighty years old. Young, virile Adam Paige wouldn't snore. And he probably wouldn't fall asleep, either.

Quit stressing and go, she told herself. Adam was probably early, waiting in the reception area for her to greet him.

Sure enough, he was there. As Sarah approached, he stood. Today he wore tan trousers and a matching shirt. Although he looked more stylish than he had the week before, he still exhibited the same rugged appeal. Both the makeup artist and her client checked him out from their vantage point. And, of course, Tina watched with a dreamy smile, probably thinking Sarah was the luckiest girl in L.A.

Yeah, right. More like the most nervous.

"Hi, Adam," Sarah said, reminding herself it was just a facial—a procedure she had done a thousand times before. "Are you ready?"

"Sure. Lead the way."

She showed him where her treatment room was, then took

him to an empty dressing room. "Just remove your shirt and put this on." She handed him a kimono-style robe that belted in front, her friendly, professional voice intact. "And when you're ready, come to the facial room." Pointing to a rack of hangers, she added, "We encourage clients to keep their belongings with them, so be sure to bring your shirt along."

"Okay." He flashed that devastating smile, and she proceeded down the hall, taking a deep, I'll-get-through-this breath. Men might be low on her list of priorities, but this one made her tingly and weak-kneed, sensations she would prefer to do without.

Sarah waited by the treatment chair, resisting the urge to cleanse her hands again. She couldn't wash away her nervousness no matter how hard she tried. Touching Adam was inevitable, and dousing herself with an instant sanitizer wasn't going to help.

When footsteps sounded, she looked up. Adam entered the room, shirt in hand. She took it from him and hung it on a nearby hook. He wore the aqua robe she had given him, and although it was a simple garment, the pale color emphasized every striking feature. She decided his biological parents must have been beautiful, their genes creating a mixed-blood masterpiece.

"Have you ever had a facial before?" she asked.

He smiled again, his teeth white and straight. "No, but I'm looking forward to it."

"Have a seat, and I'll explain the procedure," she said, struggling to focus on her job. She hadn't been this anxious since her state board exam. This jittery inside. How much physical perfection could one man inherit?

He sat on the facial bed, his presence filling the small room. Sarah closed the door, knowing she had to. A relaxed setting enhanced the treatment.

Once she briefed him, he reclined and she draped him with a coverlet. He had chosen to keep the room quiet rather than listen to a CD from Sarah's collection. She had a variety of soft music as well as sounds from nature. She would have preferred to have a CD playing. The silence only made her more aware of her nervousness.

"I'm going to cover your hair," she told him, slipping her hands behind his neck. His hair, banded into a ponytail, felt smooth and thick. Healthy, she thought. Everything about Adam boasted strength.

After analyzing and cleansing his skin, she began the massage. She knew all the clinical benefits of a facial massage, yet when her fingers connected with his skin, she forgot each and every one.

She could have been a woman stroking her lover. A woman exploring his face, the chiseled angles and rawboned sensuality.

Each manipulation felt erotic. Rolling movements, circular friction. She touched his forehead, his cheeks, the bridge of his nose. She allowed her fingers to roam his face, the pressure light but firm, slow yet rhythmic.

Heat against heat, Sarah thought. Flesh against flesh. Adam kept his eyes closed, but he didn't sleep. Instead he moaned his pleasure—a low, masculine sound.

When she accidentally brushed his lips, he wet them afterward. She swallowed and moved down his chin, his neck.

Mesmerized, she became aware of every breath he took, every muscle that twitched, the rise and fall of his chest, the flutter of his eyelids.

He made another low sound and shifted his weight, causing the coverlet to slip. The V on his robe gaped. Sarah was tempted to slide her hands inside, massage his chest, his nipples.

Catching her breath, she chastised herself. She had to end this now. What kind of esthetician fantasized about her client? A stranger?

A beautiful stranger.

Easing back as naturally as possible, she broke contact, lifting her hands to fill a basin with warm water.

Adam opened his eyes, blinking as though awakening from a dream. He tilted his head back and looked at Sarah.

"That was nice," he said, his voice a husky whisper.

She managed a shaky smile, uncertain of how to respond. Her fingertips still tingled, and the gaping robe still exposed his chest—gorgeous, golden-brown flesh. She even caught sight of a taut, muscular belly.

Sarah adjusted the coverlet, knowing it was her professional place to do so. Adam didn't seem to notice that his robe had slipped open, but then why would he? Most men bared their chests without modesty.

"I'm going to remove the moisturizer, then prepare a mask," she told him, an image of his navel imbedded in her mind.

She continued the procedure, shielding his eyes with moist cotton pads. They didn't talk while she applied the mask, and within an hour the treatment was complete, his skin firm and clean.

He stood and smoothed his hair, his robe still loose, the belt barely tied. "Thank you, Sarah," he said, coming forward to press some folded bills into her hand.

"You're welcome." She accepted the tip, realizing they were only inches apart. He wasn't wearing cologne, she thought, her heart fluttering in her breast. He smelled natural, like fresh-milled soap.

"Will you have dinner with me tonight?"

The invitation caught her by surprise. And so did her response. Without the slightest hesitation, Sarah agreed to share a meal with him—this tall, beautiful stranger. A man she knew she should avoid.

Adam stood in the main square of Chinatown, waiting for his date. This was insane, he thought. No matter how hard he'd tried, he hadn't been able to convince Sarah to allow him to pick her up at her apartment. She had insisted on meeting him.

He checked his watch. 7:20 p.m. She was late. Was he about to be stood up? It would serve him right, he supposed. Plenty of women chased him, and he'd gotten used to the attention. But then, that attention was based on his looks, not on the man he was inside. And he wanted more than a superficial relationship. He wanted...

What? A commitment?

Someday, maybe. But he wasn't looking for love. At least not at this time in his life. He had too many other issues, too many other goals—like finding his biological mother, bonding with his heritage. He couldn't think about love and commitment. Not until he knew who he was and where he had come from.

He released a heavy breath. So where did Sarah fit into this? Why was he so eager to see her again?

Because she fascinated him, he realized. And she could lead him to his roots. Adam knew he was lost, a ship that needed to come to port. The adoption had him feeling so damn disconnected. For the past month he had been floating. Going nowhere.

And he had the same vibe about Sarah. He suspected she was troubled, too. And that drew him to her, made him want to help. She was solid, real—so unlike the superficial women who chased him. She would make a good friend.

A good friend? he asked himself. Or a compatible lover? He couldn't very well deny the sexual spark between them. He hadn't counted on it, but it was there—lurking, hiding, waiting to be released.

Well he wasn't about to release it. The last thing he needed was to complicate a new friendship with sex. He would just have to keep those urges under control.

And just how was he supposed to do that? He had already booked another facial for next week. He wanted her to stroke him again, enchant him with her magic.

Her mystery.

Adam frowned. Already his hormones were interfering with a friendship that hadn't even happened yet. He could find another connection to his heritage, couldn't he? He didn't need Sarah to show him the way.

A beautiful, exotic woman. A dark-eyed Cherokee mystery.

Damn. Maybe he should just forget the friendship and have

an affair with her. A passionate one-night stand. That would satisfy his hormones, the unexpected lust.

Disturbed by the thought, he shook his head. Maybe it would be better if Sarah did stand him up. Then he wouldn't have to worry about their attraction.

Adam checked his watch again, then glanced up and caught his breath. It was too late, he thought. Much too late.

Beautiful, dark-eyed Sarah was already walking toward him, and all he could think about was tangling his hands in all that glorious hair and kissing her senseless.

Two

Sarah scanned the menu, wishing she could think of something to say. She wasn't good at small talk and was even worse at dating. How was she supposed to concentrate on what to order with Adam sitting across from her? A man who appeared relaxed and confident? He probably had the dating ritual down pat.

She stole a quick glance. Of course he did. Look at him. God's gift to womankind. He wore his hair in a ponytail, his clothes casual but trendy—a printed shirt and pre-washed jeans sporting a well-known label. California ranch wear, she decided, designed for the city cowboy. His rugged style appeared natural. He didn't try to attract attention. He just did.

He caught her eye, and she looked down, studied her hands.

"Did you know that they don't serve fortune cookies in China?"

She glanced up again, forcing herself to hold his gaze. "Why not?"

"They were invented in the U.S. They don't exist in China."

"Have you been there?"

"No. I read that on the Internet in a travel guide. I spend a lot of time online."

Sarah took a deep breath, told herself she would get through this date. It helped not thinking of him as a world traveler. She had never even been on a plane. "I'm glad they serve them here. Fortune cookies are my favorite part of a Chinese meal."

He smiled. "Me, too."

When his smile faded, their eyes met. They sat in a small red booth, candlelight flickering between them. His face fascinated her, but she had already touched it, explored the ridges and angles, the masculine texture of his skin. She didn't want to remember every detail, but looking at him made that impossible.

He lifted the teapot and offered her a refill. She shook her head. She hadn't finished the first cup yet.

"Let's choose a few extra entrées so we can share," he said.

"All right." She agreed even though the suggestion sounded oddly intimate. "I would prefer chicken and vegetables, though. I don't eat red meat."

He smiled at her, something he did often, she noticed.

"Me, neither," he said, his voice as easy as his smile. "I guess that means we're going to get along just fine."

Yes, she thought, if she could just get over her nervousness, tame the unwelcome flutter in her stomach.

When the waiter arrived, they ordered a variety of dishes. Adam spoke a little Cantonese, enough to surprise Sarah and please the grinning waiter. Sarah wondered if Adam had learned the language on the Internet. He appeared to know a lot more than just the history of fortune cookies.

"Ancient cultures fascinate me," he told her. "I had some training in traditional Chinese medicine. It's an integral part of their philosophy and religion. Much like the Native American culture." He lifted his tea. "I've been reading about the Cherokee."

Sarah frowned. She didn't want to discuss her heritage.

And coming from Adam, the term *Native American* sounded almost glamorous. A far cry from her roots. She was just a simple Indian girl from Oklahoma.

''Where did you get your formal training?'' she asked, hoping to steer clear of Cherokee subjects.

''First I attended a school of herbal studies in Northern California, then transferred to a university in London''

''London? You went to school in England?'' Maybe he was more of a world traveler than she had originally thought. ''Did you like living there?''

''Sure. It's a beautiful country, and the University of Westminster was an excellent school.''

His casual response made her feel even more Indian, and she hated the feeling. Adam's adoptive mother might have been Latino, but he'd been raised in a predominantly white world. Apparently his brown skin hadn't hindered his experiences. ''It sounds exciting, but expensive, too.''

''My dad was an accountant, one of those conservative guys who saved money for his son's education. We weren't rich, but I didn't go without, either.''

His adoptive father must have been an honorable man, she thought with a twinge of admiration and a sting of envy. Sarah's father hadn't saved a dime. She had struggled to pay for her own schooling.

Their dinner arrived, and they ate in silence, his gaze catching hers between bites. Feeling shy, she glanced away. His mouth fascinated her. The way he moistened his lips before he lifted the fork.

He leaned toward her, and suddenly, foolishly, she wished the table wasn't between them.

''Sarah?''

''Yes?''

''Are you enjoying your meal?''

She nodded, even though her stomach was still alive with nerves, the flutter of feminine anxiety. ''Yes. It's quite good.''

He smiled, and she took a deep breath, recalling the warmth of his skin.

* * *

Night settled in the sky, scattering stars around a quarter moon. Adam and Sarah walked through the Chinatown courtyard, strolling in and out of boutiques. Adam loved the area. A few of the vendors knew him by name. He spent a lot of time in Chinatown, purchasing herbs and admiring the culture.

He turned to look at Sarah. As many times as he came here, he had never brought a date. Not until today.

She smiled a little shyly, and he considered holding her hand. Then reconsidered when she clutched her purse strap with the hand closest to his. There was no point in pushing too hard. If something developed between them, it would happen naturally.

"Have you been to Chinatown before?" he asked.

"Once, when I first moved here."

"And when was that?"

"Six years ago. I was eighteen at the time."

Adam nodded. He could almost see her, fresh out of high school—a little Oklahoma girl heading for the golden state. She was still little, he realized. Small and feminine in a way that made him yearn to protect her. But whether or not she would welcome protection, he couldn't be sure. In spite of her petite frame, independence shone through. She didn't have to tell him that she had ventured to California alone.

Independent yet vulnerable. Suddenly Adam was reminded of the stray cats that came to his door, the smooth, sleek creatures he couldn't seem to resist. He gave them their space, but he fed them, too. And those scouting a cozy place to sleep inevitably found their way into his bed.

Adam looked at Sarah again, wondering if she would find her way into his bed. If she would nuzzle and purr, arch and stretch against him. A smooth, sleek creature he wouldn't be able to resist.

Frowning, he shook his head. She wasn't a lost kitten. And he was thinking with his libido, creating sexual scenarios on a first date. So much for not pushing too hard.

"What's your favorite thing about California?" he asked, forcing himself to clear his mind.

She stopped to gaze at a window display. "That's easy." Turning toward him, she smiled. "The beaches. I love the sand and the surf. I like to go there at dusk, when it's quiet."

She sighed, and Adam pictured her at the beach on a windy day, dressed in an oversize sweater and jeans, her waist-length hair blowing in the breeze. "You collect shells, don't you?"

She widened her eyes. "Yes. How did you know?"

Because he could see her walking along the shore, shells glinting in her hand like pieces of eight. She was, he decided, a woman who appreciated simple treasures. "A good guess, I suppose. Do you want to check out this shop?"

"Sure."

They entered the boutique and scanned the crammed interior. It held a collection of goods, many of them jewelry and trinkets, shiny items meant to attract a woman's eye. Sarah looked around, then wandered over to a small circular rack of clothing. Intrigued, Adam watched her.

She admired a satin dress, tilting her head as she stroked the shiny red fabric.

"It's pretty," Adam said, noting the traditional mandarin collar and intricate embroidered design.

"Yes." Her voice held a note of feminine awe.

The proprietor, a tiny Chinese woman offering a friendly smile, walked over to them. She was old, Adam thought, ancient and charming. She patted Sarah's shoulder with a gnarled hand.

"You try on," she said, her accent making her English choppy.

Sarah turned, hugged the garment in a startled reaction. "Oh, no. Thank you, though."

"We have a private fitting room." The woman pointed to a corner where an ornate brass rod housed a silky green drape.

"I'm just browsing." Sarah replaced the dress, giving it one last glance.

The old woman said, "Okay," then headed toward the front counter.

Perplexed, Adam studied his date. She had looked at the garment with longing, yet refused to indulge herself. Sarah Cloud was a mystery, a dark-eyed princess who wore plain clothes and collected seashells at dusk. He didn't know how to pursue her, wasn't sure if he should try. She confused as much as fascinated him.

"Why didn't you try the dress on?" he asked.

She crossed her arms in what seemed like a protective, if not slightly defiant gesture. "It's too fancy."

"I think it's perfect."

"Not for me."

Did everyone see her beauty but her? he wondered. Most beautiful women in L.A. were used to attention, yet Sarah didn't appear to notice an appreciative eye. Of course she wasn't from California, he reminded himself. And that alone appealed to him. Since he'd lost his parents, the City of Angels and everything it represented no longer felt right. But in spite of his European education, it was all he knew.

Sarah had asked him about England, and he had tried to respond as casually as possible. His parents had died while he was in London. He had come home to bury them, then returned to finish his studies, knowing his career was all he had left. But that hadn't been something he could discuss over dinner, not on a first date, not when he'd wanted to keep the evening light. And there was nothing light about the death of his parents—the caring, supportive family that had lied to him. It hurt so badly, sometimes he couldn't breathe.

Adam looked at Sarah and noticed her arms were still crossed. She was tense, but suddenly so was he. "Let's buy something," he said, hoping to ease the tension. "You pick out a souvenir for me, and I'll choose one for you."

"You're kidding, right?"

"Nope." And he intended to con her into the red dress. "Come on." He led her to the other side of the store. "Find something you think I'd like."

Baffled, Sarah wandered through the tiny boutique. She didn't know what to choose for Adam. She wasn't an experienced shopper. And the only items she collected came from the sea. She didn't buy shells; she lifted them from the sand, even broken and chipped ones.

He smiled at her, and her stomach unleashed a flurry of wings. Beautiful butterflies, she decided. It wasn't nerves this time. It was the flutter of attraction.

Curious about his upbringing, she wanted to ask him about his mother and why he was determined to replace her with the woman who had given him up. But she decided now wasn't the time for that sort of conversation.

Maybe she was curious about Adam's mother because she missed her own. Sarah didn't have anything to remember her mother by, no outdated dresses, no feminine little keepsakes. Her father had burned everything. But that had been part of their culture, the old Cherokee way. A path she no longer followed.

Sarah looked up at Adam. He watched her. Closely. Maybe too closely. Before he could ask what she had been thinking about, she returned to the business at hand. She still had to find him a souvenir.

Scanning the shelves, she caught sight of a teapot. But not just any teapot. This one was adorned with a hand-painted dragon. The serpent's body shimmered with gold, and its eyes were set with shiny red stones. Yes, she thought, a powerful creature spun from legend. A man like Adam would slay this beast, assume the role of the protective knight, the fairy-tale prince.

She lifted it, turned it in her hand. The serpent's eyes shined back at her. The detail was exquisite. The dragon seemed alive, ready to breathe a burst of iridescent flames. She could almost feel the heat. The scorch of fire.

"This," she said. "Do you like it?"

Adam blinked. "It's a teapot, Sarah."

"It has a dragon on it," she pointed out.

"Yeah, but it's still a teapot."

She stifled a smile. He looked as if she had just squelched his masculinity. "You drink tea, so what's wrong with a teapot?"

"Nothing, I guess. It's just not what I figured you'd choose."

She touched the serpent. "I think he's dangerous." Like the way Adam made her feel. Suddenly she was caught up in the moment, in the fairy tale she had created in her mind.

Adam studied the teapot, and the winged flutter erupted in her stomach again. And when he took a small step toward her, the motion intensified.

"Okay. I'll take the dragon," he said. "But I want you to try on that dress."

Her heartbeat jumped. "Why?"

"Because I want to see you in it."

"It won't look right on me," she said, feeling suddenly foolish. "I'm not a red satin kind of girl." She wore mostly pastels, simple skirts and blouses constructed of washable fabrics. Never red. And never satin.

"You'll never know until you try it on."

Was he challenging her? Baiting her? Either way, she knew she had to prove him wrong. Sarah considered herself a practical woman. She had no use for such a luxurious garment. It wouldn't fit her looks or her lifestyle.

"Fine. I'll try it on." She turned and headed toward the clothing rack, knowing Adam followed. Retrieving the dress, she darted into the fitting room without glancing back.

She closed the curtain, removed her wedged sandals and unbuttoned her blouse. Slipping off her skirt, she eyed the dress. It looked much too bright next to her mint green ensemble. The dress zipped in back, so she peeled it open and stepped into the opening. The moment the fabric touched her skin, she shivered. It felt cool. Slick. Almost wet.

Fighting those sensations, she forced herself to continue. She couldn't reach the zipper to close it all the way, nor could she attach the tiny hooks that fastened behind the collar. She fumbled with them, then gave up and studied herself.

The woman in the mirror startled her. Nothing about the image seemed familiar. Her waist-length hair spilled over red satin, like onyx melting over rubies—jewels from the fairy tale she had created. Tilting her head, she ran her hands over her body. Even with the zipper partially undone, the dress molded to her curves.

Decadent. Sensual.

Wrong, she told herself, suddenly nervous. This wasn't her.

With a pounding heart, she fastened her sandals and emerged from the fitting room. She would prove to Adam the dress wasn't right. She would…

…slam into his gaze and lose her breath.

He stood tall and handsome, watching her, his stare bewitching. The knight. The fairy-tale prince. The dragon slayer.

"I told you it was too fancy," she said.

"No," he countered quietly. "It's perfect. Let me buy it for you."

She shook her head, but he persisted. "Wear it now, Sarah. Wear it for me."

How in God's name could she refuse? Deny the husky pleasure in his voice?

Realizing the zipper was still undone, she chewed her lip. "I…um…couldn't zip it all the way. Will you ask the saleslady to help me?"

He smiled. "Does that mean you're going to let me buy it for you?"

She nodded. "Yes. Thank you. I've never owned anything like this before."

Adam moved closer. "I can zip it for you."

No, she thought. Her heart was already thumping against her ribs. And her stomach. That wild winged flutter. "But it has these tiny hooks." She placed her hand on the back of her neck, trying to explain, trying to keep him from coming any closer.

His smile turned boyish. "I think I can manage."

He didn't give her a choice. He approached her, so she turned around. How many women had he dressed? she wondered. Or undressed?

"Lift your hair," he said, his voice quiet once again.

Decadent. Sleek. Dangerous. The words spun in her head, making her dizzy.

She pulled her hair to one side, felt him touch her. His hands were deft, steady and controlled.

He zipped the dress, then went after the hooks, his breath brushing her nape. A shiver raced up her spine, but she wasn't cold. She was warm. Much too warm.

"All done."

"Thank you."

She turned and found herself inches from him.

He moistened his lips, and she swallowed. Was he going to kiss her? She wanted him to, yet she couldn't imagine letting it happen. Not here. Not in this tiny boutique. There were other customers, and the saleslady watched them from behind the counter.

Sarah stepped back and lifted her arm where the price tag dangled. "This needs to be cut."

He nodded, but didn't say anything. He was staring at her. Fixated, it seemed, on her mouth. Finally, he blinked and smiled.

Still a little dizzy, she returned his smile, and they walked to the front counter. He paid for his purchase with a credit card. She with cash. The old woman removed the tag on the dress and packed the teapot in a sturdy box. Sarah, wrapped gloriously in red satin, accepted a shopping bag with her old clothes folded inside.

They stepped into the night air, and she filled her lungs, chasing away the dizziness. An array of buildings surrounded them, a blend of ancient architecture and modern accents.

"Where did you learn to speak Cantonese?" she asked Adam, as he guided her toward a secluded bench.

"From coming here and talking to the people." He placed his package on the ground and waited for Sarah to sit. "But I only know conversational phrases. Languages aren't easy to grasp unless you use them all the time."

She nodded. She only remembered bits and pieces of the Cherokee dialect, words her mother had spoken. But that seemed like a lifetime ago.

They sat quietly, stars glittering in the sky, a small breeze cooling the summer air. Sarah enjoyed the silence until

Adam's gaze became too intense. She shifted a little, uncrossed her legs, then crossed them again, unsure of what to do with herself. The dizziness returned—the shaky, wild, fluttery sensation.

She looked away, pretended to study a building, her pulse racing.

Would sex make her feel this way? she wondered. Hot and hungry? Excited yet nervous? Sarah was a virgin—a woman who still lived in the shadow of an old-fashioned upbringing, keeping herself pure for love.

Or was that a lie? she asked herself. Was she saving herself for the right man? Or using her virginity as an excuse to protect her heart?

"What are you thinking about?"

Adam's question startled her. "Nothing important," she responded, knowing she couldn't tell him where her mind had wandered.

"I was thinking about dragons," he said.

"What about them?"

His voice turned quiet, a little husky. "The embroidery on your dress. I didn't realize it before, but it's a dragon."

"It is?" She glanced down, saw the image come suddenly to life. What had looked like an intricate pattern was actually a gold serpent twining around her breasts, her tummy, her hips. And Adam's gaze followed every curve, desire flashing in his eyes.

She couldn't stop what was happening, nor did she want to. They moved in perfect harmony. Synchronized, slow—dancers coming together at the same moment. She wet her lips. He slid his hands into her hair. She made a kittenish sound, and he kissed her.

Pleasure caught at the back of her throat, then flowed through every vein, every cell, every muscle. She grew hot. Needy. Her flesh burned, her nipples ignited. She wanted him to caress her, slay the dragon scorching her body.

He did. He touched, stroked, ran those clever hands over the fire. She had never felt so helpless, yet so completely alive. A smoldering kiss in public. It wasn't proper, but God help her, she didn't care.

They were in their own world, and nothing could penetrate it but passion. His tongue swept her mouth—a mating—over and over. The motion was sexual. And that was what she wanted.

She had needs, strong, overwhelming needs. She wouldn't lose her heart. Sex wasn't love. She could sleep with him tonight.

Sleep with him? Was that what she wanted? To lose her virginity to a man she barely knew? A man obsessed with his newly discovered Cherokee roots? A man romanticizing the culture she'd left behind?

Her head reeling, Sarah pulled away from Adam's kiss.

He made her flesh tingle, her heartbeat accelerate, but she couldn't be with him. No matter what her mother had said, modern warriors didn't exist. And neither did dragon slayers.

"Sarah, what's wrong?"

"I think it's time for me to go," she responded, clasping her nervous hands in her lap. She needed to escape this moment, the spicy taste of his kiss still lingering on her tongue.

"But why? Tell me what's wrong."

"Nothing. I just want to go home." She stood, lifted her purse. She couldn't explain, couldn't ease his conscience. He hadn't offended her. He had aroused her, made her feel too good.

He rose from the bench, his gaze searching hers for the answer she refused to give. "I'll walk you to your car."

"Honestly, Adam. I'll be fine. Thank you for dinner. For the dress." Something she should have never accepted. Gathering the bag of her old clothes, she left him standing at the bench, Chinatown dazzling around him.

Three

A week passed, and Adam still battled his emotions. His work day had ended, but he sat in the conference room at the clinic, checking his watch. Then rechecking it. In twenty minutes, he had an appointment with Sarah. He hadn't spoken to her since their date, and he'd expected her to reschedule his facial, refer him to another esthetician. But she hadn't done that.

Of course not. She was too professional to turn away a client, to let personal feelings interfere with her job.

And what exactly were her feelings? he wondered. To him, their kiss had seemed so right, so naturally erotic, especially when she'd made those sexy little sounds. Like a stray kitten, he thought, mewling in satisfaction. Now that damn fantasy wouldn't go away.

Maybe she didn't want to be the object of his desire, the woman he lusted after. Adam frowned. Had he really put his hands all over her? Yeah, he had. And even though he longed to do it again, he still owed her an apology. That kiss had been a little too wild, too hungry for public display.

An apology would set things right. They could be friends, couldn't they? They didn't have to get romantically involved. He could lay his urges to rest, but he couldn't let Sarah go. Not completely.

He was too caught in the mystery surrounding her. Why was she hiding from her heritage? What could have possibly happened to turn her away from her roots? Adam needed to know. Being Cherokee was their link, a bond he hoped to strengthen.

He left the clinic and entered the salon. The blond receptionist grinned when she saw him. He returned her smile, but just as he approached the desk, he spotted Sarah coming around the corner.

The blonde spoke up first. ''Sarah, your five o'clock is here.''

''Thank you, Tina,'' she responded, shifting her gaze to Adam.

He walked toward her, and she slipped her hands in her pockets. She wore a white lab coat over her clothes, but it didn't make her look clinical. Instead she looked pure—a dark-haired, dark-eyed angel.

''Hi,'' he said.

''Hi,'' she repeated, her voice fighting a strained note. ''Go ahead and change, and I'll meet you in the treatment room.''

''Okay.'' He knew the receptionist was watching, and he knew it made Sarah even more uncomfortable than she already was. He should cancel the facial, let her off the hook, but he needed some quiet time with her, to apologize without an audience.

Five minutes later, he entered the treatment room, shirt in hand. He hung it on a nearby hook and waited for Sarah to acknowledge him. She was still setting up, filling disposable containers with creams and lotions.

She turned, and their eyes met. Silence, still and awkward, engulfed the room. Neither spoke. Adam became aware of everything—the pounding of his heart beneath the robe, the hitch in Sarah's breath, the way her hands shook.

He had no right to put her through this. He had to ease the

tension. Walking toward her, he managed a smile, even though his heart picked up speed. Being near her did that to him, he realized. And it wasn't a comforting thought, trying to calm a woman when he wasn't particularly stable himself.

Sensuality sizzled between them. Nervous and edgy, maybe. But it was there, a thickness in the air he couldn't deny. Couldn't control.

"Let me help," he said, reaching for one of the disposable containers.

"No, it's okay, I can..."

Their fingers brushed, an innocent touch that sent shock waves through his unstable heart, his yearning body.

Sarah must have felt it, too. She pulled back, knocking over a nearby jar. It rolled onto the floor, spilling a citrus-scented lotion.

"Damn it." Her voice shook as badly as her hands. She dashed over to the paper-towel dispenser and tore one in her haste. "I can't seem to do anything right today."

Because of me, Adam thought. Because their attraction was so intense.

She knelt on the floor and began soaking up the mess. He lowered himself beside her. "It was my fault," he said, taking the paper towels away from her. "I startled you."

"It was an accident." Avoiding eye contact, she released an audible breath. "I'll get something to clean up the residue." She went to a cabinet and returned with a spray cleanser and another wad of paper towels.

They worked side by side, concentrating on the task at hand. They didn't look at each other, didn't speak. Instead they gazed at the vinyl floor as if the pattern held great importance.

"I think we should cancel the facial," he said, when the overwhelming silence became too much to bear.

"I think so, too." She sat back on her heels. "I'm just not myself today. I almost called in sick."

Which said it all, he thought. She had been anxiety-ridden about seeing him, enough to make herself ill. His apology was long overdue.

"Sarah, I'm sorry. I didn't mean to get carried away last week. I shouldn't have kissed you the way I did. And certainly not in public."

She twisted a dry paper towel. "I...um...we both got carried away. It wasn't all your fault."

"Then why don't we start over?" He stood and offered her a hand, trying to keep his voice casual, his heartbeat steady.

She accepted his hand, but let go the moment she was on her feet. Leaning over, she picked up the soiled paper towels, then tossed them into the wastebasket. "I don't think we should go out again. I don't think it would work."

"I meant as friends." He tried not to frown. The rejection stung, even if he had been prepared for it. "I know you're not comfortable dating me. But I think we have a lot in common, and I'd like to be friends."

She sent him a small smile. "That's a nice thing to say."

"Then you're willing to start over?"

Sarah nodded, although a part of her could still taste his kiss, feel the heat of his body next to hers. Struggling with the image, she sanitized her hands, wringing them together. In spite of their attraction, friendship was best. Dating Adam was out of the question.

Why? she asked herself. Why was she going to deprive herself of his kiss, his touch?

Because it might lead to sex, a step she wasn't ready to take. How could she become intimate with a man obsessed with finding his Cherokee family when she had left her own behind? And then, of course, there was her virginity. She couldn't pretend that her moral upbringing didn't matter. She had made a promise to her mother. And she couldn't forget that youthful vow.

Don't give yourself to a man unless he's special to you, unless you love him.

But how will I know the difference?

You'll know, sweet Sarah. You'll know.

She could see herself sitting on the edge of a lace-draped bed, gazing at her mother, her head filled with wonder. It could have been yesterday. Or it could have been a lifetime ago. A dreamy twelve-year-old girl who had just experienced her first menstrual cycle.

I'll wait for the right man, Mom. I promise.

She blinked, looked at Adam and noticed how stunning he was—the planes and angles of his face, the broad shoulders, slim hips. And his smile, that warm, genuine smile.

Yes, he was handsome, but she wouldn't fool herself into believing he was the right man.

"Sarah?

"Yes?"

"Will you have dinner with me tomorrow night?" He held up a hand as if to fend off an expected protest. "A friendship dinner at my house. Just a casual meal." He flashed that devastating smile. "What do you say?"

"You're offering to cook for me?"

"Well, sort of." His grin turned a little sheepish. "I'll probably just throw some sandwiches together. Maybe a salad."

Sarah laughed. "How can a guy who eats health food not know how to cook?"

"Oh, I don't know. He lives on veggie burgers. The frozen kind you pop in the microwave." He smiled at her again. "So, will you come over tomorrow night? Suffer through one of my bland meals?"

"Yes," she said, charmed by his honesty. Besides, she thought, curiosity had gotten the best of her. She couldn't help but wonder where he lived.

He lived in a guest house in Sherman Oaks, not too far from Sarah's apartment. She smoothed her blouse, then knocked on the door. She had actually stressed about what to wear, then decided on jeans and a plain blue top. Everything she owned was simple, she supposed. Everything but the red satin dress.

Adam opened the door and stunned her senses. Classic rock played on the stereo, and his jeans were faded, the knees fraying just a little. She heard a loud "meow" and watched a black cat brush her leg as it darted past.

"Hey, Sarah. Come on in. Don't worry about Darrin," he added, apparently referring to the cat, "he's allowed to go out."

Sarah entered the house and took in her surroundings—hardwood floors, heavy oak furniture and tall, leafy plants in every corner.

The clean, masculine decor suited him. As always, Adam wore his long hair secured in a ponytail.

Handing him a small packet, she said, "It's fresh honey. For your tea. I didn't know what else to bring."

"Thanks. I guess you're not going to let me forget about that teapot, are you?"

"What?" She blinked and realized he was teasing her. "You're an herbalist. You're supposed to brew your own tea."

She gave a start when something moved. Another cat, she told herself foolishly as a furry being pounced onto the back of the sofa. This one was white with big curious eyes.

"How many cats to do you have?" she inquired, petting the friendly creature.

"There's usually five or six around here. Most of them are strays, so the number changes. Some just visit and others have decided to stay. Cameo is a permanent resident. She's expecting a litter soon." He nodded to the sturdy feline. "She showed up at my door pregnant. There wasn't much I could do."

But spoil her, Sarah supposed. Cameo looked pampered and well loved.

"Dinner won't be long," Adam said. "I was in the middle of fixing the salad, and the spaghetti is almost done."

"Spaghetti? I thought we were having sandwiches."

He shrugged. "I figured boiling some water and opening a jar of sauce wouldn't be too hard."

She laughed. "Can I help with anything?"

"Sure. The table still needs to be set."

His roomy kitchen displayed a garden window filled with

potted herbs. The appliances were white, the butcher-block table just big enough for two. She hung her purse on the back of a chair and inhaled the cooking aroma. Apparently he'd added fresh oregano to the store-bought sauce.

"Dinner smells wonderful."

"I'm figuring it out." He smiled. "Would you like something to drink? Water? Milk? Juice?"

His beverage selection pleased her and so did the fact that she didn't see a bottle of wine breathing on the counter. She avoided alcohol, even with dinner. "No thanks, I'm fine."

The CD on the stereo shifted from classic rock to vintage country, and she realized his taste in music was as diverse as her own. Stray cats and eclectic songs. She couldn't help but like him.

He pointed out the appropriate cabinets and drawers, and she set the table, feeling surprisingly relaxed. His plates and bowls were heavy stoneware, his silverware stamped with a geometric pattern. She turned and spotted the dragon sitting on a cluttered oak shelf. Its jeweled eyes glowed back at her.

Adam removed the pasta from the stove and dumped it into a large serving bowl.

And then he winked, jarring her composure with a perfect white smile. She had to tell her woman's heart to behave. It flipped in her chest, forcing her to catch her breath. He was just too handsome for his own good.

"Dinner's ready, sweet Sarah."

Sweet Sarah. Stunned, she stared at him, her jittery heart flooding with emotion. Her mother used to call her that.

"Lemon?"

"I'm sorry, what?"

"Do you want lemon?" He poured her a glass of carbonated water, held it up.

"Yes, thank you." She told herself it was coincidence. It didn't mean anything. He didn't know about her nickname, didn't know that it made her ache for childhood dreams and fairy-tale wishes. The beauty her father had destroyed.

They sat across from each other, a ceiling fan turning slowly overhead.

Refusing to focus on her jumbled emotions, Sarah started a conversation. "Didn't you just move into this house about a month ago?"

Adam nodded. "About the same time I started working at the clinic. Regardless, I'm due for a vacation. I haven't had any time off in years."

"So did they agree to give you some time off even though you're new?"

"Yeah. A couple of weeks in August."

"I was thinking about taking a vacation this summer, too. Sleep in and be lazy. Sometimes it feels good to do nothing." She placed her napkin on her lap. "So what made you decide to switch jobs anyway?"

"The new facility has more to offer. There's a yoga studio and a natural pharmacy in the building. There's also a masseuse and a variety of practitioners." He poured dressing on his salad, then glanced up. "I would love to open a wellness center someday. Of course, there are some things I would do differently."

Sarah understood. She often thought of opening her own skin-care salon. She tasted the spaghetti, alternating bites between her salad.

"Adam, why is it so important for you to find your biological mother? Why would you want to replace your parents with the woman who gave you up?"

"I never said I was trying to replace them. But damn it, I don't understand why they didn't tell me that I was adopted."

So he was hurt, she thought. And confused. "Maybe they were protecting you."

He made a face. "From what? Come on, Sarah. I had the right to know."

She sighed. "I hate to say this, but there's a good chance that your biological mother won't want to see you. She might feel as though you're interfering in her life."

He lifted his water, took a sip. "Then that's a chance I'll have to take. Besides, I think most women give up their babies because they're unable to care for them, not because they don't want them."

"It was a closed adoption."

"That doesn't mean anything. My mom could have been forced to give me up. She could have been too young or too poor. Or it could have been one of those tragic-type love stories. It's obvious my father was white. Maybe the difference in their cultures kept them apart." He reached for a breadstick, dipped it into a bowl of marinara sauce. "I'm not going to quit searching. After I find my mom, I'm going to look for my dad. I want to know both of them."

Sarah shook her head. Did he have foolish notions about reuniting his parents? Bringing lost lovers back together?

"You're still skeptical," he said.

She shrugged. "It's my nature, I suppose."

"But you would probably do the same thing if you were in my situation. Uncovering the circumstances of my birth will fill a void in my life. I'm part Cherokee, Sarah. I belong to a nation of people I know nothing about."

"Maybe your biological mother didn't want you to be raised by an Indian family."

"That's possible, I suppose. But if that's the way she felt, then I need to know why. Don't you think I have a right to know about my culture, learn everything I can?" He paused, pointed to the plants crowding the window sill. "I've devoted most of my adult life to alternative medicine, but that didn't come from the way I was raised. My adoptive mom grew herbs for cooking purposes, but I took it a step further. I studied about their healing properties on my own. Isn't it possible that's the Cherokee in me?" He met her gaze, his voice taking on a wistful tone. "Maybe there was a medicine man in my family."

Sarah sighed. She respected the healer in Adam, but he was caught up in the Indian mystique, glorifying it in a way that would only lead to disappointment. She knew firsthand that the old ways were lost. Her father was living proof of the Cherokee lifestyle today—false promises and alcoholism. There wasn't a medicine man on earth who could take away the pain William Cloud had caused.

When the opportunity arose, Sarah changed the topic of

conversation. She didn't want to talk about being Cherokee, didn't want to think about it or relive it in her mind.

After dinner, Adam and Sarah sat on the patio, the sky sprinkled with stars, the summer air cooled by a soft, intermittent breeze. Adam admired his companion, thinking how beautiful she looked—her hair a long, luxurious curtain, her eyes as dark and mysterious as the night. No wonder she had come to the City of Angels. She was one of them, he thought. A lost angel.

Something was wrong in her life, and he wanted to fix it, make her pain go away.

"Do you eat sweets anymore?" she asked.

Adam quirked an eyebrow. Her question seemed out of the blue, but everything about Sarah Cloud was unpredictable. "No. At least I haven't in a long time."

"Me, neither. But don't you ever want to cheat?"

He couldn't help but smile. "Yeah. Every once in a while I get a craving."

"Me, too. Chocolate eclairs are my favorite. I love the custard filling."

She made a hungry little moaning sound, and Adam pictured her mouth sinking into the rich, creamy pastry. Damn it. Now he wanted to touch her, slide his arms around her waist, ease his body next to hers, slip his tongue…

He studied her lips, the full, alluring shape. Kissing wasn't an option. He had agreed to friendship. No romantic entanglement.

Then why couldn't he convince his hormones of that?

He sipped his tea, hoping the honey-flavored brew would ease his craving, give his mouth something to do. The taste of her, the fevered flavor of their forbidden kiss, still lingered in his mind.

"Do you want to cheat next time?" he asked.

Her voice turned soft. "Are we talking about dessert?"

"Yes," he responded. "We won't be so guilty if we do it together."

She looked at him from across the table, and like magnets

drawn to metal, their gazes locked and held. Sarah pushed her hair off her shoulder, and Adam gripped the handle on his cup. They could move, make unimportant gestures, but they couldn't take their eyes off each other. Couldn't stop staring.

Suddenly the world around them ceased, sounds and scents fading. She felt it, too, he thought. The sexual pull. The heat that wasn't supposed to happen. They weren't talking about chocolate eclairs.

"I don't think cheating is a good idea," she said, breaking their unnerving stare.

"Yeah," he agreed, his voice huskier than usual. "We have more discipline than that."

She folded her hands on her lap. "Of course we do."

They sat quietly then, and Adam noticed the world had returned. The breeze blew a little stronger, stirring scents from his garden. He turned toward the plants and studied the small crop, needing to focus on something other than the attraction he had vowed to ignore.

"I read that when traditional Cherokees gather wild herbs, they ask a plant for its permission to be gathered, then leave a small gift of thanks," he said, thinking it was a beautiful practice. He wondered how it would feel to leave a shining bead on the ground in place of a plant.

"Was that in one of your text books?" she asked.

He shook his head. "I subscribe to a Cherokee newspaper. I get it online, in digest form, and they post cultural tidbits in every issue. Unfortunately my education didn't include Native American practices, at least not to any degree."

"The elders pass along things like that."

"I don't know any elders," he said, watching her tight expression, the one that came over her face whenever he mentioned their heritage. "You're the only Cherokee I know."

"I can't help you, Adam. I don't follow the old ways anymore."

He scooted his chair forward. "Why not?" he pressed, hoping to uncover her mystery, unveil the true woman, the soul behind the quiet, exotic beauty.

She didn't respond. Instead she reached for her tea and held the mug, drawing comfort, it seemed, from the warmth.

He saw sadness in her eyes, the loneliness reflected in his own. They were meant to be part of each other's lives, he thought. He wouldn't let this lost angel fly away.

"I don't think being Cherokee is anything to be proud of," she said finally.

He didn't know how to react, so he waited for her to continue. She did, after she tasted her tea.

"When I was young my mother filled my head with all of those romantic notions about the old ways. I was taught to believe in the unity of family and have pride in my heritage." She met Adam's gaze, her voice distant. "Cherokee men were supposed to be warriors—their role to remain strong and provide for their wife and children."

"So who let you down, Sarah? Was it your father?"

She nodded. "When I was fourteen my mom died unexpectantly from an aneurysm. It was awful. I missed her so much. And so did my dad, but he buried himself in his grief. He didn't consider how I felt or how much I needed him. He just kept saying that he didn't want to go on without her."

For a moment Adam thought about his own parents, about the fact that they had died together. "I know how it feels to lose a parent. I lost both of mine, but maybe it's even harder losing a spouse, the person you planned to spend the rest of your life with."

Sarah gave him a hard stare. "Please don't make excuses for my father."

"I wasn't. I'm just trying to understand."

"What's to understand? My dad started drinking. He turned to alcohol for solace and let me fend for myself most of the time because he was too drunk to take responsibility."

Stunned, Adam only stared. This wasn't what he'd expected. All this time he had been wondering what plagued Sarah. And now he knew. It was her father's battle with alcoholism, a struggle Adam remembered well.

Frowning, he pictured himself before the addiction had set in—a lean, somewhat shy youth influenced and impressed by the ''in'' crowd. Parties, drinking games and teenage sex. He'd been tempted. And he'd fallen hard.

Should he tell Sarah? Admit that he'd drunk his way through high school?

Adam blew a heavy breath. Yes, he should tell her. But not now, not while she was finally opening up, revealing her troubled heart.

Besides, he wanted Sarah to think of him as someone she could lean on, and blurting out that he used to drink didn't seem to be the answer. Eventually he would talk about himself, explain that he wasn't like her father anymore. Adam had been clean for eleven years.

''Didn't anyone intervene?'' he asked. ''Try to get your dad some help?''

''Yes, but you can't force someone into sobriety.''

Adam knew she was right. His parents had instilled ''tough love,'' more or less forcing him into rehab, but he'd stayed sober on his own. ''So your dad wasn't willing to quit?''

''He tried, I suppose, only not hard enough. Steadily he got worse. We were never rich, but his job as a mechanic provided a middle-class lifestyle. Eventually his drinking destroyed that, too. He started tipping the bottle at work and lost his job. I learned soon enough what it was like to be a poor downtrodden Indian.'' Her breath hitched, as unsteady and edgy as her words. ''He never did regain regular employment, but he continued to offer promises of sobriety. And for the longest time I believed him.''

''But you lost faith.'' Adam recalled how worried his parents had been. There was always the fear that he would slip up.

''I was tired of false promises. I left when I was eighteen, came to California to start over. It's the best thing I've ever done.''

He wasn't inclined to think so, but he kept that thought to himself. Starting over didn't work if you left your heart behind. And Sarah's was still in Oklahoma, wishing her dad had come through.

"So you haven't seen your father or spoken to him in over six years?"

"That's right." She formed a steeple with her hands, much in the same manner Adam had been taught to pray. "Whenever my dad attempted to stop drinking and failed, he blamed his alcoholism on genetics. Indians can't help it, you see. It's in their blood. That certainly gave me a new perspective on being Cherokee." She tightened the steeple, lifted it to her chin. "Everything my mother told me was just illusion. Warriors don't exist anymore. Holding onto the old ways is pointless."

Sarah was making excuses, Adam thought sadly. She'd turned away from her heritage as a means to distance herself from a painful childhood. Rather than view her father as a man, she saw him as a fallen warrior—something intolerable in her mind.

Adam gazed up at the sky, at the stars shimmering in the heavens. Warriors were only human, men prone to fault—a fact Sarah needed to accept. Being Cherokee wasn't the cause of her father's demise and ignoring her culture wouldn't erase the despair he had caused.

A star winked from above, and Adam made a solemn vow. Somehow he was going to help this lost angel find her way home. And in the meantime, he'd keep his past a secret. Sarah might overreact to an addiction that had afflicted him years ago.

Four

Adam arrived at Sarah's apartment on Sunday afternoon. He had called ahead, so she was expecting him, but he still felt a little apprehensive. He didn't want to come on too strong, didn't want Sarah to know how easily she stirred his hormones. Adam was doing his damnedest to stick by their friendship agreement.

She opened the door and invited him in. "What did you bring?" she asked, eyeing the box he carried.

"Just some things I wanted to show you," he responded, hoping this was the right thing to do.

He placed the box on the floor and lifted the African violet he had tucked in the corner. First order of business, he thought, handing her the small potted plant. "This is for you."

"Thank you. It's lovely."

"My landlady grows them." And its exotic beauty reminded him of her, but he didn't say so.

He met her gaze, and she clutched the plant to her breast.

This sweltering summer day she wore a white T-shirt and denim shorts. She had shapely legs, a deep shade of copper, just the way he imagined the rest of her. And her feet were bare, her toenails painted a soft shade of pink. Barefoot women enticed Adam, the sexy, natural quality it seemed to give them.

She broke eye contact first, the flower still pressed against her body. "Make yourself at home, and I'll put this on the windowsill."

She headed for the kitchen, choosing just the right spot for the violet. He could see her from where he stood. Her hair was straight and dark, as thick as a midnight sky, swaying as she moved.

Because the image made him want her, he shifted his attention to her apartment. It was modern, with almond-colored carpeting and high ceilings. She had furnished it with a beige sofa and a glass-topped coffee table. The paintings on the walls displayed muted watercolors—a foaming seascape at dusk, a vase of willowy flowers, a white gazebo—serene, pretty things women enjoyed.

He noticed a small basket of seashells on the coffee table and smiled. He knew they were her way of connecting with nature, of breathing in the ocean and letting it flow through her veins. Like a wave. Warm and slow and mesmerizing.

Suddenly his body went taut, hungry with liquid heat. His belly tightened in a blatantly sexual pull, pressing lower, dangerously low. He had to stop wanting her, craving what he had vowed to avoid.

She returned from the kitchen, and he wished he was the sort of man who could go to another woman for relief, fall into bed with the first warm, willing body who came his way.

But even so, he knew that wouldn't work. It was Sarah he wanted, Sarah he longed to touch.

"I'm sorry," she said. "I'm being a terrible hostess. I didn't even offer you a cold drink."

"I'm fine. I don't need anything." Nothing but to get her out of his system, which he didn't see happening anytime soon. Here he was, at her home, intending to ask her to take a vacation with him—a woman he barely knew.

They settled onto the sofa, the box he'd brought on the table in front of them.

She peered into it curiously. "So what did you want to show me, Adam?"

"It's more or less my research material, literature I downloaded from web sites or photocopied from books."

"About adoption?"

He shook his head. "It's mostly Cherokee stuff." When she frowned, he continued, keeping his voice light. "There's also some information about Tahlequah. I called the Chamber of Commerce, and this is what they sent me." He lifted a large white packet bearing a black-and-white feather logo. It contained pamphlets about lodging, restaurants and schools, a couple of maps, pictures of recreational spots.

She didn't make a move for the packet, so he opened the flap, removed a brochure. "I'm going to Tahlequah in August, Sarah." Pausing a beat, he searched her gaze, smiled a little. "And I want you to go with me."

A stunned expression replaced the disapproving frown. "I can't do that."

"Why not?"

"Because I..." She released an audible breath, her explanation drifting. "Are you planning to search for your mother?"

"Yes. I realize she might not live in Oklahoma anymore, but she could still have family there. And I was born in Tahlequah. I want to see what's it like, absorb whatever I can." He paged through the brochure. It contained information about the Cherokee Heritage Center. "You're familiar with the area, Sarah. You could be my guide."

"I don't think that's a good idea."

"I'll pay your way. And I'm not asking you to stay with me." He kept his gaze trained on hers and saw her eyelids flutter. She had captivating eyes, long pretty lashes. It was all he could do not to lose himself in them. "We'll get separate rooms."

"I wasn't worried about..."

Her copper skin flushed, and he realized how shy Sarah was, how innocently sensual. That, God forbid, made him want her again.

He looked away, gained his composure. This trip wasn't a whim. He hadn't conjured it as a ruse to be near her. He honestly believed it could present a new beginning for both of them. He could search for his mother, and Sarah could get reacquainted with her roots. She needed to see her dad one more time—ask for an apology, insist he get help.

Rather than push the issue, he gave her a measure of space, time to adjust to the idea of going back to the place she had left behind. "You don't have to make a decision right now. Just promise you'll think about it."

"I won't change my mind, Adam."

He shrugged, sent her a friendly smile. "You might. And if you don't, then I'll make the trip alone."

"You should let it go," she said. "Pretend you never stumbled upon those adoption papers."

"I can't do that." He would search until his dying day, search until he met the people who had created him, looked in their eyes and saw a piece of himself. Did he have his mother's cheekbones? His father's hands? "I know you don't understand. But my adoptive parents are gone, and now I'm alone. I need answers."

"What if you don't like what you find?"

"Then I'll deal with it. Life is full of challenges. And mankind has flaws. None of us are perfect."

"You are," she said, stunning him nearly speechless.

"Where did you get that idea?"

"You're tall and handsome and smart. It's hard to find fault."

"You need to look deeper, Sarah. I'm no different than anyone else."

"But you are," she countered. "You're not only handsome, but you have a good heart."

Adam felt a rush of guilt. A good heart, maybe, but not an honest one. He still hadn't told her about his unholy past.

"Sarah, I—"

What was he going to say? He used to pimp beer? Steal whiskey? Belt back a shot or two before school?

Suddenly he couldn't bear to admit the truth. Because deep down, he knew it would destroy the clean, tender emotion stirring between them.

"I'm just an average guy," he managed, telling himself it wasn't a complete lie. For the past eleven years, he'd lived a pretty normal life.

"Not to me. I've never known anyone like you."

Immediately they both fell silent, the kind of quiet that marked an awkward moment. She chewed her bottom lip, and he studied the archway that led to her spotless kitchen. Slats of gold streamed through the blinds, shooting filtered sunlight into the room.

He wanted to touch her, slide his hands down her arms, feel the pulse at her wrist. But instead he lifted the Tahlequah packet and removed the entire contents. The papers made a ruffling noise, and Sarah turned toward the sound.

The brochure on top caught Sarah's eye, and she noticed a heading that read "Self-guided tour of historic Tahlequah." Adam wanted her to serve as his guide, return to Oklahoma for two weeks.

Home. He wanted her to go home.

A burst of panic constricted her throat. She couldn't go back. Wouldn't go back, especially with him. He confused her emotions, reminding her of starry Oklahoma nights and the Cherokee warriors her mother used to talk about.

Caught up in the image of a warrior, she studied him. His hair was combed away from his face, secured at his nape in a thick ponytail. She had never seen him with his hair down and couldn't help but wonder how it would look flowing over his shoulders.

Adam shifted the papers on his lap, reached for a map and unfolded it. "Where did you live?" he asked.

Sarah forced herself to look at the map, to quell the anxiety in the pit of her stomach. She leaned into him. She could smell the faint aroma of the soap he used. She had seen a bar of it in his bathroom, knew it contained extracts of pine and European mosses.

"In this area," she said, picturing the friendly middle-class neighborhood: Sunday-afternoon barbecues filling the summer air, children's bicycles parked hastily on freshly mowed lawns, teenage boys tinkering with hand-me-down cars. "They used to come to our door and ask for his opinion."

Adam glanced up from the map. "What? Who?"

Sarah blinked, realizing she had spoken her thoughts out loud. "Some of the teenage boys in our neighborhood. My dad would help them customize their cars, make them louder or faster or whatever it was they were trying to accomplish." She shivered at the memory. Happy times, before her mother had died, before her father had crawled into his vodka-steeped hole.

"Your dad must have been a good mechanic."

She shrugged. "He was, I suppose." But *was* was the operative word. Like everything else, he had let his career fall by the wayside. After his wife had died, nothing mattered to William Cloud.

"I really want to go here," Adam said.

She glanced at the map again, saw that he referred to the Cherokee Heritage Center.

"Have you been there?" he asked.

She nodded, knowing she couldn't avoid Adam's questions. He had such raw need on his face, a thirst to hear about anything that would put him in touch with his ancestry. She sincerely hoped his quest wouldn't end up hurting him, but she had her doubts. Not just because of the Indian aspect, but because most adopted people who searched for their biological families ended up with ill-fated reunions, strangers with nothing in common but the blood that ran through their veins.

"My mom used to take me to the Heritage Center," she said finally. "It was one of her favorite places. The prayer chapel affected her the most. It's dedicated to the Cherokees who lost their lives on the Trail of Tears." And now the chapel reminded Sarah of her mother, a woman who died believing in dreams.

"You must miss her terribly," he said, as though reading her mind.

"I do, but I've learned to go on."

"Do you miss your dad at all?"

She lifted one shoulder, lowered it in a partial shrug. "I miss the way he once was, I suppose. But now I realize that wasn't really him. He tried to be what my mother wanted him to be. She was the traditional Cherokee, the one who spoke the language and followed the old ways."

Adam sat quietly for a moment, then said, "I appreciate your talking to me about this. I know it's not easy for you. But it's been tough on me, too. I feel like I'm on the outside looking in. I don't even know if I'm supposed to say *Native American* or *Indian.*" He picked up the brochures, slipped them back into the oversize envelope. "I don't want to do or say the wrong thing."

He was trying so hard to find his place in the world, she thought. This perfect, beautiful man. "Use whatever term you're comfortable with."

"I notice you say *Indian.*"

"That's what I'm used to."

"It's a little confusing," he said.

She had to smile. "Don't worry about trying to be so politically correct, and you'll get along just fine. You could never offend anyone, Adam."

He smiled back at her, and her stomach fluttered. That gorgeous, white smile. No, he could never offend, only charm.

"I guess you're what's considered an urban Indian," she said, explaining when he gave her a curious look. "Someone who wasn't raised on a reservation or in a traditional environment."

"Yeah, but I'm sure the other urbanites know more about their culture than I do."

"Not necessarily. There are plenty of elders who didn't pass on the old ways. They grew up with the stigma of being Indian, and some of them thought it would be easier to spare future generations the same fate. So as the years went by, holding onto the culture became less important.''

''But times have changed. I read that they're even teaching some of the native languages in colleges now.''

''Things haven't changed that much.'' At least not for Sarah. The stigma was still there, deep in her bones.

He reached for her hand, touched it. ''I wish I could make it better for you.''

Sarah shivered, but she wasn't cold. A heat, an incredible warmth, flowed through her. His touch, his hand on hers—that simple gesture made her want him.

He could make it better, she thought, if he would kiss her again. Unable to stop herself, she leaned into him.

He moved closer, too. Only he moved slowly, cautiously, questioning her gaze, asking for permission with his eyes.

''Yes,'' she whispered, an instant before his lips brushed hers.

He was gentle, reverent. He slid his hands to her waist, held lightly. She didn't want to close her eyes, didn't want to lose sight of him, but a dreamy sensation washed over her and she yielded to it, her eyelids fluttering.

No longer could she see him, but she could feel him—every movement, every tingle, every erotic tremble he incited. The skin over his cheekbones was taut, his jaw freshly shaven. She lifted her hand and skimmed his hair, the smooth, silky texture that led to that carefully secured ponytail.

As she cupped the back of his neck, he sucked her bottom lip, sucked until she moaned and fisted his shirt, pulling him even closer.

They knocked over the box he'd brought, spilling envelopes and papers onto the carpet. Neither paid attention to it. Instead they went a little crazy, their mouths meeting over and over, tongues diving and dancing.

The room spun like a carousel, but she didn't care if she was confused and dizzy. All that mattered was him. This man. This incredible, perfect man.

''Adam,'' she said his name out loud, breathed it through another spiraling kiss.

With both hands still grasping his shirt, her mind wandered into sexual delirium. What would it be like to unbutton all that rough denim? Place her hand on his chest? Let his heartbeat thud against her palm?

Would his skin feel as golden, as warm as it seemed radiating through his clothes? Her mind continued to spin, and he lifted her onto his lap, so that she straddled him.

As the buttons on his fly grazed her zipper, moisture, hot and honeyed, settled between her legs. From the friction she thought. They were rubbing against each other, denim pressing denim—his jeans, her shorts. He skimmed her bare leg, and Sarah's nipples went hard and achy. She wanted him to touch her there, too. Caress her with those fire-tipped fingers.

Suddenly a noise jarred her—a loud, persistent ringing.

Sarah thought it was a warning bell screaming in her head, but when Adam pulled back, she realized he had heard it, too.

Struggling to gain her composure, she blinked through blurred vision. She was still dizzy, still drugged with feminine arousal. Adam seemed dazed, too. His eyelids looked heavy, and his breathing sounded raspy, as though he couldn't quite steady it.

"Was that the phone?" he asked.

She glanced around her apartment, hardly recognizing it. Why wouldn't her eyes focus, her heart quit pounding? "I don't know." Where was the phone? she wondered.

The sound buzzed again, and recognition shot through her. "It's the doorbell. Someone's at the door."

Instantly the room came into view. The afternoon sun blared through the blinds, and Sarah squinted at the box they had knocked onto the floor.

Remembering the brochures from Tahlequah, she stood. Adam wanted to take her to Oklahoma, bring her back into the world she had left behind.

What in God's name had she been thinking, encouraging him to kiss her? Run his hands over her body?

Adam rose from the sofa, a portion of his shirt untucked and slightly rumpled from where she had tugged on it. Sarah pulled air into her lungs, knowing he was aroused beneath the button-fly jeans.

He was so incredibly gorgeous. A tall, dangerous temptation.

"I have to get the door," she said.

"Then I'll clean up."

He knelt to right the cardboard box, his voice lower and huskier than she would have liked.

Crossing the room, she avoided his gaze. She wouldn't allow herself to look at him again, get drawn into those hypnotic eyes or that warm, wet mouth. His sex-tinged voice was torture enough. She could still taste him, and her nipples remained hard, her flesh tingling.

She paused at the door, took a calming breath. Maybe a zealous youth selling magazine subscriptions waited on the other side, someone friendly and safe she could invite into the apartment, use as a shield between herself and Adam.

Placing her hand on the knob, she opened the door.

"Oh, thank goodness you're home."

Vicki Lester sighed from apparent relief. She was Sarah's neighbor, an easy-going woman who looked uncharacteristically frazzled. Her curly red hair was pinned haphazardly to her head, ringlets springing against her freckled face.

Sarah stepped back, inviting Vicki inside. "Are you all right?"

"No. Yes. I mean, I'm fine, but my baby-sitter just called in sick."

"Where are the girls?"

"At a friend's house, but I have to pick them up soon." Vicki turned, apparently catching sight of the man in Sarah's apartment. "Adam," she said, her voice less jittery. "I didn't realize you were here."

Adam and Vicki knew each other, of course. She was the one who had told him about Sarah in the first place. And she had questioned Sarah about him later, asking her what she'd thought of him.

Adam stepped forward, and Sarah noticed his shirt had been neatly tucked into his pants, even if the pre-washed denims still rode low and sexy on his hips. Keeping her gaze above his belt buckle, she averted them from the button fly. She didn't want to be reminded that she had been straddling his lap, rubbing herself against him like one of his cats.

She didn't want Vicki to figure it out, either. The other woman, she suspected, had wanted them to get together from the beginning. She doubted it had been a deliberate matchmaker attempt, but a hopeful one just the same.

Adam stood beside Sarah. "I just stopped by for a visit," he said to the redhead. "So what's this about your babysitter?"

Vicki pushed a rebellious curl away from her face. "She's sick and can't watch my daughters. And here I am scheduled for a seminar in Arizona tomorrow. I'm flying out tonight, or I will be if I can find someone to stay with the girls." She blew a tired-sounding breath. "And I just got a promotion, too. My boss will be fit to be tied if I miss this seminar."

Sarah sympathized with Vicki's plight. The thirty-five-year-old divorcée worked hard to provide for her daughters, especially since her ex-husband was a deadbeat dad who shirked his financial responsibilities. And if there was one thing Sarah detested, it was men who neglected their children.

"I can stay with the girls," she offered before Vicki had to ask. "I have Sundays and Mondays off."

The redhead gave her a sturdy hug. "You're a lifesaver. I swear I'll pay you back somehow."

"I'd be glad to help out, too," Adam said. "If you don't mind having a big guy like me sleeping on your couch."

"Are you kidding?" Vicki grabbed him for a hug. "The more responsible adults the better. I hate leaving the girls overnight as it is." She stepped back and grinned. "And I'm sure my couch will survive."

But what about me? Sarah thought. How will I survive being in the same house with Adam all night? She glanced back at the sofa, the spot where she and Adam had practically mauled each other.

They would be baby-sitting, she reminded herself. She wouldn't be spending the night with him all by herself. Two bright-eyed little girls would be there. How dangerous could that be?

"What time should we come by?" she asked Vicki. Baby-sitting aside, the *we* part sounded oddly intimate, as though she and Adam were a couple.

"About 5:00 p.m. I already have a casserole in the fridge for dinner, so all you have to do is bake it." She adjusted her handbag. "The girls are supposed to be in bed by 8:30, but I can't guarantee they'll go willingly."

"Don't worry," Sarah assured her. "Everything will be fine."

Vicki departed, offering her thanks again. Once Sarah and Adam were alone, she became overly aware of his masculine presence, the size of his hands, the muscles in his arms, the way they flexed when he moved.

"Have you met Vicki's children?" she asked, before silence threatened to swallow them whole.

He shook his head. "No, but she's told me a lot about them."

Sarah shifted her bare feet. Silence again, the only sound the hum of the central air conditioner. She couldn't think of anything else to say, and she didn't know quite where to look.

Adam checked his watch. "I should get going. I'll meet you at Vicki's apartment at five, okay?"

"Okay."

He headed toward the couch, picked up the box containing his Cherokee research. "Bye, sweet Sarah. I'll see you later."

The nickname hit her square in the chest, jump-starting her heart. Every time he said it, she felt young and innocent.

She met his gaze. "Bye, Adam." Closing the door after him, she leaned against it and slowly, very slowly, caught her breath.

Five

By 5:30 p.m. Vicki was on her way to the airport, and Sarah and Adam were alone with two little girls. Sarah set the dining-room table and watched the kitchen activity with interest.

Mandy, the eight-year-old, hadn't said more than a few quiet words. She stood at the counter while dinner was being prepared, filling a restaurant-style napkin dispenser. She was a serene child, with strawberry-blond hair and fair skin.

Dawn, the six-year-old, had the same light complexion, only her nose was dusted with freckles and her hair, as red as a fire engine, grew from her head like a curly mop.

She had volunteered to help Adam fix a salad, so she wiggled beside him, eager to work. Tearing the lettuce with gusto, she grinned up at him, displaying a wide, friendly gap between two slightly crooked front teeth. Her vibrant personality was as animated as her Raggedy-Ann looks.

Although she had been bombarding him with questions, he didn't seem to mind. He answered her patiently, all the while giving her something to do. Sarah learned that red was

Adam's favorite color and that he liked to count the stars at night and watch the news in the morning. He chatted with Dawn, but still seemed completely aware of Mandy, the timid eight-year-old who kept stealing glances at him when she thought he wasn't looking.

Mandy, Sarah realized, had developed an instant crush on Adam. The fact that she was a child hadn't immunized her to his charm.

Adam opened the refrigerator, then turned and caught Sarah's eye from across the room. He smiled, and the persistent winged flutter started up in her stomach. At that he's-so-gorgeous moment, she knew exactly how little Mandy felt.

They shared dinner twenty minutes later, gathered around a glass-topped table. Vicki's apartment was similar to Sarah's, only homier. She supposed it was the youthful touches, the adolescent artwork attached to the refrigerator door and the colored pencils and toys the girls left in the living room. The apartment seemed lived in, the attractive furnishings exhibiting signs of wear. Sarah's environment seemed lonely by comparison.

Mandy continued to study Adam through her lashes, although she remained quiet, eating the tamale pie her mother had prepared earlier. When Adam winked at the child, Sarah's heart warmed. He knew—sensitive, kind, gorgeous Adam knew—the little girl wanted him to notice her.

"Is your real name Amanda?" he asked.

She nodded.

He buttered a slice of bread, set it on his plate. "Do you know what Amanda means?"

She shook her head.

"It has a Latin origin," he told her. "And it means 'much loved.'"

"How do you know that?" she asked, watching every move he made.

"I had a girlfriend named Amanda. She was pretty and blond, like you."

That bit of personal news appeared to please the child. She

accepted the compliment in a shy, ladylike fashion, dropping her gaze and smiling into her plate.

Sarah, on the other hand, found herself wondering about Adam's Amanda. Pretty and blond conjured a tall, blue-eyed California-girl image—so unlike herself. And although his former girlfriend shouldn't concern her, she couldn't stop the sudden snap of unwarranted jealousy.

"What does my name mean?" Dawn asked, air whistling through her front teeth.

Adam tilted his head and studied the younger girl. "Hmm. I'll bet it has something to do with the start of a new day." He lifted his fork, sent her a smile. "Have you ever watched the sunrise at dawn? It's mighty pretty."

Dawn grinned, glanced at Sarah, then back at Adam. "Do you know what Sarah's name means?"

He turned and met her gaze. She wanted to look away, but couldn't. His eyes, those warm brown eyes, had her sinking into their depths.

"Princess," he said quietly. "It means princess."

Sarah knew the origin of her name, but on Adam's lips it sounded gentle, sensual, like part of a fairy tale. The princess and the dragon slayer. What would happen if she let herself fall into that fantasy?

She would get swept away, she thought, pulled into a world that held no realm of reality. Lifting her water, she broke eye contact. She, of all people, knew fairy tales didn't exist.

"The name Adam is from the Bible," Dawn said, clearly fascinated with the subject.

"Yes, it is," he responded. "That's why my parents picked it for me."

The chatty little girl scratched her freckled nose, smearing tamale sauce across her face. "And Sarah's parents must have called her Sarah 'cause they thought she was a princess."

Adam's voice turned husky, just enough for Sarah to feel the masculine sound slipping through her bones.

"I have no doubt that's the reason," he said. "No doubt at all."

She gazed at the dragon slayer named Adam, the man who

dreamed of finding his parents, of reuniting old lovers. Maybe fairy tales should be allowed, at least for tonight. After all, they were spending the evening with two bright-eyed little girls.

The two bright-eyed little girls didn't want to go to bed, even after hours of their favorite board game. But a second helping of ice cream finally convinced them to bathe and put their pajamas on.

They shared a frilly pink room that reminded Sarah of being a child herself—sugar and spice and everything nice. That was, she thought, a long time ago.

Mandy and Dawn were each in their own bed, the covers tucked around them. Dawn kept a worn-out doll with her, and Mandy watched Adam with stars in her eyes. Somehow he had managed to give the smitten eight-year-old special attention without neglecting her younger sister.

Adam sat on the edge of Mandy's bed and looked up at Sarah. "Why don't you tell the girls about the Cherokee Little People. I would do it, but all I know is what I've read. You're probably more familiar with them."

She blinked, then stepped forward. Adam had just tapped into her childhood. Her mother used to talk about the Little People, telling Sarah about them. Of course, it wasn't common practice to discuss them after nightfall. But apparently Adam wasn't aware of that.

She took a seat on Dawn's bed, and the child gazed at her with expectation. Mandy and Adam watched her, too, waiting, it seemed, to be drawn into the world of Cherokee superstition.

She decided she could talk about the Little People at night. Particularly since the old ways were no longer a part of her life.

"They're called *Ynwi Tsunndi,*" she said. "And they live in rock caves on mountainsides." With a wave of unexpected emotion, she paused, suddenly uncomfortable about breaking tradition. "Most Cherokees don't talk about them after the sun goes down. I'll tell you what I know, but after tonight, you can't mention them in the evening ever again."

Dawn and Mandy made that solemn vow, and Adam sent Sarah an apologetic look, realizing he had erred. She dismissed his blunder with a gentle glance. If the Little People truly existed, they would forgive a man like Adam.

"Are they smaller than me?" Dawn asked.

Sarah nodded. "They barely reach a man's knee. But they're handsome, and their hair falls almost to the ground."

The anxious child interrupted again. "Are they nice?"

"Very nice," Sarah said, smiling at Adam when his expression softened. "They're helpful and kindhearted, and they like kids. If a child gets lost in the mountains, the Little People will take them back to their parents." She brushed a lock of hair off her shoulder. "They help sad boys and girls, too."

Clearly enthralled with this information, the six-year-old pushed her blanket away. "Are they like leprechauns?"

"Sort of. Sometimes they can be mischievous, but they don't chase pots of gold. The Little People spend most of their time drumming and dancing. But you're not allowed to search for their home. If you do, they'll cast a spell on you and make you dazed for the rest of your life."

Dawn shook her head vigorously, sending red curls dancing around her face. "I won't try to find their house."

"They don't have a house," her sister said, as though trying to sound more grown-up than her eight years. "They're not real. It's just a story."

"They do too have a house," the younger one insisted. "They live in a cave in the mountains. The Little People are real, aren't they, Sarah?"

She caught Adam watching her, the man searching for his roots. "There are a lot of Cherokee people who think so," she said. "And you can never be sure if they're around, because if they don't want you to see them, they become invisible."

"See." Dawn made a face at her older sibling.

Mandy frowned, then turned to Adam "Do you think they're real?"

He patted the child's ankle through the blanket. ''I think the world is full of magic, especially in the forests and mountains. So I would just as soon not disturb the Little Peoples' home. I wouldn't want to be dazed for the rest of my life.''

When Mandy agreed that the Little People might actually exist, he leaned toward her and asked for a hug good-night, telling the girls it was time for sleep.

She hugged him, and when her head hit the pillow, Sarah thought she looked a bit glassy-eyed. Adam's charm had dazed the eight-year-old far more than a spell from the Little People ever could.

He hugged Dawn as well, and Sarah followed suit, embracing both children. She turned off the light, and Adam led her out of the room.

He had brought a box of herbal tea along, so they brewed a pot and sat on Vicki's floral-printed sofa, sipping the mint-flavored drink.

He stretched his legs, looking devastatingly male, a bright blue T-shirt tucked into the waistband of stylish jeans. Sarah found herself wondering if they buttoned or zipped, then turned away, embarrassed by the provocative thought.

''I'm sorry,'' he said. ''I didn't know that you weren't supposed to talk about them at night.''

Sarah turned back. Because he was glancing around as though invisible beings might be watching him, she smiled. Her mother would have adored him.

''It's okay. Like you said, you didn't know.'' She sipped her tea, savoring the mint. ''But traditional Cherokees don't describe them as being magical or supernatural. Spiritual beings are a part of their everyday world.''

''Really?'' His expression turned thoughtful. ''To me, it all seems like magic. Everything about the Cherokee is so beautiful, so wondrous.''

Oh, yes, she decided. Her mother would have adored this man.

They both fell silent, companionable quiet between them. Tonight she couldn't fault him for wanting to know about his heritage.

He placed his cup on the coffee table and rolled his shoulders. The movement rippled his T-shirt. Sarah couldn't help herself. Her roving eyes strayed to his jeans again. ''Do you plan on having kids someday?'' he asked.

She chewed her bottom lip. The question didn't seem out of place, not when they had just tucked two little girls into bed. ''I'm not sure. I adore children, but marriage has never really been a conscious thought.'' At least not until now, she realized, wondering what sort of husband Adam would make. Sarah had abandoned her girlish dreams long ago, but Adam was renewing a part of her that ached for the past. The happy times, the years she believed in love.

How had she gotten so cynical? So grown-up and jaded?

Adam shifted in his seat, drawing her attention back to him. ''I want as many children as my wife is willing to give me,'' he said. ''And that's one of the reasons I'm determined to find my biological parents. They're part of who I am, a legacy I can pass on to my kids.''

''What about your adoptive family? That doesn't seem fair to them. They're the ones who raised you.''

''Having a relationship with my biological parents won't diminish the memory of my adoptive parents. I intend to tell my children about them. I have photo albums filled with pictures.'' His voice turned quiet. ''It hurts that they didn't tell me the truth about the adoption, but I still love them.''

As a wave of sudden sadness drifted through the room, Sarah brushed his hand, offering comfort. He glanced out the window at the darkness outside, and her heart went out to him—this tall, handsome man who was all alone in the world. Sarah was alone, too, but she had made the choice consciously.

His childhood had been so normal, she thought. So different from hers. And Adam's parents had never meant to hurt him. They had wanted him for their son. To Sarah, adopting someone else's child was a loving, caring act.

''Have you ever been in a relationship serious enough to consider marriage?'' she asked.

''No. I've been in a couple of fairly serious relationships

before, but I've haven't met anyone I considered spending the rest of my life with.'' He smiled a little. ''I've never been in love, but I'm sure I'll know when it happens. I'll know who the right woman is.'' He paused, trapped her gaze. ''What about you, sweet Sarah? Ever lost your heart?''

''No.'' She shook her head, fearful she could be losing it now. Everything about Adam seemed so right.

A Cherokee knight. A dragon slayer.

Breaking eye contact, she rose. She was falling into the fairy tale she had created, and she had to stop herself from tumbling too far. ''I should get ready for bed. The girls will probably be up early.'' And she couldn't spend the rest of the evening imagining what kind of husband Adam would make. ''I'll bring you a sheet and a blanket for the couch.''

''I need a pillow, too.''

She went down the hall, and when she returned with the bedding, she noticed he had cleared their tea cups from the coffee table. He stood beside the sofa, in his stylish T-shirt and jeans. His thumbs were hooked in his pockets—a stance that made the female in her take notice.

She placed the bundle on the couch.

''Thanks.'' He smiled at her, something he did far too often. ''I'm going to shower, then watch TV for a while. I'll keep it low so it doesn't bother you.''

''I'm a heavy sleeper,'' she said, disturbed by the image her mind had conjured. Adam taking a shower in one bathroom while she bathed in another. They would be naked at the same time, in the house. A flush of heat crept up her neck.

She lifted her hand, felt the fire spread. The image wouldn't go away. In her mind's eye she saw him—his athletic body glistening with water, that long brown hair loose and wet.

It was time to end this, cool her skin, bid him a proper, if not impersonal, good-night. But just as she prepared her escape, he said her name in a voice as smooth and rich as cream.

''Sarah. Sweet Sarah.''

She didn't move, not a single muscle. Her feet froze to the floor.

He took a step toward her. "We still haven't talked about what happened earlier."

For a moment, she feared she would do something humiliating, like faint. She couldn't seem to catch her breath, get enough oxygen to her brain. He expected her to talk about the way they had kissed that afternoon, rubbed and caressed through their clothes?

"We're just friends." The statement sounded foolish, even to her own ears.

He glanced up at the ceiling as though collecting his thoughts. When he brought his gaze back to hers, his eyes were intense, hypnotic. "I keep telling myself that very same thing. We're just friends. There's nothing happening between us." He laughed a little, a rough, textured sound that faded as quickly as it came on. "That's a lie, at least for me. I can't help myself. I want you. And I can't pretend that I don't." He moved closer, enough to put them inches apart. "I even fantasize about you wearing that red dress, the one with the dragon on it. Only you're naked under it. Naked just for me." He touched her cheek, then drew back. "You're my midnight seduction, sweet Sarah."

Her heart thumped wildly. She wanted to kiss him, seduce him, feel the dragon branding her skin. Mist and moonlight, she thought. Fairy tales and fantasies. God help her. She craved all of that and more.

Nerves tangled in her stomach, coiled then twisted into chains. Should she tell him that she was a virgin? That her experiences were limited? Would it shock him? Make him view her differently?

"I want you, too," was all she could manage to say before she turned and walked away, her lungs fighting for air.

When she reached the master bedroom, she sat on the edge of the bed, her legs wobbly. She had left the door open, and a short time later, she heard water running down the hall. Adam was taking a shower.

Sarah stood and closed the door, imagining what it would feel like to slip into the tiny stall with him, slide her hands all over that strong, muscular body. Live out her erotic fantasy.

She began to remove her clothes, but as she picked up her robe, she headed for the bathroom just a few feet away.

Wanting Adam didn't mean she had the courage to take him.

Adam squinted into the morning light. It blasted through the window, drenching him in its blinding glow. He had left the drapes open last night. Mostly because he hadn't slept well and the moon and stars had seemed like good company.

He didn't need to analyze his restless night. He knew the cause. Sarah—sweet, sweet Sarah. Her erotic admission still played in his mind.

I want you, too.

Last night had been torture. His mouth had all but watered, hungry for the taste of a dark-eyed, dark-haired woman. His midnight fantasy. His lust-driven seduction.

Rubbing his eyes, he rose and began to fold the sheet. The blanket came next, and when they were both stacked neatly on the sofa, he headed for the bathroom, an overnight bag in hand. Sarah and the girls were still asleep, but he assumed they would awaken soon, which meant he should brush his teeth, wash his face and comb his tousled hair. He looked like a man who had been up most of the night. Shaving would help, too, he supposed. He pulled his hand across his chin, felt the roughness. His beard stubble wasn't heavy, but it was still there, peppering his jaw.

Adam went through his grooming routine, aware of every move, his muscles rolling and bunching. He still felt a tingle of eroticism, and he was doing his damnedest to shake it. There were children in the house, and that made him guilty as hell. How did parents do it? he wondered. How did they lust after each other when their kids were stumbling out of bed, pajamas rumpled, security blankets and stuffed animals trailing behind them?

Adam left the bathroom, his hair slicked back and banded into its usual ponytail, a cotton shirt tucked into a pair of loose, comfortable khakis. Maybe some cartoons would knock the heat out of him. He would turn on the TV and wait for the kids.

He didn't wait long. They came into the living room just as he had pictured them, rumpled and sleepy-eyed. Curls sprang from Dawn's head, like the spiral noodles his mother used to smother in red sauce. On the child's feet were slippers that sported tiny pink pompoms.

Spotting him, she grinned and wiggled her nose, sending freckles dancing across a pixie face.

"Hey, pumpkin," he said. "How are you?"

"Good, but there's something important I have to say." She moved closer, taking each step with caution. "It's daytime now, so it's okay to talk about the Little People, right?"

He nodded, grateful the child had taken Sarah's warning seriously. Adam wasn't one to dismiss ancient beliefs.

"The Little People sneaked into our room last night," Dawn announced quietly.

He couldn't help but smile. "Really?"

"Uh-huh." As she bobbed her head, noodles bounced in disarray. "But I didn't hear 'em 'cause I was asleep."

Adam looked past her, catching Mandy's gaze. The eight-year-old stood back, watching him through intense blue eyes. He was used to women getting spongy over him, but not young girls. It was, he decided, a responsibility he couldn't ignore. Innocent hearts broke much too easily.

"Did you hear the Little People?" he asked her, hoping she would say yes, treat her baby sister to a thrill. Dawn's heart was innocent, too.

"Of course not."

Adam withheld a frown. Mandy was shy and pretty and much too self-conscious. She needed to believe in magic and legends and spiritual beings. Last night he had convinced her that the Little People might exist, but apparently this morning she felt foolish about the whole thing.

"Just because you didn't hear them doesn't mean they weren't there," Dawn said, eager for her sister to verify her story.

Mandy spared the younger girl a tolerant glance, but when Dawn's eyes began to water, the tolerant look turned sisterly.

"I suppose they could have climbed up the balcony," she relinquished. "And the neighbors wouldn't have seen them if they were invisible."

Bouncing, Dawn said, "I knew it! I just knew they sneaked in."

Adam thanked Mandy with a pleased smile. She blushed something fierce, but returned his smile with one of her own.

He watched cartoons with the girls, feeling calm and fatherly. But the moment Sarah came into the room, his nervous system went haywire. His mouth was suddenly dry, his heart beat faster, his palms turned clammy, uncharacteristic reactions he couldn't seem to stop.

Her hair was freshly washed, long and damp and fragrant. He could actually smell her shampoo, or at least he thought he did. His imagination may have conjured the botanical perfume.

Dawn greeted Sarah enthusiastically, recounting the tale about the Little People sneaking into the house last night.

"Even Mandy says so," the younger girl proclaimed.

Sarah smiled, and Adam studied Mandy's reaction. The older girl didn't say much, but she watched Sarah through those young, serious eyes. It was obvious that the child admired the Cherokee woman, maybe even imagined herself growing up to be like her.

There were already similarities, he thought. Not in their appearance, but in the way they moved, talked, kept themselves distanced from others. They were both beautiful, both mysterious and challenging.

Sarah had yet to glance his way. Last night she'd claimed she wanted him, but this morning she avoided his gaze. Years from now, Mandy would probably do the same thing to some smitten young man. Adam already sympathized with the guy.

"What should we have for breakfast?" Sarah asked the girls.

"Pancakes," came the joint reply.

Sarah tossed that luxurious damp hair behind her and rolled

up her sleeves. She wore no makeup and plain clothes, but to Adam, she could have been a barefoot siren—a beguiling forest nymph with copper skin and exotic eyes.

She finally looked up and met his gaze. "Good morning," she said.

The simple greeting hit him square in the solar plexus. He nearly lost his next breath, then cursed himself for wanting her so badly.

"Do you need some help with breakfast?" he asked.

"Sure."

Her tone sounded casual, but he sensed a flutter of nervousness behind it. Good, he thought. He wasn't the only one suffering, feeling awkward and unsteady.

The girls remained in front of the TV, and Adam and Sarah headed for the kitchen. Their baby-sitting duties wouldn't end until this evening, so they still had hours and hours to go. Adam decided he'd better get used to the sensation humming between them, the erotic vibration that had become thick and much too tangible.

She rummaged through the cabinet, found a box of instant pancake mix, then began searching for something else.

"I can't reach it," she said, indicating a mixing bowl on a high shelf.

Adam moved in beside her and retrieved the bowl. It hadn't been his imagination. Her hair was gloriously fragrant, a blend of cloves and carnations. No wonder she teased his libido. Carnations were a known aphrodisiac—a sweet, spicy flower that increased sexual desire.

I'm doomed, he thought, wishing he could pull her into his arms, tangle his hands in her hair, kiss her until they both gasped for air.

"Will you dice some fruit?" she asked.

"Adam?" she asked when he didn't respond.

"Yeah?"

"Would you rather make the pancakes?"

He stepped back, away from her. "No. I'll dice the fruit." He didn't have the slightest idea how to make pancakes, and now wasn't the time to learn.

Wielding a paring knife, he set about his task. And although he told himself to ignore her, he kept stealing glances. Every so often she stole glances at him, too—those dark eyes catching his for an instant, as quick and jumpy as his heartbeat.

She mixed the pancake batter with a brisk motion, but when she stopped to taste it, to lift a dripping dollop to her mouth, a white-hot flame ignited in his belly.

I've got it bad, he thought, deliberately shifting his gaze to the cutting board.

He focused on the fruit, on the apples and bananas and summer peaches. He wasn't a teenager saddled with raging hormones. He was a twenty-nine-year-old, a grown man capable of controlling primal urges.

Satisfied he had won that battle, Adam peeled an orange, his hands deft and steady. Much more relaxed, he took a deep breath, let it out slowly. The mental reminder that he was pushing thirty seemed to do the trick.

The patter of little feet caught his attention. Dawn skipped into the kitchen, red curls bouncing to keep up. He glanced down at her slippers and smiled. The pompoms danced, too.

Little girls. Daughters. He wanted a house full.

"Are the pancakes ready?" the child asked.

"Just about, sweetie," Sarah said. "Why don't you and your sister set the table?"

Suddenly the morning turned noisy and chaotic, with silverware clanking and young voices chattering. Sarah flipped pancakes while Adam poured glasses of milk and served fresh fruit.

They ate in the dining room, cartoons flickering in the background. Adam looked across the cluttered table at Sarah. Her hair had begun to dry to a glossy black sheen, as soft and elusive as a raven's wing.

The feeling that rushed his system wasn't lust. It was something more akin to romance, to family. He wondered what it would be like to make a life with her, to brush her lips tenderly, to watch her tummy swell with his child.

Soon, Adam thought, as guilt consumed him, soon he would have to tell Sarah the truth about his past. He couldn't keep deceiving a woman whose father was an alcoholic.

A woman who had managed to become his obsession.

Six

Vicki returned a little after 9:00 p.m., looking like a travel-worn businesswoman in a navy-blue suit and silk blouse. Her curly red hair was coiled into a tidy French twist, but pale shadows dogged her eyes.

''How was the seminar?'' Sarah asked.

Vicki plopped down on the couch and sighed. ''Good. Long. I'm glad I was only scheduled for one day.''

Sarah sat beside her. ''The girls are asleep already.''

The other woman slipped off her pumps. ''I hope they didn't give you any trouble.''

''They were perfect angels.'' This came from Adam, who stood in the living room a little awkwardly.

Sarah knew the feeling. Since the children had gone to bed, she and Adam didn't know what to do with themselves, where to focus their gazes, what to talk about.

Vicki looked up at Adam and smiled. ''Thank you. That's just what a mother wants to hear.''

''No problem. It's the truth.'' He shifted his stance, smiled back at her. "Do you have any more luggage in the car? I'd be glad to get it for you."

"No, but thanks." She pointed to a leather satchel. "That was it."

"Okay, well..." He smoothed the front of his hair, pulling his hand toward his ponytail. "I should get going." Vicki started to rise, but he held her off. "No need to walk me to the door."

"Thank you so much for helping out," she said. "I owe you one."

He reached for his overnight bag. "No you don't. Just give the girls a hug from me in the morning."

"Will do."

He nodded to the redhead, then turned his gaze to Sarah. "Bye," he said, his eyes locking intimately with hers.

She brushed imaginary lint from her pants, felt her heartbeat skip and stumble. Why did she have to lose her breath every time he looked at her? Why couldn't she remain cool and calm, sophisticated like most California women?

"Bye, Adam." She gave him a shaky smile.

"Yeah. See you." He headed for the door, opened it, then closed it quietly behind him.

Sarah found the breath she had lost, let it fill her lungs. She waited a few minutes, giving Adam time to make it to his Jeep. She wanted to be sure he was he gone before she started down the steps to her own apartment.

Glancing at her watch, she checked the time, watching the second hand make its hasty sweep. "I should get going, too. Give you a chance to relax."

"Oh, no you don't." Vicki placed a firm hand on her knee, holding her in place. "You're not going anywhere until you tell me what's going on between you two."

"Going on?" She shrugged, tried to make light of her attraction to Adam. "Nothing's going on. We're just friends."

"Right." The other woman struck an austere pose. "And I'm the Queen of England. Come on, girl, 'fess up. If Adam had stayed much longer, the windows would have fogged. I know sexual tension when I see it."

Sexual tension. Even the phrase made Sarah warm. Excited. Confused. Her emotions swirled around the room, closing the walls, boxing her in. "Do you think we could step outside? Maybe have this chat on the balcony?" She needed air, a cool evening breeze to take away the heat.

"Sure." Vicki popped up, grinned and began pulling pins out of her hair, dislodging the professional twist. "Go take a seat out there, and I'll meet you in a minute. I've got to get out of these clothes."

Vicki went to her bedroom, and Sarah opened the drapes and walked onto the balcony. Standing near the rail, she gazed out at the city. The San Fernando Valley looked pretty from above, lights twinkling as far as the eye could see.

Which light was Adam's? she wondered. Was he home yet? Feeding the cats that purred at his feet?

Sarah closed her eyes and felt the wind touch her face—softly, ever so softly, like a lover's tender kiss. The air was cool but the heat remained. It was inside her, warming her blood, igniting her cells, making her think of him.

She opened her eyes and moved away from the rail. Sitting in a patio chair by a tiny glass table, she waited for Vicki to join her. Maybe talking about her feelings would help.

The other woman came onto the balcony wearing jeans and an oversize T-shirt. She sat in the other chair and drew her knees up, curls rioting around her face. She cocked her head, sent Sarah a woman-to-woman smile. "Well?"

"Adam said that he wanted me," she admitted, frowning a little.

"And that's bad?"

"No, not really. I mean, I told him that I wanted him, too."

"So, why were you two acting so strange? Sounds to me like you got it out in the open."

"It was awkward." Sarah turned to study the city lights, watch them sparkle against the night. "But that was my fault. I could barely look at him the next day. I've never said anything like that to someone before."

"You're kidding, right?"

"No." She turned back. "He's the first man I've wanted that badly. I'm still a virgin, Vicki."

"Oh, my." The redhead blinked, pushed a mass of curls away from her eyes. "That's not what I expected to hear. Most women your age..." Her words trailed, then resumed with an obvious question. "What made you wait so long?"

"My traditional upbringing. My mother had this long talk with me about saving myself for the right man."

"And you think Adam might be the one?"

"Yes, but there's more to it. Part of the reason I waited so long was to avoid an attachment." And now her heart was betraying her. She knew men weren't always what they appeared to be, yet Adam seemed so perfect. So gallant. So noble. "I want him, Vicki, but I'm afraid of taking that first step." Because once she did, there would be no turning back.

The redhead squinted. "Your virginity shouldn't be an issue, Sarah. First time or not, there's still the possibility of an attachment. Most women don't have sex for the sake of entertainment. It means something to us."

"You think I waited too long?"

"No, but you can't protect your heart forever. Eventually you have to take a chance. If you don't, you'll be alone for the rest of your life."

She let out the breath she'd been holding. "Deep down I know you're right, but I'm still confused."

"So what are you going to do?"

Suddenly pensive, Sarah glanced up at the sky. The moon was nearly full, a silver ball lighting up the valley. "I don't know," she said, wondering how it would feel to give herself to Adam, to feel his weight against her body, to lift her hips and take him deep inside.

"I just don't know," she said again, her voice blending quietly into the night.

Sarah entered her apartment, grateful she had left a low light burning. Looking around, she wished she had a companion, a cat maybe, a frisky little creature that would be happy to see her. As it was, her home seemed much too quiet.

Unsure of what to do with herself, she turned on the TV for background noise and unbuttoned her blouse. A long, soothing bath was her remedy for just about everything, including bouts of loneliness. The scent of the body oil she favored combined with a tub of warm water usually managed to lull her into a peaceful kind of solitude.

Sarah filled the tub and removed the rest of her clothing. Standing in front of the mirror, she pinned her hair up. With a sigh, she immersed herself in water.

And thought about Adam.

As she slid the washcloth over her body, she imagined his hands—those long, masculine fingers—caressing, touching her in erotic places. Her breasts, her belly, between her thighs. She imagined him leaning over her, their lips meeting, tasting—the kiss openmouthed and carnal.

Tender. Passionate.

Rising a short time later, she reached for a towel and wrapped it around herself. For a reason she couldn't quite explain, she didn't dry her body. Instead she went into her bedroom and sat on the edge of the bed.

Maybe she wanted the air to dry her skin, absorb the heat she was feeling. Sarah tilted her head, pushed away a strand of hair falling onto her shoulder.

Her closet door was open, displaying a simple wardrobe—A-line dresses, functional blouses, serviceable slacks. White, beige, a touch of mint green, a scatter of denim.

The red serpent stood out like a neon sign. Like cherries in the snow. Sex with a long, lean warrior—a dragon slayer.

Striking. Mouthwatering. Forbidden.

He wanted her to seduce him. But could she? And if she did, would she lose her heart? Would she look into his eyes and see her future?

Maybe, but it didn't matter, because Vicki was right. Sarah couldn't hide from attachments for the rest of her life. And Adam wouldn't hurt her. He was kind and decent and strong, a man who respected women, who wanted a family someday.

And wasn't that what her mother had meant by the right man? Adam had all the old-fashioned qualities Sarah admired.

Yes, she thought. She was going to make love. Tonight. With Adam.

With shaky hands, she dried her damp skin and reached for the dress. This wasn't a mistake, she assured herself, taking a deep, cleansing breath. She wasn't a Victorian virgin, nor was she naive. She had lived a cautious life, judging men with a keen, realistic eye.

Unzipping the dress, she stepped into it, allowing the satin to slide over bare flesh. Her hair came next. She released the pins and brushed it to a glossy sheen. It fell to her waist in a heavy blue-black curtain.

Because she wasn't overly skilled at applying cosmetics, she added subtle touches, hoping to soften strong Cherokee features. A coat of mascara lengthened her lashes and a copper-colored blush, flecked with a shimmering powder, highlighted her cheeks. On her mouth, she wore a natural infusion of Jamaica flowers, rosewater and cocoa butter. Sarah smiled. The ruby stain felt as sinful as being naked under a satin dress.

She dumped the contents of her purse onto the bed and placed her wallet and keys into a gold mesh bag. On her feet she wore gold sandals. Both were simple summer items, but tonight they looked exotic.

Reaching behind her, she realized she hadn't finished zipping the dress or latching the tiny hooks. Fumbling, she gave up. She was going to remove the garment anyway.

To keep herself calm, she sucked on a fruit-flavored candy and breathed a gust of sweetened air.

Cherries in the snow. The image came back like a sleek, sensual temptation. She couldn't turn back now. She wanted him far too much.

Arriving at Adam's house, she parked and sat behind the wheel for a long, drawn-out moment. The tree-lined street was quiet, the nearly full moon shining high in the sky.

Finally she went to his front door and rang the bell, convincing herself there was nothing to be nervous about.

He didn't answer right away, but when he did, her heart leaped for her throat. His hair was loose, his chest bare. And on his hips, a pair of drawstring pajama bottoms rode just below his navel.

Instantly she knew she had gotten him out of bed.

He pushed a stray lock of hair away from his face. She couldn't have imagined his hair more beautiful than it was. Rich and brown, it fell to his shoulders, as smooth and touchable as mink. Suddenly she became overly aware of being naked under the form-fitting dress.

"Sarah." He stared at her. "I can't believe you're here."

When he stepped away from the door in a silent invitation, she entered the house and stood near a wall, unsure of how to proceed.

A cat circled her feet, rubbing its sleek fur against her legs. It was the mama cat, she realized. The white one expecting a litter.

Sarah didn't move, and neither did Adam.

"You look incredible," he said.

"Thank you."

A breeze swept through the room, and she saw that the windows were open, white sheers billowing like a seductive ghost. The house was quiet, with shadows streaking across hardwood floors. The area rug in front of a tiny gas fireplace presented a wash of pale color in the dim light.

"I've never done this before," she said.

"Gone to a man's house in the middle of the night?"

"Yes. No. I was talking about sex."

He came toward her and stopped when they were inches apart, his gaze riveted to hers. "This will be your first time?"

She nodded. "Are you surprised?"

"Yes." He lifted a hand, brushed her cheek. "But—" He paused, and then frowned a little.

Nervous, she studied his troubled expression. Was he going to refuse to be with her? Send her away? "Is that a problem?"

"No. I'm honored, sweet Sarah, that you want it to be me. But I—"

"Shhh." She pressed a finger to his lips, warmed by his concern. Even though Sarah told herself the old ways no longer mattered, virginity was revered in her culture. A traditional Cherokee man would consider her offering a gift.

They were almost touching, the space between them filled by the mewling cat. "I'm naked underneath," she told him, her nipples grazing the satin. "This is your seduction, Adam." And his chivalry made it even more exciting. More meaningful.

His breath hitched, the pulse at his neck jumping. "Sarah—"

"Tell me about your fantasy. Tell me how this scene plays out."

He closed his eyes, opened them a second later. "I can't."

Because of her virginity, Sarah thought. And because he was struggling to control the primal urges she saw brewing in his eyes.

"Then do it, Adam. Make it happen."

That seemed to be more than he could bear. Pushing the dress from her body, he let it slide to the floor. Cool air shocked her skin, and then his hands were on her, warm and erotic.

Slowly, ever so slowly, he backed her against the wall, and an immediate thrill, an inexperienced fear rushed through her. She could feel his sex, hard and heavy, through the lightweight sleepwear.

The cat had vanished, so she knew the purring she heard was rising from her own throat.

Sarah couldn't describe the sensation of being pinned against a wall, his mouth holding her captive, sucking gloriously on an aching nipple.

Reaching into his hair, she grabbed hold.

He kept moving lower, that determined, wet tongue sliding over bare skin. When he dropped to his knees and looked up at her, she touched his cheek.

There was no time to be shy, to glance away timidly. He told her to watch, and she did, her gaze fixed on his handsome face.

He loved her, deeply, thoroughly, allowing her to feel like

a woman—a twenty-four-year-old seductress. Beautiful, cherished, lusted after.

She climaxed against his mouth, shattered like glass—edgy, sexy shards of colored glass. She didn't care if she was coming apart, losing pieces of herself, because soon the glass melted into wet, syrupy waves.

Sarah rode the current, the world spinning around her. And when it ended, all she could do was tremble and whisper his name.

Adam rose to his feet and held her next to his beating heart. She buried her face against his neck, felt the warmth of his skin, the silky length of his hair.

"Lie down with me," he said.

She accepted his hand, and he led her to his unmade bed.

Everything, including the summer air, seemed fresh and crisp. A cool, herbal scent drifted in from the garden. Even his sheets smelled like the wind, the grass and the trees. Or maybe it was him—this natural healer with magic in his touch.

His kiss felt like enchantment, a sensual bewitching. And his body…

She roamed his chest, sliding her hands over muscle and sinew. Catching the drawstring on his pajama bottoms, she tugged. He accommodated her, shifting his hips as she removed the cotton barrier. And when he was naked, she slid her hand between his thighs.

The sound he made, the rough vulnerability, the catch in his breath, gave her power. He was battling to hold on, struggling not to plunge into her hard and deep. His blood was swimming, she thought. Pulsing through his veins in fiery bursts.

"Adam?"

"Not yet," he said. "Not this fast."

She looked up and met his gaze, and what she saw melted her.

Tenderness. So much tenderness.

"I don't want to hurt you," he said.

"You won't."

He settled his long, fluid body next to hers. Sarah studied the emotion on his face, knowing she couldn't stop the need between them, the closeness, the attachment.

"I'm so glad I waited," she said, sighing when he skimmed her cheek. He looked strong and virile, a dragon slayer with a kind and tender heart.

A man capable of capturing a woman's lonely soul.

Seven

Adam inhaled the fragrance of her skin, her hair, the scent of woman and flowers, the sweet, spicy aphrodisiac that made his blood tingle.

He slid his hands over her waist, down the curve of her hips. And then he closed his eyes, his conscience troubling him once again. How could he do this? How could he make love to her without telling her the truth?

Adam opened his eyes and saw her looking up at him. Because this mattered, he thought, brushing her lips in a tender kiss. This moment, this feeling. She had offered him a gift—a sweet, beautiful seduction. And he couldn't stop the passion, the need building between them.

Sarah arched her back, and he tongued her nipple. Her breasts were small and round, sweetly inviting. The darkness of her areolas fascinated him, the color deep and rich, like red earth touched by the sun.

She caressed him, too. Ran her palms over his shoulders, across his back, pulling him closer. Craving more, he pressed his belly to hers, felt that smooth, slick rush of flesh against flesh, limb against limb.

Adam straddled her, and she looked up at him. With silent anticipation, they watched each other, hearts pounding. Reaching into the night stand, he removed a foil packet.

She helped him put the condom on, their fingers brushing.

"Take me inside," he whispered when they were safe.

She stroked his face, lifted her hips and welcomed him.

Heat, moisture—that feminine tightness that made men crave this incredible feeling poured over him. And then there was resistance, just a little, just enough to remind him that he was her first.

He paused, lowered himself to nuzzle her cheek and pushed deeper. She turned her head and kissed him, took his tongue as he took her virginity.

Expecting her to tense or gasp in pain, he stopped and waited, giving her time to adjust to the hardness, the heaviness, the discomfort he assumed she would feel.

They weren't kissing anymore. They were staring into each other's eyes, their bodies joined in stillness.

It was, Adam thought, the most intimate moment of his life.

"It doesn't hurt," she said, a smile playing on her gorgeous mouth. "It feels good."

That smile, those ruby-stained lips, were nearly his undoing. He pushed himself deeper and rocked their bodies, making them both warm, wet and wondrous.

A mild breeze blew over the bed and stirred earthy scents throughout the room. Her skin was scented, too. And her hair, the flowing curtain of Cherokee hair. The unmistakable blend of cloves and carnations rose from it, seducing him.

Sweet, sweet Sarah. He couldn't get enough. Not nearly enough.

He could feel her desire, feel it building and swaying, turning into hot, fresh need. It flashed through him like lightning, a bolt as electrifying as a frayed wire.

They kissed. They danced. They made love. She moved

with him, stroke for stroke, finding his rhythm, becoming one with him.

He thought he heard her gasp, thought she was climaxing when the first shudder hit him. But he couldn't be sure. He was too far gone, steeped much too deeply in Sarah and sex. Her legs were wrapped so tightly around him, he couldn't think, couldn't focus on anything but the intensity of his release.

Afterward, he fell into her arms, and she stroked his sweat-slicked back and held him. Neither spoke, but their bodies were still joined, so words didn't seem necessary.

Adam closed his eyes. The moment drifted like the wind, as fresh and serene as the evening air. Flowers bloomed in her scent, in her long, silky hair. He turned his head and kissed her neck, deciding he could sleep there, his body buried deep within hers.

She shifted beneath him, and he lifted his head to look at her.

With her ebony hair spilling over the pillow, and her eyes as dark as the night, he thought she was the most beautiful woman in the world. And tonight she was his.

His lover. His lady.

She shifted again, so he released her from his weight, already missing the intimacy. Climbing out of bed, he headed to the adjoining bathroom. He removed the protection and discarded it, thinking condoms were a necessary nuisance. After cleaning himself, he brought Sarah a fresh washcloth, dampened with warm water.

"I thought you might need this." He knew there were spots of blood on the sheets, possibly a little on her inner thighs.

"Thank you."

He crawled back into bed beside her, and because she held the washcloth as though embarrassed to use it in front of him, he took it from her and slid it between her legs, dabbing gently.

"Are you sore?" he asked.

"No, not really. But that still feels good. Soothing."

Adam liked the idea that he was her first. He supposed it

was a macho way to feel, but it made his past seem cleaner somehow.

His past. His deception. He had to tell her.

"May I use your bathroom?"

He blinked, tried not to frown. "Of course."

She rose, taking the damp cloth with her. He couldn't tell her now, not on the heels of lovemaking. Adam gave in to the frown. So when? When would he bare his guilty soul?

A few minutes later, Sarah returned, a towel covering her nakedness. She sat on the edge of the bed, jet-black hair spilling down her back. In the morning, he decided. He would tell her in the morning.

He touched her shoulder. "Will you stay the night?"

"I can't." She turned to look at him. "I didn't bring anything with me."

"Like what?"

She laughed a little. "Pajamas, a toothbrush. You know, things a person might need."

"I have one of those travel toothbrushes that's never been opened. You can use that. And you can sleep in one of my pajama tops. I only wear the bottoms anyway."

Color rose to her cheeks. "What about underwear?"

He managed a lopsided grin. "Boxers?"

She returned his humored smile. "Okay."

He provided the necessary items, and she dressed in front of him, looking a little shy. They climbed into bed and cuddled, the way new lovers often did.

And when she fell asleep in his arms, Adam closed his eyes and inhaled the fragrance of her skin, wishing morning would never come.

The light of dawn was gray, dim and shadowy, like a poltergeist peeking through the curtains. Adam had already showered, dressed and brushed his teeth, but Sarah looked beautifully rumpled. The sheets were tangled around her legs, and her hair spilled over the pillowcase like rain.

He stood beside the bed, too guilty to give her an impulsive kiss, a good-morning nuzzle.

She squinted and sat up. "I can't believe I have to work today."

"I know. Me, too. But we have plenty of time for tea. Breakfast, too, if you're hungry." Although he couldn't possibly eat, depriving her of food didn't seem fair.

"Tea's fine."

"Then go ahead and freshen up, and I'll make it."

"Thanks." She sent him a sleepy smile. "Do you have some sweats or something I could borrow? I hate to wear that dress home."

"Sure." He pointed to the chest of drawers. "Just help yourself." A more experienced woman would have prepared herself for an overnight seduction. She would have brought a change of clothes, undergarments, toiletries.

Adam left Sarah alone and headed for the kitchen. After selecting a lemongrass tea, he tore several mint leaves from a windowsill plant, then set the water on to boil.

When she entered the room twenty minutes later, a fragrant brew steeped in the dragon teapot. On this gloomy morning, he'd decided to make use of the souvenir she'd chosen for him.

He stood at the counter, and she came up behind him and put her arms around his waist. Turning, he gave into the need to hold her, hugging her close.

Maybe she wouldn't react as strongly as he feared. Maybe he was worrying for nothing.

They separated, and she poured her tea and reached for the honey. He watched, taking note of how much sweetener she used. Suddenly her habits mattered, little things couples learned about each other.

She wore a pair of his sweatpants and a plain white T-shirt. The gray pants were rolled at the waist, and her budding nipples were slightly visible through the thin shirt. She had never looked prettier.

Adam led her to the living room, and they sat on a leather sofa the cats had clawed. He glanced up at the scratching post and saw Cameo sleeping in one of the cubbyholes. Darrin snoozed nearby, and Samantha and Tabitha were curled in a chair by the fireplace. No one seemed to mind that a woman was occupying his time, but maybe they sensed how special she was. The last woman Adam dated hadn't been partial to cats.

"What are you thinking about?" she asked.

"How much I like you." And how much he hated to spoil the companionable quiet between them. "Sarah, there's something I need to tell you."

She leaned forward. "You look so serious."

"It's a serious subject." He placed his cup on the coffee table, forming the dreaded words. "I used to have a drinking problem. Years ago, when I was a teenager."

Stunned, Sarah felt as if she'd been kicked. In the heart. With steeled-toed boots. The pain was so fierce she had to catch her breath. She'd trusted this man. This noble, kind, perfect...fraud. "A drinking problem? What's that? A sugar-coated way of saying you're an alcoholic?"

"I've been sober for eleven years."

Somehow that didn't matter right now. What mattered was that she had become emotionally and physically involved with a man who had the same disease as her father. "How convenient that you waited until *after* I slept with you to tell me."

"I tried to tell you last night. That's why I hesitated, that's why—"

"Damn you." She gripped the armrest. Even his chivalry was fake. Somehow that hurt even more. "You had plenty of opportunities to come clean, long before last night." She had confided in Adam, told him things about her childhood she had never admitted to anyone. And he had listened, never saying a word.

"I'm so sorry." He reached for his cup, set it back down again. "I couldn't bear to spoil what was happening between us, and I was afraid you would overreact. I'm not like your dad, Sarah. I'm sober, and I don't have the slightest desire to drink. It was just something associated with my youth."

And he was in denial if he thought he was immune, that it could never strike him again. "The trigger could be out there,

Adam. A reason, an excuse, that would make you want to drink again.''

''No way. It's not like that with me. It was a teenage addiction.''

She couldn't believe she was having this conversation with a man she'd made love with. She wanted to cry, to call herself a fool and him a bastard. All the sensuality, the warmth, the closeness from last night felt like a slap in the face.

''I'm sorry,'' he said again. ''I've been so guilty about keeping this from you. To some degree, I understand what you went through with your dad. My parents had a hell of a time with me.''

One of the cats mewled and stretched, then found its way onto Adam's lap. He stroked its fur absently. Sarah watched him, blocking out images of his hands, those strong, skilled hands, caressing her body.

Unwilling to sit next to him, she took the chair opposite the couch.

''It started during my sophomore year,'' he said, as she shifted in her seat. ''We moved, so I had to switch schools.''

Sarah wanted to say she didn't care, but a part of her needed to hear the details, needed to hear him say them out loud. She couldn't walk away until she knew every last bit of the truth. He owed her that much.

He continued, frowning as he talked. ''It was a strange time for me. I had matured, you know, getting taller and broader. Better looking, I suppose, and girls at the new school noticed me.'' The cat slept on his lap, loyal and serene. ''Popular girls,'' he added. ''The really pretty ones the jocks usually claim.''

The betrayal stabbing Sarah's heart came back tenfold. Pretty girls. This wasn't what she wanted to hear. ''So how did that lead to drinking?''

''I got invited to the in-crowd parties, and I wanted to fit in. No one pressured me, but everyone else was doing it. And it felt good hanging out with the popular kids.''

''So you overindulged?''

''Yeah. And it was so unlike me, such a contradiction to

how I had been in the past. But I was overflowing with testosterone and going through a rebellious period. Suddenly I was tired of doing homework and abiding by my parents' rules."

Sarah couldn't relate. Her teenage years had been spent trying to keep her father from adding vodka to his orange juice in the morning and blubbering lame apologies at night. She had craved the normalcy Adam's parents had provided, the parental discipline that had been their right.

"At first I only drank on weekends," he said. "And I would come home after my mom and dad were already in bed."

She took a long, aching breath. "When did your parents figure out what was going on?"

"When it progressed. When I got caught swiping a pint of whiskey from a local market." He looked up from the cat. "My folks had been nagging me about my flippant attitude and the hours I was keeping, but they didn't know I was drinking before school." He rolled his shoulders, his voice tight. "But then I wasn't stumbling around drunk. Most of the time I was just catching a buzz to get through the day."

The image he'd painted made her ill, but she continued to listen.

"My parents threatened to send me away to one of those schools for troubled teens. But instead, I agreed to see a drug-and-alcohol counselor and participate in family therapy. I was sure I could con my way through that."

"And did you?"

"Not really, no. My counselor wasn't easily fooled. And by then, neither were my parents."

She thought about all the times her father had duped her. "I'm glad your mom and dad didn't let you take advantage of them."

"I know. But I did change. Eventually I sobered up for good, and I began looking forward to college, to making something of myself. Holistic medicine was a natural transition. I needed to live a clean life, and I was already experimenting with herbal remedies." He trapped her gaze. "I haven't taken a drink in over eleven years, Sarah. And I'll never go down that road again. I'm not a rebellious teenager anymore.''

How could he be so sure? Plenty of alcoholics went through long periods of sobriety. There was no guarantee.

''I have to go. I don't want to be late for work.'' She stood, wishing she wasn't wearing his clothes. She needed to wash his scent from her body, push away the lingering memory of his tenderness.

Once again, a man she cared about had taken advantage of her heart. Only this time, it wasn't her father. It was Adam Paige. Her supposed friend. Her handsome, attentive lover.

Five days passed, and Sarah insisted she didn't care. She hadn't contacted him, either. She didn't want a relationship with a man she couldn't trust. And it wasn't as if she was deliberately staying home, sitting by the phone. She rarely went out after work. She hadn't changed her schedule, intending to be available for another I've-been-sober-for-eleven-years apology from Adam.

Carrying her dinner into the living room, she picked up the remote control and turned on the TV. Since she couldn't concentrate on a program already in progress, she chose a music channel, hoping to immerse herself in pop tunes.

The moment she cut into her chicken, the phone rang. She stared at it, debating whether to answer it. When she finally placed her hand on the cradle, she decided that if it was Adam, she would tell him she was busy.

''Hello?''

''Sweet Sarah.''

The nickname caught her off guard, but she did her best to hold her ground. ''I wasn't expecting to hear from you. I was just getting ready to have dinner.''

''Oh. I'm sorry. I didn't mean to bother you. I just wanted to tell you that Cameo had her kittens. God, Sarah, they're so amazing.''

Once again, she was caught off guard. He sounded like a

proud papa, his husky voice filled with awe. "How many?" she asked.

"Eight. They kinda look like little rats at this point, but Cameo thinks they're pretty special."

And so did he. She suspected the cat had given birth in his room, maybe even on his bed. "Congratulations," she said.

"Thanks. Will you come by and see them?"

Suddenly, saying no didn't feel like an option. She wrapped her dinner in aluminum foil and slipped her feet into a pair of sandals. Who could refuse to visit a litter of kittens? Certainly not a woman whose empty apartment was crying out for a pet.

Adam answered the door with a cautious smile, and seeing him again set off a primitive reaction, tightening her nipples beneath a simple cotton bra. His hair was banded into a ponytail, and a blue T-shirt clung to his chest, but she knew what he looked like naked with his hair flowing over his shoulders.

"The kittens are in my room," he said.

In spite of their awkward reunion, Sarah melted. A wooden box sat in a secluded corner. But not just any box. This one had been customized with a nest of cloth strips and a makeshift curtain.

"I put this in the laundry room weeks ago, but Cameo wouldn't go near it until I moved it in here." They knelt in front of the box, and Adam opened the curtain a little more. "Sarah came to see your babies," he told the cat in a soft voice.

Cameo meowed in response, and Sarah peeked in. The new mother lay on her side, and the kittens either nursed or slept in a huddle. They came in a variety of colors, including black, white, gray and combinations thereof.

"Were they born today?"

He nodded. "I called you as soon as I knew they were all okay. I had to help a little. She had three of them so close together, that she seemed to be struggling to get to all of them in time. One of them didn't look like it was breathing, so I cleaned the membrane from its face and cut the cord." Adam sat back on his haunches. "I hated to intervene, but I didn't know what else to do. I was afraid she might reject it after that, but she didn't. She seemed grateful for the help."

"Then apparently you did the right thing. You know, I was thinking about getting a cat. A kitten." And now she wanted the one he had saved. "My house gets pretty quiet. I could use the company."

"That's great. I'd love for you to have one. In six weeks you can have the pick of the litter."

"Thank you."

So polite, she thought. So proper. His bed was a few feet away, but they were acting as though they hadn't made love, hadn't rubbed and kissed and put their hands all over each other.

"Do you want a male or a female?" he asked.

"I'm not sure," she said, wondering about the one he had saved. "I guess I can decide later."

"That's fine with me." He sent her a lopsided grin. "Because I don't have the slightest idea how to sex kittens. It's not real obvious, like with puppies."

"Or humans," she said, feeling warm.

"Yeah, them, too." His smile faded, and they stared at each other.

The secluded corner was much too confining. Their knees brushed, an innocent touch that had Sarah fumbling for something to say.

The windows were open, but nothing stirred. Nothing but the tender sounds coming from the nursery box. Kittens mewling and suckling.

"I should go," she finally managed, pulling herself to her feet.

He followed suit, but they didn't get far. They made it to the hallway before they stopped, their eyes drawn like magnets. When he moved closer, she had to tell herself to breathe.

"I thought about calling you so many times," he said, his voice tinged with emotion. "I wanted to go to your house, visit you at work. Tell you over and over again how sorry I am."

Her heart pummeled her chest. "Then why didn't you?"

"Because I was trying to give you some space."

There was less than an inch between them now, and the air she struggled to breathe was as thick and humid as a summer night. The hallway was dim and narrow, but suddenly it seemed like the most sexual place on earth. How could this be happening? How could she still be attracted to him?

"Don't ever deceive me again," she said.

"I won't."

He moistened his lips, and a shiver streaked down her spine.

"Sarah?"

"Yes?"

"Are we still friends?"

She knew she should say no. Erasing Adam from her life was the safe, sane thing to do, but she couldn't let him go. Not completely. "Yes."

"Thank you. That means a lot to me."

He skimmed her cheek, her jaw, the curve of her neck. They were close, so close their lips were nearly touching, nearly meeting in a kiss that would melt like honey and sizzle like fire.

Drawing strength from the ache in her chest, from the memory of being wounded, Sarah stepped back, away from Adam, away from the warmth, the heat, the sensuality of his caress.

No matter how much he stirred her blood, she couldn't take the chance of losing her heart, of letting him hurt her again. His past made him too much of a risk.

"We can be friends," she said. "But not lovers. What happened between us was a mistake."

No, it wasn't, Adam thought, as Sarah crossed her arms. Making love, holding each other, feeling warm and tender—that wasn't a mistake.

"I understand," he told her, knowing he couldn't push the issue. Sarah struggled with intimacy, and he had blown her trust by deceiving her. And now, he supposed, he seemed dangerous in her eyes. A Cherokee with a history of alcoholism. He had two major strikes against him, but damn it, he couldn't change his past or the Native blood running through his veins.

At least she had agreed to remain friends. Adam couldn't bear losing her for good. And if they spent enough time together, Sarah would see him for the true person he was. Wouldn't she?

"Do you want to cheat?" he asked.

"What?" She blinked, then stared at him with a confused expression.

"Cheat. You know, eat something sweet. I bought some chocolate eclairs yesterday."

"You did?" She tilted her head. "Why?"

"Just in case you decided to forgive me." And because he had fantasies about her mouth, about watching her eat something rich and creamy. He couldn't seem to get her out of his system, and his urges had been going from sinful to soft in a heartbeat.

Sex. Summer seductions. A house in the country. Dark-eyed, dark-haired babies.

All of it involved intimacy, and all of it involved making love with Sarah. The idea of needing her so badly scared him, but he couldn't let go. They deserved a chance to explore the emotions that had begun to unfold, the attachment that could make a difference in their lives.

He reached for her hand, breathed a sigh of relief when she didn't pull away. "So, are you up for a chocolate binge, sweet Sarah?"

She gave him a nervous smile. "I guess so. I mean, you already bought the eclairs. There's no point in letting them go to waste."

"Good." He led her to his kitchen, and when she stood near the window, he saw a beautiful, beguiling woman.

Her cheekbones caught the light, and her hair cascaded to her waist, as sleek and compelling as nightfall. Everything about her looked exotic, especially the shape of her eyes. They tilted at the corners, giving her a bewitching quality.

Yes, Adam thought. That was the description that fit the way he felt.

Sarah Cloud had bewitched him, lulled him into a quiet, confusing enchantment.

Eight

Sarah agreed to spend Sunday afternoon with Adam. It was their day off, and the sun shone bright and pretty. He hadn't told her what they'd be doing, but he'd said it would be a casual outing.

She sat across from him in his Jeep, the wind blowing through her hair. He drove like most Californians—fast and aggressive. There was a time when freeways made her nervous, but she had gotten used to the quick lane changes and congested traffic.

He exited on a winding off-ramp that took them into an area showcasing equestrian shops and exclusive ranch homes.

"Come on, Adam. Where exactly are we going?"

He stopped at a red light and grinned. "To look at the paint I'm going to buy."

"You ride?" She didn't know why that surprised her. He certainly looked the part with his sexy-fitting denims and golden skin.

"I've been riding since I was a kid," he said. "I had a

horse up until I got into trouble. And then, well, things sort of changed after that.''

With silent understanding, she nodded. His drinking had interfered with the simple pleasures of life. ''Where did you board your horse?'' she asked, knowing he had grown up in a suburban neighborhood.

''At a facility not far from here.''

''And is that where you're going to board this new horse?''

''Yep. For a while, anyway.'' He turned onto a street that led to the hills. ''Eventually I plan to buy my own place. As many acres as I can afford. I've always wanted to have horse property.''

They passed a fancy stylized home, displaying an attractive barn, a riding arena and a hot walker. Sarah raised her eyebrows. ''You don't plan on buying around here, do you?''

Her question made him laugh. ''Are you kidding? I have some money, but I'm not rich.'' Soon his laughter faded, his voice serious. ''I inherited a fair amount from my parents. But even with the investments I've made, it's not enough to buy a ranch in this area. We're talking millions to live here.''

A gust of warm air tousled Sarah's hair. She pushed the flyaway strands away from her face and reached for the bottled water they had brought along. ''Then where are you going to go?'' She knew there was more affordable acreage in California, even if most of it was desert.

He turned to look at her. ''I was thinking Oklahoma.''

A knot formed in her stomach. ''You've never even been there.''

He stopped in front of a large estate and killed the engine. ''I know, but it seems like the only thing I have, the place where I'm supposed to be. California hasn't felt like home for a long time, Sarah. I've stayed because I didn't know where else to go.''

''What about your job?''

''I can always find work. I'm good at what I do, and there are people who follow the holistic path everywhere. There has to be a clinic in Oklahoma that would hire me.'' He leaned his head against the seat. "I just don't think I can handle living in California much longer."

Not now that he knew he had been born in Tahlequah, she thought. Knew that he might have family in Oklahoma. "I guess taking that trip will help you decide."

"Yeah, especially if I find my mom." He skimmed her hand. "I wish you would agree to come with me. I don't want to go alone. I really need you there."

"I—" Panic welled in her chest, hard and fast and shaky. Her heartbeat stumbled and tripped, then bounced back with thundering beats. Going home scared her, and so did the fact that he had just told her that he needed her. "I can't think about this now."

"Okay." He turned to gaze out the window, his profile strong and strikingly chiseled. "It's still over a month away. I won't push you."

Because her heart was still thundering, she drank small sips of water, battling jittery nerves. "Why are we parked here? Is this where your new horse is?"

He nodded. "I gave the current owner a deposit."

"So you're paying off the balance today?"

"Yep."

He turned toward her, and she wondered if he would actually find his mother in Oklahoma. And if he did, would he discover that his alcoholism was genetic?

They exited the car and headed toward the barn. The woman who greeted them was tall and fashionably slim, with short blond hair and an aristocratic face that had been aged a little too early by the sun. She looked wealthy and well bred, a lady born to the California equestrian set.

Her name was Carol, and she was the divorced mother of two college-age daughters. Carol also appeared to find Adam attractive, but that didn't surprise Sarah because females of all ages and lifestyles were drawn to him. Unfortunately, Sarah found herself admiring him, too. He stood tall and broad-shouldered, his body hard and lean and muscular, the sun playing off his hair, highlighting various shades of brown.

The horse he had chosen, a sorrel overo paint, was as striking as the man. And it was a mare. She had expected it to be a gelding, but Adam had bought himself a gentle-eyed female.

"We call her Cee-Cee," Carol told her. "It was our nickname for Sienna's Pride."

The mare, Sarah also learned, had belonged to Carol's oldest daughter and was primarily used as a trail horse, which was exactly what Adam wanted.

"He'll take good care of her," she said.

Carol motioned to the stall and smiled. "Yes, I suspect he will."

Sarah turned to find Cee-Cee nuzzling Adam's neck like a long-lost lover. Even the horse had developed a crush on him.

Within three weeks, the kittens had grown into eight little balls of adorable fluff. Some were developing faster than others, and Sarah's favorite, of course, was the most independent one. She named him Groucho because he had black slashes above his eyes that looked remarkably like big, animated eyebrows. He was also the baby Adam had saved, and that made him even more special.

Sarah and Adam sat on the floor in his room, the kittens stumbling around their feet. Groucho wandered in another direction, but Cameo latched onto him and dropped him back into the thick of things. The mama cat kept her eye on everyone, including the humans playing with her young brood.

Adam glanced up and said, "Groucho could be a girl, you know."

"No way." She reached for her favorite kitty. "Look at that face. This one's definitely a boy."

He grinned. "It's got nothing to do with faces, sweetheart. It's the other end that counts."

"Smart aleck." She turned Groucho over in her palm and rubbed his belly. The kitten batted his tiny paws in response. "Maybe it's time we tried to figure this out. Where's that book you bought?"

Adam made his way to the nightstand and retrieved the book. When he returned, he flipped through the pages until he came to the breeding section. "Determining the Sex of

Your Kittens.'' He announced, then read the paragraph to himself and regarded Groucho with a perplexed expression. ''We're supposed to elevate his tail and view him from the rear. If he's a male, his...um...area is supposed to be lower than a female's, and it says you should be able to feel his—'' he made a face only a man could make at a time like this and finished his sentence, ''—testicles.''

Biting back a smile, she handed him the kitten. ''Here. You can do that.''

''Gee, thanks.''

Groucho didn't seem to mind the examination. If anything, he looked amused. Sarah could have sworn his eyebrows waggled.

Adam's expression didn't change. During the procedure, he kept that uncomfortable look on his face. Somehow that made Groucho's comical eyebrows even funnier.

Sarah coughed to cover a giggle, and Adam shook his head.

''I'm feeling around for testes, and you're laughing.''

''Sorry. Couldn't help it.''

''Yeah, well, I'm not getting this. I think I need to compare kittens. Maybe find a female first.''

Sarah lost the battle to remain serious, and soon her giggling had Adam laughing, too. But even through their silly fit, he finally figured out what he was doing. Groucho, he discovered, was indeed a boy.

''Told you.'' Sarah beamed and kissed the top of the kitty's head. ''He's a regular little stud.''

''Yeah, I guess he is.''

The mama cat decided the visit was over when most of her babies started bumping into her, insisting it was time to nurse. Adam and Sarah rounded up the kittens and placed them in the nursery box, leaving Cameo alone with them.

''Come on,'' he said. ''Let's go fix a snack.''

They entered the kitchen, and she leaned against the counter. ''So what are we going to make?''

He washed his hands and turned back to face her. ''Fry bread.''

Sarah was startled. She had no idea Adam was familiar

with fry bread. "I don't know how to make it," she said, which was more or less the truth. She had never actually prepared it herself. And just the smell alone would remind her of the intertribal powwows her mother had loved to attend. She wasn't up for a painful trip down memory lane.

"I have a recipe," he said. "And I bought everything we need yesterday."

"As far as I know, fry bread is a Navaho dish," she said. "So if you're looking for a Cherokee experience, this isn't it."

"Really? Well, I got the recipe from a Cherokee newspaper, so that's good enough for me. Come on, Sarah. You know what a lousy cook I am. I can't do this without you."

Further argument was pointless. Adam was already gathering the ingredients. Sarah washed her hands and dried them on a paper towel, telling herself it was only a snack. It didn't have to remind her of lost dreams and faraway powwows. She could separate the past from the present.

A persistent cat meowed at the back door, so she answered the summons while Adam searched for an appropriate frying pan. She knelt on the tiny porch and placed a bowl of dry cat food on the bottom step. The feline was a war-torn tom who never came into the house. He wouldn't let anyone touch him, but he wasn't too proud to accept a free meal now and then.

She watched him, wondering if he was the father of Cameo's kittens. The tom's bluish gray coat was the color of a rain-shrouded sky. Secretly she called him Storm. The name seemed to fit this wary stray.

He looked as though he had been in a fight recently, but she knew he wouldn't allow himself to be doctored. Sarah understood his need to be alone, to choose solitude over the emotion and turmoil that came with being part of a family.

The tom studied her with knowing green eyes, and she smiled. He seemed to understand her, too. To respect her for keeping her distance, for not trying to lure him with pretty words and promises of forever.

I should have been a cat, she mused, leaving the hungry tom alone.

Going back into the house, she saw that Adam waited for her.

"Who was it?" he asked.

"The gray tom."

"How did he look?"

"A little battered. Like he's been in another fight."

A frown creased his forehead. "I know cats are independent, but that one worries me."

Trust Adam, she thought, to want to stitch the cuts, heal the bruises, give the tom a warm place to sleep. "He appears to be able to take care of himself."

"Not if a car gets him."

Sarah met Adam's gaze. Those tender brown eyes could melt a woman's heart, leave her as warm and molten as wax. He protected everyone—the dragon slayer who took in strays. Deep down she knew Adam hadn't intended to hurt her. But as much as she valued his friendship, being intimate with him still frightened her.

"Have you named him?" Adam asked, referring to the wary tom.

She tucked her hair behind her ears. This conversation was going in a direction that made her uncomfortable. She would never say Storm's name out loud. To do so would lay too much claim. "No," she lied. "Have you?"

"No, but if he knew where you lived, he would visit your house, too. They all would."

"Groucho's coming home with me, remember?" And Groucho was probably Storm's son. That gave her an attachment to the roaming tom, a bond she couldn't deny. They were almost like family. Her and Adam and the cats.

Sarah glanced at the stove. This wasn't supposed to happen. She wasn't suppose to feel this way. "I thought we were making fry bread."

He smiled and reached for her hand, drawing her closer. "We are."

The recipe was simple—flour, salt, water, baking powder and powdered milk. They measured the ingredients and mixed them into a bowl. While the oil heated, they shaped the bread.

The recipe claimed size was a matter of preference, so Adam's palm-size mounds came out bigger than Sarah's.

Standing side by side, they flattened the dough into disks, then placed them in the oil, turning each one as it browned.

Adam had flour on his chin. Sarah gave him a motherly "tsk" and brushed him clean. He grinned and rewarded her with a playful hug. He seemed so happy, so incredibly pleased to have her in his kitchen, sharing a simple but important moment of his life.

The fry bread, she supposed, made him feel more Indian. Adam wanted so desperately to belong, to be accepted into a culture that had yet to recognize him. He wasn't registered with the Cherokee Nation. Officially he wasn't a member of the Western or Eastern Band. He didn't have an enrollment number linking him to his ancestors. All he had was an aging document stating his mother's name and heritage.

"It's almost ready," he said.

Sarah turned back to the task at hand. The recipe produced four servings. Adam drained their bounty in a brown paper bag lined with napkins, and she inhaled the fried aroma.

Tea steeped in the dragon pot. It smelled wonderful, too. Man, mint and fry bread. It was, she thought, a heady combination.

A combination that seemed to wrap itself around her reluctant heart.

The following Sunday, Adam invited Sarah to Mason Ranch, the boarding facility that housed his horse.

Sarah exited Adam's Jeep and looked around. Ancient oaks offered shade and scenic trails led to a hilltop view. A roping arena sat on one side of the property, wash racks and lockers on the other. Mason Ranch was an urban-cowboy facility, catering to boots, buckles and well-worn denim.

And today, Adam fit the bill. Gorgeous Adam in a pair of slim-fitting Wranglers. Just the sight of him made her blood tingle.

He entered Cee-Cee's stall, and the paint greeted him with

friendly eyes and a bobbing head. Sarah stood on the other side of the gate and watched them.

"She probably thinks we're going for a ride," he said. "I've been taking her into the hills nearly every morning."

"You come here before work?"

He nodded and pushed against Cee-Cee, who was nudging him for attention. "You should see this place at dawn, Sarah. It's incredible."

"I'll bet it is." She pictured the sun rising over the hills like a ball of fire. "Do you hit traffic on the way back?"

"A little. But it's worth it." He lifted Cee-Cee's halter and slipped it over her head. "I cut it close, though. I have just enough time for a quick shower before I go to work." Buckling the halter, he spoke to the mare now, his voice deep but gentle. "It's not going to be like this forever. Someday we're going to have our own ranch. Aren't we, girl?"

A place in Oklahoma, Sarah thought uncomfortably. She was going to lose Adam to the world she'd left behind. Lose him? He was only supposed to be her friend, not a man she hoped to keep. "You're not moving for a while."

"Actually, I might find a place this summer." The mare's neighbor, a big bay gelding, poked his nose over the rail. Adam smiled at the curious horse and led Cee-Cee out of the stall. "I've already contacted a Realtor in Oklahoma. They're going to show me some property while I'm there." He paused, looked over at her. "I wish you would agree to take that vacation with me."

Sarah closed the gate, and they fell into step, with Adam leading the paint. She didn't want to talk about this. The day was much too nice to ruin.

They continued on the path that led to the lockers, passing a picnic area rife with benches. She decided the best course was a silent one. Rather than respond to his comment, she let it drift between them, float until it disappeared.

Cee-Cee didn't shy away from the wash rack. She allowed Adam to hitch her to a post without the slightest fuss. Sarah had pictured the mare dragging her hoofs like a stubborn child. Cee-Cee, with her gentle eyes and flashy coat, was a bit on the spoiled side.

"She really is a good horse," Sarah said.

"Yeah, she is." Turning on the hose, he let the water run for a moment. "How long has it been since you've ridden?"

"Years. Since I was a kid. Some of my friends had horses."

"Do you miss it?"

She studied the paint. "Yes, I suppose I do." It was a difficult admission to make, but she chose to be honest. Sarah had stopped riding after her mother died, and there were moments she longed for the simple pleasure of a dusty trail.

They soaped down the mare together, their clothes taking a good portion of the dirt. Cee-Cee had decided to dance after all, whinnying as she did. Sarah had to laugh. The horse wasn't spooked. The big overgrown baby was singing in the shower.

While Cee-Cee basked in the sun, Adam and Sarah dried themselves with the same towel. Watching him tackle his damp shirt, she had to tell her hormones to behave. With a Western hat dipped over his eyes, he looked sexier than lust-driven sin. All denim and all male, she thought. Muscles bunched in his arms and a buckle glinted at his waist.

"Adam?" a man's voice said. "Is that you, Paige?"

They both turned, and then Adam grinned.

"Hey, Dan. What a surprise." He clasped the other man's hand in a friendly shake. "Do you board here?"

"Sure do."

Dan was lanky and blond, with hazel eyes that crinkled when he smiled. Beside him was a young Mexican woman, very pretty and very pregnant. A little boy held her hand, his skin a light shade of brown. Sarah assumed they were a family.

Dan turned to the woman. "Angie, you remember Adam, don't you?"

She nodded and smiled. "From the league, right?"

"Yes, it's nice to see you again."

Once all of the introductions were made, Sarah learned that

Adam and Dan had played basketball on the same city league six years before. She was also told that Dan and Angie had been married forever and had named their son Jordan because Dan was a die-hard basketball fan.

Adam knelt to greet the boy. ''Hey, partner. Do you ride?''

Jordan bobbed his head, tipping the cowboy hat he wore. ''I ride with my daddy, and I get to hold the reins.''

''Pretty cool. How old are you?''

The child held up three fingers, but said, ''Four.''

''He'll be four in September,'' his mother clarified.

''Yep.'' Jordan's hat teetered again. ''And that's when I'm gonna be a big brother. My mom's havin' another boy. We know 'cause the doctor took a picture of him inside her tummy.'' The child made an expressive face and leaned into Adam. ''It showed his pee-pee and everything.''

''Oh, yeah?''

Adam broke into a grin and glanced up at Dan, who flashed a that's-my-kid smile back at him. Sarah and Angie just laughed.

''Do you got a horse?'' Jordan asked Adam.

''Yeah. She's right over there. Do you want to meet her?''

''Sure.'' The three-year-old reached for Adam as if they were life-long buddies. ''What's her name?''

He balanced the child with ease. ''Cee-Cee. And she loves carrots. We can feed her one, okay?''

Sarah could only stand back and marvel. Jordan clung to Adam's neck while the boy's parents watched with proud smiles. Jordan already knew how to feed a horse, so Adam praised him for being such a good cowboy. Cee-Cee cooperated as well, reaching for the carrot with a delicate nibble.

They looked right together, Sarah thought. The man, the child and the big, flashy paint.

Dan finally told Jordan it was time to go home. The boy whined but agreed that his pregnant mom should take a nap. Sarah suspected Jordan would be napping before long, too. He insisted he didn't need one, but heavy eyelids indicated otherwise.

"You should barbecue with us one weekend," Angie said, extending the invitation to both Sarah and Adam.

Before they could respond, Dan chimed in. "Yeah, that would be great, except I'll bet Adam's still a health-food nut."

"That's right, I am. But I have been known to cheat." He bumped Sarah's arm and grinned.

They bantered a little more, laughing and joking. Sarah joined in, even though she felt a little strange. The other couple acted as if she and Adam were living together, as if they were on the verge of a major commitment.

But they were just friends, she thought. Friends who had been one-time lovers.

A few minutes later Jordan waved goodbye as his dad carried him to their car. The little boy's hat bobbed, as big and floppy as his grin.

Adam returned the child's wave, then leaned against a hitching post. "He's quite a kid, isn't he?"

"Yes, he is." Sarah squinted into the sun. Jordan was no longer visible. He was strapped in the back seat, tinted windows shielding him from view.

"He looks like us."

Blinking, she turned. Adam stared at her, his eyes intense. How many times had he watched her like that? So tender, so earnest.

"Us?" she all but stuttered.

"Like he could be our son."

This wasn't a conversation she wanted to have. Friends didn't imagine what their children would look like. Couples did that, people in serious relationships.

"Adam—"

He touched her cheek, his fingertips gentle. Whatever she intended to say was lost. The world stilled. She couldn't see anything but him. And the face of a dark-haired, dark-eyed child.

Their child.

"I think about it, Sarah. I think about having babies with you."

Closing her eyes, she fought the image. His words, those romantic words, pierced a part of her that already ached—the part that knew it wouldn't work.

"I think it's time to go," she said. "It's hot, and I'm tired. And…" She couldn't bring herself to talk, not here. Not beneath a blue sky and a bright yellow sun. Not with giant oaks offering quiet shade and horses whinnying for attention. It was all too beautiful to spoil.

Masking a tight expression, Adam stepped back. He should have kept silent, kept his feelings to himself. Sarah would barely look at him, and damn it, that hurt.

"I'll take Cee-Cee back to her stall."

"That's fine. I'll wait here."

Untying the horse, he led her across the dirt and down a tidy row of pipe stalls. In the distance, the hills rose to the sky, edging the heavens in a wash of color, a setting that seemed almost surreal.

"What should I do?" he asked the paint. "How do I get her out of my system?"

Cee-Cee nuzzled him as he opened the gate, and he had to chuckle. "Offering to take her place, are you?"

Why did he have to fall for a female who didn't want him? "They chase me," he told the horse. "Women actually chase me." But not Sarah. Whenever he tried to close the gap between them, she widened it even more.

Unbuckling Cee-Cee's halter, he found himself being nudged. The mare poked and prodded, and he realized he was being patted down for carrots. "And here I thought you loved me." He reached into his pocket and handed her the last bite.

When he exited the stall, Cee-Cee's neighbor tossed his head, sending his mane flying. The gelding was courting her, Adam thought, showing off proud and pretty.

"Don't bother," he said under his breath, feeling cynical and hurt and much too male.

Sarah stood right where he'd left her. She gazed at the sky, and he wondered what she was thinking. Maybe it was over between them. Maybe this was it. The subject that would pull them apart for good.

Babies. The possibility of a future. Something deeper and more meaningful than friendship.

Damn it. His heart ached something fierce. "Let's go," he said.

They climbed into the Jeep without uttering a single word. The freeway was busy, so he concentrated on the SUV in front of him, shifting gears when the traffic came to a blinding halt.

"Great," he muttered. He couldn't wait to get the hell out of the city.

Sarah tucked a strand of hair behind her ear. "There's probably an accident up ahead."

"Yeah, probably." He couldn't see anything but a sea of cars and graffiti on an overhead pass. The concrete jungle on a typical day.

They moved at a snail's pace, but once they reached the holdup, Adam's breath lodged in his throat. There was indeed an accident, a collision on the other side of the road. He caught a glimpse of flashing lights and mangled metal, emergency vehicles and clean white stretchers.

Turning away, he thought about the plane crash that had taken his parents' lives. He wanted to reach for Sarah's hand, hold it tightly in his. Life was too short to lose what mattered. Adam missed his parents, missed the loving, caring people who had raised him as their son. They hadn't told him about the adoption, but they had seen him through the roughest time of his life.

"It looks bad," Sarah said.

"Yeah, it does."

He was grateful when the traffic picked up and they left the accident behind. He didn't want to dwell on funerals and cemeteries and sympathy cards you wished you didn't have to open.

Sarah's sprawling apartment complex sat in the heart of the Valley. Adam entered through the security gate and parked in a visitor's spot. He noticed a fenced playground beside the clubhouse. Kids were welcome and so were dogs, as long as they weighed under thirty pounds. There were two swimming pools and lots of restrictions. He wondered if Sarah ever felt stifled.

"Do you want to come in?" she asked.

He hesitated, simply because he hadn't expected an invitation. "Are you sure you're up for company?"

She brushed his hand. "We need to talk, Adam."

"All right." Something akin to fear gripped his belly. Was this it? he wondered. The talk that would end his chance of winning her over? The we-shouldn't-see-each-other-anymore speech? Our relationship is getting too complicated? I don't want to have babies with a guy who used to drink?

They walked to her door in silence, activity stirring around them. Most of her neighbors either barbecued on their tiny patios or headed to the closest pool, towels and suntan lotion in tow.

Once they were inside, Sarah offered him a cold drink. Still a little sweaty from grooming the horse, he accepted a tall glass of cranberry juice, finishing it in several long swallows.

He sat at her dining room table, waiting for the ax to fall. She sat across from him, sipping her juice.

He wanted to jump up, stretch his legs, roll his shoulders. His muscles were tight, his body on edge. He needed a shower, a therapeutic spray of warm water to take his mind off what was happening.

"So?" he said, meeting her gaze head-on. The sooner this ended, the sooner he could go home, close his eyes and try to forget.

"What you said earlier—" she paused to take another sip, ice cubes crackling in her glass. "It was nice, Adam. A nice thing to say."

Stunned, he blinked, losing sight of her for an instant. "Really? I thought it upset you."

"It scared me. And it still does. We're not supposed to have these kind of feelings for each other. We're not supposed to fantasize about what our children will look like."

"Why not?" He leaned into the table, wishing he could

touch her. ''We're young and healthy and single. It's normal. Men and women get attached. That's what life is about.''

''But it won't work.'' She shook her head, and he wondered if she was trying to shake off her emotions.

''Why won't it work, Sarah?''

She pushed away her juice, leaving a streak of moisture across the glass tabletop. ''I promised myself a long time ago that I would never get involved with an alcoholic.''

''And I promised myself I would never drink again. It's not a problem in my life anymore, and it shouldn't come between us.''

''You're obsessed with Oklahoma,'' she countered.

He gave in to the urge to stand, to stretch his legs and roll his shoulders. ''It's not an obsession. I might have family there. And I've been asking you to come with me.''

She set her jaw. ''I can't go back there.''

''Yes, you can.'' He sat down again, only this time he took the chair closest to hers. ''You need to go back. For yourself. For us. For your dad.''

''My dad?''

She flinched, and he knew he had hit a raw nerve. ''Yeah. The man you haven't seen or spoken to in over six years. It's time to face him, don't you think? Tell him what a mess he made of things.''

Her jaw was still set, stiff and tighter than a drum. ''And what good would that do?''

''It might give you some peace of mind. And it might restore a little pride in your heritage. You've been blaming a whole nation of people for one man's mistakes. Your dad ruined it for you. And now you're ruining it for us.'' He inhaled, let the air out slowly. ''Didn't you see that accident today? Damn it, life is too short to waste. Your mother is gone. My parents are dead. Who do we have left?'' He answered his own question, his heart aching for both of them. ''I'll tell you who. The people who gave me up for adoption and the father who disappointed you. They're it. They're all we've got.''

She didn't respond. Instead she just stared at him, her eyes watery. And when her mouth finally moved, her words came out soft and broken, like a jagged whisper. "He sends me letters."

Adam didn't need to ask who she meant. He knew she was talking about her dad. Reaching for her hand, he felt it tremble in his. "What do they say?"

Her fingers curled around his. "I don't know. I've never opened them."

"Oh, Sarah." Sweet, confused Sarah. "You have to read them."

"They're probably full of phony promises."

"It doesn't matter. You still have to read them."

"I will," she said. "But I don't want to do it alone. Will you stay with me? Be here when I open them?"

"Of course I will." He moved closer, breathing in the scent of her hair. They might be two lonely people, adults struggling to survive without a family, but today, they had each other.

She closed her eyes, and for the longest time, they sat in her dining room, simply holding hands. For now, he thought, it was enough.

Nine

Sarah squeezed his hand. It frightened her to need someone so badly, yet she couldn't deny that at this life-altering moment, she needed a companion.

Adam. She needed Adam.

How many times had she stared at those letters, trying to garner the courage to read them?

She took a deep breath, knowing there was no point in prolonging the inevitable. "They're in my closet." Rising, she invited him to join her.

They entered her room, and he sat on the edge of her bed. Hesitating, she stood by the door and looked at him. His jeans were slightly soiled, his hair matted from the hat he had worn earlier. A faint sunburn marked his cheeks and the bridge of his nose.

"Is it because I'm Cherokee?" she asked.

He cocked his head. "What do you mean?"

"Is that why you haven't let me go? Being Indian is so important to you. And I'm the only Cherokee you know."

A frown creased his brow. ‘‘How can you say something like that? How could you even think it?’’ He pounded on his chest, then spread his hand over it. ‘‘I haven’t let you go because you live inside me. Right here, all the time.’’

Dizzy, she teetered, then held onto the doorknob for support. What he described sounded so tender, so passionate. So real. ‘‘The Cherokee have a saying—’’ she met his gaze, her pulse quickening. ‘‘They say that when you care about someone, that person walks in your soul.’’

‘‘Is that what’s happening to me?’’ he asked.

‘‘I don’t know.’’ Maybe it was happening to both of them. Maybe they walked in each other’s souls. Walked so deeply, there was no way out. ‘‘I shouldn’t have brought this up.’’

‘‘It’s okay.’’ He watched her with intensity. ‘‘It scares me, too, Sarah.’’

Were they talking about love? The emotion she’d feared all along? ‘‘I was just feeling insecure. You know, about the Cherokee thing. I had no right to accuse you of being so shallow.’’ She glanced at the top of her closet. The door was open, beckoning her to come closer. ‘‘It’s those letters, I guess.’’

He nodded. ‘‘I understand.’’

She stepped forward, reached for a small box. Removing the envelopes, she placed them on the bed beside Adam. Her father’s handwriting caught her attention. She closed her eyes, then opened them, knowing she couldn’t blink away this moment. The letters were bundled together with a rubber band. Adam picked them up and studied them.

‘‘How did he get your address?’’

‘‘I kept in touch with a high-school friend for a while. She must have given it to him.’’

He removed the rubber band. She knew the oldest postmark was from two years before, the most recent just several months ago. There were six letters in all.

Adam indicated the return address. ‘‘I’ve never heard of this town.’’

‘‘Hatcher is a small community, between Tulsa and Tahlequah. It's quiet, a little off the beaten path. I've passed through it, but never stopped."

"And that's where your dad lives now?"

"So it seems."

He handed her the oldest letter, suggesting she read them in chronological order.

She took it and tore the seal, feeling like Pandora opening that box. What if this turned out to be a mistake? What if it just ended up drawing her back into a world of pain?

Dear Sarah....

The text was short and fairly simple. He apologized in the first sentence, told her he had stopped drinking in the second.

"I've heard all of this before." She finished reading it and gave it to Adam. Opening the next envelope, her heart sank. In this note, her father admitted that he had slipped up and taken a drink, but he was going to try harder.

From there, the letters continued in the same tone. He continued to apologize, telling her how sorry he was for letting her down, for being an irresponsible parent. He loved her, he claimed, loved her so much.

"He seems sincere." Adam re-bundled the stack. "And it appears he's been sober for almost two years now. He only screwed up that once. Plus he's been attending meetings ever since."

"So he says." Sarah fingered the rubber band. It could have been fastened around her heart, constricting the beats. "I want to believe him, but these letters don't prove a thing. He's lied about being sober before." And he'd told her that he loved her before, too. So many times. "They're just words."

"No, they're not. They're his feelings. His struggle. He misses you, Sarah. He wants to do the right thing."

"You're so trusting."

"I've been there. I remember what it felt like to disappoint the people who loved me. Your dad deserves a chance to prove himself."

She gazed at Adam. His adoptive father was dead. And his

biological father was a nameless, faceless man he hoped to meet someday.

"I have to go to Oklahoma, don't I?"

He smoothed her hair, brushed a strand from her cheek. "It's the only way to know if he's telling the truth. If he really is sober."

Forcing air through her lungs, she fought to temper the rising panic. "And if he isn't?"

"Then we'll deal with it. Together."

Together. The word melted over her like a balm. She leaned into Adam, and he held her. Close. So very close. He understood how much she needed his support.

She nuzzled his neck, and he stroked her back.

"Will you stay here tonight?" she asked.

He leaned back to look at her, to touch her cheek. "You know I will."

They stared at each other, and while silence engulfed the room, Sarah told herself she couldn't keep punishing Adam for his teenage rebellion. Eleven years of sobriety was a long time.

"I have to go to my place to get a change of clothes," he said finally. "And I could use a shower, too."

"You can shower here."

He sent her a seductive smile. "With you?"

"Yes." She wanted to hold him, feel his nakedness against hers.

They made it to his house within twenty minutes. He opened the front door and a wall of "meows" greeted him. One eager tabby jumped straight into his arms. He laughed and stroked its mottled coat. "I guess everybody's hungry."

No, Sarah thought. It wasn't food they were after. It was him.

And she couldn't blame them. She wanted to be near him, too.

Adam gave the cats canned food. He spoiled them, she supposed, but all of them had come from the streets. They deserved to know that someone cared. As a youth, Sarah had often felt like a stray herself, a tattered girl who had lost the comfort of home.

Could she really go back to Oklahoma and see her father? And what about forgiving him? She wasn't sure if her heart was capable.

While Adam packed an overnight bag, Sarah visited with Cameo and the kittens. Groucho peeked over the box at her, his eyebrows quirked at a curious angle. She decided he was contemplating his escape, anxious to develop the skills that would enable him to climb out.

"You're going to be a handful," she told him.

Cameo meowed and sent her a look that said he already was. Sarah grinned and reached for the fluffy little monster. She couldn't wait to take him home. Glancing back at Adam, she cocked her head. He sat at his computer, punching keys.

"What are you doing?"

"Just getting online for a minute."

"What for?"

"To check my e-mail." He studied the screen. "Plus I thought I'd see what kind of airline rates were available. Maybe I can get us a deal." Turning to look over his shoulder, he met her gaze. "You're not going to have any trouble getting time off in August, are you?"

"No." Her schedule was more or less her own. She leased a treatment room from the salon, booking her own hours. "Do you really think we need to get our tickets so soon?"

"Why?" His gaze turned suspicious. "Are you thinking of backing out?"

"No." Yes. Maybe. She wasn't sure. "I've never been on a plane before."

"Really?" The look in his eyes softened. "How did you come to California?"

"On a bus." Which made her feel unsophisticated and poor. Of course that was exactly what she was at the time. A down-and-out Indian with an alcoholic father.

"I can do this tomorrow." He shut down the computer and came toward her, clearly sensing her mood. "Don't change your mind, Sarah. I don't want to go to Oklahoma without you. We both need this.''

When he gazed directly into her eyes, she thought about how kind and caring he was. ''Okay.'' She made the vow quietly, her heart fluttering on a wing and a prayer. Somehow she would summon the strength to go home.

Adam stood beside Sarah in her sunny bathroom, shedding his clothes. She turned on the water and adjusted the nozzle to accommodate his height. The shower stall was separate from the tub, barely big enough for one person, let alone two. That made this more stimulating. When he joined her in the confined space, skin brushed skin.

They managed to share the water and the soap. He used her shower gel, lathering his body. She scrubbed, too, washing away the emotion and exhaustion of the day. He could almost see her muscles relax.

She ducked under the spray and saturated her hair. It clung, wet and ropy, to her breasts, like twines of licorice. He imagined putting his mouth there.

He knew he could make love to her, but he wanted to wait. He wanted to fantasize while she touched herself, while she soaped her arms and belly, the V between her legs.

There was nothing more beautiful than a naked woman, especially one who had no idea how exquisite she was.

She washed her hair, and he stood, fully aroused, watching her. Sarah's shampoo smelled sweetly of carnations, the aphrodisiac that had become her signature.

Minutes later, he lathered his own hair with the same shampoo, and even that felt erotic. Her sexual scent was on him now, spicy and fragrant.

She turned, and her nipples grazed his arm. He made a rough sound, but it couldn't be heard above the pounding water. When she looked up at him, trapped him with those dark eyes, he struggled to breathe.

She reached for him, and he knew he was lost.

Sleek and slippery, they rubbed and kissed, like otters

splashing in the sea. He licked moisture from her skin, opened his mouth and let rivulets run onto his tongue.

She brought his head to her breasts. He latched onto a nipple and sucked. Hard. So hard, she clawed his shoulders and moaned.

Soaking wet, they stumbled from the bathroom to her bed, desperate for each other. Sunlight spilled into the room, bathing them in a late-afternoon glow. Still kissing, they shoved the quilt away, finding the sheets cool and inviting.

He wanted to crawl all over her, devour every luscious curve. Taut and erect, he spread her thighs and penetrated her, heat flooding his loins.

He moved, and she moved with him, taking him deeper.

Sex. Sensation. Incredible lovemaking.

It felt different this time. Warmer, wetter, even more intimate.

And then they looked at each other and realized why. They were completely naked, joined with no protection between them.

Adam groaned, then withdrew, even though he ached to stay right where he was.

"Maybe I should get on the Pill," she said.

He stroked her hair. It was still wet and clinging to her skin. "That isn't natural. It isn't good for your body."

She arched against him. "Then what?"

"A holistic method."

She kissed the side of his neck. "They're not foolproof."

"Nothing is." He turned his head and captured her lips. They were discussing birth control, yet they couldn't stop touching. "I wish we could forget about it."

"We can't."

"I know." He knew, but he wanted to lose himself inside her, spill his seed and make a baby. Now. Right now.

The urgency should have stunned him, but it didn't. He was beyond analyzing his feelings. When she was this close, all he could think about was keeping her, holding on and never letting go.

"We need a condom," she reminded him.

"Later." He pushed her down and buried his face between her legs. She gasped on contact, and he tasted her, over and over, delving into warm, wet heat.

Her stomach quivered, her hips bucked. Half crazed, she panted his name and tugged on his damp hair.

Yes, he thought. If he couldn't make a baby, then he wanted it wild.

Slick and sweet and wild.

He reveled in her reaction. Dark-eyed, smooth-skinned Sarah. In that climactic moment, that hot, sexy moment, she belonged to him. Flesh and blood and soul.

She needed him.

When he tore into the condom, they were more than ready. She straddled his lap and impaled herself, riding him until the rest of the world shattered and disappeared.

The sun had yet to rise, but Sarah was awake. She sat up in bed, and Adam stirred beside her.

"What's wrong?" he asked, his voice groggy.

She squinted at the clock. "It's later in Oklahoma." And that meant it was daylight there. "I should call my dad and get it over with."

He turned on the lamp, illuminating the room in a pale glow. "Have you been up all night?"

"More or less." She couldn't lie, not with Adam watching her through concerned eyes. She had lain awake, listening to him breathe. Everything was moving too fast. Her feelings for Adam, her fear of going home. She had made promises, and now she couldn't turn back, no matter how much she wanted to.

Sarah studied her companion. His hair fell loose about his shoulders. He looked sleepy and tousled, a rumpled male wrapped in mauve-colored sheets. Her room wasn't overly feminine, but it was still a little too girlish for a man like Adam.

"I can make some tea," he said. "It might help calm your nerves."

"Okay." Anxious, she watched him climb out of bed.

Sarah felt as if she were tumbling down a hill, her heart sliding straight into her stomach. She eyed the phone and wished she could turn off the light and forget this was happening. She didn't want to talk to her dad, and she didn't want to need Adam so badly, either. But, damn it, here she was, unable to stop the spiral of emotion suddenly consuming her life.

Being alone all these years had been so much easier.

She picked up her father's letters and paged through them again. When Adam re-entered the bedroom, she met his gaze.

"I was looking for his number," she said.

He placed her tea on the dresser. "I'll wait in the living room. I'm sure you would rather do this by yourself."

"No, I wouldn't. Truthfully, I'd like you to stay." She lifted the tea and took a small sip. It contained just the right amount of honey. They had already gotten to know each other's habits. "I'm going to ask my dad about your mom. See if he's heard her name before."

Adam sat on the edge of the bed. "Thank you. I know how difficult this is for you."

"I'll be okay." She dialed the number and listened to the rings. They sounded lonely and faraway. The voice that answered had her gripping the receiver. She recognized her father's graveled tone instantly.

"Hello?"

"Dad, it's me."

"Sarah? I hadn't expected...I can't believe..."

His words drifted, and she envisioned him drinking a cup of strong, black coffee— a brew much more potent than her chamomile tea. Did he have a hangover? Was his skin sallow? His eyes swollen? She wanted to picture him sober but couldn't quite manage it.

"I can't believe you actually called," he said finally, forming a more coherent sentence. When she didn't respond, he asked if everything was all right.

No, she thought, it wasn't. Her heartbeat was racing out of control, her imagination battling scenes from the past.

"Everything's fine."

They talked, but not deeply. Their conversation was strained, both unsure of how to communicate with the other. It became a little easier when she mentioned Adam.

"He's a friend," she said. "And he's looking for his biological mother. He doesn't know much about her. We were hoping you could help."

Sarah's father didn't know anyone named Cynthia Youngwolf, but he promised to question some old acquaintances, ask around the Cherokee community.

When the call ended, she glanced at Adam. He sat quietly, watching her with a gentle expression. It was a look she had come to know well.

"I did it," she said. "I talked to him."

"How did he seem?"

"The same. Different. I don't know. I couldn't tell if he was sober."

"I guess we'll find out soon enough." He skimmed her cheek. "You must be beat. Do you want to try to go back to sleep?"

"I don't think I can."

"Then how about some breakfast?"

Sarah glanced at the window. "It's still dark out."

"I don't mind. Do you?"

"No." She reached for her robe, wondering when she would stop relying on Adam.

Maybe never, she thought, with a flicker of warmth and a twinge of fear. Whatever was happening between them felt right. Scary, but right. Maybe being alone wasn't all that great after all. At least now she was alive, her blood crackling with energy.

They walked into the kitchen together, Sarah wrapped in a terry-cloth robe and Adam half-dressed, his pajama bottoms riding just below his navel. They looked like a couple, she thought, two people who slept in the same bed, shared the same chores.

"Sarah?"

"Yes?"

"What's his name? You've never told me your dad's name."

"William," she said, sensing her life, as well as Adam's, was about to change. But whether those changes were good or bad, she couldn't be sure. She took a deep breath and opened the refrigerator. They would have to go to Oklahoma to find out.

Ten

August was hot, particularly in Oklahoma. But Adam didn't mind. He enjoyed the heat, the land, the place that was part of his history. Sarah sat beside him, quiet one minute, chatty the next. They were headed down a narrow dirt road, passing crooked wood fencing and fascinating old farmhouses.

This was their second day in Oklahoma. Their first had been spent battling jet lag and two delayed flights. By the time they had checked into a motel room in Hatcher, all they cared about was a half-way decent meal and a reasonably comfortable bed.

"Do you think they're okay?" she asked.

He knew she meant the kittens they had left behind. "Sure. Babette will take good care of them." Babette was Adam's landlady, an eccentric old woman who had been a Hollywood starlet in her heyday. She was a little strange, with her thinning bleached hair and fake eyelashes, but he trusted her. She had cats of her own.

Sarah shot him a teasing grin. "Do you know what Babette said about you?"

"What?" he asked, wincing a little. From the expression on Sarah's face, it had to be something embarrassing.

"That she rented to you because you have a great butt."

He kept his eyes on the road and tried not to envision his landlady checking out his backside. "Please tell me you're kidding."

"Sorry. It's the truth. She even asked me about your performance in bed. Wanted to know if you were as good as you looked."

Mortified, he felt his cheeks burn. "I hope to God you didn't answer her."

"Of course I did." Sarah laughed. "I told her you were even better. The poor old woman nearly died on the spot."

Adam shook his head, letting the ridiculous remark go. He figured Sarah was camouflaging her anxiety with humor. The road they traveled led to her father's residence, and he supposed William Cloud waited just as nervously for their arrival.

Following the directions written on a scrap of paper, he turned onto another dirt road. In the distance was a small, rough-hewn house.

"This is it," he said.

Sarah nodded, her breathing audible. She looked suddenly vulnerable, with her flowing black hair and dark, deep-set eyes.

Adam wanted to make this moment easier, but he knew there wasn't anything he could say or do that would change her past. She had to face her father, take control of the hurt and betrayal.

He steered the vehicle toward the graveled driveway. The house appeared old but well kept, the land surrounding it flanked by hills.

It was a simple country setting—a wooden porch, a large bed of grass and scattered trees reaching for the sky. The tiny town of Hatcher was dusty yet charming, a world rife with farmers, ranchers and blue-collar workers.

They knocked on the door, and a medium-built man answered the summons. His graying hair was cut short, his eyes as dark as midnight. He looked as if he had lived a rough life, the lines in his face premature. Adam had no doubt he was William Cloud.

"Dad," Sarah said quietly, making no move toward him.

William lifted his hand to touch her cheek, but dropped it before making contact. "You're all grown-up," he said.

"Yes, well...this is my friend, Adam." She offered an introduction quickly, and the men shook hands.

William's grip was strong and steady, and Adam prayed Sarah's father was as sober as he appeared.

"Come in." The other man stepped back, and Sarah and Adam entered his home. The living room was tidy, with paneled walls painted white and hardwood floors polished to a slick shine. The furniture bore slightly worn cushions and a few scars, but it looked inviting.

"I have pop," William said. "Would you like one?"

Sarah didn't respond, so Adam accepted a soda to be polite. They gathered in the kitchen, around a table with mismatched chairs. It made the old-fashioned room seem sort of art deco, although Adam doubted that had been William's intent. The furniture had probably come from a flea market and had been purchased out of necessity rather than style.

William pointed to a multi-paned window. "See those hills? That's where the rich people around here live. Society types who drive luxury cars. I work at a garage up there." He glanced at his daughter. "They're decent folk, and they treat me right."

Adam assumed that was William's way of saying that he was a respected citizen, a man who had battled the bottle and won. Sarah didn't look impressed or convinced by her father's words, but he understood why. She had been through hell and back with her dad, much in the same way his parents had struggled with him. Trusting an alcoholic wasn't easy.

William turned to Adam. "So you're looking for your biological mother."

"Yes, I am."

"That's good. Family is important." He drew a breath. "I've been doing what I can, asking some old friends if they've ever heard of her. I haven't had any luck, but I'll keep trying."

"Thank you. That means a lot to me. It feels a little strange, being born into a culture I don't know much about."

The older man cocked his head, then chuckled. "As long as you don't tell anyone that your great-grandmother was a Cherokee princess, you'll be fine."

Adam grinned. Sarah had already explained that myth. It seemed just about everyone claiming to have Cherokee blood also claimed they had descended from royalty. But the fact was there were no Cherokee princesses, at least not in the true definition of the word. In years past, Cherokee men had used an endearment for their wives that roughly translated to princess. The royalty fable had become a long-running joke in Indian country.

"Sarah's name means princess in Hebrew," Adam said, smiling at William.

"That's right, it does." The other man quirked an eyebrow. "I guess that means my daughter is a true Cherokee princess."

"Very funny." Sarah looked at her dad, and they both sputtered into nervous laughter.

When their laughter faded, silence engulfed the room. Adam decided it was time to go for a walk. Expressing an interest in the landscape, he rose from the table, leaving father and daughter alone.

He stepped onto the porch, hoping they would take this opportunity to talk.

Sarah sat in silence with her dad, barely meeting his gaze. She didn't know where to begin, what to say, even where to look. Everything in his house had changed. There wasn't one stick of furniture she recognized. Even her father seemed different. Older, she supposed. The lines around his eyes were more pronounced, the shape of his face more angular. His hair hadn't thinned, but it bore an abundance of gray.

How was she supposed to do this? How could she speak her mind when her mind was in a fog? She wanted to hate

William Cloud, to shout at him, but another part of her wanted to lean against him and cry.

"Maybe I should check on Adam," she said, searching for an excuse to escape.

"Why? Is there something wrong with him?"

She twisted the hem on her blouse. "No...I just—"

"He's more than a friend, isn't he?"

Blinking, she stilled her hands, clasping them on her lap. "I don't think that's any of your concern." And she didn't want to admit that she was falling in love, at least not out loud, and certainly not to her wayward father.

"I'm sorry. I didn't mean to upset you. It's just the way you look at him. The way he looks at you." William's voice turned soft. "It was like that with your mother and me. I still miss her."

"I miss her, too."

"She knew I was an alcoholic."

Sarah felt the blood drain from her face. "What are you talking about?"

"I was a drinker when I met her. I've been fighting this practically all of my life."

"And she married you anyway?"

"She loved me."

Sarah's heart lurched, stunned by the frightening pattern, the parallel between herself and her mother.

No, she thought. It wasn't the same. Her situation with Adam was different. He was sober. He wasn't fighting the addiction anymore. "So the whole time you were married to Mom, you were drinking?"

He shook his head. "No. I was on the program. I messed up a few times, but she was there to help me through it."

Betrayal gripped her stomach, twisting it into a painful knot. "And neither one of you ever thought to tell me?"

"I didn't want you to know. Your mother was always talking about the old ways, a man being a warrior and all that. I didn't want to spoil that image for you."

Sarah's eyes burned, but she refused to cry. Lifting her

chin, she swallowed the lump in her throat. "But you did spoil it. After she died, you ruined everything."

"I know. I'm so sorry."

He met her gaze, his dark eyes filled with apology. And something else, she thought. Shame? Sorrow? Loneliness? She couldn't be sure. She had seen the look before, given in to it so many times in the past.

William picked up his soda, drank from the can and placed it back on the table. "I know what it's like to live with an alcoholic. My mother...your grandmother...I don't think she was sober a day of her adult life."

And she had died when Sarah was just a toddler. "You never talked about her. I just assumed that it made you sad, that you missed her."

"My mother was a miserable woman. Bitter. Dirt poor. My father wasn't any better, but he didn't stick around long enough to matter." He glanced out the window. "I was ashamed of where I came from, of who I was."

She followed his gaze to the hills. A part of her understood all too well. "You daydreamed about being rich. And white."

He nodded. "I didn't have any pride in my heritage, not until I met your mother. She was my salvation."

The way Adam is mine, she thought, aware of the irony once again. "Adam's the one who talked me into coming here."

"Are you glad he did?"

"I don't know." Adam had a way of making everything seem all right, but she wasn't sure if it was. "Are you really sober, Dad?"

"Yes. Do you believe me?"

"Not really, no."

"I can't say as I blame you. I've lied before."

"Yes, you have." And she knew how it felt to have him abuse her trust. She couldn't let her heart go, not this time, not so easily. "Why did you move away from Tahlequah?"

"Too many memories," he responded. "And you weren't there anymore. I didn't want to live in that house without you."

"I like California. I've made a life for myself there."

"So you don't miss Tahlequah?"

She missed the way things had been before her mother died, the parental bond, the sense of belonging. "I'm taking Adam there tomorrow."

"I hope he finds his family."

"I hope so, too," she said, turning to look out the window again.

Sarah glanced at Adam, who paged through books at the museum gift shop. They had spent two days in Tahlequah. Yesterday they'd searched for information about his mother and today they'd toured the Cherokee Heritage Center.

She knew the Tsa-La-Gi Ancient Village had fascinated him the most. It was her favorite part of the tour, too. A living museum, the village recreated the lifestyle of the Cherokee during the sixteenth century, a time when being Indian seemed beautiful and romantic. As the "villagers" had gone about their daily routine, Adam and Sarah had envisioned their ancestors preparing food and making arrowheads, weaving baskets and playing stick ball.

Maybe it was okay to feel safe with someone, she thought, to love a man the way she loved Adam. He made Tahlequah seem like a magical place. When she was with him, she didn't dwell on the pain from her past. Even the prospect of seeing her father again wasn't so frightening.

"Look at these." Adam displayed the books in his hand. "Cherokee medicine. Can you believe it? This one is filled with natural plant remedies."

"That's great." Suddenly emotional, she reached for his arm and held tight. "Everything's going to be all right, isn't it?"

"Of course it is." Studying her expression, he kissed her forehead. "We have each other, don't we?"

She breathed in his scent, the herbal soap he used on his skin. "And we're going to find your mom. Maybe not on this trip, but eventually we'll find her." They had to, she thought. Because Adam needed a connection to his roots. He needed to know who he was and where he had come from. Now that she was home, she knew how important that was.

"This means a lot to me," he said. "You being here, helping me look for my mom."

"I know."

He paid for his books, and they headed to a restaurant Sarah recommended. It was a small diner, but the food had a hearty, home-cooked quality. They scooted into a vinyl booth and scanned their menus.

"I've had a good time today," he said.

"Me, too. I wish yesterday had been more productive, though." Their search for Cynthia Youngwolf had led nowhere. No one seemed to remember her, and the tribal office wasn't able to accommodate them. There were over 200,000 enrolled members of the Cherokee Nation. Locating a woman who had given her son up for adoption nearly thirty years before wasn't a simple task.

"How many Youngwolfs are on the final rolls?" she asked, referring to the data Adam had found on the Cherokee enrollment compiled between 1898 and 1914.

"Eleven. But there's no way to link me to any of them."

That was true. The only way for Adam to receive a Certificate of Indian Blood was to provide birth records that proved he was related to someone on the final rolls.

"We should start bright and early tomorrow," Sarah suggested, knowing they couldn't give up hope. "Maybe go to the library first. See if they have any old high-school annuals."

Adam sipped his water. "That's a great idea, but I wish I knew how old she was when I was born. I have no idea when she went to high school."

"We'll just have to cover a couple of decades. And since Youngwolf doesn't appear to be a very common name around here, that should help."

If they found a picture of her in an old yearbook, then they might be able to locate some of her classmates. Someone must have kept in touch with her, Sarah thought. People just didn't fade into oblivion. News about Cynthia would turn up sooner or later.

Adam sat across from Sarah thinking how beautiful she was, how vital she had become to him. He couldn't imagine living without her, but now wasn't the time to tell her how he felt. The diner was noisy and crowded, hardly the right atmosphere for a man to spill his heart.

"We should check out the private schools, too."

He blinked and picked up his fork, pulling himself back into their conversation. "For information about my mom?"

She nodded. "I know of a Christian academy that's been around for quite a while. She could have gone there."

"I hadn't thought of that." And he couldn't begin to express his gratitude. Sarah finally understood how important this was to him.

He cut into his turkey and watched her do the same. They had a lot in common, he thought. They enjoyed the same foods, the same kind of movies. And they were more than compatible in bed. Every time they made love, they clung to each other afterward, as if neither could bear to let go.

He still wanted to make a baby with her, to see her tummy swell with his child. It would be the ultimate connection, a bond that could never be broken.

"Adam?"

"Hmm?"

"What are you thinking about?"

You, he wanted to say. Us. Our future.

"Family," he told her, deciding it was close enough to the truth. "I keep wondering who my dad is and if he still lives around here. He could have gone to high school with my mom. Or he could have been her college sweetheart." And since arriving in Oklahoma, Adam had looked at strangers with interest, realizing they could be his biological parents.

"It's too bad you don't have a copy of your original birth certificate. Your father's name was probably on it."

"Believe me, I tried. I contacted the hospitals in the area, but they couldn't help. I also checked with the Department of Health Services. The records in cases like mine are sealed.

The only birth certificates available are the ones that have been amended.''

''We should still go the hospitals and question the staff. There might be a doctor or a nurse who remembers Cynthia.''

Adam had no idea if he was born in the Tahlequah City Hospital or in the Indian Hospital, but he was willing to talk to whomever would listen. ''You're right. I mean, how many unwed mothers could there have been in those days? Of course, it's been almost thirty years.''

''True, but someone might direct us to a retired employee.''

Lifting his water, he smiled. ''Thanks for helping, Sarah.''

She smiled back at him. ''You're welcome. Do you want to go for a drive after we eat? There's still some historic sites you haven't seen.''

''Sure.'' He glanced out the window and saw the town where he had been born, the streets and sidewalks, the parks and rivers. He had parents out there somewhere. And he had Sarah. He wasn't alone anymore.

''Do you know when abortions were legalized? '' he asked, wondering about the past.

''I'm not sure, but I think the Supreme Court ruling was in 1973.''

''So what were women doing before then?''

''Going to Mexico, I guess.'' She tilted her head, sending him a curious look. ''Why?''

''I'm just glad my mom didn't do that. I'm glad she chose to have me.''

''Me, too.'' Her eyes turned a little misty, but she kept eating, the buzz of the diner swirling around her.

It was a strangely intimate moment, Adam thought. Noisy yet quiet.

Thirty minutes later, they finished their meals, then climbed into the SUV. She drove this time, taking him on a private tour of her hometown. She pointed out sites of interest, historical homes and buildings, the architecture ranging from Victorian to more modern styles.

When they stopped in front of a cemetery, he turned to look at her.

"My mother is buried here," she said. "Do you mind if I visit her grave?"

"Of course not."

She opened her door. "Will you come with me?"

He nodded, then walked across the lawn with her. His adoptive parents were buried in a place just like this one—grass and trees and marble headstones. He knew how it felt to grieve, to kneel on the ground and blink back tears.

Sarah stopped in front of a stone marker, and Adam read the inscription: Nancy Lynn Cloud. Beloved Wife and Mother.

"Someone left flowers." A fresh bouquet spilled onto the grave like a rainbow of love and remembrance.

"It must have been my father." Her voice broke a little, and Adam put his arm around her.

"She knows we're here," he said, certain he could feel Nancy Cloud's spirit.

"Do you think she knows what's happening between us?" Sarah asked.

"Yes." He touched her cheek as she turned to face him. "I'm sure she's watching over us right now."

"It doesn't scare me so much anymore." She looked directly into his eyes, the sun shining on her skin. "I like the feeling."

"So do I." He knew they were talking about love, making a declaration in front of the woman who had given Sarah life. It seemed fitting somehow. "I want to marry you. I want you to have my babies."

She leaned into him, soft and warm and beautiful. "I want that, too."

They didn't talk on the way back to the motel, but he didn't mind. They had already spoken from their hearts. And Sarah had just agreed to become his wife.

The world was a perfect place, he thought, and life couldn't get much better. Love was everything Adam Paige had always hoped it would be.

* * *

The following morning was warm and quiet. Adam breathed against Sarah's hair, and she wondered how long they had slept in this position. Spoon-style, she supposed it was called, his front to her back.

She moved her bottom deliberately, then smiled when he groaned. Apparently he was awake, too. Awake and aroused. She could feel him through the lightweight pajamas he wore.

She turned to face him, to brush his lips. He looked gorgeous, his eyes sleepy, his hair loose and just a little messy. A night-tousled male. Rumpled and sexy.

Was this really happening? Had she really agreed to marry him?

Yes, she thought, tasting his kiss, she had. And she wasn't sorry. She loved him so much, she actually hurt inside.

He nibbled her jaw, and she imagined mornings like this for the rest of her life. And now, she wanted all of him, every powerful muscle, every hard, virile inch.

"Adam?"

"Hmm?"

"How come you've never asked me to—" she paused and toyed with the drawstring on his waistband, "—you know?"

He blinked those sleepy eyes, but she knew he understood the question. Oral sex. An image of the act danced between them like firelight. He did it to her, but she had yet to reciprocate.

"I'd never ask you to do that," he said, his voice shy yet crackling with heat.

It was a stimulating combination. The sound of sandpaper over sun, coarse and warm all at once. In response, she skimmed her hand up and down his belly, making his muscles quiver.

"What if I offered?"

He moistened his lips, then looked at her mouth, studied it with a very quiet, very masculine longing. When he lifted his gaze, they stared at each other. "That's different. I mean, well…"

Sarah couldn't help herself. She had to ask, had to hear him admit it out loud. "So, do you want me to?"

He looked at her mouth again, and her nipples ignited into red-tipped sparks. "Yeah," he said, his sinful voice even raspier. "I do."

With a small, feminine smile, she kissed his chest, moved her hands slowly down his body. And as she tugged on his pajamas, his breath rushed out.

He seemed anxious, maybe even a little nervous, and that thrilled her. She ached to create a new moment between them.

A slick, sensual journey. An erotic awakening.

He was perfect—bronzed and naked and unbelievably hard. His chest narrowed into lean hips, and his legs were long and muscular. A line of hair grew from his navel to his sex. Fascinated, she followed it with her finger.

Adam watched her, knowing his heart pounded much too fast. She was teasing him, making him wait, making him want so badly he could barely breathe. Her lips, warm and tender, cruised over his belly. And then her tongue. So wet, so stimulating.

He was dying. And soon, he thought, soon, he would slide straight into heaven. He fisted the sheets and lifted his hips. Or was it hell? he asked himself, as her hair, that long, luxurious curtain, caressed his thighs. She was an angel, a devil, a vixen who had captured his soul.

Nothing mattered but her.

He was desperate to be touched. Loved. Laved. He chanted her name, over and over in his mind. *Sarah. Sweet, sweet Sarah.* Her mouth was on him now. There, right there.

He struggled to control the urgency, struggled to keep himself from falling too far, but he knew he was losing the battle.

Sensation slammed into sensation, as fast and violent as a storm. His breath crashed in his lungs, his blood pumped heat through his veins

He had to stop her. Now.

Fighting the fury, he gripped her shoulders and pulled her up. Her nightgown was in the way, so he grabbed the fabric and nearly tore it in his haste.

They tumbled over the bed, and he yanked open the drawer and fisted a condom. And then he tried, damn it, tried to tear the package, but he couldn't quite manage it. Sarah was stroking him, milking him with those smooth, skilled hands.

"You shouldn't do that," he rasped. She still wore her panties, and his climax was ebbing, rising like a wave.

"It's okay."

"But I can't…not yet…not…"

"I want you to." She pressed her stomach to his and held him, giving him permission, encouraging him to spill, warm and wet, onto her skin.

And when it happened, he shuddered in her arms and let the moment, the incredible closeness, sweep him away.

Eleven

Three days later, Sarah and Adam sat at the table in their motel room, sharing a makeshift breakfast of fresh fruit and granola bars. They'd showered, but had yet to dress. Both wore terry-cloth robes. Like a happy couple, she thought, lounging on a quiet morning.

Peeling an orange, she glanced up at him. He lifted an apple to his mouth and smiled. Perfect Adam. It was difficult to picture him as a rebellious youth, a teenage boy stealing whiskey and lying to his parents. He was so grounded now, so centered.

"I can't believe we haven't found out anything about your mom," she said.

They had searched, but there was no sign of Cynthia Youngwolf, not one single clue. No one at the hospitals remembered her, nor did the library in town have any old high-school annuals available. The librarian had suggested checking with the schools themselves, but that hadn't panned out, either. Both high schools were closed for the summer.

"We haven't gone to the university yet. She might have been a student there. There's still a lot of ground to cover."

He was right, of course. Their search wasn't over.

Adam took a swig of bottled water. "I'd still like to buy some ranch property around here, Sarah. Are you okay with that?"

Suddenly nervous, she filled her lungs with air, then let it out slowly. "Yes." She wanted to make a life with Adam and that meant coming to terms with her past, with making some kind of peace with her father. "I haven't spent much time with my dad. I should go see him today. I think it's his day off."

"That's a good idea." He reached for her hand, squeezed it. "Everything's going to be fine, sweetheart."

"I know," she said, even though she felt a niggle of fear. But with Sarah, there were always little jabs of worry. It was her nature, she supposed.

Abandoning breakfast, Adam shed his robe. "We can meet here later."

"Are you going to the university?"

"No. I'd rather wait for you to do that."

"Then what are you going to do?"

He grinned. "Go see a Realtor. They've already got a list of properties to show me."

"We only have one car," she pointed out.

"I can walk. The realty office isn't far from here."

Adam was dressed before Sarah, but it was easier for a man to throw himself together. All he needed was pair of jeans and a T-shirt to look gorgeous. Her ritual consisted of quite a bit more.

He buckled his belt and reached for his shoes. "There's a nice seafood restaurant down the street. How about some swordfish tonight?"

"Sure." She curled a mascara wand around an eyelash, doing her best to prevent it from clumping.

"Feel free to invite your dad."

"Okay."

After lacing his ropers, he patted her bottom. She laughed

and nearly poked herself in the eye. "You better get out of here before I end up with an injury."

"Yes, ma'am." He faked an Oklahoma twang. "I'll see you back here around five."

She watched him go, feeling like a schoolgirl. Her heart was fluttering in her chest. Just like the patter of little feet, she thought. Someday she was going to have his babies.

And there was nothing to worry about, she told herself as she dialed her father's number. This wasn't a dream. She wasn't going to wake up and find everything gone. They had already picked out names for their children. And Adam was meeting with a Realtor, looking for a home.

What could be more stable than that?

Her dad's line was busy, so she went back to her makeup. When she called again, he answered.

"Hi," she said. "It's me. I was wondering—"

"Oh, God. I was just going to call you."

Her fluttering heart skipped a beat. "Why? What's going on?"

"Nothing. I mean, I don't want to talk about it over the phone."

He's been drinking, she thought. His voice sounded shaky, his words unsteady. How could he do this? And what excuse would he come up with to ease his conscience?

"Can you come over, Sarah?"

She wanted to say no. She wanted to tell him to go straight to hell. "Yes," she said instead.

"Will you come alone? I don't want Adam—"

"He isn't here." But she wished he was. She didn't know how she was going to handle this without him.

The drive to Hatcher took forever. The roads to her father's house were long and dusty, and in spite of the air-conditioned vehicle, her palms were sweating.

He met her on the porch, reaching out to take one of her clammy hands.

He looked distressed. And with her father, that meant a shot or two. Or three, she thought, releasing a pent-up breath. "How many have you had, Dad?"

"What?" He backed away, releasing her hand. "Is that what you think this is about?"

She crossed her arms. The sun was beating down on her back. She had prepared herself for the heat, worn a sleeveless shirt and fastened her hair in a single braid, but the humidity stuck to her like glue. "Isn't it?"

"No. This has nothing to do with me. It concerns Adam."

Skeptical, she tilted her head. "Really? How so?"

"I found out about his mother, honey. And his father, too."

Her knees nearly buckled. "I'm sorry. I thought—"

"It's okay. Come inside and we'll talk."

She sat on her dad's old-fashioned sofa and waited for him to sit beside her. But instead, he paced the floor, then stopped to drag a hand through his hair. It must be bad, she thought. Really bad.

"Are they dead?" she asked.

William frowned. "His father is."

"And his mother?"

"She's in Tulsa."

Then it can't be that bad, Sarah told herself. As long as Cynthia Youngwolf was alive, there was hope. "Is she sick?"

"No." He sat beside her, sinking into the corduroy cushions. "She's a widow and has other children. Two grown sons and a school-age daughter."

Sarah's heart stuck in her throat. Adam had brothers. And a little sister. She tried to picture them, wondered if they were as beautiful, as perfect as the man she loved. "They don't know about him, do they?"

"No, they don't." He stared straight ahead. "I'm sorry, honey, but Adam's mother doesn't want to see him."

"Why?" Anger caught her hard and fast. She didn't have any sympathy for Cynthia Youngwolf, not if the woman was going to hurt Adam. There had been a time when Sarah thought he had been wrong to search for his family, but she felt differently now. "This isn't fair. All he wants is a chance to meet her. He deserves that much."

"Honey, you don't understand."

She narrowed her eyes. "Then make me understand. Tell me why she doesn't want to see her son."

"I will," he said. "But how in God's name we're supposed to tell Adam, I don't know."

When Adam walked into the motel room, he shot Sarah and William a big smile, pleased that her father had decided to join them. "So we're on for dinner?" He couldn't wait to tell them about the properties he had seen.

"We need to talk." Sarah, sitting on the edge of the bed, looked up at him. She seemed sad, he realized suddenly. He glanced at William, who stood near his daughter. His expression was equally somber.

"What's going on?"

"I found your mother." William stepped forward. "And I'm going to start from the beginning, because I don't know how else to do this."

Adam sat in a chair by the desk. In that instant, he knew: Cynthia Youngwolf had refused to meet him. All of Sarah's old warnings came scrambling back, tenfold.

I hate to say this, but there's a good chance that your biological mother won't want to see you. She might feel as though you're interfering in her life.

Preparing himself for the worst, he maintained his composure. He would listen to whatever William had to say, and when it ended, he would give his mother the time she needed. Eventually, it would work out.

When William's breath hitched, he wanted to tell the other man that everything would be okay. He understood how difficult this had to be for his mother. She wasn't expecting to hear from him. It had to be a shock.

"You weren't born in a hospital," William told him. "A midwife delivered you. Her name is Margaret, and she's the one who told me about your mother. Margaret is an old woman now, but she never forgot Cindy Youngwolf."

"Cindy? Is that the name my mom uses?"

He nodded. "Yes."

"Whose house was I born at?"

"Cindy's aunt's. You see, your mother wasn't from Tahlequah. She lived in Oklahoma City at the time, but she had an aunt here. So when her family found out she was pregnant, they sent her to stay with a relative."

"How old was Cindy?" he asked, trying to picture his mother.

"Eighteen. She was a quiet girl who kept to herself, but she told Margaret about what had happened to her."

He sat forward in his chair. "What do you mean?"

"I wish I didn't have to tell you this."

Sarah glanced away, and Adam's stomach fell. Why wouldn't she look at him? And why was her father so reluctant to talk? What the hell was going on? "Just say it."

William bit down on his bottom lip. "Cindy claimed that she was raped. That a white boy had forced her to..." The older man glanced up at the ceiling. "But in those days, if a girl flirted with a boy, she was held accountable, too. The police discouraged her from filing charges. She was a minority, and he came from a well-to-do family. That's the way things were back then."

"No." Adam shook his head. "The midwife has my mother mixed up with someone else." This sordid, sickening story didn't belong to him. "My mother and my father were—" in love, he wanted to say. His eyes stung, but he fought the urge to cry. "They..." When his voice broke, he looked at Sarah and saw that her hands were trembling. "Oh, God. Who are they, William? Who the hell are my parents?"

"Cindy Youngwolf is your mother. And your father was a twenty-year-old college boy."

"I don't want to be related to him. I don't..."

"I'm sorry."

Adam battled a wave of nausea. His mother, his eighteen-year-old mother, was sexually assaulted. By his father. His conception was a vile act, the most degrading of human crimes. "How could he do that to her? How could he..." The nausea worsened, so he stood and made his way to the sink. He wanted to vomit, but he knew it wouldn't help. He couldn't purge his father's sin.

Turning, he faced William again, feeling shamed and dirty. "Who is he?"

"A college boy," the other man said again, his voice filled with sorrow.

"What's his name? What's the bastard's bloody name?"

"I don't know. If it's any consolation, he's dead. Margaret said that he's been dead a long time."

"Good." It didn't help, not really, but he unclenched his fists. If his father wasn't dead, he would have called him out, taken vengeance for Cindy. And for the disgusting circumstances of his birth.

When Sarah started toward him, he backed himself against the sink. She was crying, blinking furiously to stop the flow. Who did she see? he wondered. Who was he to her now?

"Don't touch me." He held up his hand to ward her off. She was too pure to come into contact with him, too soft and beautiful. His blood was tainted. He could feel it running through his veins like a sewer of filth.

He hadn't been prepared for this, for something so dirty. And by searching for Cindy, by showing up nearly thirty years later, he had brought the memory back to her, the ache and the horror of being violated.

"Do you think my mother tried to wash him off her skin?" he asked, his mind clouding with heart-wrenching images. "Do you think she rubbed her body until it was raw?" Because no one answered, he continued to talk. "That's what I've heard women do after they're raped. They try to make themselves clean again."

"You have to stop thinking about that," William said. "Your mother went on with her life. She got married, and she had other children. She's widowed now, but her daughter is only twelve. And her sons are close by."

A lump clogged Adam's throat. Cindy had given birth to other babies, children she wanted. He tried to be glad for her, but all he felt was pain. He was the one she had given away, the baby who had grown in her stomach like a cancer.

He was the rape.

"I want you to go home," he told William. "And I want you to take Sarah with you."

"No." She was still crying, her hands still trembling. "I love you, Adam. Let me stay with you."

He closed his eyes. He needed to send Sarah as far away as he could. She pitied him now, but before long, her skin would start to crawl. She would look at him and see the cancer. He was no longer the man she loved. He couldn't give her sweet, clean babies. His genes were soiled.

How could she stand to look at him? Even think about touching him?

"Please." Opening his eyes, he implored the other man. "I need some time alone."

William took charge, insisting his daughter pack an overnight bag. She gathered a few toiletries and whispered a shaky goodbye.

Adam turned away and waited for them to leave, and when they were gone, he caught his reflection in the mirror.

Without thinking, he raised his fist to the glass and shattered it. Blood dripped down his wrist, but he didn't care. It was his father's face that he had just destroyed, and he never wanted to see it again.

At dawn, Sarah stared at the flickering image on the television set. She had covered herself with a blanket, but felt no warmth from it. All she could think about was Adam.

A shadow crossed the room, and she turned to see her father.

His hair was wet from a recent shower, the salt and pepper strands combed away from his face. "You haven't slept, have you?"

She shook her head. "What are you doing up so early?"

"Getting ready for work." He sat beside her and handed her a cup. "I don't have any tea, but I thought you might need this."

"Thanks." Accepting the offering, she brought it to her lips. It was coffee, diluted with cream and sugar. She let the liquid seep into her bones, chasing away the chill.

"It's morning now," he said. "It would probably be okay to go see him."

"That's what I was thinking." She turned to look out the window, where the sun peeked through the blinds, sending slats of light across the hardwood floor. It could have been a rainbow, but she knew better. "Is he going to be all right?"

"Of course, he is. He has you, doesn't he? You'll help him get through this."

"Just the way I have you." She smiled at her father, remembering how she had cried in his arms the night before. "Are my eyes still puffy?"

"Yeah, but it doesn't make you any less pretty."

"I love you, Dad."

"I love you, too." He squeezed her knee. "Now go on, get yourself together. There's a man who needs you more than I do."

She stood and sipped her coffee. And at that moment, in the light of dawn, with cartoons playing on TV and the taste of caffeine on her tongue, she knew William Cloud was sober.

He winked at her, and she saw her daddy—the strong, proud warrior who used to tuck her in at night. Before she broke down and started crying again, she headed for the shower, reviving herself for Adam.

An hour later, Sarah unlocked the motel-room door. The bed was still made, the curtains drawn tight, keeping out the light. She stepped farther into the darkness, willing her eyes to adjust. Placing her purse on the desk, she turned, her heart catching on a gasp.

"Oh, dear God."

He was asleep on the floor, his bloodied hand staining his shirt. The mirror above the sink was smashed. Shards of glass littered the counter, glinting dangerously.

She knelt on the carpet and touched his shoulder. He flinched and came awake, jerking when he saw her.

"Shhh. It's okay. I'm just going to clean up your hand."

He didn't protest, so she wet several washcloths in the tub and sat on the floor in front of him. There were slivers of glass under his skin and gashes deep enough to worry her.

"You might need stitches."

He pulled back. "It doesn't matter."

It did to her, but she didn't press the issue. Tending him the best she could, she removed the glass with a pair of tweezers and cut the corner of a sheet for a makeshift bandage.

He didn't look like himself. His eyes were empty, so vacant she feared he had lost his soul. Beautiful Adam, she thought, blinking back tears. Her dragon slayer was dying inside, slipping into a dungeon of darkness and pain.

"It will get easier," she told him, bandaging his hand. She considered drawing him into her arms, but sensed he wouldn't welcome her sympathy. His shoulders were broad and rigid, a man keeping himself at bay. "You won't feel this way forever."

He met her gaze without really looking at her. "I don't care."

But he did, she thought. He cared too much. He wanted his mother to forgive him for something he had nothing to do with. "You were a baby. It wasn't your fault."

"She's ashamed of me. I'll always be something vile in her mind."

"She doesn't even know you. If she did, she would be proud of the man you've become."

He drew his knees up, putting a shield between them. "She should have had an abortion. She should have ended it a long time ago."

"No." Sarah shook her head, wanting to shake him. "Don't you say that. Don't you dare." Because it meant that he didn't think he was worthy of life. And he was. If anyone deserved to be happy, to be loved, it was Adam.

"I'm so stupid." He wrapped his arms around his legs, putting pressure on his hand. Blood seeped through the bandage, staining a portion of the white cloth a crimson hue. "I fantasized about my parents. About how in love they must have been."

"Your other parents were in love. The ones who raised you, Adam. They were your *real* parents."

He looked up, fear in his eyes. ''Oh, God. They knew, didn't they? They must have known.''

''It doesn't matter—''

''The hell it doesn't.'' The fear turned to fury, flashes of fire and anger. ''All those years, all that time, they knew. When I became a problem, they must have worried that they'd made a mistake, that they'd adopted the wrong child.''

''Stop it! They loved you. Don't degrade their memory like this.''

''So what am I supposed to do? Pretend that my father didn't rape my mother? Pretend that Cindy isn't refusing to see me? Am I just supposed to go on with my life, feeling normal?''

Sarah couldn't swallow her shame. Adam's world had just shattered. Everything he cared about had been stolen from him, and she didn't have the words to comfort him. Suddenly loving him wasn't enough. ''I'm sorry. I wish I could take the pain away.''

''You can't. No one can.''

Cindy Youngwolf could, she thought. The older woman could meet her son. She could look into his eyes and help him feel human again. But how was that going to happen? Adam's mother didn't want to have anything to do with him.

He came to his feet, and she could see how dizzy he was. He leaned against the wall for support, then steadied himself, rigid once again.

''I need to clean up this mess,'' he said. ''And I have to tell someone at the front desk that I'll have the mirror fixed.''

So proper, she thought, so decent. He might be battling a deep state of depression, but he was still concerned about doing the right thing.

''I'll help.'' She reached for the trash can and began filling it with broken glass. His blood had dried on the counter, and the sight of it made her eyes water. ''What are you going to do about your hand?''

Focusing on their task, he shrugged.

''You should see a doctor.'' She wet a cloth and wiped the counter. ''Will you do that, Adam? Will you see a doctor?''

"I guess." He turned to look at her. "Thank you, sweet Sarah, but you should go. You shouldn't be here."

Sweet Sarah. The nickname shot through her like an arrow, piercing the part of her that ached for him. "Come to my father's house with me. It's quiet there." And maybe, just maybe, being in the country would help him heal. "It was so pretty this morning. The sun rises over the hills, and the air smells like horses and hay and flowers. And my dad's neighbor has kids. A boy and a girl. They're part Indian. Like you."

"I'm not part anything anymore." He touched her cheek with his injured hand, brushing her skin with the bandage. "But you…you're so beautiful. Your blood is so pure."

"My blood is no different than yours."

"It's pure," he said again. "Pure Cherokee. I'm what society used to call a half-breed. I don't belong to either side."

She understood what he meant, and because she did, she didn't know how to respond. His mother wouldn't acknowledge him, and his father wasn't worth being related to. It was so unfair. He deserved better. So much more.

He dropped his hand. "Go home. Go back to your dad's, and I'll see a doctor. I'm not going to hurt myself again."

But he wanted to, she thought with despair. He wanted to.

Adam returned from the doctor's office, his hand stitched and bandaged. He'd rented another car so he could distance himself from Sarah. He needed to be alone, to deal with his feelings in his own way. He couldn't share anything with her, not even something as simple as a rental vehicle.

Squaring his shoulders, he entered the motel lobby, intending to get this over with as quickly as possible. He wasn't in the mood to chat with strangers, to fake a smile or return a casual hello.

The lobby was fairly busy. The clerk waited on an older man, and a young couple with a trio of active kids gathered brochures and planned their day.

To keep himself from making direct eye contact with anyone, Adam studied the floor, hoping he appeared as unapproachable as he felt.

When the room finally cleared, he walked toward the desk.

"Hey. How ya doin'?" the clerk said, recognition in his upbeat tone, an indication that he recalled checking Adam and Sarah into their room.

Suddenly Adam didn't know how to explain the situation. Keeping his bandaged hand below the counter, he frowned. He'd told the doctor he'd cut himself on some glass, but this was different. He'd damaged property. This wasn't about his injury.

"I broke the mirror in my room," he said, keeping it honest and simple. "I apologize, and I'm more than willing to replace it."

The clerk measured him with a curious stare, and Adam caught his own blunder. He shouldn't have come in here with a dark cloud hovering over his head, with a don't-mess-with-me stance. He should have called, handled it over the phone.

"Is everything all right?" the other man asked.

"Yeah. It was an accident. You can bill my credit card to fix it."

"And that little lady you're with is all right, too?"

Stunned and immediately sickened, Adam felt his stomach roll. Did the clerk think he had hurt Sarah? Was that the sort of person he appeared to be? A man who abused women? A man like the bastard who had spawned him?

"She's fine."

"So long as she didn't cut herself, too. I noticed your bandage when you came in."

Adam blinked, realizing he'd misunderstood the clerk's concern for Sarah. Was this how he'd react for the rest of his life? Guilty and paranoid about his father's sin? "My hand isn't as bad as it looks."

"Well, then." The other man's posture relaxed. "Why don't I get you checked into another room while we get that one squared away?"

"Thank you."

Five minutes later, Adam exited the lobby, his breath clogging his lungs. He returned to the old room and packed his belongings along with what Sarah had left behind.

And when he entered the new room, he panicked. What was he supposed to do? Stare blindly at the TV? Pace the floor like a caged animal? Struggle to block the fear? The paranoia?

Damn it. The walls were closing in.

He needed to go for a drive. He needed…

His next thought hit him like a fist. A drink. He needed a drink.

No, he told himself as he headed toward his car. No. He was clean, sober. He'd followed a holistic path, healing his mind, respecting his body.

Adam dug the key out of his pocket and ran his thumb over the serrated edge. Big deal. Big damn deal. His adoptive parents were dead, his father was a monster, and his mother couldn't bear to see his face. How holistic was that?

He unlocked the door, slid behind the wheel. And then there was Sarah, he thought. Sweet, sweet Sarah. She had been right from the beginning. They should never have gotten involved, never made love, never fooled themselves into believing everything would be okay. She was too good for him, too wholesome and pure. And if they stayed together, he'd only end up ruining her life.

Like a man possessed, a man losing his soul to an old, familiar demon, he pulled out of the parking lot.

He would buy a bottle of whiskey and go back to his room. And when it was over, when the amber liquid warmed his gut and the edges of his nightmare turned a misty shade of gray, eleven years of sobriety wouldn't mean a thing.

Twelve

That evening, Sarah sat on her father's porch, watching the sun set. The sky was a haze of mauve, streaked with slashes of red and melting streams of blue. It reminded her of fire, of flames burning in the heavens. And in her heart.

If only she could make things right for Adam. She had been trying to reach him for hours, leaving messages at the motel. The man at the front desk had told her he'd switched rooms, which made her feel a little better. At least he wasn't staring into the remnants of that broken mirror.

Should she drive over there? Or would that upset him even more? He seemed determined to keep her at bay, to handle this crisis on his own. She suspected he was sitting alone in the dark, refusing to answer the phone.

William came outside and set a plate on the table positioned beside her. "It's that wild rice medley your mom used to make." He pointed to the dinner he'd prepared. "It was your favorite when you were little. You never cared much for burgers and fries and that sort of thing. You always went for the healthier stuff. It was hard to believe you were my kid. I thrived on junk.''

She picked up the plate and managed a grateful smile. He'd added zucchini from his neighbor's garden to the recipe, and there was a heap of coleslaw and diced apples on the side. ''This is perfect. Aren't you having any?''

He wrinkled his nose. ''No way. I made myself a sloppy Joe. I'll be right back.''

He returned with his meal, and when he bit into the sandwich, bits of the stuffing fell out the sides and landed back on his plate in a saucy mess. He'd given himself potato chips as a side dish and a can of grape soda to wash it down. Sarah sipped bottled water and marveled at the man William Cloud had become.

''I know you're not drinking any more, Dad. And I'm proud of you.''

''Thanks.'' He wiped his mouth. ''It's been a long, dark road, and I don't have any intention of going back.''

''I should have stayed here. I should have been more supportive, the way Mom was.''

''No. You did the right thing. You were young, with your whole life ahead of you. I had no right to put you through that kind of misery, to make you ashamed of me and your heritage.'' He went after a handful of chips, his actions more casual than his words. ''Now I go to a meeting every day. Sometimes twice a day when temptation rears its ugly head.''

''You've come a long way.'' And it made her glad that he was her father, that he was the man her mother had fallen in love with.

''Adam used to drink,'' she admitted, knowing it was time to confide in her dad. ''But he's been sober for eleven years.''

William startled, his soda teetering for a moment. ''I'm surprised you got involved with him.''

''I almost didn't. But I've learned to trust him.''

Silence bounced between them then, the sky still blazing with fiery hues. The fragrance of summer misted the air, and Sarah breathed in the scent.

''I love him so much, Dad.''

"I know." Balancing his plate on his lap, William frowned into his food. "But are you sure he won't drink again? He is going through a rough time."

As an image of Adam sleeping on the floor loomed in her mind, she shivered. Broken glass and blood. That's how he felt, she realized. Shattered and wounded.

But that didn't mean he would turn to alcohol, she told herself, as a stab of fear jabbed her chest. Adam knew better. He was stronger than that. "I used to think the trigger was out there somewhere, that he might fall, but he said it would never happen."

"And you believe him?"

She nodded. Loving him meant that she had to believe him, had to trust his words, his promises. "Everyone who used to drink doesn't falter." And Adam deserved her support, her faith in his sobriety. "Eleven years is a long time."

"I'm sorry. I had to ask." William released a heavy breath. "Maybe we can convince him to stay here. He should be around family."

"I already tried." Sarah looked up at the sky, suddenly aware of what she had to do. Family was exactly what Adam needed. "Did you talk to Cindy Youngwolf?"

"No. Margaret is the one who called her and told her about Adam. And then she relayed their conversation back to me."

"But you have Cindy's number?"

"Yes. It's listed in the book, under her husband's name. Why? What are you going to do?"

"I'm going to call her," she said, praying the other woman would take the time to listen.

Adam stared at the bottle, at the whiskey he'd purchased hours ago. He hadn't broken the seal, hadn't opened it.

It sat on the dresser like a cool, dark temptation. He wanted it so badly, yet he couldn't bring himself to take that first drink.

Because of Sarah. Because he'd promised her he would never deceive her again. And drinking behind her back would have been the biggest deception of all.

He glanced at the phone. How many messages had she left? Three? Four?

He had to call her, he realized. He had to tell her the truth.

Adam dialed her father's number, keeping his back to the mirror. He'd been avoiding his reflection all night, avoiding the image that sickened him.

"Hello?" Sarah's voice came over the phone, soft and sweet and gentle.

"Hi. It's me." The guy losing his self-respect, the liar, the cheat. He reached for the bottle, felt the familiar shape beneath his fingers. "I'm sorry I didn't call you back sooner."

"Oh, Adam. I have so much to tell you. Can I come by?"

"It's late, Sarah. I don't want you driving over here." And he didn't want her in this room, in the place where he battled the urge to get sloppily drunk. "I rented a car today. I'll head over that way, okay?" So he could tell her in person, look into her eyes and admit what he'd almost done.

"Okay. I love you," she said.

A lump formed in his throat. He loved her, too. More than he had a right to. "I'll be there as soon as I can."

Feeling clumsy and awkward, Adam laced his boots, then cursed his injured hand. And when he stood, he noticed the trembling.

Was he nervous? he asked himself. Or was he experiencing a psychological withdrawal? A mental reminder of the shakes, the edginess that came with the addiction?

Being seventeen years old and craving one shot, just one stress-relieving drink, wasn't something he was likely to forget. Nor was shivering until his teeth rattled.

Adam grabbed the rest of Sarah's luggage and put it in the trunk, along with the whiskey, the proof he needed to set her free, to convince her that loving him was a mistake.

When he arrived at her father's house, she waited for him on the front steps, looking like a little girl in an oversized T-shirt and baggy jeans. She'd plaited her hair into a single braid, leaving the angles of her face unframed. Her eyes seemed darker and deeper, he thought. Her cheekbones more striking. The backlight from the porch bathed her in a soft, buttery glow.

He moved to the back of the car, prepared to open the trunk, to show her the bottle. He couldn't drag this moment out, make either one of them suffer longer than necessary.

She stood and came toward him. "I'm so glad you're here. I talked to your mother, Adam. I talked to Cindy."

He froze, the trunk key imprinting his thumb. "What?"

"I called her." She drew a breath, gauged his troubled expression. "Please don't be mad. I wasn't trying to interfere."

"I'm not mad." He was stunned. Guilty. Sick at heart. He'd spent the day lusting after a drink, and Sarah had contacted his mother. "What did she say?"

"Truthfully, not much. She didn't want to discuss anything personal over the phone. I think her daughter was there."

He closed his eyes, and then opened them a second later. He wouldn't let his mind conjure an image of his mother's youngest child. His little sister.

Sarah moved closer. "Cindy agreed to meet with me tomorrow." She lifted her eyes to his, held him tenderly within her gaze. "And I'm going to tell her about you. About how kind and decent you are."

God help him, he thought. He longed to touch Sarah's cheek, to stroke her skin and profess how much he loved her. But her good intentions didn't change who or what he really was—an alcoholic conceived from rape. "Don't glorify me to my mother. I bought a bottle of whiskey today, right after I switched rooms."

Dear God. Fear, shock, a dizzying pain gripped Sarah's heart. Her father had warned her, but she hadn't seen it coming. Her love for Adam had blinded her, the fairy tale, the fantasy she had created in her mind.

Needing to sit, to collect her emotions, she found her way to the steps. She couldn't fall apart. Not now.

"Did you drink?" she asked.

"No." He shook his head. "I wanted to, though. A lot."

But he didn't, she thought, as her heartbeat stabilized. He

hadn't let himself go that far. He was still living by the vow he'd made to stay sober. The warrior in Adam was fighting the addiction. "You're going to be all right. You'll get through this. I can help you."

"How?" He turned, paced a little, stopped to look at her. "You can't make the craving go away. You're not me, Sarah. You don't know what it feels like. How badly I wanted to open that bottle."

She inhaled the summer air, telling herself to think, to say the right thing. All those years with her father hadn't prepared her for this moment. She wasn't supposed to have fallen in love with an alcoholic. Yet Adam, troubled Adam, lived inside her.

She glanced up at the sky, saw a scatter of stars twinkling against the night. Was there anything she could say or do that would lessen his fears? He seemed so lost, so broken. "You should get professional help. My father goes to meetings. You could—"

"No." He cut her off. "I'm not...I can't..."

He paced again, trampling grass beneath his shoes. His hair was loose, flowing to his shoulders, and his eyes were dark and shadowed. She could see that he hadn't slept, hadn't eaten. She wanted to reach out and hold him, but she knew she couldn't coddle his addiction.

"Why won't you see someone, Adam? You've done it before. You know therapy can be effective."

He dragged a hand through his hair. "It's different this time."

"Why?"

"It just is."

Because of his parents, she realized. His biological parents. Therapy would mean talking about them, admitting out loud why he had the urge to drink. His father had raped his mother, and now his mother was rejecting him.

Sarah thought about Cindy. The other woman hadn't made any promises on the phone. She hadn't agreed to meet Adam, but she had made arrangements to talk to Sarah, to discuss the son she'd given up. It was a start, a hope to cling to. If

Sarah could convince Cindy to give Adam a chance, then maybe he could find the strength to heal.

She looked up at him, saw that he watched her. "Are you hungry?" she asked. "I can heat some leftovers."

"Thanks, but no. I can't deal with food right now. Maybe I just need to get some sleep."

"You can stay here," she offered.

"No. I can't." He came forward and sat beside her. "You promised yourself you'd never get involved with an alcoholic, and that's what I am. A man craving a drink."

Sarah forced herself to breathe, to fill her lungs with oxygen. She wouldn't lose him, not like this. Not to an addiction, to a bottle of whiskey. He was worth so much more than that. "I'm not giving up on you. Or on us."

He touched her cheek, then drew back quickly, his injured hand shaky. "So you're still going to meet with my mother? Tell her what a great guy I am?"

"Yes, I am. And I'm going to be here if you need me." She noticed the professional bandage on his hand, pleased that he'd seen a doctor. "But I'm asking you to destroy the whiskey you bought. Throw it away. Pour it down the sink. Whatever you have to do to get rid of it."

"What if I give it to you?"

She blinked. "What?"

He gestured toward the car. "It's in the trunk. I brought it with me. And I brought the rest of your luggage, too. The stuff you left at the motel."

She ignored the pain, the clench in her heart. Adam couldn't bear to have her staying with him. He had chosen solitude over love.

He placed her suitcase on the porch. And when he handed her the unopened whiskey, she fought a burst of panic, realizing how close to the edge he really was.

Stay strong, she told herself an instant later. Focused. Adam's mother was most likely the key to his salvation.

But would Cindy Youngwolf listen to what Sarah had to say? Would the other woman agree to meet her son? Or would Sarah have to give Adam more hurtful news?

She glanced at the whiskey and frowned. Maybe she was placing too much importance on Adam's mother. Cindy could ease the part of him that ached, but she couldn't stop him from drinking. Only Adam could conquer his addiction.

"I'll call you tomorrow," she said. "After I see your mom."

"Thank you." He looked directly into her eyes. "Aren't you worried that I'm going to buy another bottle?"

"I trust you," she told him. Maybe even more than he trusted himself. Because if she gave into the panic and lost hope, then he would, too.

The following afternoon Sarah drove to Tulsa. She found the park Cindy Youngwolf-Nichols had directed her to and got out of the car.

Anxious, she sat on a picnic bench and placed two small cartons of orange juice on the table. The air was warm, even in the shade. Checking the time, she turned to watch the activity on the playground. A group of kids took turns on the slide, and a toddler clapped his chubby hands and grinned as his mother pushed him on one of the baby swings.

Did Cindy live nearby? Was this the park she had taken her own children to? Or was this on the other side of town, away from those who knew her? Cindy's address wasn't listed in the phone book.

Within minutes a woman came toward the bench. Sarah assumed she was Adam's mother simply because she wore a yellow blouse—the color Cindy had said she would be sporting.

Nervous, she stood to greet her. "Hello," she said, when they were close enough to hear each other. "I'm Sarah."

"Hello." The other woman stood a little awkwardly. Attractive for her age, she was trim, with dark hair cut into one of those easy-to-care-for styles that fell just below her chin. Neither tall nor short, her height measured somewhere in-between.

Because Sarah searched for a family resemblance, she found several. Brown eyes, Indian cheekbones and a mouth that managed to look full and feminine on Cindy, yet wickedly sensual on Adam. Yes, she thought, this woman was his mother.

"I brought some juice."

"Thank you." They both sat, and Cindy accepted one of the plastic containers without opening it. "So Adam is your fiancé?" she asked, reaffirming what had been briefly discussed over the phone.

"Yes, but he's pulling away from me." Trying to convince her not to love him, she thought. And refusing to get help for his struggle, for the battle to stay sober.

"I'm sorry if he isn't taking this well, but this hasn't been easy on me, either. My other children don't know about him. I never even told my husband. I agreed to meet with you because—" Pausing to twist the gold band on her left hand, she trapped Sarah's gaze. "I need for you to understand why I can't see Adam. Why it would be better to leave things as they are."

"That's fine." She would let Cindy say her piece, then she would say hers. She wasn't going to argue with Adam's mother, but she couldn't bear to watch the man she loved suffer, either.

"Giving up a child was the hardest thing I've ever done, but I did it for the right reasons. I wanted him to have a better life than I was able to provide."

"And that's the only reason you didn't keep him?"

"No." The other's woman's gaze turned candid. "It was also because of what his father did to me."

Silent, Sarah waited, knowing she was about to hear the whole ugly story.

Clasping her hands, Cindy placed them on the table. "He was very handsome. Johnny, that was his name. Tall and broad, with the most stunning smile I had ever seen."

"Where did you meet him?"

"At the diner where I worked. Some of the local college students hung out there, so it was an exciting job for me. I was a senior in high school, trying to look more grown-up. I flirted with Johnny, but so did other girls. He got a lot of attention. And he had a wild streak, a rebelliousness that fit the times. We were the generation that was going to change the world.''

Sarah glanced at the playground again. Laughter drifted through the air, as warm and happy as sunshine. No one would ever know, she thought, that two women were sitting below a bright blue sky, discussing the man who had raped one of them.

''One night, after my shift, Johnny asked me to go for a drive. I barely knew him, aside from the little bit of flirting that we'd done, but I wasn't about to refuse. He seemed so nice, so charming.'' Lifting her hand, she smoothed her hair, even though there wasn't a strand out of place. ''And when he took me into a secluded area, I thought 'Oh, my. He's going to kiss me.' He did, of course. But then everything changed. He started tugging at my clothes, pushing me onto the back seat. I said no, and suddenly he wasn't Johnny anymore. He wasn't the charming boy with the stunning smile.''

''I'm so sorry.'' Sarah could almost picture herself in Cindy's place. Naive and young, being abused by someone she had trusted.

''When he was done, I was in tears, and he kept telling me to quit making such a big deal about it.'' She drew a tight breath. ''Later I discovered that my thighs were bruised. And I had a bump on the back of my head because he'd shoved me against the window.''

''Did you tell anyone that night?''

''No. I should have, but I was too ashamed. My parents were asleep, so I crept into the house, took a scalding bath and cried like a baby. When I finally got the courage to tell my mother, the bruises were gone.''

''It was too late then,'' Sarah found herself saying.

''Yes, it was. The police said it would be my word against his. One of them even asked me why I was out to ruin Johnny's life. He was just a college kid, and he came from a good, upstanding family.'' Anger flashing in her eyes, she shook her head. ''Needless to say, my parents convinced me to drop the charges. We were supposed to forget that it ever happened.''

But they couldn't forget, Sarah thought. Not when Cindy turned up pregnant. ''They sent you to Tahlequah to have your baby.''

She nodded. ''And while I was gone, they moved from Oklahoma City to Tulsa, so that when I came back, I could start over. A new town, a new life.''

''It couldn't have been that simple.''

''I did what I had to do, including giving my baby up for adoption. And later, when I'd heard that Johnny had crashed his fancy new car, I prayed that he had done what he felt he had to do, that he had died out of guilt. But that wasn't the case. He'd been drag racing with some buddies and lost control.''

''Adam isn't anything like Johnny,'' Sarah offered, watching Cindy twist her wedding ring again. ''He's good and decent, the kindest person I know. And this is killing him. With every day that passes, he dies a little more. His spirit is breaking, and I don't know what to do about it.''

The other woman's eyes filled with tears. ''Tell him I'm sorry. Tell him I did what I thought was best, what my family expected me to do.''

''He needs to hear that from you. He needs to know that you don't hate him.''

''Oh.'' Cindy rocked forward, touched a hand to her heart. ''I've thought about him over the years, at Christmas and on his birthday. He's always there. I haven't forgotten about him.'' Clutching her blouse, her voice shattered a little. ''I even nursed him. My aunt told me not to, but I did it anyway. I needed to hold him before they took him away.''

Sarah's chest constricted. ''He has no idea. He doesn't have that memory.''

''He's not supposed to. He has other parents now.''

''They're dead. They were killed in a plane crash when he was in college. You're all he has left.''

''Oh, no,'' Cindy whispered before her tears fell. ''What am I going to do?''

"Meet your son," Sarah told her. "If you don't, neither one of you will ever be the same."

With her emotions riding her sleeve, Sarah parked in her father's graveled driveway, unlocked the front door and stepped inside. She wanted to see Adam in person, but she'd offered to call rather than crowd him. Trusting him meant just that. She couldn't police him, even though a part of her wanted to. The whiskey incident had scared her more than she was willing to admit.

She set down her purse and picked up the phone. Adam answered on the second ring, which told her he had been waiting anxiously.

"Cindy agreed to meet you," she said.

"Oh, God. When? Where?"

"This Tuesday, at her house. Her other children won't be there, so it will just be you and her."

Fear jumped into his voice. "What about you?"

Sarah sat forward. "Do you want me to go with you?"

"Yeah. I mean, as long as you don't mind. You've already met her, and…"

He was nervous, she realized, anxiety-ridden about facing his mother. She pictured his troubled expression, pictured him pacing the motel room half the day. Was his hair banded into a ponytail? Or was it loose, a little messy? She wished she could touch him, run her fingers over those razor-edge cheekbones, that rugged jaw.

"Of course I don't mind," she said.

"Thank you." He paused, released an audible breath. "And, Sarah?"

"Yes?"

"You didn't tell Cindy, did you? You know, about what's been going on with me?"

"No. I didn't think that was my place." She leaned back, closed her eyes, suddenly nervous herself. How much time would pass before he lost the urge to drink? Before he felt whole again?

"Is she pretty?"

"What?" She opened her eyes, realized he was asking about Cindy. "Yes, she is. I think you're going to like her. She talked about when you were born. She held you, Adam. And nursed you."

"Really?" His voice turned soft, a little shy, and Sarah had to smile.

"Did she mention her other kids?" he asked.

"Only that they don't know about you. She didn't tell me their names."

After a moment of silence, he posed another question, shooting it like a bullet. "What about him? Did she say anything about him?"

"Yes," Sarah said, choosing her words carefully. Adam wasn't ready to hear details about his father. The wound was too fresh, the pain too raw. She suspected Adam had inherited bits and pieces from Johnny, physical traits that defined their gender. But none of that mattered. Cindy wouldn't look into her son's eyes and see the man who had hurt her. "His name was Johnny. He died in a car accident. He was drag racing with some buddies."

"I hope he suffered," Adam said, his tone cold and hard.

Sarah didn't respond. Hatred could destroy a person's soul, and Adam was still teetering on the edge of destruction. Despising a dead man, she thought, wasn't going to help him heal.

Thirteen

On Tuesday afternoon Adam opened the motel-room door and stepped back so Sarah could enter.

''I'm not quite ready,'' he said, stating the obvious. He sported a pair of tan trousers, but his chest was bare, his hair still loose. Adam rarely lingered over his appearance or criticized his wardrobe, but today he'd been doing both.

''That's okay. There's still time.''

Sarah smiled, and he imagined holding her, breathing in her scent. He missed the feel of her, the warmth of her skin, the taste of her kiss. And today she reminded him of a gypsy with her shining black hair and glittering gold hoops. She rarely wore jewelry, but when she did, it enhanced her exotic appeal. He wanted to put a diamond on her finger, but he didn't have the right.

''How are you?'' she asked.

''Better.'' Adam knew she was referring to his urge to drink. ''It's not as strong as it was.'' But it made him realize how severe his addiction was, how he had downplayed the seriousness of it all these years.

"As long as you're okay."

"I'm hanging in there." He reached for a polo-style shirt and lifted it over his head. Turning, he headed for the mirror to band his hair into a ponytail. Combing the dark strands, he tried not to wince. His injured hand ached with the movement, and it shamed and frightened him that he was capable of such aggression. He wasn't the same man, and he knew Sarah deserved better.

When his hair was neatly fixed, he stared at his reflection and saw a stranger staring back at him. A ball of nervousness tightened his stomach. What if Cindy found him offensive. What if…

He spun toward Sarah, who waited at the desk, busying herself with a book he had left there.

"I don't think I can do this."

"What?" She whipped her head up. "Oh, my goodness, why?"

"I might have his face." He couldn't bear to resemble the man who had shattered a young woman's innocence. "My mother might look at me and see him."

"No, she won't." Sarah came to her feet and walked toward him, brushing his arm.

"How can you be so sure?"

"Because you look like Cindy. You look like a Cherokee."

"Thank you," he said, even though the knot in his stomach wouldn't loosen. No matter what Sarah said, he knew Johnny was inside him.

Wouldn't Cindy realize that, too? And if she hated his father, if her skin still crawled when she thought about him, then how could she accept the son who carried his blood? And how could Sarah? How could any woman?

"I'll get my shoes." He suspected Sarah knew more about his father than she'd told him, but he wasn't going to press her for information. He wasn't going to make her talk about the man who had tainted his genes.

Sitting on the edge of the bed, he laced a pair of leather ropers, then decided to change his shirt. "This one itches."

He peeled the garment from his body, knowing it wasn't the fabric. He didn't feel comfortable in his own skin anymore.

Adam chose a Western shirt, tucking it into his pants and threading a belt through the loops. Sarah watched him, and he felt self-conscious and nervous all over again.

They left the motel, and he offered to drive. The ride was long and quiet, but once they reached Tulsa, she read him the directions to Cindy's house. And when he parked in front of a tidy suburban home, he willed his heartbeat to steady itself.

The woman who answered the door was slim and pretty, with golden skin and hair the color of night. She wore her years with grace and style, reminding Adam of his other mother. And at that heart-clenching moment, he thought about how much he missed his parents, wishing they were standing here beside him. Unsure of what to do or say, he let Cindy take the lead.

"Hello, Sarah," she said, then turned to him. "Oh, my. You must be Adam."

He nodded, waiting for her to extend her hand. But she didn't. She just stood, staring at him, looking at every feature. Silence rose between them, like a ghost drifting on the wind.

He wanted to say something, to break the haunting, but he found himself staring at her, too. He did look like her, he realized. He saw the slant of his cheekbones on her face, and they had the same mouth, only hers was softer, painted with a peach-colored lipstick.

She wasn't as small as Sarah, but she was still a fine-boned lady, telling him that his father had been a big man. Adam stood taller and broader than most. Suddenly a sick feeling came over him, a need to apologize.

"I'm sorry about what happened to you," he said, his voice as raw as his throat.

Cindy blinked. "That was a lifetime ago." Reaching out to touch his cheek, she skimmed lightly. "Were your parents good to you, Adam? Did they treat you right?"

"Yes." He wanted to capture her hand and hold it, but she was already pulling back. "I loved them very much."

"That's what I wanted for you. A good life." Seeming a

little shaken, she smoothed her blouse. "Where are my manners? Come in, please, both of you."

Adam hadn't realized that he and Sarah were still standing at the door, the Oklahoma sun shining on their backs.

Cindy offered them a seat in a formal living room. Her home was bright and pleasant, with a vase of fresh-cut flowers on the fireplace mantle and a lavender-and-blue afghan folded over a melon-colored sofa. She appeared to favor pastels.

"I made coffee," she said. "And sandwiches. Would either of you like something to eat?"

"Yes, thank you." Adam spoke first. He wasn't hungry, and he normally steered clear of caffeine, but he'd heard it was rude to refuse food in an Indian home. He had no idea if Cindy followed the old ways, but he still worried about offending her.

"Can I help?" Sarah rose from her chair.

"No. No. I've got it. I'll just be a moment." The older woman headed toward the kitchen, and Sarah resumed her seat.

She and Adam glanced at each other, but didn't speak. She sent him a reassuring smile, and he wished things had turned out differently. He had caused sweet Sarah nothing but heartache.

Cindy returned with a tray, placing it on the coffee table. She poured the coffee and told them to help themselves to the food. The sandwiches, filled with a variety of meat and cheeses, were cut into small wedges, the serving platter garnished with greens and vegetable sticks.

Still nervous, Adam chose turkey and cheddar, then scattered some celery onto his plate. "This looks great."

"Thank you." She handed him a cup of coffee. "Did Sarah tell you that I have other children?"

"Yes, she did." He didn't see any photographs on the walls, but he assumed they were in a less formal room. A den, perhaps, where the family gathered in front of the TV. "I'm aware that they don't know about me."

"I'm going to tell them, but it might take some time. Rachel is only twelve."

Rachel. He imagined Cindy's daughter with big dark eyes and a pretty smile. "I understand."

"I'm not sure how they'll feel about all of this."

"You don't have to tell them." He poured milk in his coffee and tried to ease her mind. She looked as nervous as he was. "I don't want to make things difficult for you."

"They should know. I should have told them before now. Secrets can destroy a family. And I want them to meet you." She tilted her head, studying him. "You're their brother."

It was, he thought, the nicest thing she could have said. He smiled, and they both let out the breaths they'd been holding.

The conversation turned to small talk, with Sarah joining in. And when they rose to leave an hour later, Cindy hugged him.

Adam's mother felt soft and delicate in his arms, but at that tender moment, all he could think about was how much he hated the man who had hurt her.

Two days later, Adam drove to the garage where Sarah's father worked. He entered the office, telling himself he had to do this. He'd made some monumental decisions, and it was time to follow through.

A middle-aged man sat at a cluttered desk, the phone pressed to his ear. He nodded to Adam and signaled a gesture that said "I'll be with you in a minute."

He wore a dark blue uniform, and Adam assumed he was one of the mechanics who worked there. Checking his watch, he realized it was nearly noon. He hoped he hadn't missed William on his lunch hour.

"What do you need?" the other man asked, returning the phone to its cradle.

"Is William Cloud around?"

"I think so. Just a second."

Adam waited while the mechanic paged Sarah's father. This was the right thing to do, he reassured himself. The only thing to do.

William entered the office through a door that led to the automotive bay. They stared at each other for a moment.

Adam hadn't seen the other man since the day William had told him about the rape.

Sarah's father spoke first. "It's good to see you."

"Thanks. You, too. Do you have a minute?"

"Sure."

Since the other mechanic still occupied the office, they walked outside and stood near the front of the building. The garage was located in Arrow Hill, a wealthy community showcasing mansions and historical homes.

"I have something to ask you." Adam noticed that William watched him, waiting for him to state his business. He wasn't sure how the other man felt about him. They had barely gotten acquainted, which made this moment even more difficult. "I was wondering if I could go to one of those meetings with you tonight. AA or whatever it is you attend."

"Of course you can." William's expression softened. "So, have you stayed clean, Adam?"

"Yeah. But it scares me that it's become an issue in my life again. I never expected it to happen, not after all these years." He turned, met the older man's gaze. "And I've never been to a group meeting. I had private counseling when I was a kid."

"It's not so bad. In fact, it helps to know there's others out there. That they're struggling to get by, too."

"That's what I figured." But the idea still made him nervous, talking about himself to strangers, admitting that he had a problem. "I realize I can't hide from the truth. I need to get it out in the open."

"So have you told my daughter?"

"No, but I'm stopping by your house next." Which meant telling Sarah that he couldn't marry her. He hadn't officially broken their engagement, and he feared she was still clinging to false hope, to a fantasy about him that no longer existed. Adam was a changed man, born into a darkness he couldn't deny. Cindy was a kind and caring woman, but he was still Johnny's son, too.

"William?"

"Yes?"

"No matter what happens, I want you to know that I love Sarah. That I would never hurt her deliberately."

"She loves you, too. The way her mother loved me." The older man leaned against the building, but his gaze didn't falter. He kept his eyes trained on Adam. "And that kind of love is rare. One in a million."

I know, Adam thought, frowning at an oil stain on the ground. And that's exactly why he didn't deserve it.

Sarah and Adam strolled along her father's property. Hills rose in the distance, limestone mansions jutting from grassy cliffs. The rich, the working class. It was here that their worlds joined. Sarah was glad her father had chosen this area. It suited him.

Turning to look at Adam, she brushed a lock of hair from her face. Two days had passed since they'd met with Cindy, and now their time in Oklahoma was nearly over. She couldn't believe so much had happened within the span of two weeks.

"Our flight is scheduled on Tuesday," she said, praying that their relationship would resume once they got back to California. Adam was still withdrawn, at least around her.

He stopped, his boots layered with dust. "I'm not going. Not yet, anyway. Cindy asked if I could stay a little longer. We're trying to get to know each other before she tells her other children about me."

"That's good." Sarah told herself this wasn't the end. If anything, it was a new beginning. He would get to know his family and return to California a happier man. And then they could make plans for their future, decide where they were going to live, how many babies they were going to have. "So you rearranged your schedule at work?"

"Not exactly. I told them I wouldn't be coming back." He bent to pick a yellow flower, to hold the stem between his fingers. "I'm going to find a place here, focus on getting myself together. When I go back to California, it will be to pack and arrange to have the animals brought here. I have some time to find a job in Oklahoma. I've got money put away."

"What about us, Adam?"

"I can't marry you, Sarah. You know as well as I do, we're not meant to be."

She struggled to mask the overwhelming pain, the ache squeezing her heart. The man she loved was leaving her. For good. "Why? Because you had the urge to drink?"

"That's part of it." He handed her the flower, then stepped back as if he'd crossed an invisible line. "I'm going to a meeting with your dad tonight, but the idea of admitting that I'm an alcoholic makes me nervous. I've been hiding from it. Pretending the disease would never affect me again."

"You'll do fine." She knew how important sobriety was to him. He'd gotten through the darkest moment of his life without a drink. He wouldn't falter now.

She brought the daisy to her breast. "I trust you, Adam. And I'm willing to stand beside you, to help you."

"I know. And that's what makes this so difficult." He frowned, turned to study the hills. "You deserve better, Sarah. You deserve the kind of stability I can't give you. A home. Children."

Stunned, she only stared. He no longer wanted children? A house in the country? How could a man change that much? How could he walk away from the woman who loved him?

Because, Sarah told herself a moment later, she didn't fit into his world anymore. She had been part of a dream, a fairy tale that had turned into a harsh reality. Adam was battling an emotional crisis, and she had no right to intrude on the time he needed to spend with his new family. They had become his focus, not a wife and children.

"I understand," she said, blinking back tears. She wouldn't cry, wouldn't beg him to include her in his life.

He stuffed his hands in his pockets, his voice raspy. "So, what are you going to do?"

"Go back to California. My dad is getting along just fine. He doesn't need me fussing over him." She took a deep breath, fought the ache where her heart used to be.

"Have I thanked you?" he asked.

"A few times." She longed to hold him, to stroke his face, his hair, those broad, troubled shoulders. "I know you appreciate what I did." Convincing his mother to see him, she thought. That was the only bond they still shared.

He met her gaze, and she noticed his eyes still seemed vacant. He would win the battle, she reminded herself. He would be whole again someday. His new family would help him heal.

At the sound of shuffling feet behind them, they both turned.

"Hi, Sarah." Dillon Hawk, the fourteen-year-old boy from next door, came forward, holding his little sister's hand. She trotted along, her tiny face smudged with dirt.

"We picked some vegetables for your dad." Dillon handed her a brown paper bag, and his sister squinted into the sun, gazing up at the adults.

"Thank you. My father's at work, but I'll give it to him as soon as he gets home." After taking the bag, she introduced Adam to the kids.

He shook Dillon's hand, then knelt to greet the toddler.

"Hi," he said.

"Hi," she repeated, grinning at him.

"Her name is Rebecca," Dillon announced with pride. "But we call her Becky. She's almost two."

"Two," Becky confirmed.

She was adorable, Sarah thought, with her tanned skin and twin ponytails. A mixed-blood, just like Adam. And they seemed enthralled with each other—the big man and the tiny girl.

Sarah chatted with Dillon, telling herself she would survive this moment, the sight of Adam with a toddler who looked as if she could belong to them.

When the children finally left, Becky rode in her big brother's arms, waving and saying goodbye.

As they disappeared, Adam watched them go. "So they live in the farmhouse across the way?"

"Yes. Their father, Jesse, is a veterinarian. He has a practice behind their house and acreage that leads to the hills."

"It looks like a great old place. Full of country charm."

She nodded, realizing it was the kind of house Adam used to want. "Their mother is pregnant again. I guess they intend to have a passel of kids now that they've found each other again."

"What do you mean?"

"Jesse and his wife were separated before Dillon was born, but they're together now." Happy, she thought. Her father's neighbors were blissfully wed.

"Oh." Adam fell silent as they walked, heading back to the house.

When they reached the front porch, Sarah placed the bag of vegetables on a wooden step. A small breeze blew, stirring scents of an Oklahoma summer. She could smell hay, horses and flowers, like the one in her hand—a tiny yellow bloom from the man she would always love.

"Sarah?"

"Yes?"

"I'm glad you understand why we shouldn't be together, why you should have those babies with someone else."

Sarah's heart lurched, bumping her ribcage with a heavy knock.

Suddenly it all made sense. Every last, lonesome detail. He was letting her go because of Johnny. Adam still thought the blood that flowed through his veins was tainted. Meeting Cindy hadn't eased his greatest fear.

Sarah sat on the porch, and he stood by the rail, with those dark, vacant eyes.

"It's Johnny, isn't it? He's the reason you don't want to get married and have children?"

"He's my father, Sarah."

"He's a biological figure," she countered. "Not a father. There's a difference."

"But I inherited things from him. My height, the way I'm built. I'm not just Cindy's son. He's inside me, too."

"No, he isn't. You're nothing like him. And in truth, you

don't know anything about him. Maybe he was hurt or abused himself. Maybe he lashed out at Cindy because of his own insecurities, his own pain."

Adam made a tight face. "How can you excuse what he did so easily?"

"I'm not. By God, I'm not. But just because he was rich doesn't mean he came from a nurturing environment. He ran his car off a cliff, Adam. What does that say? Supposedly he was drag racing and lost control, but how can anyone really know what was going on in his mind at the time? Maybe he hated himself. Maybe deep down he wanted to die."

His expression remained tight. "And maybe he was just a selfish bastard."

"Maybe," she agreed. "But he doesn't matter to me. I'm not judging you by his actions. You're the same man you were before we found out about this. The same kind, honorable man. Your blood is pure, Adam. Pure and good." She stood, came toward him. "And I want to have *your* children. I want them to be part of me, part of us."

"Do you realize what you're saying?" His voice sounded rough, flooded with emotion.

"Yes, I do. And I should have told you before now, but I was trying to make things right between you and your mother. Once she accepted you, I thought everything would be okay, that you would stop blaming yourself for what Johnny did."

He sat beside her. "How do I forget? How do I block those awful images from my mind?"

"I don't know. But you need to stop punishing yourself." She looked at the flower in her lap. It was so fragile, she thought. Like the human spirit. "If a woman you cared about was raped, and she had a baby, would you hate that child? Would you think it was dirty? That it didn't deserve to be loved?"

"Of course not. I wouldn't blame an innocent life."

Sarah moved closer, touched his shoulder. "But don't you see? That's what you've been doing. Twenty-nine years ago, *you* were that baby. You were that innocent life."

Stunned into silence, Adam stared at his bandaged hand.

Could it be that complicated, yet that simple? Was he destroying himself because he was trying to destroy Johnny? Kill a man who was already dead?

He lifted his gaze to Sarah and felt the sting of tears burn the back of his eyes. "I tried to right a wrong with hatred. I ignored the good my adoptive parents instilled in me."

"It's still there, Adam." She placed her hand over his heart. "Right there."

Blinking, he forced back the threat of tears. He hadn't cried throughout this whole ordeal, and damn it, he wasn't going to embarrass himself with watery eyes now.

He covered her hand with his, and while the sun shone bright in the sky and leaves fluttered on the trees, they felt his heartbeat, letting it flow through both of them.

"You had me fooled," he said, recalling the day they'd met. "You seemed like this confused little angel with a broken wing. But here you are, strong and beautiful and whole."

She smiled. "I don't know about the angel part, but I was confused. And if I'm strong and beautiful, it's because of you. You inspired me to give my dad a chance, to forgive him."

Adam thought about her admission, and then frowned. "I don't think I'll ever be able to forgive Johnny. I don't think I have that much good in me."

"Yes, you do."

How could she believe so strongly in him? Trust so deeply?

"Think about your parents, Adam. They didn't tell you about the adoption because they didn't want you to know about Johnny, to feed on the rage and shame you would feel."

He glanced up at the sky, then met her gaze, looked into her eyes and saw his future shining back at him. "Maybe I'll be able to pray for his redemption someday," he said, his voice breaking a little. "Maybe that will take the anger away."

She leaned into him, brushing his lips. "You're going to be fine. You're going to heal from all of this."

He tasted her kiss, the gentleness and the beauty in it. She was his soul, his heart, everything good inside him. Adam closed his eyes, opened them a moment later. "I love you, sweet Sarah."

"I love you, too. And I want to have a life with you."

His chest warmed. "Me, too."

She stood, held out her hand. "Then come inside. Be with me."

He looked up at her, immortalizing this moment in his mind. He knew what she was offering, what she was asking him to do. Sarah wanted to make a baby, to seal their union with everlasting life.

And he wanted that, too. More than he'd ever wanted anything. Accepting her hand, he let her lead him. It felt right to be needed, he thought. To be loved.

He smiled as she locked the bedroom door. Love gave you power, strength in yourself.

With a feminine touch, she began to undress him, baring his chest, unzipping his jeans.

Together they caressed and held, encouraging silk and sensation. And when they were naked, he took her mouth, long and slow. A kiss of friends, of lovers, of dreams and heart-filled promises. In each other's arms, they were home, safe and loved, where they belonged.

He licked her nipples, tasted and savored. Her hair fanned the pillow as his tongue slid over bare skin. Gold washed over the bed, the color of glitter, of sunshine and light.

He settled between her thighs, waiting to consummate their vow. "Say it, sweet Sarah. Say you'll marry me."

"I will." Lifting her hips, she took him inside, eager for the warmth, the deep, stirring penetration. "I'll marry you."

They linked their fingers, then moved in a dance as fertile and rhythmic as spring. He could feel life pulsing between them, the baby they were sure to create. Anxious and aroused, she gripped his shoulders, urging him to increase the tempo. And when he spilled into her, their worlds joined.

Afterward, Adam lowered himself into her arms and nuzzled her neck. She smelled like the wind and the grass and everything natural. Her hair felt like the flutter of a raven's wing against his face, her skin sleek and smooth.

"I want to have two ceremonies," he said, thinking about the future they had just sealed. "One in a church and one that represents the old Cherokee way."

Stroking his back, she slid gentle fingers up and down his spine. "There isn't just one Cherokee way. Different regions had different practices."

"Really? Like what?" He rolled onto his side, taking her with him.

"Sometimes it was up to a holy man whether a couple married. If he forbade their union, they would split up."

He frowned. "Forget that. I'm not going to let anyone take you away from me."

"There was also the proposal that was decided on by the maiden's mother. If the mother consented, the young man was allowed to share the maiden's bed."

He gave her a boyish grin. "I'm already sharing your bed."

She traced the shape of his smile. "And you declared your love at my mother's grave site. That meant a lot to me, Adam."

"I wanted her to know." For a moment, they were both silent, wrapped in a cocoon of emotion. He brushed a lock of hair from her cheek, and she moved close enough to increase the rhythm of his heart.

"We could exchange gifts," she said finally. "But it involves our parents. Your mother is supposed to give you something symbolic to offer me, and my mother is supposed to give me something to offer you. But since my mom is gone, my dad could take her place."

"That's perfect." It would be a new beginning for all of them, a way to bridge the gap that had separated them. Adam had found his mother, and Sarah had made peace with her father. And in nine months, he thought, sliding his hand over her tummy, there would be a child to bring their families even closer.

"Thank you." He leaned in to kiss her. "For believing in

me.'' For being there when he fell, when the addiction and the fear nearly destroyed him. ''I'd be lost without you.''

''Me, too.'' Her eyes turned misty, but he knew they were tears of joy. From now until forever, Sarah Cloud and Adam Paige would have each other.

He kept his hand on her tummy and smiled. As the Cherokee would say—she walked in his soul, and he walked in hers.

Epilogue

Sarah stood in the kitchen with Adam's spirited sister, preparing for an important party. She baked chicken while Rachel put the final touches on a relish tray. The counter was laden with food, from cheese and crackers to a frothy cake decorated with sugared roses.

Sarah took a deep breath. A garden window displayed a variety of potted herbs, enhancing the eclectic aroma.

Oklahoma was home again, and she couldn't imagine being anywhere else. Adam had opened a clinic in Tahlequah, an establishment that offered small-town warmth and holistic medicine. Sarah was also part of the business, adding natural skin-care remedies to the services. Everything she and Adam did, they did together.

Their charming old ranch house was filled with cats, and their yard flourished with plants. Two horses shared a small barn, whinnying every morning to greet the day. It was, she thought, the most beautiful place on earth.

"It smells good in here." Adam came up behind them, his boots sounding on the clay-tiled floor.

Sarah and Rachel shared a smile, then turned to acknowledge him. Sarah's heart bumped lovingly. He stood tall and proud, a boyish grin tilting his lips. She knew how much he enjoyed family gatherings, and today was special. So incredibly special.

"So how are my two favorite women?" he asked.

"We're fine," Rachel said, arranging carrot sticks just so. "Busy doing women stuff."

"So I guess that means a guy can't mooch a snack or anything?"

"Not on your life, buster. This is party food." With a satisfied smirk, the fourteen-year-old returned to her task, her hair swishing across her shoulders.

Adam winked at Sarah, and her heart thumped again. Was it possible to fall in love all over again? To see the sun and the moon in your husband's eyes?

"I invited Jeremy to come by," he said. "And his parents, too."

Sarah nodded. Jeremy was one of the teenage boys from the youth center where Adam volunteered his time. He'd developed a warm relationship with the Cherokee boy, but they shared a common bond. Both were recovering alcoholics, only Jeremy's struggle was more recent. Of course, Adam never forgot his challenge, and he never missed an opportunity to help someone in need.

Sarah's father remained strong and sober as well. He had even begun to date, courting a woman who appreciated his quick wit and easy manner.

Everyone was settled, she thought, happy and whole. Adam's mother would be arriving soon to help with the party, and his brothers were probably buying last-minute gifts. They visited regularly, watching sporting events with Adam and yelling at the TV the way men often did.

Sarah checked on the chicken, and Adam glanced at the clock.

"Do you think the birthday girl is awake yet?" he asked.

"I don't know." She smiled and closed the oven. "Should

we go see?'' From the anxious expression on her husband's face, she knew he was itching to hold their daughter.

Hand in hand, they exited the kitchen and headed toward the nursery. Slipping quietly inside, they stood near the crib, silently awed. Kaylee Marie Paige napped with her bottom in the air and an empty bottle by her side. A cap of dark hair fell across her forehead, and her cheeks were rosy against golden skin.

Adam moved closer. ''I can't believe she's already a year old.''

''I know. But it's been an incredible year.''

''Yeah.'' He smiled at his wife. ''Being parents suits us.''

Just then, Kaylee roused, peeking at them through sleepy eyes. Adam reached out, and their little girl came to her feet, anxious to cuddle in Daddy's arms. He lifted her from the crib and held her close, brushing her cheek with a soft kiss.

Moving to stand beside her husband, Sarah said a silent prayer, thanking the Creator for each and every blessing He had bestowed upon them.

This, she thought, as Adam and Kaylee drew her into a family hug, is what life was all about.

* * * * *

Harlequin Mills & Boon

Texas Cattleman's Club: Lone Star Jewels

Don't miss any of the titles in this compelling miniseries

- **Jennifer Greene**
  1. Millionaire M.D.
  July 2001

- **Sara Orwig**
  2. World's Most Eligible Texan
  July 2001

- **Cindy Gerard**
  3. Lone Star Knight
  November 2001

- **Kristi Gold**
  4. Her Ardent Sheikh
  November 2001

- **Sheri Whitefeather**
  5. Tycoon Warrior
  December 2001

Books only available from Harlequin Mills & Boon for 3 months after the publishing date.

Call **1300 659 500** to get your copy today.

Information above is correct at time of printing

DES

Available this month from

Harlequin Mills & Boon®

Desire Duos

Provocative & Seductive Romances

2 stories in each volume

Sheri Whitefeather
Tycoon Warrior
&
Sheri Whitefeather
Cherokee

Alexandra Sellers
The Sultan's Heir
&
Alexandra Sellers
Undercover Sultan

Peggy Moreland
Slow Waltz Across Texas
&
Shirley Rogers
A Cowboy, A Bride & A Wedding Vow

AVAILABLE FROM

Target • K-Mart • Big W • selected Coles supermarkets • bookstores • newsagents

OR

Call Harlequin Mills & Boon on 1300 659 500 to order now for the cost of a local call. NZ customers call (09) 837 1553.

Shop online at www.eHarlequin.com.au

SUBSCRIBE TODAY *AND TAKE ONE BOOK FREE!*

Enjoy one FREE Harlequin Mills & Boon Desire book when you agree to trial our home delivery service.

Plus you'll also receive a gorgeous Austrian Crystal Pendant FREE just for giving us a try!

By subscribing to Harlequin Mills & Boon Desire you'll enjoy:

✓ The convenience of books delivered to your door every month
✓ Savings off the cover price every month
✓ Exclusive Competitions, Free Gifts, Author News, and much, much more.
✓ Friendly Customer Service Team to answer your calls
✓ No Obligation, No Minimum Number of Purchases - No Risk at All!

It's so easy! Mail this coupon FREE to:
Harlequin Mills & Boon
**** Reply Paid 63360, CHATSWOOD NSW 2067**

FREE POSTAGE & HANDLING

------------------------------------NO STAMP REQUIRED------------------------------------

Yes! Please send me a FREE Harlequin Mills & Boon Desire book, PLUS my **FREE** gift - a gorgeous Austrian Crystal Pendant. Then send me 2 brand-new books every month delivered directly to my door. Bill me at the low price of just $10.15 per book - that's a total price of $20.30* including GST. That's the complete price, and if I wish to cancel my subscription all I have to do is write or call Harlequin Mills & Boon within 10 days. I understand that accepting the books and gift places me under no obligation ever to buy any books - they are mine to keep forever. Plus, my Harlequin Mills & Boon Desire subscription is completely flexible - I can always return a shipment, suspend or cancel at any time. I am over 18 years of age.

DZ1JBS

Mrs/Ms/Miss/Mr ____
PLEASE PRINT

Account number (if known)____________________________________

Address____

____P/code__________

Daytime Tele. No. (__________)_________________________________

Signature____

Offer not available to current Harlequin Mills & Boon Desire subscribers.
Harlequin Mills & Boon reserves the right to refuse an application and change the terms of this offer.
Offer expires 29 March 2002. Offer available in Australia and New Zealand only.
* NZ Price $24.10. Terms & Prices subject to change without notice.
** NZ Address: FREEPOST 3805, Private Bag 92122, Auckland 1020.

Your free book may differ from the one pictured above

adma DIRECT MARKETING CODE COMPLIANT
APPROVED TRADER NZ DIRECT MARKETING ASSOCIATION

NDES

Available next month from

Harlequin Mills & Boon®

Desire Duos

Provocative & Seductive Romances

2 stories in each volume

Ann Major
Cowboy Fantasy
&
Sara Orwig
Cowboy's Secret Child

Peggy Moreland
Hard Lovin' Man
&
Annette Broadrick
Marriage Prey

Katherine Garbera
Baby At His Door
&
Kathie Denosky
His Baby Surprise

AVAILABLE FROM

Target • K-Mart • Big W
selected Coles supermarkets
• bookstores • newsagents

OR

Call Harlequin Mills & Boon
on 1300 659 500 to order now
for the cost of a local call.
NZ customers call (09) 837 1553.

Shop online at www.eHarlequin.com.au

CONT04

10 reasons why you'll love getting your books delivered direct to your home:

♥ ♥ ♥ ♥ ♥ ♥ ♥ ♥ ♥ ♥

- ♥ You can add even more love and romance to your life with wonderful books that always have a happy ending - and ma you feel great.
- ♥ You can choose romances from 13 different series - there's something to suit every taste!
- ♥ We don't charge for Postage and Handling - it's FREE
- ♥ Our home delivery saves you time at the shops.
- ♥ We reserve your books and deliver them well before they a available in the stores - so you never miss out on the best romance reading.
- ♥ There's no risk and no obligation - you don't have to buy a minimum amount of books and you can cancel or suspend your subscription at anytime!
- ♥ You can order directly from our internet site *www.eHarlequin.com.au*
- ♥ You feel special because of our numerous competitions, newsletters, Prize draws and Free Gifts!
- ♥ Our delightful customer service team really do care about y - they're always more than happy to chat and answer questions about your account.

Call our friendly customer service ladies now fro anywhere in Australia on 1300 659 500 for the cost of a local call! [New Zealand:(09)837155

TEMP

Available this month from

Harlequin Mills & Boon®

Temptation Duos

Sexy & Exciting Romances

2 stories in each volume

Leslie Kelly
Relentless

&

Jill Shalvis
Aftershock

Kate Hoffmann
The Mighty Quinns: Conor

&

Barbara Dunlop
Forever Jake

AVAILABLE FROM

Target • K-Mart • Big W
• selected Coles supermarkets
• bookstores • newsagents

OR

Call Harlequin Mills & Boon
on 1300 659 500 to order now
for the cost of a local call.
NZ customers call (09) 837 1553.

Shop online at www.eHarlequin.com.au

Has he been reading your Blaze™ books?

Harlequin Books turns up the heat with ***Blaze***™... A scorching new series available at your favourite store. Get your hands all over one soon... *Can't wait? Get a sneak preview right now at eHarlequin.com.au*

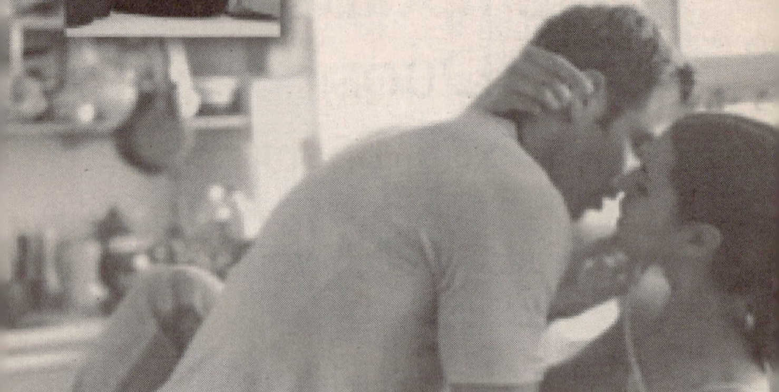

AVAILABLE FROM

Target • K-Mart • Big W
• selected Coles supermarkets
• bookstores • newsagents

OR

Call Harlequin Mills & Boon
on 1300 659 500 to order
for the cost of a local call.
NZ customers call (09) 837 155

Shop on-line at www.eHarlequin.com.au

Harlequin
lills Boon

CLLNOV

Christmas with A Latin Lover

hree gorgeous Mediterranean men are about to propose seasonal
'ductions – and mistletoe marriages – in these sensational
ew stories by three bestselling authors.

IN STORE NOVEMBER

'HE CHRISTMAS EVE BRIDE

Lynne Graham

'hen Rocco Volpe suggests Amber should be
s mistress, she turns him down! But Amber
iickly changes her mind – for little Freddy's
ke. Rocco might believe Amber had once
etrayed him, but he still wants his baby son...
nd Amber!

SPANISH CHRISTMAS

Penny Jordan

'hen Meg Scott spends Christmas with Spanish aristocrat Don
hristian Felipe Martinez, she finds that, though he's injured, his
ody is in full working order! Meg is thrilled by his passion – but
unned by his announcement that they'll be married by New Year!

'HRISTMAS IN VENICE

Lucy Gordon

fter months apart from her Italian husband, Francesco Bartini,
nia returns to Venice knowing she will inevitably see Francesco.
nia has accepted that their marriage is over. But when Francesco
alises she's eight and a half months pregnant, he's determined
win back his wife...

AVAILABLE FROM

Target • K-Mart • Big W
• selected Coles supermarkets
• bookstores • newsagents

OR

Call Harlequin Mills & Boon
on 1300 659 500 to order
for the cost of a local call.
NZ customers call (09) 837 1553.

Shop on-line at www.eHarlequin.com.au

summer HEAT BLOCKBUSTER

4 Sizzling Summer Romance

IN STORE DECEMBER

Hot On His Trail
Linda Winstead Jones

Lost But Not Forgotten
Roz Denny Fox

Millionaire Boss
Peggy Moreland

His Witness, Her Chi
Ann Voss Peterson

The temperature's rising..

AVAILABLE FROM

Target • K-Mart • Big W • selected Coles supermarkets • bookstores • newsagents

OR

Call Harlequin Mills & Boon on 1300 659 500 to order for the cost of a local call. NZ customers call (09) 837 155

Shop on-line at www.eHarlequin.com.au

HOR02

Harlequin Mills & Boon

MILTON BLACK'S HOROSCOPES 2002

AVAILABLE IN OCTOBER

WANT TO KNOW HOW TO MAKE 2002 A SUCCESSFUL YEAR?

Then this is the guide for you!
Join Milton Black, Australia's most respected astrologer for over 34 years, as he takes a look into the future and what it holds for you.

This fantastic guide gives you:

★ An overview of the whole year ahead
★ Month-by-month predictions ★ Daily charts
★ Hair and beauty tips by the stars
★ Star sign compatibilities
★ Destiny hints and lucky lotto numbers...
and much more!

AUST $5.95 (incl. G.S.T.) NZ $7.50 (incl. G.S.T.)

AVAILABLE FROM

Target • K-Mart • Big W
selected Coles supermarkets
bookstores • newsagents
from October 2001.

OR

Call Harlequin Mills & Boon
on 1300 659 500
for the cost of a local call.
NZ customers call
(09) 837 1553.

Shop on-line at www.eHarlequin.com.au

Harlequin Mills & Boon

GOFNO

Gifts of FORTUNE

The Fortunes Of Texas:
A family whose Christmas legacy is greater than mere riche

Let bestselling authors Barbara Boswell Jennifer Greene and Jackie Merritt enthra you with a Texas-size celebration Determined to repay the people who stoo by him in his darkest hours, Ryan Fortun bestows on them three special gift intended to bring love and th promise of family..

IN STORE NOVEMBER

Barbara Boswe
The Holiday Heir: Ryan gives wealthy shei Nico Tanefi his prized signet ring with hopes tha the brooding ruler can woo back his ex-fiancée..

Jennifer Greene
The Christmas House: Two strangers are each given a home – only it's the same house! Can Ryan's matchmaking scheme pull these orphans together?

Jackie Merrit
Maggie's Miracle: Two million dollars allows researche Dr. Maggie Taylor to hire her sexy rival to her cause, onl *his* cause is loosening her tightly leashed passio

AVAILABLE FROM

Target • K-Mart • Big W
• selected Coles supermarkets
• bookstores • newsagents

OR

Call Harlequin Mills & Boon
on 1300 659 500 to order
for the cost of a local call.
NZ customers call (09) 837 1553.

Shop on-line at www.eHarlequin.com.au